Y0-EBB-318

TO KISS
EARTH
GOOD-BYE

TO KISS EARTH GOOD-BYE

INGO SWANN

Foreword by Dr. Gertrude Schmeidler

HAWTHORN BOOKS, INC.
PUBLISHERS / *New York*

TO KISS EARTH GOOD-BYE

Copyright © 1975 by Ingo Swann. Copyright under International and Pan-American Copyright Conventions. All rights reserved, including the right to reproduce this book or portions thereof in any form, except for the inclusion of brief quotations in a review. All inquiries should be addressed to Hawthorn Books, Inc., 260 Madison Avenue, New York, New York 10016. This book was manufactured in the United States of America and published simultaneously in Canada by Prentice-Hall of Canada, Limited, 1870 Birchmount Road, Scarborough, Ontario.

Library of Congress Catalog Card Number: 73-21321
ISBN: 0-8015-7774-8
1 2 3 4 5 6 7 8 9 10

To Polly, who bore me this time, and to those who wish matter, energy, space, and time to be barriers no longer, this book is respectfully dedicated.

CONTENTS

FOREWORD ix
ACKNOWLEDGMENTS xiii
INTRODUCTION xv
THE STARSHIP AZALIA, by Alma Geovese xix

I   NERVOUS FRONTIERS   1
II   PSYCHOKINESIS   31
III   OUT OF BODY   63
IV   PROPHECY   129
V   TO KISS EARTH GOOD-BYE   173

SELECTED BIBLIOGRAPHY 199
INDEX 209

FOREWORD

Ingo Swann is a remarkable man. He has extraordinarily strong psychic ability; he is thoughtful; he is fluent. Hearing him speak is a special experience, and this book offers a similar experience to readers. It tells about some of his accomplishments and some of his ideas. It is frank, so far as it goes—mercilessly frank at times. And if it does not answer all the reader's questions, it is in good company; there is probably no book that does.

As with other complex persons, one grows to know Ingo only slowly. He gives and withholds different parts of himself at different times. When I first met him, he withheld. We were in a group of his friends and acquaintances and he sat monolithic in a chair, letting conversation swirl around him—a large, blond man who watched pleasantly but seldom joined in the chatter or the activity. From that first meeting I had only two impressions of him: that the others thought he had outstanding psychic gifts, and that I knew nothing of what he thought.

Some weeks later I was surprised and pleased when he telephoned me at my office. He had an offer to make: that I do research with him. He wanted the research done under careful conditions, which I could specify, in order to learn about an ability that he had begun to think he possessed —an ability so striking (if it truly existed) as to boggle the mind. He thought he had found, in informal tests, that he could change the temperature of distant objects.

The proposal that we study this together left me torn between two sets of reactions. One, of course, was "no." It sounded like a wild goose chase, studying the impossible with a stranger. It would take time and I was busy. It would take money for equipment, and research money was in short supply. And besides the whole idea was ridiculous, wasn't it?

The other reaction was "yes." Here was someone his friends believed to be psychic, who proposed working in the laboratory under controlled conditions that I was to make as tight as possible. A psychic who asks for strict controls is a rara avis, and few of us are willing to let a rare

FOREWORD

bird fly away unobserved. As for the impossibility of what he asked me to investigate, long exposure to parapsychology had left me inclined to think well of the advice of Lewis Carroll, that Oxford mathematician and philosopher of the absurd, who told us to believe three impossible things before breakfast. I hadn't taken Carroll's advice, but the inclination was there, and here was a chance for a compromise. I could wait until after breakfast, then study (if not necessarily believe) one impossible thing.

The "yes" prevailed. After some further talks I ordered the equipment we would need: thermistors (sensitive devices for measuring small temperature changes) and a bridge to connect them with a polygraph (which would trace out the record of any temperature change that occurred). The equipment arrived, we set it up, and then Ingo came to the laboratory to see what would happen when he worked with it.

You may want to be able to visualize us. In all but one of our sessions Ingo sat in front of the polygraph so he could watch the readout. Quiet and relaxed, he made almost no movements. At his left, several feet away, was the thermistor he was trying to change. At his right I sat, stopwatch in hand, telling him when to rest, when to try to make it hotter, when to try to make it colder. Between me and the polygraph was a colleague, Larry Lewis, who made sure that the machine ran properly and recorded the timing. It was a quiet scene. Almost the only activity was the machine's, with paper rolling through it and its needles jiggling slightly as they traced the changes that "should not" have occurred.

You also may want to know the details of the procedure. In our first series the thermistor Ingo tried to change was free in the air, but another thermistor was attached to Ingo's wrist to determine whether his body temperature varied with the hotter or colder instructions. (If it did, this could have caused the thermistor change, but it did not.) In all later series the thermistor was sealed into a thermos bottle so it was insulated from the air. To make sure that my instructions did not merely anticipate temperature changes that occurred naturally, all instructional periods were equally long (forty-five seconds) and every series followed a preset, counterbalanced order (rest, hotter, rest, colder, rest, colder, rest, hotter, rest, colder, rest, hotter, rest, hotter, rest, colder) for one of the two series in each session, and its mirror image (rest, colder, rest, hotter, etc.) for the other. This order was arranged so that progressive changes or simple cycles of change would not distort the hotter versus colder comparisons.

And before our eyes the "impossible" happened. Both visual inspection of the record and careful statistical analysis showed that again and again (in seven of our ten series) there was a significant correspondence between what I told Ingo to do and what the record traced. For each of five of the series the difference between the record of rising temperature in the "make it hotter" periods and of falling temperature in the "make it colder" periods was so great that it would be expected to happen by chance only one time in a thousand. To have such changes even once, in a thermistor insulated in a thermos that was twenty-five feet away from Ingo, would be a strong indication of paranormal ability; to have it happen so consistently seems conclusive evidence. It is true that the temperature differences were small (seldom showing a change of one degree in the period of forty-five seconds) and the changes were not uniformly in the instructed direction, but the overall pattern was unequivocal.

It seems to me that the only possible interpretation of this project is that Ingo by his psychic ability changed the temperature of a distant insulated object—or else, and just as striking, that by his psychic ability Ingo changed the electric current or the pen's motion so that the record showed the desired temperature change.

The most dramatic effect was unanticipated. It came in our second session, one in which Ingo and I were in a room several yards from the polygraph so that Ingo's brain waves could be recorded. The thermistor was in a thermos bottle on a table five feet from us. As Ingo and I were talking before the tests began, he started (he told me later) to wonder just where inside the thermos the thermistor was. He then tried to locate it mentally—he "probed" for it.

Lewis was at the polygraph, checking that the brain wave records were clear and occasionally glancing at the thermistor readout. One of these glances showed him that, instead of its usual straight line which meant the temperature was constant, it showed an abrupt perturbation so large as to indicate a change of about a degree of temperature in a few seconds. He naturally thought this must mean we had opened the thermos, wondered why, and came tearing into the experimental room to find out what was happening. But he found that neither of us had moved and the thermos was untouched. Apparently the abrupt change in the recording had come when Ingo, sitting quietly in his chair, made a psychic probe into the thermos to locate the thermistor. This is a man with a powerful mind!

FOREWORD

And here is the book he wrote. It is partly an autobiography—it tells of his family background and early psychic experiences, of how as an adult his interest in psychic matters was rekindled by a chinchilla, and of his later psychic successes in the laboratory and outside. It shows his deep concern with achieving both better control of the processes involved and better understanding of them. It describes how hard he works at both self-analysis and analysis of others' reports. It summarizes his reading, and how he thinks historical records relate to the facts and theories of parapsychology.

Its major theme is one with which I heartily concur—that psychic phenomena are natural events to be understood in the framework of science. His own words are, "The path of understanding things psychic has . . . led away from the usual occult, mystical, and even mythic sources." There are many variations on this theme. He emphasizes that scientific theories must change to include psychic happenings; that we can apply psychic abilities even before we understand them; that with understanding we can use them better; that we should be less inhibited or negative in the way we think; that creativity may partake of or be close in its functioning to psychic ability; that consciousness can travel far from the here and now in both space and time.

The book is disturbing, both in what it reports and in the theories it propounds. It is like a series of conversations in which Ingo talks more or less freely about what is uppermost in his thinking—and, just as would happen in a wide-ranging conversation, there is much that makes me want to interrupt and query or contradict. There is also much that I find impressive, most of all the way Ingo tests out some of his most astonishing ideas—first thinking about his observations, then developing a theory, then working out an application of the theory, then testing that application and finding strong confirmatory results.

The book is provocative. I would expect other readers, like myself, to be sometimes stimulated into a desire to argue and sometimes stimulated into admiration and respect.

Gertrude R. Schmeidler
Department of Psychology
The City College of the
City University of New York

ACKNOWLEDGMENTS

There are so many books these days dealing irresolutely with the paranormal that I hesitated to add yet another. Many suggested I write this book, however, and to get some idea of what kind of information I should include, I solicited advice from many respected parapsychologists. Those who were kind enough to reply to my query suggested that my personal viewpoint would be the most informative and that I should throw aside fear of parapsychological criticism, and even caution. For their suggestions, then, I am indebted to Dr. Rex G. Stanford, Dr. Stanley Krippner, Dr. K. Ramakrishna Rao, Dr. Jose M. Feola, Professor Frederick C. Dommeyer, Dr. Arthur C. Hastings, and to Professor Hans Bender for drawing my attention to several important nuances.

The establishment, in any scientific sense, of a parapsychological phenomenon requires the combined and cooperative efforts of many. My deepest appreciation must go to Janet Mitchell, who for three years has given her selfless help and assistance even to the smallest details in the many projects in which I have been involved. I was both grateful and honored to have the wise counseling of Dr. Jan Ehrenwald and Dr. Gertrude Schmeidler, who not only gave many important suggestions for experimental design but worked closely with me herself. I am extremely honored by the support and interest of both the staff and trustees of the American Society for Psychical Research, especially that of Dr. Montague Ullman, without whose guidance I could not have gone on, and Dr. John Wingate and Arthur Twitchell, as well as Dr. Karlis Osis. At Stanford Research Institute, which courageously moved into the arena of this controversial research, I am grateful for and enheartened by the confidence placed in me by Dr. Charles A. Anderson, Dr. Don R. Scheuch, Dr. Bonnar Cox, Dr. H. E. Puthoff, and Russell Targ, and by the members of the immense SRI staff who made my stay and work there an unforgettable epoch in my life.

Too numerous to be mentioned here are those who have contributed

ACKNOWLEDGMENTS

supportively to my courage and determination, and there are some who cannot at this time be mentioned but without whose help and encouragement I should have faltered many times. I express my thanks to Alma Geovese for permission to quote her lovely song and poem "The Starship Azalia," which pulls me psychically into the infinite future ahead, and to Manly P. Hall for permission to quote in part his poingant poem "The Hymn of Death." Any researcher must be grateful for America's wonderful libraries, especially that grand old pile, the New York Public Library.

INTRODUCTION

In the ordinary run of things the game of consciousness revolves around the rules governing the games of the senses and the ideas of man, himself existing in a physical universe.

This is the universe of all things material, of the physically oriented senses, the world in which every thing and all events are held to be explainable and workable in terms of material causes and effects. In this material universe, and also within the ideas that hold it in place, the game of material sensations and acquisition of things material is played by the "haves" against the "have nots." This universe therefore requires only two major conditions—the condition of the victor and the condition of the victim.

The game of consciousness is set within the confines of the physical and sensorially perceived universe. In order to be in this game, each man and woman is said to have barriers to consciousness, barriers limiting perception only to things material. But barriers can exist only if there are innately things to be debarred from. Thus the game.

But actually there are universes within universes within universes. Even in terms of material consciousness, universes are often seen to move across, adjacent, contrariwise, and upside down in relation to other universes. And there are worlds of thought and existence beyond the barriers of present concepts of the mind, of consciousness, and of ideas of man himself.

In some individuals these barriers shift askew, disobeying the rules, moving into strange combinations or perhaps collapsing altogether. Then the perceiver senses beyond the merely physical, accedes to immaterial, nonmaterial universes where material organization and rules—if they still exist—are not the be-all, end-all of awareness.

Across the minds of men and women flow tides of changing consciousness, fluctuating, undulating, giving birth to new concepts, growing fields of ideas, and seeking undiscovered vistas to move toward. Sometimes these fluctuating, undulating components of awareness erupt in spectrums of glittering achievement, at other times in vortexes of dehumanizing trauma.

Yet, everywhere and in all times, consciousness seeks the thrill of living, of sensation, of experience. To this search in any given age the quality of life itself brings the challenge: to triumph, to win, to succeed, to do better, or to lose, to fail, to be controlled; to create, to envision, to imagine, or to destroy, to change things, to dominate.

With the ordinary progression of life the individual's ideas of himself and of others serve to turn the cogs of society and enterprise. Work, play, success, failure, adventure, discovery—all these comprise the elegance and the drama of human consciousness.

In all these human enterprises or failings, consciousness itself takes its cues from what it receives from the eyes and ears; its rewards and punishments also are of the senses, usually pleasure or pain.

But it is no longer merely a matter of belief or disbelief but of fact that there are universes in addition to the sensorially perceived material universe. In trying to solve many mysterious riddles present in quantum physics, many physicists have become impressed with the existence of immaterial realms that suggest an equal amount of probable structure as do the sensorially perceived realms. Today the physicist must cope with universes beyond the physical.

But there have lived many individuals whose consciousness slipped over and away from accepted material barriers, individuals who participated in the game of other spaces, other dimensions.

There, in the immaterial, invisible to the eyes and silent to the ears, sometimes above and beyond pleasure and pain, the rules governing matter, energy, space, and time amazingly rearrange themselves. And the mind, the perceiving entity, the being, is no longer locked into the cycles of the material universe—the inevitable motion of birth, youth, maturity, descent into age, death, and decay.

Consciousness can then reach out, perhaps toward the future, viewing it stalwartly as prophecy, or into the past as retrocognition, viewing things long gone in the material sense. It can cut across arrangements of matter in many startling forms of psychokinesis or even poltergeist, or rearrange energy in forms of healing, miracles, or apparitions that befuddle the eye. It "listens" to "sounds" that the eardrum cannot monitor; it perceives "things" that exist on other wave-lengths; it "feels" situations beyond thought. It can, perhaps, exist without a physical body at all, and move and communicate in thought alone. These possibilities engender raptures of an existence beyond or in addition to the birth–decay cycle of matter and all things dependent upon material idealisms.

In other ways, drawing from the vast domains beyond the senses, it surges through the social fabric in forms of invention, philosophy, and humanitarianism to stagger the minds of the materialistically bound. Out of these invisible realms come mathematics, geometry, and physical calculations beyond the material. It decorates and illuminates material existence with the transcendence of art, poetry, dance, and song. It inspires certain men to take illogical but successful actions, and helps others to find fulfillment in places and ways different from their upbringing or their fortune.

In some way or manner each person is affected by the unexpected, unfamiliar magnitudes of his consciousness. Twice, at least, everyone experiences passing along the shifting barriers of consciousness; life and death attest that the being passes through barriers of consciousness, into and out of life.

And down at the bottom line of the contract called life, everyone knows that these two markers of life—birth and death—do not constitute the front and back door of consciousness; it is surprising that people still argue about it.

Whatever viewpoints individuals may hold, consciousness is and remains. What each person decides to do about it is usually his own business, but in each being there is a wonderful universe, if each would only have a look at it. There in the immanent magnitudinous nature of consciousness lies a beauty, a meaning, and a freedom only hinted at in the most profound of books. The barriers to it lie only in the ideas man holds of himself; and, since this is so, these barriers give up easily, being barriers only as long as they are thought to be barriers.

It is fashionable at this time to call the immaterial manifestations of consciousness "psychic."

Perhaps this is a good word, but it is of recent vintage, barely a hundred years old. Throughout the long history of man on this Earth, there have been many who acceded to consciousness of things beyond material relationships. What we call psychic probably has been called by many other

INTRODUCTION

names in other times, and doubtless different individuals have sought special interpretations to dignify their thoughts about it. Invective and diatribe have been hurled, religious or philosophic wars have been waged, science has conflicted with religion, and men of different faiths, creeds, and imaginations, their worlds of ideas challenged, have viewed each other with mistrust or misgiving.

But this only reflects some of the uses to which consciousness has been put; there seems to be only one thing that can be conscious, and that is what *is* conscious. Perhaps this includes you. And, barring your own ideas about the extent of consciousness, probably you can be conscious, and aware, of everything.

The Starship Azalia
by Alma Geovese

Way up high
In the Starship Azalia
Stars stream by
In a black velvet sky—

Energy flows
In the Starship Azalia
In the depths of the ship
Where the fountain glows—

Will we find our people waiting
    with welcome in their eyes,
Souls we'll recognize?

Will they give the ancient greeting
    of the constant Double Sun—
That's where our Life was spun!

Way up high
Where the star clusters gather
We drift through
Where the Sun Stars are blue—

PART I

Nervous Frontiers

> He liked watching the glorious stars, thinking "there must be myriads of worlds out there." Then one night he shifted his awareness toward and into himself. "By God," he whispered, but only to himself, "there are myriads of worlds there, too!"

At the august American Society for Psychical Research in New York, the small room in which the "psychic" event was expected to take place did not seem suitable. There was an artificiality about it, a stiffness that made the room seem forlorn.

If anything, the dull yellow walls, perhaps painted that color to inspire "intellectual" proceedings, seemed empty if not somewhat grimy. At one end the room's natural light was blotted out by heavy and definitely grimy draperies, with most illumination coming from two kitchen-style fixtures overhead. At the other end was a drapery-shrouded unit for closed-circuit television.

A nondescript couch lay in one corner, used by other subjects who needed to drop into a deep meditative mood or trance state to try to accomplish their psychic adventures. A few other pieces of furniture, neo-Salvation Army in character, populated the remainder of the room.

This room was part of what once was a gracious front room in the town house the society now occupied. It had been partitioned into three smaller chambers and named the Chester F. Carlson Research Laboratory. Carlson, inventor of the Xerox process, had an interest in things psychic and over the years gave a good deal of money to the society.

From an adjoining cubicle came the familiar, if not comforting, clacking of the EEG (electroencephalograph) machine sounding a cadence to its computer printout. The subject, his head pasted with several electrodes, sat in the dull yellow room awaiting the moment when all would be in order and the experiment could proceed.

As usual, he felt somewhat foolish. He was about to try the impossible once more. Over his head by several feet, up near the ceiling, a small platform hung suspended. On that platform, out of sight, were the "targets." The subject was imprisoned in the chair in which he sat, the electrodes on his head feeding through the wall behind him into the EEG equipment clacking away in the next cubicle. If he moved his head very far, he would disconnect from the machine.

He was supposed to try to "float out of his body" and, wafting upward, attempt to view what was on the platform.

While he waited, he gazed once more at the three framed art works on the opposite wall. The largest, crooked as usual, was an original seascape, a sort of stormy scene in green showing people in boats adrift on a somber ocean. To the right was another painting by the same artist, of some flowers looking as if they were waiting to be born. But to the left was a reproduction of Van Gogh's marvelous *Sowers*, a lone farmer casting seeds in the beautiful light of a strange setting sun. The subject gazed into the marvel of that setting sun, wondering where Van Gogh's head had been at to create such a small, exotic vision. His eyes then dropped to study the small radiator beneath the reproduction, itself painted dull yellow and perched at an odd angle on the even duller yellow carpet.

To escape the inane yellow of the room, he shifted his awareness outside the building, to the elegant and misty gray of a New York winter afternoon. It was January 12, 1972, approximately 3 P.M.

With his "other" awareness he could barely perceive the dark canyon of buildings forming West Seventy-third Street. He noticed a brilliance flowing from Central Park, where the light was apparently bouncing on trees and openness, emanating into the street somewhat like a mist of silent molecular bubbles. His awareness flashed momentarily up through the overcast and smog. There he perceived the sun, brilliant, already sinking in the west. The sky above the clouds was a pale blue, almost a shimmering silver sheen. A familiar sense of freedom ran through his consciousness, a sense of freedom—from when? Or from where?

Sounds in the building pulled his consciousness back to somewhere in the proximity of his head. He was bored with waiting. He lit a cigar, sniffing the delicious aroma, a smell that probably was an acrid stench to others.

Then everything was suddenly ready. The machinery was functioning properly. Now it was all right for him to "float" up and view the target.

Without extinguishing his cigar, holding it lightly between two fingers, he tried consciously to locate the target up at the ceiling. It involved only a moment's slight shift of attention, a feat about as difficult as shifting thoughts.

His "seeing" seemed to flux in and out of the visible light spectrum. From blackness through red, suddenly a brilliant white. There it was— briefly he saw what lay on the platform. As usual it was divided into two parts, and as usual, with his paranormal perception having anything but 20/20 vision, he could barely make it out. Definitely an unfamiliar form. But it was long and black, lying on something red, almost circular in form.

On the other half of the target was what appeared to be a circular arrangement, almost like a bull's-eye, a real "target." Could it be? Could the experimenters have put something as simple as that, as contrasted to the esoteric designs they usually thought up, designs one had to ponder carefully even when viewing them with real eyes? Yest, he decided, it was a bull's-eye.

This perceptive awareness had suffered itself to be pinpointed for a brief moment. Now suddenly it expanded again to encompass much more: voices in other parts of the building, someone climbing the stairs in the corridor outside the laboratory, slush flooding through some plumbing, the noises of New York sonorously roaring outside the building.

Puffing a fresh cloud of blue-white cigar smoke, the subject took a clipboard awaiting him and sketched out what he had seen "up there." And then the experiment was over. It had taken just sixty seconds from start to finish.

He was unplugged from the machinery in the next room. Now expectation floated around him and the others as a high ladder was brought and the targets taken down from the platform.

Several people gazed in silence at the actual targets compared with the subject's response, the drawing attached to the clipboard.

The long black thing was a black leather case holding a letter opener and a pair of scissors, indeed an unfamiliar shape, lying on a red, heart-shaped background. The other target was a bull's-eye. There were four numbers that the subject had not "seen." (Both the target and the subject's response for this particular experiment are shown in Figure 13.)

After the targets were seen, the expectation abated.

There was no residue of excitement. By now the subject was used to the attitudes at the American Society for Psychical Research.

One person volunteered that it was probably only telepathy—the subject had tuned in somehow to the mind of the person who had constructed the targets. Another said it was only clairvoyance and not a real out-of-the-body phenomenon at all. There also was some muttering about this success being nothing but a "floating fantasy with clairvoyant abilities."

The subject lit another cigar and went to examine the strip charts of his brain waves to see if anything significant had occurred *there*.

Only telepathy?

Only clairvoyance?

As if such rare abilities utterly abounded within these august rooms, or anywhere else for that matter. As to the "floating fantasy" possibility, well. . . .

And so the difficulties went.

Of course the subject himself seemed to have broken all the rules. Who ever heard of a psychic attempting a near-mystical event from within a cloud of cigar smoke? And he did not go into a trance or sit in fabulous meditation to "float" up and out. When he attempted to "perceive" the targets, he did not manifest in an "astral" form, nor quiver and shake as his "consciousness" separated from the physical body. And the "event" usually lasted only a few seconds, hardly profitable enough to try to capture on closed-circuit TV tape.

And even more horrifying was the fact that the subject himself had voiced doubt that the experiment would particularly establish the validity of an out-of-body phenomenon, as contrasted to other possible explanatory hypotheses. But it was the experiment the American Society was running at the time, and he had agreed to do it.

To him it seemed enough that it could be done, that an individual could sit in one place and perceive things at another. The construct of consciousness that would explain this might be a long time in coming, might even turn out to be not telepathy or clairvoyance at all but some unknown, unimagined human potential. With all due respect to noble researchers long in the field, the field was by no means played out. There was yet much to discover about man, about consciousness, about human potential.

If one could by any means at all transcend space and separate perception to perceive things at locations other than those accessible to the physical senses, definitions and terminology became a moot question. According to the hypothesis at the American Society that governed this "platform" experiment, the human being might be capable of operating independently of and away from the physical body. If this could be adequately demonstrated, it might be assumed that that same "part" of the personality also could be conceived of as leaving the body at death and continuing to exist.

This was an experimental hope, however, an assumption for which evidence was being sought. This assumption—which had yet to be proved—assumed that the center of the projection is capable of perceiving from the point of view of the location in space to which it has projected itself, rather than from the subject's actual eye level.

As grand as this hypothesis might be, to the subject who sketched his response that day it seemed miniscule compared to the potential integral to the act of perceiving something "away" from the body, whether it be called "telepathy," or "clairvoyance," or a "floating phantasmagoric center." No, the introduction of argumentative hypotheses, the use of possibly outdated terminology and old-fashioned ideas only served to deflate meaning.

The subject himself did not claim that his ability to perceive things distant from the body was an out-of-body phenomenon. Nor telepathy, nor clairvoyance, for that matter.

The fact that the target was adequately perceived without the use of the ordinary senses seemed to him enough to indicate that the human is possessed of abilities that might cause the total image of man to quaver a little. And viewing, however successfully, the targets on a suspended platform was an artificial situation, more convenient to researchers and theorists than to the experient. The results of the experiment could be shredded into speculations about telepathy, clairvoyance, and so forth, and in other ways drawn and quartered, eventually to be served up as a hypothetical situation more significant than meaningful or revelatory.

These silent thoughts coming to an end in his mind, the subject finished surveying the yards of brainwave recordings. There were some meaningful deviations among the brainwave patterns, deviations that he supposed would not be easily acceptable to brainwave theorists.

He made an appointment for another experimental session. The cumulative results of these experiments were not to be collected for several months. When they were complete, eight sessions considered unimpeachable from an experimental point of view would be submitted for independent judging. The judge correctly identified all eight drawn responses with the correct target. A statistical delineation indicated that this could happen by chance only once in 40,000 tries. This seemed a good beginning.

Leaving the American Society, the subject noticed on his way to the subway that not all his perceptions had settled back into the accepted mode. Above, through the intervening mists and smog, he perceived that the quarter moon was riding high, faintly visible in the dwindling rays of the sun, which had just descended beneath the western horizon. To his mind's eye, or whatever, the heavens above the cloud cover had turned a lovely chartreuse, an ethereal green, almost exactly the sky Van Gogh had painted, which could be seen in the reproduction hanging in the experimental chamber.

To him, all argumentation, speculation, and hypothesis aside, it had been an important day. If the results of the experiment were unclear to the researchers, they were good enough to convince him of one important understanding.

"Yes, yes," he breathed, dipping into the stale air of the subway system. "It *is* possible! It *can* be done!"

The life of this author is being lived at a time when "Spaceship" Earth, probably an ecological disaster already, also is beginning to crack apart from other pressures.

It is too dreary to go into what these pressures are, and most people are bored with facing unsolvable problems anyway. Others have devoted time and research to describing them, and there are plenty of sources to read. Most somehow hope that the coming plagues of human ineptness are not really there—or, if they are, will be taken care of shortly.

Of these plagues the psychological ones are perhaps the most virulent, and central among these is the one called "loss of self."[1] Hardly anyone knows who he is any longer, and it is increasingly difficult to get any information on this matter.

As the mind tries valiantly to whiz across the face of Earth, the mental tendrils of the weak in spirit must tend to wilt as they seek comfort in platitudes invented during Victoria's reign or perhaps disappear altogether into the vast and cloying, if comforting, folds of various mysticisms. But the courageous few, escaping somehow from the *pathetic fallacy*, the wilting idea that ascribes human traits and feelings to nature, attempt to point out that many answers to human plights might come out of investigating man's supposed greater abilities and that, by extending his mental or even psychic capacities, man might be led to increasing creative confrontations.

Of course these reputed "greater abilities" are nowhere very well delineated. And descriptions of them tend to get mixed up by gossip, supposition, superstition, elegant philosophies, dreams, fantasies, and scientific ramblings.

It is clear that Earth has allowed almost every possible natural frontier to be conquered and developed, and men everywhere have benefited to some degree. But it would be philosophically foolish to say that there are no more frontiers. There are plenty! Of all possible future frontiers remaining there are at least two left to be fulfilled, two frontiers not of this Earth: the touching of life somewhere among the glittering star systems populating the "out there" and the frontier represented by the living, seemingly endless mind of man himself. Of these two it is hard to say which is the more breathtaking or the more feared. Both give everyone the jitters.

Aside from UFOlogists and certain flying saucer contactees, whose tales can easily and safely be allocated by proper and respectable society to the lunatic fringe, there has always been a small portion of the scientific community that has speculated on the possiblities of extraterrestrial life and intelligence.

Two stars relatively near Earth, 70 *Ophiuchi* and 61 *Cygni*, have been studied closely. Their observed dynamics offer empirical evidence that they possess small, nonluminous bodies—planets. Another type of study, an

[1] See Charles A. Reich, *The Greening of America* (New York: Random House, 1970), p. 9.

analysis of right-ascension stars and their small but regular variations, makes it possible to conclude that at least sixty of these stars probably hold planets. A rough general calculation of stars carrying planets in this galaxy shows that some 67 percent of the glittering specks populating the Milky Way, a paltry 130 billion, are capable of having associated planetary systems.[2]

As vast and as exciting as extraterrestrial life possibilities are, if certain intelligences should suddenly decide to visit and hove into orbit around Earth in a fleet of spaceships, probably a full million people would drop dead from fright. Certainly current governments would consider that they had something to worry about besides harassing each other over territorial frontiers, oil supplies, and mixed ideologies. And what of religious concepts, already moldering with discontent? Earth would be very nervous indeed.

And this confrontation might not be so far away in time. If *Pioneer 10*, having passed Jupiter and now headed for the great beyond out there, should happen to be acquired by vehicles plying the legendary trade routes between star systems, possibly the captors would like to see just who placed the strange squiggles on it. *Pioneer 10*, launched on March 2, 1972, from Cape Canaveral, carries a plaque with diagrams of the human female and male, and directions on how to locate Earth within the Milky Way system.

And, although it is hard for thinking people to put much credence in psychic prognostications, if certain modern-day prophets are to be believed, the time is drawing near when the first extraterrestrial will, publicly at last, set foot on terra firma, probably somewhere in the southern part of the United States. This is, naturally, mere prophetic speculation at this time, but a speculation that excites and electrifies a certain group of men working on "unified" predictions, a new direction in attempting use of mental potential.

Whenever or however this event comes to be, doubtless there will transpire a goodly amount of dramatics.

[2] N. F. Reyn and N. N. Pariyskiy, "Katastroficheskiye gipotezy proiskhodzheniya solnechnoy sistemy," *Uspekhi Astronomicheskikh Nauk* (1941), pp. 137–156; A. N. Deych, "61 Lebyedya, kak troinaya systema," *Priroda* 33, nos. 5–6 (1944), p. 99; E. Holmberg, "Invisible Companions of Parallax Stars Revealed by Means of Modern Trigonometric Parallax Observations," *Meddelanden Fran Lunds Astronomiska Observatorium,* Series 11, no. 92 (1938), p. 23.

The other frontier, man's own inner self, is equally inflammatory. Hitherto the volatile situation represented by the potential of mind and consciousness has been adroitly handled by individuals and groups who told others what was possible and not possible, and especially what was respectable and what was beyond the pale or around the bend.

But, frankly, aside from a few moments of grandeur viewed best as history, the general human mind, if potentially grand, also has managed to accumulate enough crap to cause ten Earths to flounder. If the mind is blank at birth as some psychologists and philosophers claim, it is amazing how, in the short life-span of the individual, it becomes so rapidly possessed of obdurate incapabilities that bring about not only individual unhappiness, misfortune, and death but the demise of societies and civilizations as well.

The physical or materialistic explanation for this default would have to hold that one's synapses and electrochemical circuits do not fire off in sublime working order at all times. This idea holds general sway among "respectable" mentors and authorities today, the disorders of the mind supposedly originating in trauma of one sort or another (usually thought to be sexual trauma).

The mystic perhaps would hold that one has not yet attained or "evolved" to heights of wisdom and therefore is still mucking around in base desires and goals. Yet others will announce, with fire in their eyes, that in all likelihood one is suffering perdition, the condition of final spiritual damnation and ruin, while still others drivel on about karma, fate, destiny, and the fact that everything is predetermined anyway.

Ho hum, ad infinitum, ad nauseam!

No, no! All these ideas of mind seem only to stricture the potential of consciousness too tightly, so tightly that ordinary mortals cannot grow, expand, and touch the innate largesse of their own being, which all people know is within them. Granted many individuals, their synapses misfiring or their alleged karma catching up with them, do sometimes go bonkers and create confusion among their fellow men. But, even so, this is no sign that all people whose imagination and consciousness wander beyond the immediate barriers of ideas of consciousness are bonkers.

Without the experience of the fluctuations of consciousness innate in the human makeup, we could never have meaningful discovery, invention, music, art, humanitarianism, and so forth.

TO KISS EARTH GOOD-BYE

One Sunday afternoon in May 1765, for example, one James Watt was strolling along in a Glasgow park, allowing his consciousness to fluctuate all over the place. He suffered a "vision" in which he saw a steam engine in all its working detail. The next day he built it complete in less than twelve hours, harnessing, for better or worse (and some say worse), the power of steam and giving impetus to the industrial revolution. Not long ago, Pablo Picasso suggested something akin to special fluctuations of awareness when he indicated that genius is an error, a chance departure from the ordinary.

But it is not an "error" that brings about an increased chance of awareness. The "error," if it exists at all, lies in the arbitrary concepts governing the boundaries of consciousness, and especially the embargos placed upon it by educative processes, authority, or respectability.

Human history is so replete with extraordinary occurrences, many developing into fascinating and beneficial discovery, that today it really seems nonsurvival and unhumanitarian to consider that the total spectrum of human consciousness already has been discovered. This is neither obvious nor true.

It is obvious, though, that in relation to what is possible and not possible, there are basically two types of intelligences: those (rare) who are truly interested in, and unafraid of, discovery in all things, including the mind and man's potential, and those (common) who sit around and pontificate on how impossible everything is. These latter types seem to hang around everywhere, in all walks of life, and to pontificate on anything to do with the mind and how man thinks and activates consciousness.

During the last three years in which I have been involved in various psychic research projects at a number of places, I have found it possible to surmise that this latter type of intelligence dominates the scene at a ratio of about 85 percent. To such types I have playfully given the generic name of *psychosis impedimenta,* which indicates that they are possessed of a quality of intelligence that cannot *believe* a lot of things and hence feel compelled (thus the term "psychosis") to try to stop and disprove what they cannot believe is possible. But for easier reference such types can be referred to as "bloopers."

It also has been my privilege, and often a distinct honor, to meet and talk with individuals to whom the universe holds boundless hope and beauty. These types are almost spectral in nature, and with them the barriers to consciousness, discovery, even adventure, disappear and life takes on a glittering quality. Such a person is a *homo novis* (new human), always *building* and foreseeing in his visions and discoveries. I like to refer to such people—privately, of course—as "star-busters."

A particular realm in which bloopers jump about a lot is that of things psychic. The psychic realm is composed of all extraordinary manifestations not explainable in ordinary terms, and it befuddles those who insist that extraordinary potential does not exist. It is usual to find things psychic viewed in one of two ways: by adherents or devotees, who lavish raptures about potential, meaning, and excitement or by detractors, who hold that all is trickery and believers are freaks, or at least somewhat around the bend (which may be true in some cases).

But, aside from the quibbles and diatribes between believers and detractors, real psychical phenomena, like rainstorms or tornados, seem to occur with or without the interest of either group. Believers, of course, are always concerned and excited by psychical potential, while such an event creates consternation in the detracting camp.

At this point in time part of the frontier of the endless human mind, or perhaps even the entirety of it, is represented by the challenge of things psychic. In the past this frontier has been characterized more by the jests and jibes flung at it by adherents of the extremely solid, materialistic scheme of things. For a few very good reasons, mostly as a result of the discovery of nonmaterial interactions in physics, this recalcitrant attitude has shifted somewhat. Interest in discovery and advancement in things paranormal is waxing almost majestically at the public level.

If one were to labor over a definition of the word "psychic," it probably would be a very long time before any agreement might occur. To say that something is above, beyond, or outside normality is hardly a definition or contribution since discussion, debate, polemics, and diatribes could extend at length just to determine what is and is not "normal."

In my experience something paranormal is something that is not within an individual's usual boundaries of awareness. This might as well, in some cases, concern the mysteries of how the plumbing works, how the government survives, how it is that one cannot communicate with one's wife, or what it is scientists think they are doing for humanity. Things psychic constitute a mere fraction of all paranormal carryings-on.

But interwoven among argumentation as to what does or does not constitute paranormal, or even the so-called normal, there always have been instances and occurrences of awareness and events fluctuating at the edges of ordinary or accepted definitions of consciousness.

There always have been people who felt they could communicate with plants, the "green thumb" people whose communication might not have been verbal but an emotional situation to which the plants seemed to respond, offering luxuriant growth, blooming flowers, and magnificent fruit to please their gardeners. The possibility that plants have emotional response systems is now pretty well established through continuing research in this direction after the work first done by Cleve Backster, the former CIA interrogative specialist.[3]

Backster is one of the leading polygraph experts in the United States and is familiar with emotional response criteria in humans. He also is a dramatic, intense, and well-motivated person who feels there is more to life than what is in the stomach and between the covers of books or the legs, and he is eager to follow the intuitive directions his mind and existence suggest to him.

One day, in his stereotyped Manhattan offices, he was inspired to hook up to a galvanometer a rather dramatic-looking *Dracaena massangeana* and found tracings that suspiciously resembled emotional response characteristics. His further exploration of this matter, bringing down upon his head many diatribes and lampoons, has now brought forth an impressive amount of data and the sentient plant possibility has been taken up in earnest by hundreds of experimenters the world over, including experimenters in Russia.

Backster's experiments are significant in that the results provide evidence that there exists—not only within plants but possibly in all organic and

[3] See Peter Tompkins and Christopher Bird, *The Secret Life of Plants* (New York: Harper & Row, 1973).

inorganic matter—a life impulse capable of responding negatively or positively to the environment. Plants, microorganisms, human sperm, even some forms of inert substance respond—that is, they exhibit marked variations while hooked up to galvanometers and EEG equipment, suggesting responses to life termination of other specimens, to threatening negative mental thoughts from people in the environment, and to prosurvival factors such as warmth, light, food, and nutrient rewards.

Since its inception Backster's work has attracted attention of one sort or another all over the world. He is penetrating deeper and deeper into this unseen world of plant, microorganism, and cellular communication and response systems; his samples also including chicken eggs, human sperm, whole blood, and specialized animal tissue *in vitro.*

The establishment of emotional or other reactions in substances hitherto thought not to have any is in itself not particularly psychic. But in individuals who have exhibited a penchant for perceiving such implications through some sort of extra awareness, a psychic ramification can be said to exist. Many people talk to their plants, aware that their communication is being received. The famous Luther Burbank, so successful in crossing and selecting new plants to breed, was accused of talking to his plants. At first he confessed this ability to communicate with his specimens only to a very few people, but toward the end of his life he was more open and admitted that he was convinced the plants could understand him.

During the long years in New York when I was seeking to be an artist, my aesthetics, techniques, and expressions yet needing to develop, I earned a living in the United Nations at a job that in itself was uninteresting. There, at the seat of international parleys on weighty matters, I decided to study and research certain aspects of existence far removed from wars in the Middle East and racism in South Africa. I was curious about the rumored efficacy of prayer on plant growth, an idea that was being discussed heatedly at the time.

Into my office I dragged a *massangeana,* and, placing it in a sunny spot in the secretariat's eastern exposure overlooking New York's East River, I advised it emphatically that there it would be safe and it was all right to grow, that nothing would harm it—all the good things a plant might like to hear. Considering that I had discovered this plant in a cold and barren store selling for two dollars with at least half of its long, spiked leaves brown and falling, all this benevolence seemed a charitable thing to do, and it would be easy to judge results—if there were any.

Every day I gave it some water, talked to it a little, brushed dust off its leaves, and watched it grow like mad. Naturally I was inspired to extend all sorts of communications to it, asking it whether it had enough water, whether it was warm enough, and what it would like to be named. It is not necessary to describe how some of my co-workers responded to this strange set of activities.

For reasons I would never care to explain to doubting Thomases, I came to conclude that this plant possessed something of a dramatic personality, and I agreed to call him Lucifer—this idea of a name seemed to originate more with it than with me.

As the months dragged on through several world conflicts, I came to notice that when Lucifer was feeling chipper his leaves strutted horizontally outward in a vigorous manner, but when he was down and out they drooped, sometimes almost vertically down his stalk. Thus, each time this drooping occurred, I usually inquired of him what was wrong.

In this way I became aware of the plant's ability to project something akin to mental image pictures, which I received dubiously at first. But when I followed the suggestions contained in these images, his situation usually changed within hours and his leaves once more stood out with satisfaction.

Once, for example, when I had been working in another part of the building for a few days, I returned to my desk to find a sorry sight indeed. Lucifer seemed in extremely bad condition, his fronds hanging utterly dejected. He was screaming his head off that while I was away several ladies in the office—which sometimes worked two shifts—had all taken his care in hand and each gave him water every day and night. He was almost drowning. He wanted a sign placed in his pot not to water him. The sign was promptly placed, and in a matter of two hours he was obviously chipper as hell, even though his soil was yet extremely soggy.

At another time no remedy seemed to work and the "pictures" coming from Lucifer seemed exceedingly confusing. His graceful leaves hung dejectedly and he seemed to be ranting something about the necessity of a penny being placed in his pot—a request that did not make sense for me until, after discussion with a "green thumb" lady whose desk was at the front of the office surrounded by all sorts of vegetable wonders, we decided that Lucifer was starving for copper oxide. Whereupon he promptly got not one but five pennies placed in his pot—and he recovered his dramatic posture in a matter of hours.

When I belatedly resigned my job at the United Nations to cast myself on the waters of chance in the world of art, Lucifer had grown too tall to conveniently take out of the building except in a truck, so I left him there. I later heard that he finally pressed against the ceiling and his budding nodule was cut out to encourage him to grow outwards instead of up.

Personally, I would never care to argue the reality that plants and men can communicate via something akin to thought transference, preferring to discuss the matter only with those of the same persuasion, such as research chemist Marcel Vogel, a liquid-crystal expert working at International Business Machines in Los Gatos, California.

Vogel and I have held many interesting conversations about such possibilities. Vogel is convinced, and has demonstrated—at least sufficiently to establish a trial hypothesis—that plants do pick up intentions from humans. This idea, even as a trial hypothesis, is staggering enough since, if the evidence is anywhere near correct, plants seem to have a sentient, thinking nature, capable of recognition at least in matters of life and death.

Of course, most humans do not seem capable of responding to mental images sent out by plants. Nonetheless, Vogel's experiments, done as expertly as Backster's, are today yielding vastly impressive results, results that must in one way or another begin to alter man's concept of his mental and psychical abilities.

These new discoveries and probabilities are likely to create a vast difference in how man surveys the vegetable life kingdom on Spaceship Earth. But a retrospective view will suggest that the communicative potential always was there, dependent upon how any given individual felt about it. Many people simply went ahead and communicated in their way with plants, even if others said it was impossible.

Another area where presumed psychical abilities have always lain quite close to accessibility is the area of so-called "eyeless vision." This area, however, is also accessible to magicians and tricksters, so much so that many have been exposed as hoaxers when they claimed this effect as a psychical ability.[4] But aside from the stage magicians who have performed excellently blindfold from a stage and research subjects caught at trickery, there are research reports that suggest a positive view allowing that a certain extrasensory capacity is innate in man, sometimes brought to the fore only through determination or circumstance. The negative view has to hold, of course—that all is trickery even if it cannot be proved so; this is one manifestation of blooperism.

One positive report, a recent one, involves a subject who had a box placed around his head to preclude visual cues and rather consistently could distinguish the difference between black and red paper when it was uncovered.[5] When the papers were covered with thin clear plastic he could yet distinguish the color, but not when the papers were covered with picture glass. There is some hesitation in this report to draw a conclusion as to exactly how it was that the subject managed to distinguish between the two papers, hinting that possibly the perception hinged on the subject's sensitive cutaneous perception of infrared radiation and not on touch or ESP. However such static conclusions, cagily put, are characteristics of parapsychological research. The subject, in some manner other than the usual, did manage to distinguish between the colors.

Another report describes the abilities of a twenty-one-year-old woman.[6] Her eyes were blinded by goggles and Kleenex, and her hands plunged into a box whose contents she could not see even if her eyes were uncovered. She could tell the difference between cards of four colors—blue, yellow, green, and red construction paper—but only if there was light on them.

Many experiments along these lines have been done, usually with sighted people, all yielding exceedingly significant results. A poignant confirmation of this type of sensitivity was established recently as sixteen totally blind volunteers at Rosary Hill College in Buffalo, New York, undertook to tell colors in an ESP experiment. As the end of eight weeks experimentation neared, after a lot of guesswork, most of the volunteers

[4] For a report on this type of trickery, see Martin Gardner, "Dermo-optical Perception: A Peek Down the Nose," *Science* 151, no. 3711 (February 11, 1966), pp. 654–657.

[5] See C. B. Nash, "Cutaneous Perception of Color with a Head Box," *The Journal of the American Society for Psychical Research* 65, no. 1 (January 1971), pp. 83–87.

[6] See J. Z. Jacobson, B. J. Frost, and W. L. King, "A Case of Dermooptical Perception," *Perceptual and Motor Skills* 22, no. 2 (April 1966), pp. 515–520.

were able to tell the difference between white and black consistently, and then even between red and green. One of the subjects began to be able to differentiate the outlines of doorways and furniture.

Douglas Dean, an eminent and respected parapsychologist, a former president of the Parapsychological Association and a teacher of computer programming and statistics at the Newark College of Engineering, has run a statistical evaluation on the results of these experiments with blind subjects. Dean is an energetic, indefatigable, devoted parapsychologist, interested in the creative potential of human psychical gifts. He indicates that the statistics show not only a result far above chance expectation (some 65 to 75 percent) but also that a visible learning process was taking place within the subjects as they endeavored to discern the color of the targets.

For centuries skeptics have denied that living tissues (or anything else, for that matter) can emit radiations that the senses cannot perceive. Of course, in some ways, this skepticism has been rudely disabused, especially in matters of X-rays and nuclear radiations. But the skepticism concerning either so-called psychical emanations or perceptions of them is still paramount.

The widespread interest in Kirlian photography—that is high-voltage, radiation field photography—must come as a sort of low-keyed denouement for this skeptical drama.

Although there were some predecessors investigating the effects of "electrophotography" before Semyon and Valentina Kirlian accidentally discovered in 1939 that a high-voltage wire sparking across a piece of film left a picture, the current interest in the field obviously stems from the work of this Russian man and wife team. The Kirlian device is basically a Tesla coil connected to two metallic plates between which an object and film can be placed.

Many beautiful flares and coronas are produced around the objects and recorded on the film when high-voltage current passes through the plates. Flares and energy bubbles also emanate from human fingertips when they are placed on the film. Conservative interpretation as to what is taking place holds that these marvelous effects are not psychical in nature but merely a new way of viewing electrical coronal discharge. In all fairness to scientific procedures, aside from personal convictions as to what is going on, it could not be stated arbitrarily at this time that these effects are either physical or nonphysical in nature. The hard work of discovery has yet to be done.

Professor William A. Tiller, an elegant, introspective man interested in creative, nonmaterial aspects of existence, and also head of the Material Science Department at Stanford University, has begun to ask proper questions as to the nature of the Kirlian effect.[7] These lights, auras, emanations, energy bubbles progress magnificently from just about anything that can be photographed in the Kirlian manner. Tiller suggests that extremely careful experimentation should be developed to ensure meaningful observation and discovery about the real nature of these impressive flares and coronal auras. He indicates that the "streamer phenomenon or corona discharge" might account for the effects but adds that, even if there should prove to be a definite physical mechanism involved, this would not arbitrarily eliminate an additional nonphysical correlate (see Figures 1 and 2).

Whatever the physical and nonphysical implications of the beautiful Kirlian effects, it should be acknowledged even by hardened skeptics that sensitives the world over have always reported "seeing" emanations from living as well as inert materials. One of the first investigators to try to treat the subject scientifically was Baron Karl von Reichenbach, who in 1840–1844 tested many "sensitives" who consistently reported seeing flares, bubbles, and emanations from almost everything, including living things and especially bar magnets, these perceptions often taking place in totally darkened rooms.[8]

Baron von Reichenbach was a noted scientist in his own right, but when he presented his findings officially he was looked at askance and relegated to the "lunatic fringe," as have been so many researchers in the field of possible nonmaterial phenomena. The von Reichenbach work, though, is impressive testimony not only to the existence of emanations in the environs of living as well as nonliving substances but also to the capacities of certain individuals to report upon these emanations.

[7] W. A. Tiller, "The *Light* Source in High-voltage Photography," *Proceedings of the Second Western Hemisphere Conference on Kirlian Photography, Acupuncture and the Human Aura.* New York, February 1973.

[8] Freiherr Karl L. F. von Reichenbach, *Physico-Physiological Researches on the Dynamics of Magnetism, Heat, Light, Electricity and Chemism, in Their Relations to Vital Force* (New York: J. S. Redfield, 1851), and *The Odic Force: Letters on OD and Magnetism* (New Hyde Park, N.Y.: University Books, 1968).

In 1911 Dr. Walter J. Kilner of St. Thomas' Hospital of London designed a dicyanin screen that reportedly rendered the human aura to natural sight. This screen was made of a solution of coal-tar dye between two pieces of glass hermetically sealed. Several attempts have been made to reproduce Kilner's work,[9] but none seems to have been as successful as his.

The rather beautiful Kilner auric representations show differing layers of surrounds, often egg-shaped, encompassing the entire body. This latter effect became the usual arrangement reported by people claiming to "see" auras (see Figure 3).

The astonishing similarities between the beautiful Kirlian effects and descriptions by sensitives suggest that a trial hypothesis should be established. Yet, looking back through history on this subject, the reports of sensing or perceiving the magnificent "energy" fields and fluxes around bodies and things are so numerous that this type of perception might almost be taken as a common rather than a paranormal ability. And, after all, even if the emanations are to be called "cold electron," or whatever, an emanation is an aura and there really should be no problem about that. The real question is whether individuals utilizing so-called extrasensory methods can perceive auras.

The world of children does not match very closely the carefully guarded parameters of the respectable, social adult. No one really cares about the perceptions of the child—only that he should somehow be brought into proper conditioning and respect. Anything untoward involving a child can be attributed to vivid imagination and fantasy. Slowly, pervasively, restrained by parents, teachers, religionists, and finally the unyielding social fabric itself, the child is settled into the system. No one really knows what a human unimpeded by conditioning and learning would become.

But childhood, and the many mysterious happenings that truly characterize it, is extremely interesting. Sometimes the brave adult reflects upon it, even drawing from it certain assurances that can be found nowhere else.

As a child I used to watch with great fascination the fluttering forms of color sparkling from objects and people—from my mother, father, grand-

---

[9] Walter J. Kilner, *The Human Atmosphere; or the Aura Made Visible by the Aid of Chemical Screens* (New York: Rebman, 1911).

mothers, and ordinary people, as well as from caterpillars, leaves, rocks, and so forth. As might be expected, describing these marvelous rainbows and energetic flares to my peers left me very impressed with the fact that one was not supposed to see such things, and certainly not talk about them if one did.

Eventually my response to such perceptions faded from consciousness, and many years passed before I once more began to solicit them. These perceptions did not seem to be the same as the marvelous auric envelopes described by Kilner, but they did resemble several effects reported by von Reichenbach.

Many years later, in 1962, after spending several years discovering that it was quite a difficult goal, if not an absolutely insane one, to try to arrive in the New York art establishment, I made an energetic decision to retreat into myself and at least paint what I enjoyed. I had spent my first years in New York in sort of a studentship guise, striving to equal famous artists, and thus had not really produced anything "original."

The insanity of this situation dawned on me, and I began to pay attention to my own aesthetic trends, among which was, of all things, an appreciation of flowers. Now in the successful New York art world of 1962, any artist worth his paint would not consider painting flowers; to do so was tantamount to a successful Freudian psychiatrist suddenly taking up druidism.

Whatever it was I was trying to impress the members of the art establishment with, they were having none of it anyway, and hurting a little with the sting of rejection, I decided to paint flowers—wonderful, brilliant flowers of all shapes and varieties, including, of course, the magnificent, scintillating undulations of "light" and "energy" that swept in and out of the blossoms. This effort produced a series that I called *Les Fleurs Fleurs*, many of which were sold at nominal sums to friends and individuals who felt they could not do without them.

Finally flowers dwindled in interest before the advancing onslaught of a far more complex and strange array of ideas and visions. My inward eye turned to human figures, and another series of works, executed between 1963 and 1966, resulted.

These paintings were for the most part composed of elongated nudes, gigantic males and females, all with blue skin and burning red eyes, possessing fantastic energy shells and glittering, undulating rainbow auras, and shooting out radiant streamers and bubbles. The one gallery dealer I had acquired, who was working assiduously (so he said) to sell my earlier, more mundane, strongly surrealistic works, cast an oblique eye on these new productions, and not long after that we parted company (see Figures 4, 5, 6, and 7).

The first Kirlian photographs I saw were some of the marvelous renderings displayed at the First Western Hemisphere Conference on Kirlian Photography, Acupuncture, and the Human Aura, held in New York in May 1972 under the sponsorship of Judy Skutch of the Parasensory Foundation. There I was extremely astonished to view high- and low-frequency photographic results of coronal conditions that resembled almost exactly the flows, flares, and bubbles I had begun to paint nearly ten years earlier.[10]

Naturally, painting auras of one sort or another is not really new; it was especially prevalent during the Middle Ages. Direct contemporary perceptions of auric surrounds are unusual, however, especially as such subjective content is and has been discouraged in modern art appreciation and acceptance.

Several years later, having begun an independent search for other artists interested in using things beyond the physical senses as subject matter, I came across an amazing collection of research devoted to this very subject. By studying the notes and photographs of this research representing the work of over 2,000 *living* artists (1930–1974) from sixty-four different countries, I came to feel at home with my own visions. All these artists demonstrated an interest in and portrayal of various paranormal perceptions and a beautiful, often lilting aesthetic.

Among these artists, Helmut Zimmerman of Germany gives a cogent example of his viewing of radiances beyond the scope of the physical eye. Of his *Mandala of the Soul* (Figure 8) he says:

> One may begin the understanding of this painting by regarding it as an X-ray film which presents the frontal view of a standing human figure. It is an interpretation of human nature in terms of latent centers of psychic energy which lie along man's vertebral axis. It is an attempt to represent not man's outward appearance but what he

[10] See Stanley Krippner and Daniel Rubin, eds., *The Kirlian Aura* (Garden City, N.Y.: Anchor Books, 1974), pp. 170–177.

perceives or feels to be his existing self as he looks within. Every brush stroke resulted from something which I felt within me.[11]

The inner senses of man, the boundaries of consciousness, are extremely difficult to perceive. Probably this is because man exists in the midst of his perceptual and creative greatness but puts "shoulds" and "should nots" around himself, never daring to disagree to any great length with social and academic arbiters. But a great deal of blockage comes from the carrying forward of once meaningful (but no longer useful) concepts.[12]

Contemporary ideas on parapsychology, if once functional in the situations they served, are already outworn and nonfunctional. This history can best be found in the example of the famous Rhines, Dr. J. B. and Louisa E., who were continually having to define and describe basic parapsychological dilemmas and paradoxes.[13]

I am personally convinced that the "problem" represented by things psychic, if indeed it is a problem, is not the strangeness or paranormality of extrasensory ocurrences but the ways men permit themselves to perceive, the ideas held by society, groups, or even the individual about human potential. In other words, things psychic are not basically a scientific "problem," but a social one.

One of the greatest excitements of this current age is that man has pushed back almost every other frontier on the planet and is now up against his own idea of himself. Courageous people can be counted on to push into this frontier, and already the actions of a few star-busters can be felt.

[11] See Raymond and Lila K. Piper, *Cosmic Art* (Ingo Swann, ed.) (New York: Hawthorn Books, forthcoming).

[12] See, for instance, Jan Ehrenwald, "Parapsychology and the seven dragons: a neuropsychiatric model of psi phenomena," *Parapsychology: Today's Implications, Tomorrow's Applications,* The American Society for Psychical Research Symposium, May 1974, in press.

[13] Louisa E. Rhine, "The Establishment of Basic Concepts and Terminology in Parapsychology," *The Journal of Parapsychology* 35, no. 1 (March 1971), pp. 34–56; J. B. Rhine, "Psi and Psychology: Conflict and Solution," *ibid.* 32, no. 2 (June 1968), pp. 101–128.

In the past, things psychic referred essentially to strange goings-on, supernatural or mystical events disdained by the so-called "thinking" man. Now, however, the entire conceptualization of things psychic is undergoing an extraordinary change. The push is on.

In additon to including just legendary concepts like clairvoyance, psychokinesis, telepathy, and precognition, the idea of things psychic now tends to include such things as vastly enhanced performance in emergency situations, concentrated studies in intuition, creativity, awareness, and empathetic communication. People who have absolute color sense or musical pitch, or other extraordinary and specialized abilities such as being able to sense the difference between regular and counterfeit bills, above-average success in business and money-making, extraordinary acceleration of learning in children—all these are now being investigated as procedures of consciousness that can well be described as psychic or psychically oriented. And the accepted idea of mental phenomena, characterized by the straitjacket that nineteenth-century materialism engendered around man's concept of his mental prowess, is beginning to loosen.

In its grandest sense, as a trial hypothesis, the term "psychic" could well be redefined as the individual's awareness of himself as well as his capabilities of performance in the everyday working sense and in the so-called paranormal arenas. Hitherto, things called psychic have included only events or occurrences that stood out from the straitjacket; the term has excluded more usual abilities in perception and experience.

Yet I have had sufficient experience in research to be able to suggest that the most exciting and extraordinary of psychical abilities are built firmly upon good control of so-called ordinary abilities, and that operational forms of either ordinary or extraordinary abilities seem totally dependent first on how one thinks of oneself and then on how one perceives the rest of the universe, both the seen and the unseen parts.

In a way, like the artist or composer if he is to be truly original, the psychic must have the courage to separate himself from what has gone before in order to know himself and his potential in a more complete sense. If the artist, businessman, poet, or psychic allows himself to depend too much upon the visions and works of predecessors, the impact of his self-understanding dwindles accordingly.

This originality can be extended to life itself since most individuals are seeking some sort of self-expression and fulfillment, whatever their goals or professions.

When one knows he is beginning to touch upon the deep reservoirs of self-existence, of self-expression, of self-management, life begins to become excellent and exciting; a future appears in the form of growth, blossoming of potential, extensions of awareness, and a knowledge that one will be able to succeed, to complete and achieve goals.

The realm of things psychic, if cursed by the skeptic, also holds the seeds of grand human potential—potential yet to be discovered, potential that needs to become familiar. Things psychic present to things scientific an almost unending series of problems and controversies since things scientific are based almost solely upon what the eyes and ears can perceive. It is an almost impossible task to investigate the subjective universe using as criteria the rules governing the objective universe. Both these universes exist, but their spaces are different.

For many years now this conflict has been monitored by the neoscience called parapsychology; this science has tried valiantly to discover something about things psychic, but with a few exceptions it has only succeeded in grinding the diamond into a dust pile while trying to capture the sparkle.

In the science of parapsychology, only those thought qualified by training and expertise were officially permitted to speak of and draw conclusions pertaining to modern concepts of the paranormal and the psychic.

For the most part, because the field of psychology had claimed supremacy in all matters of the mind and human rationale, most workers thought qualified in parapsychology were those trained in psychological theory and practice.

The individuals least consulted on matters of theory or interpretation of research results were those performing as subjects.

Today this arbitrary arrangement shows some signs of change. Certain parapsychologists have softened their approach. One or two have expressed a desire to give increasing consideration to the possibility that persons possessed of seemingly extraordinary abilities might also contribute some clues as to how their abilities might be revealed most fruitfully.

If this compromise is visible in a few, they are but few. The overall vista of psychical research is still heavily influenced by parapsychologists who hold that only they, as trained psychologists, or at least as experienced researchers, are qualified to give advice and reach conclusions.

In all likelihood, therefore, this book, written by a subject, will not receive the approbation of the majority of parapsychologists, especially those who feel that only years of psychological training equip one to speak in depth about the subject.

It is probably best, therefore, to consider the thoughts and musings in this book as representing a personal document, or a tirade if one wishes. Parts of this book are, of necessity, autobiographical, but not in the strict sense of autobiography.

A few personal experiences are necessary in hopefully establishing the various nonmaterial realities that have drawn this author, through the years, more and more toward the "paranormal," toward things "psychic," toward the nonmaterial aspects of life. These recorded experiences are more by way of an anamnesis—a gentle recalling of things past.

If the track record of successful psychical discovery in parapsychology had illuminated science with continuous understanding, probably there would be no desire to write this book.

But without wishing to appear critical in examining the collected evidence, it is possible to conclude that the track record of illuminating discovery in parapsychology is akin to a dismal flop. Few, if any, far-reaching conclusions can be drawn from the tremendous volume of research, reports, and theory published so far.

No irony or invalidation of parapsychologists' work and efforts is intended. Many established researchers in the field bemoan this obvious nonresult, as in fact did one of the founding fathers of psychical research, the honorable William James.

It seems not to have dawned upon most researchers that the problems constituted by things psychic might not be solely a scientific matter at all but one that carries significant philosophical, and possibly metaphysical or even aesthetic, connotations.

In this dank age dominated by materialistic doctrine in science, however, philosophical, metaphysical, and aesthetic processes have dwindled into almost nothing, and consequently cannot be well used as investigative or cognitive tools, as it seems they once were.

Additionally, when things psychic finally are seriously entertained among scientists, strenuous efforts are sometimes made to locate the psychic event, the paranormal human occurrence, in the vast, imposing, beautiful realms of the mystical or the occult—when it seems obvious, to this author at least, that the psychic feat is ever more closely aligned with the necessities of material existence, with trying to get along in life, and certainly with the problems some individuals confront in trying to understand themselves in relation to the vast, monolithic scenario of existence itself.

In parapsychology there is a tremendous gap between the desire to know about things psychic and the ability to know how to understand them. The serious lack of cogent results seems to indicate that parapsychologists are not asking the right questions in the first place. Some serious change in attitude or approach seems necessary if the science is to result in growth instead of stasis.

In parapsychology, as in anything, there are both strategy and tactics. If the strategy is too far removed from the realities it is expected to deal with, the tactics utilized within it will yield insignificant results.

The tactic heretofore has been to capture a subject exhibiting some paranormal potential and grind that subject through the research mill governed by fashionable, but by no means conclusive, strategic ideas of human possibility. The paranormal potential in the subject—if indeed it was there in the first place—usually was extinguished promptly and the subject himself fed out the back door in some sort of pulp form.

Subjects who presumed to protest this treatment or method of research and sought to contribute an idea or two were regarded rather horrifically, and usually invited not to return. Where the subject survived the research with his psychic abilities intact, his results hardly ever survived the argumentation engendered as researchers set about trying to construct explanatory rationales.

Yet, in spite of the multitudes of failures, a science of parapsychology has resulted. This must be held as solely due to the dedication of a few visionary men and women to whom apperceptive appreciation should be extended. Their apperceptive contributions have given meaning and importance in numerous ways, and in some cases have established a value without which hardly anything can progress: the value dignity holds in the face of adversity.

The science of parapsychology has slipped over into other disciplines. Researchers in the fields of energetics, biology, and physics have been involved increasingly with ascertaining the meaning of situations that—in their variable characteristics of matter, energy, space, and time—are not dissimilar from situations long of fundamental interest to parapsychologists.

If the inquiry into the paranormal components of the human being is expanding, the weight of acceptability of research results must come about based upon standards hard won as well as upon new discovery. These standards include independent judging of results as established by parapsychologist members of the Parapsychology Association, which in turn is a member of the American Association for the Advancement of Science.

Individual claims may have flexible degrees of credibility in personal and certain social situations. In science, however, if momentous discovery is hoped for in this highly questionable field, experimental results must bear the test of time and conform in the long run to scientific standards.

Because of the illusive nature of things psychic, parapsychology so far represents an oblique approach to the topic. But the minimal data accumulated are sufficient to indicate that the psychic premise is personal to every man. In this light the appearance of psychic superstars who know or care nothing of science, philosophy, or humanitarianism seems anachronistic. The appearance of psychic scientists or philosophers, on the other hand, seems to fulfill the beck and call of a creative future.

The boundaries now constituted by the problems emerging in quantum (nonmaterial) physics seem similar to the boundaries delineated by things psychic. Consequently these two fields of paradoxical interest are probably destined to influence each other increasingly.

The problem in physics is to somehow establish a new order of physics that is bound to disagree in some fundamental aspects with the historical notions that underlie present-day physics.[14] In terms of parapsychological, or psi, interests, the present quasi-comprehended psi factors implying factors beyond current concepts of space and time are not compatible with physics.

[14] Many sources review the problematical situations created by physical discovery. The dichotomies created by quantum discovery were elucidated around 1920. A recent synopsis can be found in David Bohm, "Quantum Theory as an Indication of a New Order in Physics: Part A, The Development of New Orders as Shown Through the History of Physics," *Foundations of Physics* 1, no. 4 (1971), pp. 359–381, and "Part B: Implicate and Explicate Order in Physical Law," *ibid.* 3, no. 2 (1973), pp. 139–167.

But it cannot be said that studies in physics are complete; the total range of relationships in the universe has by no means been scrutinized, as increasing discovery indicates.[15] Until these two do meet in a future of science yet undiscovered, the problem centers more around philosophical or sociological aspects, as has been mentioned quite often.

The science of man's non-physical abilities is, apparently, in some sort of prenatal condition.[16] Yet there are foreshadowings of discovery, of which currently little understood psi factors must be held indicative. There is no doubt that the history of science is beleaguered by examples attesting to the ever-prevalent nonsurvival condition exhibited by many men who powerfully hold the world in the image they expect to see it.[17]

[15] See, for instance, Rémy Chauvin, "To Reconcile Psi and Physics," *The Journal of Parapsychology* 34, no. 3 (September 1970), pp. 215–218; Willem Klip, "An Experimental Approach to the Interpretation of the Quantum Theory," *The Journal of the Society for Psychical Research* 44, no. 734 (December 1967), pp. 181–187.

[16] See Willis W. Harman, "The New Copernican Revolution," *Stanford Today*, Winter 1969, pp. 7–10.

[17] Willis W. Harman, "Old Wine in New Wineskins," in J. F. T. Bugental, ed., *Challenges of Humanistic Psychology*, 1967, pp. 321–332.

PART II

Psychokinesis

> The skeptical scientist told the psychic that he would have to see a demonstration of psychokinesis to believe it. The psychic told him to move his little finger, which he did. "Did you believe it?" asked the psychic.

For the most part, modern research in things psychic is a bland, if not boring, affair. It does not offer the magic and drama of seances, the elegance of burning candles, mysterious voices, or ecstatic nocturnal gambolings for which it was so famous in earlier days.

Inquiry or endeavour into the invisible realms now takes place in rooms full of gray and stainless steel equipment. Recording devices and other esoteric machinery litter the floors and walls of chambers to which no particular aesthetic attention has been given. The catching or trapping of the illusive psychic event in science is usually a frantic affair of machines (since eyes alone are not to be trusted). The rooms in which these activities take place are expected only to be serviceable, not particularly stylish or elegant.

Such a room as this is Cleve Backster's lie-detection school on Broadway and Forty-fifth Street in Manhattan. There, during the week of October 10, 1972, I sat trying to "zap" plants with some form of mental or psychical motion. The room was a smallish, gray square cubicle furnished with steel desks and some galvanometers. One wall had a one-way, see-through mirror system where observers in the next gray, smallish cubicle could spy unseen. The *Dracaena massangeana*, the plant that had officially ushered in the age of sentient plant reactions, lurked back in a corner, by this time a monster some five feet tall.

The target for "zapping" was an ordinary, medium-sized philodendron, hooked up by a direct current system (a Wheatstone bridge circuit). On a moving strip of paper a needle was tracing the electric potential or resistance changes presumably taking place in the plant.

What was wanted in this instance was one effect that could be reproduced again and again. However, the plant was proving rather perverse, responding magnificently at first to almost any thought pattern flung at it. The idea of burning its leaves with a match caused the needle to scribble an appropriate deviation on the traceout. Several antisurvival thoughts—chopping it in half, pouring acid on its leaves, etc.—also brought expected deviations on the graph. But only at first.

Repetition of these mentally destructive activities did not bring about a similar pattern of electrical potential shift; it tended instead to register grandly at first but then to diminish and finally disappear altogether.

Backster and I watched this "decline effect," not understanding exactly why it took place. Why should the philodendron react at all unless there really was some sort of reception of the "thought" within the plant itself, and if it reacted then, why did it not continue to react to the same thought?

I had worked my way into Backster's domain as a result of meeting him at a cocktail party. In the kitchen of our hostess, a certain Zelda, a grand lady who does a great deal to bring people together, I had pinned Backster between the refrigerator and the table and explained to him what I feel must be possible as a result of certain "psychic" photographs that had been taken earlier and had turned out remarkably well.

And to Zelda's apartment, a month earlier, had come some young people with a camera and infrared film. They had been going around trying to photograph ghosts in haunted houses in the New York area. Apparently ghosts were hard to catch, even on infrared film, and if enthusiasm still shone from their eyes, there also was a certain disappointment.

The archives of psychic goings-on are full of absolutely amazing and startling photographs—visions of departed personalities, ectoplasms, thought forms, lights, sparks, even some obscene things defying description. It is also known that there are more than 200 ways of producing fraudulent photographs of this kind; for instance, bisulfate of quinine is invisible to the human eye but will appear afterward on a plate, so decorating the face of the subject with this substance produces invisible visions that "miraculously" come forth in the photograph.

When the young people came barging into Zelda's, I happened to be there. After some convivial chatter we decided to repair to Zelda's bedroom, which could be totally darkened, and take turns trying to manifest psychic energies for photographing. Our reasoning was that we *might* have a better chance of recording living energies on the sensitive film, since with the living one could at least know where to aim the camera.

Everyone was amazed, myself in particular, after the film had been developed, to find some organizations of light effects that would be hard to fake by any means. These results were submitted unofficially to some photographic "experts," who examined them and felt they could not easily be faked. (see Figure 9).*

I knew that, for my part, there was no fakery.

All I had done was sit in a chair in the dark, imbibing increasingly warm beer and trying to create energy vacuoles in my hands, around my head, and so forth.

These results were, if not bona fide science, at least fascinating. Turning the matter over in my mind for several days, I eventually came to conclude that photography was a sloppy and ineffective way to proceed. But if such energies, or whatever they were, had enough substance to record on a film, they also must have some sort of electromagnetic implications. In order to reproduce on film at all, these effects had to be locatable somewhere in the electromagnetic spectrum.

Therefore, having caged Backster in the kitchen, I explained all this to him and suggested that this type of phenomenon might be found somewhere in thermal, magnetic, or electrostatic formations that exist within the electromagnetic spectrum. A good place to start looking could be with electric potential shifts, as seemed to be demonstrated by the results of his plant research.

A few days later, in front of the recalcitrant philodendron, it was becoming increasingly apparent that, even if the plant "responded" at first, it did not continue to do so. Thus the hope for a reproducible effect declined accordingly. The plant seemed to become familiar with the "zap"; since the zap was not followed up with a real destructive effect, it seemed to get accustomed to the mental probe, deciding that since I did not mean actual harm it no longer needed to react.

Of course this type of reasoning implied that the rather bedraggled

* Photographic sessions such as that described in no way qualify as scientific evidence, the necessary controls of course being absent. The photo is presented merely as a curiosity.

philodendron somehow was in possession of analytical appreciation of the incoming intent and could "decide" by experience that, if the thought was negative, the action was not. Presumably it therefore turned its attention to more important things—such as, perhaps, the bacteria trying to nibble away at its roots or in the invisible crevices in its leaves.

I told Backster that I felt the plant had psyched me out, had discerned that I did not really mean to harm it, and so no longer deigned to cooperate.

What followed was some quite serious conversation on the nature of plant sentience and the difficulties official science would be likely to have in stomaching this possibility, a prospect that was not likely in the near future. But this was no reason to abandon the search. Instead of trying to convince the uncooperative philodendron (we tried several species of plants), I suggested that what was needed was a target that had electric potential shift characteristics but also had less "mind," had no decision-making capacity, and was less self-determined than the plants seemed to be.

Backster admitted that he had "hooked up" a lot of things, among them a specimen of "rubberized" graphite that usually was used as insulating material but gave a rather continuous, fluctuating electric potential pattern when connected to the Wheatstone bridge.

Now there is some degree of rationality in interacting mentally or psychically with living plants, but even in my most lurid imagination I had not thought of interacting with inert matter. A preliminary attempt at "zapping" this new target went a long way toward confirming my suspicion that this feat might be impossible. The readout did not shift at all, no matter what I tried.

A little defeated about the idea of electromagnetic interactions, I retreated for a few days. But thoughts about this impossible situation continued to turn around in my head. Had I not seen the photographic results? Had I not seen vegetable structures quiver and respond? At least to my own satisfaction, these things had occurred.

Several days passed, and periodically I went to Backster's to try to get through to the graphite. But the graphite proved even more recalcitrant than the plants: It did not fluctuate at all. But away from the target, going about the daily trial of existing, I was turning over countless possibilities, examining and discarding.

The center of this mental maelstrom gradually shifted from considerations of the graphite itself to considerations of how I *viewed* the graphite, and therefore matter itself.

It became possible to understand that matter just goes along its merry way, composed essentially of motion of particles. The human idea of man is that he *cannot* interact with these particles of matter, and thus he usually does not. But what of the body itself? Is it just a complex biological system that goes along without our own intention or agreement? Not likely, since usually, some of the time at least, it does what I want it to do.

Thus I came up against the barrier not of interacting mentally with the graphite but of man's idea that it was not possible. If I went past this barrier and affected the graphite, not only would I affect the graphite but if others heard of it, I would bring disbelief and disapprobation down on my head.

If I did not somehow affect that piece of graphite, I would have to step backward into the limited idea of man's potential; if I succeeded in perturbing it, I would have to contend with the wrath of man's limited ideas.

So I got sick. The headaches were sublime in their perfection. then fever, cold, and finally into bed, there to commiserate with myself about the problem caused by thinking too long on any subject.

Finally I got bored with being sick. To hell with what others thought possible. If it should transpire that the inert graphite could be affected by consciousness, they would just have to do the best they could. With this decision the cold disappeared as if by magic.

Once again ensconced across from the graphite, its electric potential fluctuating away through the Wheatstone bridge at a steady pace, I reached consciously through the intervening space between it and me and touched it, no longer caring what others would think, or if they ever thought at all.

In the space occupied by the graphite, pinned between the two small resistors to which it was attached, I felt I could sense what might be molecular motion, or at least the ever-so-slight electrostatic aura that emanates from electromagnetic motion or frequencies. This could possibly be disrupted by the psychic overlap of "intent" of hot or cold. My probe was off by almost an inch. I moved it accordingly and touched the graphite. The recording pen gave a simultaneous jog, and then in accord with the psychic probe—again, and again, and again (see Figure 10).

※

The "official" world of parapsychology is not large. With a little effort it is possible to see its peripheries and get some idea of the kinds of people that populate it. Most of those integral to the field, in their official, academic stance, are dull, and the field of parapsychology itself is characterized by a slow-moving, almost insensible lethargy.

This official academic visage provides a front that makes developments and progress inaccessible to the ordinary person, and even to the public media, which cannot interpret the "papers" very well and thus come to rely for their data upon the historical "probable trickery" of it all.

This apparently unified official front (which most parapsychologists are careful to preserve) is characteristic of the field from the uninitiated point of view. But within the field itself this unity is decidedly not the case. There are serious internecine battles that might put to shame the dramatics of battles between inhabitants of opposing star systems. Also, there is a sort of quasi-task force of individuals who devote a great deal of time and enthusiasm to taking literary or gossipy "pot shots" at independent researchers or theorists who dare to raise their heads. Their fusillades provide a continuous din.

The population of the field may be categorized into three general types, but these three types by no means include all the manifold personality types in the arena. There are, first, the venomous, defensive types, scientists who are not above cheating a little on their own behalf and attacking others accordingly. This problem has been discussed elsewhere and need not be gone into here.[1] There is the greater backbone of the field, individuals who are interested in and concerned about discovery, working diligently, and often unsuccessfully, with little or no attention. And there are the elegant few who rise far above all others and whose names will continue into the future, the results of their work accumulating, giving

[1] See, for instance, R. A. McConnell, "ESP and Credibility in Science," *American Psychologist* 24, no. 5 (May 1969), pp. 531–538.

substance and body to the increasing realities of man's paranormal potential. (A fourth personality type might be mentioned, the subjects themselves, the possessors or self-claimed possessors of abilities. But for the most part they appear to be disassociated from the "work," and some parapsychologists consider them incidental to the profession.)

Among the few who—for their grandeur of vision and accumulation of significant results— have come to stand out far above others, Gertrude Schmeidler may be one of the best known. And she can at least be trusted not to do in a subject before the start—in contrast to those whose ideas are set and inflexible.

About the time I was laboring in Backster's laboratory, worrying over the significances of fluctuating electric potential shifts in an unimpressive speck of graphite, I ran into this amazing woman at a party. There —surrounded by a multitude of voices talking about the latest scandals in the field, about who was doing what and to whom—we began talking about the possibilities that might develop from this beginning work with the graphite.

Possibilities like this are always unclear, sometimes even to the most professional of scientists. But the initial fluctuations of the graphite could, we both thought, be taken a little further if this psychokinetic effect could be reproduced under good laboratory conditions. (To the general reader, reference to this necessity is always boring. It is almost impossible, considering the ecstatic frivolity generated by the public psychic, to convey the urgent necessity for controlled research. And, suffice it to say, controlled research is ultra boring in character.)

But experimental design, as I came to learn, is one of Schmeidler's passions. And, as I also came to know, Schmeidler has an even more grand and elegant characteristic—that of being open to possibilities, of surveying them without at the same time interjecting imaginary reservations or barriers.

As the cigarette smoke increasingly clouded the environs of the party, a psychic flush setting into the faces of most, I indicated to her, "I think it is possible to get this effect."

"Well, it would be most interesting to follow up on this to see," replied Schmeidler.

"I know absolutely nothing about the necessities of experimental situations, you know," I informed her glumly, well understanding that the merit of psychic research as *research* does not lie in personal claims but in observable, verifiable, and visible data, usually in the form of graphs and other boring things.

A few days later, over the telephone, we talked again. Schmeidler accepted my wish for a strong experiment.

"If you will show me what it is you think you can do, I will see if I can surround it with a respectable experimental design," she volunteered.

And in this way the graphite business went a step further.

One of Schmeidler's earliest experimental situations was designed to try to ascertain some of the psychological conditions that tied in with ESP abilities. She pioneered with straightforward ESP tests with stringent controls. Her subjects, all of whom must have believed a little in the existence of ESP, tended to score a little above chance expectation. But into this situation entered two subjects who had joined the ESP testing only to demonstrate to Schmeidler the unimportance of ESP, and who themselves had a negative belief about it. And these two subjects scored *below* chance.

Schmeidler caught this interesting situation in hand, and developed it into what is now the famous "sheep/goats" effect: The "sheep" who hold a positive approach to ESP tend to score above chance on testing, and the "goats," the disbelievers, usually score below.

To see if this effect held up, hundreds of subjects, divided into two groups—those who believed in ESP and those who did not—were run in experimentation. The results were so consistent that it became possible to predict the above-chance score from the positive attitudes and the low score from the negative attitudes.

As Schmeidler indicates, these results gave a different view to one of the anomalies in ESP research.[2] Not only the presumed ESP abilities were now to be sought and considered but also the pro or con attitudes of the subjects and the experimenters themselves.

This sheep/goat effect has been given a lot of attention since Schmeidler first began studying it, and the experiment has been replicated

[2] G. R. Schmeidler, "Predicting Good and Bad Scores in a Clairvoyance Experiment: A Final Report," *The Journal of the American Society for Psychical Research* 37 (October 1943), pp. 210–221.

many times with the same results. In India, for example, 150 subjects, separated into the two groups, showed a highly significant difference between the scores of the sheep and the goats.[3]

In addition to being an eminent parapsychologist, Gertrude Schmeidler also has a teaching career at City College in New York. To this seat of learning, therefore, I was obliged to repair many times during the succeeding weeks. City College, in terms of aesthetics, has absolutely nothing to offer; in fact I came to refer to it as the dungeon above ground.

But in the presence of Schmeidler and a courageous young parapsychologist, Larry Lewis, who structured all the equipment necessary to run the experiments, the dreary medieval atmosphere of the dream laboratory where the experiments were conducted seemed to vanish. About once every week or so I would make the long subway trek through Manhattan up to City College, there to climb the hill after exiting from the subway, thence to climb the stairs to the experimental room in the dungeon above ground.

The graphite samples, attached to extremely sensitive thermistors, were sealed in vacuum bottles. The temperature variations were recorded in a complex bank of EEG equipment, its normal gray relieved by copious splatterings of red ink from the recording pens. After several days of preliminary attempts at affecting the graphite and the thermistors Schmeidler finally felt she had a good enough idea of the situation to begin to design the experiment.

There was a hiatus of a few weeks, and finally the call came that all was ready. And the experiment took place—a beautiful, wonderful experiment that I will remember, if for no other reason than working with such an open and farsighted personality as Gertrude Schmeidler.

The results of this series of experiments were quite positive in that the effect was seen to occur repeatedly within the structure and controls of the experimental situation. At this point the reality or verity of the effect must pass from personal claim over to the strength of the experiment itself.

Thus at this point personal claim no longer need be made on my part. Personal claim, characteristic of all people with alleged abilities, is not

[3] B. H. Bhadra, "The Relationship of Test Scores to Belief in ESP," *The Journal of Parapsychology* 30, no. 1 (March 1966), pp. 1–17.

research, and it was research and not personal claim that I was interested in from the first. Schmeidler's experiment and its results are now in print.[4] The interested reader is referred directly to that report, since in the educative process one must refer directly to the source of the observed data. (Schmeidler's procedure is described in the Foreword of this book.)

This experiment can be considered successful in that automatic recordings of temperature were repeatedly produced in target thermistors in insulated thermos bottles as far as twenty-five feet from the body. Furthermore, in providing control subjects for the experiment Schmeidler was able to discover that the effect was not unique to my attempts since another subject was able to produce similar results.

Psychokinesis ordinarily is defined as "mind over matter," a definition that seems singularly uninformed—if only because the meaning of "mind" is not at all clear within the scope of today's sciences.

The reader as well as the scientist should not be persuaded otherwise. Rushing to even the most concise of dictionaries, one is likely to discover at least thirty-one nuances defining this word. Such conglomerate definitions do not contribute much to either education or understanding in any precise sense. It is observed, though, that this type of profuse defining seems to appeal to certain people who like to dwell in and perpetuate generalities and do not at all care to dissect existence with precision.

Many years ago, even before I became aware that *I* caused volitional body movements and the body did not move me, I gave serious thought to this matter of mind. My thoughts probably would not qualify as any sort of scientific acumen, but nonetheless I arrived at certain conclusions.

It seemed that the mind's major occupation was to think, to analyze. After having "thought" about something, it was up to me to take the decisions or establish the intention to do any given thing. This led, naturally, to an awareness of the difference between myself as a decision-making

---

[4] G. R. Schmeidler, "PK Effects Upon Continuously Recorded Temperature," *The Journal of the American Society for Psychical Research* 67, no. 4 (October 1973), pp. 325–340.

entity and the mind that mechanically analyzed. Yet, if the mind had analytical capabilities, hypothetically these analytical capabilities could be used to dissect the mind itself, to understand the mind in its totality.

Upon voicing such an opinion, I was quick to discover that hardly anyone else held a similar one and I was definitely and dramatically informed that this was not possible. I was greatly shocked, and still am, that the majority of people simply refuse to consider this possibility. In some cases it is held, even to the point of fisticuffs, that the mind is not capable of understanding itself or of being used to understand even a portion of its own workings.

Yet I felt then as now that I, as an entity that observes the mind thinking, also cause it to think, depending on the topics and problems at hand.

Possibly this sort of awareness is inherent in the creative processes, especially the visual creative processes. Any artist becomes familiar to a certain degree with the picturizing capabilities of the mind, since he is continually mentally creating and destroying images relative to his artwork.

The social dangers of holding that thought can be understood as structure (mind) as well as content (what it thinks about) did not dissuade me from clinging to this opinion. If certain people did assert that it was wrong, nowhere could I find proof that it was. It was paramount in my artistic endeavors to observe continually the function of thought in relation to the topics I was interested in artistically. It was not long before I began to apply this differentiation to other areas of interest. And, naturally, it was just about this point that the turkey feathers really hit the fan with blizzard force.

I soon discovered that there were whole areas of life from which I retreated in thought, areas that—when they came into the thinking process and thus into awareness—sent shivers here and there. Among these were thoughts about genitalia, money, art gallery dealers, and the landlord. And there were other areas that also brought about discomfort, such as thoughts about where it was that I came from, about my "I-ness" as contrasted to just the body. These topics came to include such esoteric items as past lives, other worlds, the invisible motion of base matter, time differentials, imagination of things beyond reality—all the things that make one seem bonkers in the eyes of others.

After a period of confusion it was possible to understand that all these retreating tendencies must originate in another part of the mind—a part of the mind capable of vetoing analytical thought, a part of the mind that was already possessed of suppressed thoughts and immediately produced mental discomfort when touched upon. This part of the mind I came to call the "garbage bag."

For the purposes of this book it seems necessary to limit the definition of "mind" to only these two ideas of it, i.e., the garbage bag and the analytical computing part, if only to enable me to communicate to the reader some of the factors that have enabled me to participate in psychic research.

Mind seems to be, on the one hand, whatever it is that the individual uses to think with, plus, and most important, his total history of thoughts and experiences. These thoughts and experiences may be either conscious or subconscious, but whatever form they are in, they often surge up in the form of mental image pictures. When the content of those pictures is far removed from familiarity or is laden with uncomfortable experience, the thinking entity rejects them, but apparently not without some disturbance emanating from them.

Thinking, at its best, might be said to be the ability of the sentient or knowing entity to discern, quickly and without hesitation any given situation as regards at least "seeing" differences, similarities and "samenesses" that enable him to initiate subsequent action. When these comparative action processes are impeded with contents coughed up from the "mind," and especially if those contents cause the person to withdraw from action, the mind becomes an impediment.

Usually life means accepting matter, energy, space, and time as one perceives them and trying to think and plot a course somewhat in keeping with those perceptions. It is always an embarrassment to initiate a life action based upon one's perceptions and thinking, only to find that it doesn't work as expected. One either miscalculated because one wasn't perceiving matter, energy, space, and time correctly, or his perceptions were being aborted because of undue influence coming up out of the mind, influences unfamiliar and unexpected, but nonetheless there.

Aside from the negative imperatives rising up out of the hidden depths of the garbage bag, it is easy to see that one's total concept of the universe might easily be formed and monitored by past negative experiences, causing the thinking entity to withdraw and not wish to think about those negatives anymore. Thus, any given thing will be as unreal (and intolerable) to an individual as the sum contents of his mind causes him to withdraw from it. These sum contents cause the person to create opinions and viewpoints that are tolerable to him and to reject all opposing information.

A "law" becomes a law when a certain thing can be said to occur again and again, and the reasons for this occurrence, its frequency, and its sameness can be discerned and appreciated.

But there are no laws of mind established in science or sociology to any convincing degree, except to assume that a "mind" seems to be already possessed by a fetus that successfully emerges into birth. The infant predictably will grow into a physical body that is generally recognizable, with some rare fascinating exceptions; but what the "mind" that is assumed to arrive with the infant will grow into frequently quite staggers the imaginations of even the most respected philosophers and scientists, to say nothing of psychologists.

No serious thinker could entertain the ideas that psychokinesis is "mind over matter," this definition belonging to stage magicians, uneducated and superstitious people, and sensationalist writers. If one were to cling to an idea of "mind/matter," about the best that might be established, and this badly, is a mind *and* matter relationship of some sort, but even this idea is unpromising. The "mind over matter" idea really stacks up by descriptive definition as "something we don't know about over something else we don't know much about."

Psychokinesis, therefore, is more profitably described as "a process not yet known to contemporary physics."[5]

Assuming that one is trying to get through a lifetime with as little travail and trauma as necessary and as much material gain as possible —that is, to suffer less and live better—one may conclude that the less waves one makes about life the better off one will be. Possibly this attitude

[5] Haakon Forwald, *Mind, Matter, and Gravitation: A Theoretical and Experimental Study* (New York: Parapsychology Foundation, 1969), p. 1.

works for some people—for the rare few who troop around with stars in their eyes, assuring everyone that all is good and wonderful and beautiful. But for others, who cannot pattern themselves after Candide, this attitude is impossible.

In New York, for instance, one makes the decision to risk one's life by entering the subway; in Texas voracious bugs are at the crops; in San Francisco the suicide rate is the highest ever. All is not well. Over the world hangs the pall of governmental decline and ecological rape; one's children turn up with strange ideas and act even more strangely; church attendance dwindles; movies and entertainment erupt in spectacles of violence.

All these can easily be seen to descend from cause-effect situations, but cause-effect solutions and methods of dealing with them are not taught even in the most respectable universities. And today mature students graduating with piles of sheepskins (degrees and certificates) really step from an academic Eden into a barbarian territory.

It may be wondered what it is, exactly, that psychic abilities have to do with any of these problems. Frankly, one's inspired, intuitive, and imaginative abilities permit one to have a better chance of surviving.

The small, meek voices deep inside one's head, the hunches and foresights experienced by almost everyone, are part and parcel of the human's ability to ferret out a course of life for himself.

Countless people transcend the *material* barriers of matter, energy, space, and time in any number of ways.

In the first place each human manages to animate his body—a complex engine that does not animate without *intention*. This particular form of psychokinesis (matter moved by mind?) is so usual that it is not considered unusual; it is one of the psychic acts sitting on the tips of researchers' noses, but it is assiduously avoided.

Thinking itself transcends time to a greater or lesser degree. The ordinary human can compare things from the past with things in the future. Energy and space transcendence are daily accomplished in thought systems, especially systems utilized by inventors, artists, and mathematicians.

None of these events is ordinarily termed "psychic" since they all are usual and common. Only the more spectacular, usually foolish, things that selected individuals make stand out from these common psychic situations are usually called "psychic." Yet the greatest pools of psychism, of nonmaterial interaction with the material universe, can be observed just by causing one's little finger to move, again and again until one comes to understand how it is moving.

Now immaterial or nonmaterial interactions heretofore have been considered beyond the pale of understanding and possibility. Anyone who suggested that there was more to the universe than met doctrine or the eye (or sense perceptions) risked being burned, tortured, fired, demoted, ostracized, or dragged off to the nut house.

However, contrary to common beliefs and official academic standards, the decline of a total mechanical, materialistic view in the physical sciences actually began somewhere during the eighteenth century. Even prior to the eighteenth century there were several scandalous excursions away from the then forming materialistic bastion.[6]

By 1870 a young man, named William Kingdon Clifford, only twenty-four years of age, had suggested to the Cambridge Philosophical Society that a particle of matter might really be nothing more than a kind of hill in the geometry of space. Shortly after that, in 1873, while still believing in materialistic cause and effect, James Clerk Maxwell hinted that, although the electromagnetic field seemed continuous, the study of the singularities and instabilities might tend to remove the prejudice of the continuity of things.

It was only in 1900 that the full impact of these hints and suggestions began to erupt when Max Planck demonstrated that energy was *not* emitted in a continuous fashion. And in 1905, Albert Einstein proved that light came in packages called quanta.*

The physicist Niels Bohr soon was able to incorporate the fundamental

---

[6] See, for instance, Albert Einstein and Leopold Infeld, *The Evolution of Physics* (New York: Simon and Schuster, 1938), pp. 71–123.

* The scientific explanation of quantum theory, while important to the scope of the psychokinetic premise, is only touched upon lightly, and then insofar as it relates to sociological and philosophical concepts of man in the universe. Technical quantum theory is fundamentally concerned with the radiation of energy from a given substance, establishing that such radiation is not continuous and involves a unit amount of energy, called the quantum, that differs in each different substance with the vibration frequency of that substance. Before Max Planck advanced his hypothesis, emission and absorption of energy by given substances was held to be continuous.

discontinuity of the universe into his model of the atom and eventually outlined his principles of complementarity, which suggested that light—and energy—could be both wave and particle.

When Einstein produced a wave of continuity of sorts with his theory of general relativity, he ended the dichotomy of time and space. He also suggested, and eventually proved, that matter and energy share the same equation.

All these momentous events in physics meant, simply and with a pristine clarity, that the universe of materialism *dematerialized,* this being the supreme psychic event of the millenium—and accomplished not by psychics but by physicists!

The materialistic view that everything could eventually be explained by material interactions was demonstrated as decidedly incorrect. There could be events inspired in the material, objective universe by seemingly nonmaterial influences.

How these nonmaterial influences affected things was not quite clear in all cases, but at least the reality had been openly established.

The implications arising from the action of the voltaic battery, from Clifford's shocking statement, and eventually from the acute and momentous observations of Maxwell, Bohr, and Einstein, presented an astonishing vista to physicists. But, since difficulties of this nature arise frequently in the sciences, they tried to take the discoveries in stride.

Other physicists made various attempts to invoke simple generalizations of old ideas as a convenient way out of the dilemmas presented by discovery of nonmaterial interactions. But in the physical sciences such cheating goes only so far, since physical scientists eventually must respond to acute observation, and not solely to favored ideas.

In the intellectual sciences (philosophy, sociology, psychology), however, a glossed-over generality can remain in fashion almost indefinitely, since the intellectual man must utilize the qualities of intellect and awareness to observe intellectual or mental phenomena. If one observes these through a screen of glossed-over intellectual generalities, a good deal of confusion is likely to result.

And, even more pertinent in the realms of metaphysics, psychology, and philosophy, it is all too likely that any given individual will receive or perceive only the human interactions that fall within *his* given experience or imagination. It is therefore permissible to hypothesize that narrow education coupled with minimal experience and imagination will predictably result in narrow, minimal conclusions.

For this and other reasons the intellectual sciences often appear to be less science than games people play with themselves and others.

But science that proceeds along the lines of having to use the intellect and awareness to *observe* before *interpreting* usually comes up finally with real discovery.

Reviewing the fundamental principles of the quantum theory in his Chicago lectures in 1929, the Nobel laureate Werner Heisenberg indicated that although the theory of relativity makes the greatest demands on the ability for abstract thought, it nevertheless fulfills the requirements of traditional science.[7] It permits division of the world into subject and object (that is, observer and observed) and hence a clear delineation of the laws of causality.[8]

However, Heisenberg went on, where in classical physical theory it was assumed that observer-observed interaction was negligible, this assumption was not permissible in atomic physics since the interaction between observer and object caused large or uncontrollable changes in the system being observed. He did not immediately associate this discovery with thought, but just about anyone can perceive that thinking about something causes the thought itself to commence a series of almost uncontrollable changes.

Many years later Heisenberg fully indicated that the objective world in space and time no longer existed down at the atomic level. And he further noted that mathematical symbols of theoretical physics referred merely to possibilities and probabilities, and not even to facts, as was earlier suggested by twenty-four-year-old William Kingdon Clifford.[9]

---

[7] See Werner Heisenberg, *The Physical Principles of the Quantum Theory* (Chicago: University of Chicago Press, 1930), pp. 1–4.

[8] Heisenberg also dealt early on with the philosophical difficulties brought about by the introduction of quantum theory into a mechanical universe. See Werner Heisenberg, *Philosophic Problems of Nuclear Science* (London: Faber and Faber, 1952), particularly the chapter entitled "Fundamental Problems of Present-day Atomic Physics," pp. 77–94.

[9] See Werner Heisenberg, *Der Teil und das Ganze* (Munich, 1969), pp. 63–64.

Stanford Research Institute (SRI) in Menlo Park, California, is composed of an extensive grouping of buildings. Ranging from ultra-modern structures to reconverted military barracks, this conglomeration houses some 3,500 people engaged either in trying to think or in giving moral and material support to those so engaged.

Thus it is called in the popular press a "think tank," an appellation that is probably apt but in no sense gives an accurate picture of what it's all about. First, it is filled with *people*—many of them have vision, others are interested in discovery, and yet others have both qualities. Second, it is also populated with individuals who are interested in something and do not sit about merely trying to be interesting and colorful themselves.

This might seem to some a niggling difference, but actually being interested in things, as opposed to posing as an interesting creature (which is often the case among psychic superstars), is almost the difference between being comfortably human and indecently nonhuman. At SRI it was my endless pleasure to meet first one and then another in a continuing supply of individuals interested in life and things beyond their own personalities.

My first excursions to this establishment were therefore of good pleasure for me, especially after two years' exposure to a line of parapsychologists, many of whom were interested in nothing aside from their personal, and quite unproved, ideas of the psychic. Further, the people at SRI with whom I was to come into closest association were mostly physicists, so the view of the landing field of psychism upon which cognition might alight was totally different from that usually encountered in psychic research.

It was decidedly unusual for such a respectable and meritorious establishment as SRI to begin, of all things, an exploration into things psychic, and this activity did not go unnoticed by critics and the public media. Yet the arena of consciousness and the world of physics continue to draw closer together every day, and the Electronics and Bioengineering Laboratory at SRI was simply one of the first to take interest in the possibilities, albeit yet alleged, that things psychic seem to imply.

Basic to the social situation created by the possibility of paranormal perceptions is the confusion surrounding quasi-occult ideas of how it is exactly that the being perceives by these so-called esoteric means. Does one have "other eyes," other organs similar to known sensory equipment? No, I did not feel this was the case at all, even though such things as astral bodies are legion in psychic literature.

Before I was invited to SRI, as the experiments in which I became involved progressed, it seemed more likely that all one had to do in terms of awareness was to approximate, "by a process yet unknown to physics," whatever it was that one wished to perceive. In this manner I was soon somewhat abysmally entangled in such complicated things as the electromagnetic spectrum, wavelengths, and frequencies.

Whatever all this may or may not have led up to, I was reasonably convinced that, until one consciously can do this—that is, duplicate in terms of awareness what it is one wishes to perceive paranormally—all will be black and remain black. The tendency of memory to present to consciousness a "picture" of whatever is being recalled seemed close to this idea, but memory in most cases appeared to be under only a quasi–consciousness-control system, if not completely automatic.

I had become, in a few short months of active thought and participation in experiments, aware of such things as the velocities of awareness exterior to or away from sensory tactics. For example, the eyes do not record or inform the brain of the passing of X-rays, which can be and are sensed by film. Yet many people have reported suddenly "seeing" or becoming aware of the interiors of biological systems as if they had momentarily developed X-ray vision.

Could it be, therefore, I tried to reason, that we as perceptual beings are merely habitually dependent upon sensory perception and just never use the other? And, if this is the case, just where and how is it that one begins to use that other?

Among the many tantalizing possibilities that came to mind was a hypothesis that psychic perceptions, in terms of velocities, might be exceedingly swift, possibly faster than the speed of light. If this was so, basic psychic perception would pass through the physical universe as if it did not exist, much as cosmic rays and neutrinos do. But if this were so, then to consciously grasp such perceptions required a vast revision in what one could be conscious of.

Grasping at these few wisps of ideas, by no means conclusive of anything, I used plant-man Backster as a sounding board. Backster nodded enthusiastically and produced a copy of a theoretical paper by Dr. H. E. Puthoff, a senior research physicist at SRI.

Puthoff's paper began by stating:

> Recent experiments in parapsychology, especially in the Soviet Union and Czechoslovakia, have indicated anew that sufficient evidence exists to warrant serious scientific investigation. Experiments in telepathy, psychokinesis (PK), etc., are now being conducted with sufficient rigor in scientific laboratories to indicate the possibility of developing not just a catalog of interesting events, but rather a pattern of cause-effect relationships of the type that lends itself to analysis and hypothesis in the forms we are familiar with in the physical sciences. . . . A careful survey of the characteristics of certain phenomena in this category has suggested to the author a theoretical foundation within the framework of present-day scientific considerations and which lends itself to straight-forward experimental verification or rejection. We advance here on the hypothesis that "tachyon" phenomena predicted on the basis of relativistic quantum theory but not yet observed may be involved (tachyon is the name given to particles with spacelike four-momentum which presumably travel faster than the velocity of light in vacuum, the description of which satisfies the requirements of relativistic quantum mechanics).[10]

And Puthoff adds: "An argument is made that this hypothesis is the natural result of an effort to extend quantum theory to include phenomena associated with life processes."

Now from the first, as impossibilities dawned upon me as potential possibilities, it seemed that life took on a new allure if one viewed psychical phenomena as potentially explicable in the sense of increasing discovery rather than as impossible occult and magical effects.

Puthoff's ideas intrigued me, especially as he indicated:

> When one considers basic life processes within the framework of modern scientific theory, particularly modern quantum theory, two basic viewpoints emerge. One is that quantum theory as now understood is, in principle, essentially capable of encompassing the biologi-

---

[10] See H. E. Puthoff, "The Physics of Psychoenergetic Processes, Research Proposal" (1971 unpublished), p. 1. Tachyon, from the Greek word meaning "swift," originated with the Columbia University physicist Gerald Feinberg. See G. Feinberg, "Possibility of Faster-than-light Particles," *Physics Review*, no. 159 (1967), p. 1089.

cal and psychological principles of existence as manifested in life processes.

From this viewpoint, the fact that we have not done so is due simply to the complexities of analysis presented to the theorist by even the simplest of living organisms. This viewpoint we refer to as the reductionist viewpoint. Here it is considered that even the most complex of life processes can in principle be reduced step by step, through layers of complexity, to the basic principles encompassed by present quantum theory.[11]

It seemed to me that Puthoff, whoever he was, was speaking sooth, so on March 30, 1972, I fired a letter off to him. I stated in part:

> I have been working for several months now in two directions, firstly at the American Society for Psychical Research on trying to increase visual capacity by extrasensory modes and secondly at City College with Dr. Gertrude Schmeidler on certain psychotronic and psychokinetic effects. . . . In the case of paranormal perceptions I have already decided that indeed a field of vision exterior to sensory data inputs exists, but the fields of viewpoint and dimensions are cluttered with perceptic overloads and packed with black particles which seem to be, surprisingly, the physical universal itself. The problem is to differentiate between particles and certain wavelengths without the use of the eyes, at which time certain perceptual effects did begin to take place. There are, however, considerable variables yet to be considered, and I wanted to sound you out as to your having an interest in discussing these possibilities.

Having sent off my query to Puthoff, the first physicist of any merit I had approached, I waited to see what would happen.

If one is to approach psychoenergetics from a critical platform, the problems are likely to be monumental since any critical platform must be based upon prior acceptable data. Materialism does not admit of psychoenergetic effects, and hence critical evaluations proceeding from the viewpoints characteristic of materialistic opinion provide their own barriers to acceptance of nonmaterial events, even in the hypothetical sense.

[11] *Ibid.*, p. 3.

Allowing for the peccadilloes of materialistically oriented observers who take pot shots at emerging but unfamiliar and unrecognizable data, it is still possible to accede to the land of hypothesis. In terms of science it must be stressed that this land of hypothesis differs from the territory of ego-poised claims characteristic of the popular world of self-proclaimed psychics.

If science descends from its position aloof from things psychic in order to open certain possibilities for exploration, so must the psychic come away from pretentious claims of magical effects and, even in his own mind, endeavor to meet scientists at least halfway. For this to occur, the psychic or the gifted person must understand somewhat (as they usually do not) the difficulties the scientist faces in trying to structure an experiment that will allow the psychical or psychoenergetic event to be observed.

For most people, scientists or psychics, who have observed or better still experienced a paranormal occurrence, the weight of acceptance almost always moves toward the positive. Yet, even aside from this positive aura, the problem of casting the scientific net over the vast ocean of psychic occurrences and catching one recognizable fish is immense. The net, of course, is always materialistic—at least it has been so far. The psychic event, presumably being nonmaterial in nature, simply eludes the threads of the material.

Many scientists have known they had a psychoenergetic potential, often right in front of them, and have pulled their hair and shredded their fingernails while trying to figure out a way to catch it in terms acceptable to even the most liberal scientific view.* Assuming that an apparently

---

* For example, among the many psychoenergetic experiments in which I have participated during the last three years, appreciable apparently paranormal effects have been observed time and again, on many diverse substances. Many substances were selected because their known conductivity or nonconductivity had been tested: liquid mercury, graphite, gold, silver, lead, copper, bismuth, iron, porcelain, tin, and helium and nitrogen gases. Light beams and laser frequencies also have been probed, with good continuing effects produced. Several different laser beams were established as targets, the best and most continuous results obtained at 4765Å. Certain biological targets also have been established and experimented upon, a one-celled Nitella target producing the most obvious results upon being probed psychoenergetically. The difficulties encountered, aside from the dramatics of trying to interact psychoenergetically with such targets, are primarily the difficulties in creating a suitable, if not airtight, test paradigm. Thus experiments are not usually reported officially until such time as test design does meet critical requirements.

psychically gifted person is up to putting in the requisite man-hours to collaborate with earnest scientists, there are, so far, only two ways for either to be certain something has occurred.

First, the event should be reproducible, that is, every time the battering ram hits the door, the door should collapse. The weakness of this demand is, of course, that it is human not to succeed in everything all the time but in some things some of the time. Heretofore, scientists, especially those critical of things psychic, generally have demanded this approach of psychics and have been triumphant when the psychic was not able to produce the golden egg every time. The alternative approach hinges around the capacity of scientists to structure an experiment that would be immaculate in the materialistic sense, so that if a presumably paranormal event occurred it could not be attributed to some fluctuation of the experimental situation.

In the positive sense, enough research has been conducted to establish that PK does exist in any of several forms. Human interaction in (or human effect upon) such variegated areas as bioelectrical systems, fungi cultures, electrical clocks, dice (the most frequent), and resuscitation of anesthetized mice has been minimally if not positively established,[12] dependent, of course, upon how one regards the general field of things psychic in the first place.

As a result of my letter to him concerning supposed psychical movement of hypothetical particles (such is the way things like this must be described), Puthoff telephoned from California. He was indeed interested in what had been going on with Schmeidler and in the so-called "out-of-

[12] See R. M. Brier, "PK on a Bio-electrical System," *The Journal of Parapsychology* 33, no. 3 (September 1969), pp. 187–205; J. Barry, "General and Comparative Study of the Psychokinetic Effect on a Fungus Culture," *ibid*. 32, no. 4 (December 1968), pp. 237–243; W. E. Cox, "The Effect of PK on Electro-mechanical Systems," *ibid*. 29, no. 3 (September 1965), pp. 164–175; G. K. and A. M. Watkins, "Possible PK Influence on the Resuscitation of Anesthetized Mice," *ibid*. 35, no. 4 (December 1971), pp. 257–272.

body" experiments I had been participating in at the American Society for Psychical Research.

An interesting series of telephone conversations took place during subsequent weeks, earnest discussions about things "not really there," things that had never been "seen" before, things that had to be talked about within the sanctums of physics in hushed, almost secretive tones.

Where in previous dealings with parapsychologists I had encountered a sort of lethargy—coming from the fact that most parapsychologists do not care for or solicit theoretical contributions from subjects—the long-distance conversations with Puthoff began to engender an enthusiasm, an excitement. This type of excitement eventually came to be characteristic in talking with physicists who seemed almost always eager to take descriptive, even theoretical, offerings from me as a participating subject, and began to compare those offerings with what is known about the structure of the physical universe, the laws of thermodynamics, and the advancing edge of physical discovery into the discrepancies of time and space itself.

These conversations eventually reached a point where enough possibilities had been generated and it was made possible for me to go to SRI to "poke around" in association with Puthoff, with the results of this initial exploration contributing hopefully to the future establishment of a larger opportunity.

Puthoff is a rather extraordinary individual. Doubtless he has a vision. And this vision is strong enough to enable him to confront the recalcitrance of physical theory to accommodate invisible life processes, and seek to move towards this frontier. His spirit is therefore large. He and many others at SRI were to be sorely pressured by the exaggerated excitement generated in the press and among critics as a result of this eminent establishment's taking up things psychic.

But it might well be remembered that life processes, consciousness, and the advancing edge of physical discovery are continually drawing closer. It is legitimate for researchers to create trial hypotheses and investigate them. Anything that can be treated in this manner constitutes legitimate research, press and critical commentary notwithstanding.

A good deal of work was conducted along the lines of psychoenergtic effects, not only with myself as a participating subject but also with several others. Official interpretation of results must await proper presentation, a procedure that seems to take years in science.

But one incident can be described, not so much as an experiment, nor even as a demonstration, and certainly not as "proof" of anything. It is always more convenient to consider psychoenergetic or psychical things as possibilities—this is so because the source or structure of things psychic does not readily present itself. Therefore, what one witnesses in a psychic event is the result of some unexplained activity. Until both cause and effect become tangible, even theoretically, the use of the word "possibility" is the most felicitous.

As mentioned, half of the problem of researching things psychic lies in the inability of science to create an airtight experiment. The other half lies in the inability of a given subject to reproduce the psychic effect.

Usually people acting as subjects are not technically prepared to challenge the experimenter about his experiment. In a rather grand manner I informed Puthoff that as a subject I should not wish to waste my time demonstrating any hopefully psychic interaction in an experiment that had critical loopholes.

Puthoff's eyes swirled a little at this challenge. He countered with the suggestion that over at Stanford University in the Varian Hall of Physics resided one quark detector * that was immaculate in that it was, by design and thorough testing, impenetrable to outside influences. Inside this device was a stable magnetic field. If I, as a "psychic," could poke around in that magnetic field by allegedly paranormal means, this would give good evidence that something had occurred.

We repaired to Stanford University, there to meet with Dr. Arthur Hebbard, who had designed and built a good portion of this esoteric instrument.

I don't know why I assumed the quark detector would be an instrument capable of sitting on a table. Probably it was because instrumentation in the familiar sense stands around and can often be put on tables. We progressed to the basement of the Varian Hall of Physics, and thence into a largish room full of a confusion of pipes and equipment. Several moments were spent in cordialities. Finally I asked where it was exactly that the quark detector might be perceived.

---

* Physicists theorize that the proton is composed of three subparticles called quarks. These have not been located as of this writing, but the instrument at Stanford University, one of its kind, was constructed at great expense, with copious work, in an effort to capture one of these theoretical subparticles.

I was totally stunned to find that the quark detector could not be visually perceived since it was encased in an aluminum container and copper canister, as well as a superconducting shield, and in any case was buried some five feet beneath the floor in concrete. This information caused my own eyes to swirl a little. This was a breathless situation, and somehow I felt a little tricked.

To sit in Gertrude Schmeidler's laboratory and poke around at small thermistors sealed in thermos flasks was one thing; at least one could get a general idea of where the target was. But the small anger that had boiled up inside me passed quickly as I realized that here indeed was an experiment almost as immaculate as any could be.

The quark detector, and the magnetometer inside it, had been subjected to tests with large electromagnets, and no signals had been induced in the shielded portion. Prior to our arrival, a decaying magnetic field had been set up inside the shielded chamber. Its steady decay with time provided a background calibration signal that registered as a sine wave output on an x-y recorder, the frequency of the sine wave corresponding to the decay rate of the calibration field. Further, this system had been running for something on the order of an hour with no "noise." (On the day of the experiment in question, the quark-detecting function of this marvelous instrument was not in operation. This experiment pertains only to the operating magnetometer housed deep inside the various shieldings.)

I was told that if I were to affect the magnetic field in the magnetometer it would show up as a change in the output recording. A large group of people stood around waiting for the event to occur. Frankly, the urge to retreat was paramount, but I quickly understood that here was an opportunity that should not be flummoxed by a pantywaist attitude.

The distance to the invisible target beneath the floor was not much greater than the distance between me and the targets in Schmeidler's arrangement. Intervening layers of concrete, and so forth, should not make any difference if the effect had nonmaterial implications. And besides, these physicists were not going to get the best of me at this crucial point. And this last point might have provided an extraordinary psychological motivation.

Now in order for the following to be at least comprehensible (I do not ask for belief), it has to be said that I have become convinced that the seat of consciousness does not emanate from or exist solely as a result of the physical body, an opinion that I have tried to bring into reality in this book so far. It can move in terms of time and space; and, in terms of matter and energy, the act of this seat of consciousness observing them *does* cause fluctuations at the impact of observation. Further, this seat of consciousness is capable of bilocation, that is, of establishing perceptual capacities in more than one place (usually within the body, though).

At this crucial time, my body standing before the x-y recorder watching the sine wave output, I tried to move a good deal of conscious perception to the innards of that canister beneath the floor and I managed to perceive certain of its structural elements. At this point of perceptive contact the frequency of the sine wave doubled for a couple of cycles. There resulted an astonished silence from those attending, a silence that sustained itself for at least thirty seconds before a controlled pandemonium broke loose (see Figure 11, point F).

Dr. Hebbard giggled. He suggested that perhaps this variation in the sine wave output was some kind of "noise." By this time, however, I was in stride and asked that he offer a suggestion as to *what,* if anything, would not be considered merely noise. He suggested that I try to stop the entire thing for as much as, say, ten seconds.

With growing enthusiasm I poked around down in the dark chamber. I began to ask questions as to what it was I was "seeing" down there, and grabbing a pen, began to sketch out the machinery innards. When I actually located the magnetometer itself (the cavity was filled with liquid helium, dielectric gold-titanium–coated glass and a few balls of niobium used in the quark process), the impact of observation upon this part of the instrumentation stopped the sine wave altogether. I tried to sustain my intent upon this portion of the apparatus and managed to do it for the ten seconds required by Dr. Hebbard's suggestion. (See Figure 11, point B.)

Puthoff then suggested I refrain from trying to affect the magnetometer, and the sine wave immediately returned to normal. Thereafter I was asked—nay grilled—as to what I had done. In trying to explain that all I had done was to put my attention "down there," each time I so explained a part of my attention indeed went down there and the effect was re-created several times.

By this time, however, the people in the environment were beginning to come apart, and I suggested to Puthoff that we retreat somewhere for coffee. Hebbard continued to run the apparatus for over an hour after we had departed; no trace of noise or nonsinusoidal activity appeared (see Figure 12).[13]

This type of experiment allows for speculations concerning the nature of paradoxes often observed with psychoenergetically-produced phenomena. These speculations are not conclusions drawn from statistically significant information but do help contribute to conceptualizations or hypotheses around which other specific experiments might in the future be designed.

Psychokinetic phenomena, as commonly observed, appear to result from coincidence rather than as the effect of well-defined causes. However, natural causes observed as coincidence may be the effect of a series of causal links, outside the experimental boundaries, representing unforeseen lines of least resistance, but nevertheless acting as instruments of human will. Additionally, it is abysmally difficult to provoke psychokinetic phenomena on cue. Volitional performance, however, was achieved both in the Schmeidler and SRI experiments.

Since this volitional control took place within my mind before it was reflected in the instrumentation, in order to give some illuminating explanation of it, I feel it possible to suggest that human consciousness is not imprisoned in the human body, but capable of becoming coincident in two or possibly more places at any given time. The vectors of consciousness by which such strange and unfamiliar activity take place are almost always outside everyday working consciousness. But most people certainly have played the game of trying to get someone else to move their head or their hand by will alone. Sometimes some have succeeded. The provoking of the psychokinetic phenomena in the above experiments were of no different nature.

The difficulty in getting reproduceable psychokinetic effects suggests that they can be viewed as some macroscopic analog of a quantum transition, that is, as events unpredictable in time except as a probability function.

---

[13] A technical recounting of this experiment was presented formally at the Conference on Quantum Physics and Parapsychology. This report contains exact descriptions of the equipment involved and the experimental procedures. See H. E. Puthoff and Russell Targ, "Physics, Entropy, and Psychokinesis," *Proceedings of the Conference on Quantum Physics and Parapsychology, Geneva, August 26-27, 1974.* New York: Parapsychology Foundation (in preparation).

But it has to be entered into possibility that human consciousness is capable of operating both in time (that is, statistically) and also within the occluded and hardly know areas of probability. One does this by doing it. And then one quickly becomes aware of the ability of human consciousness to exert will and intention at places other than in the material body it inhabits.

In 1963 an English translation of a book by a prominent Russian physiologist, Professor L. L. Vasiliev, was published.[14] This book summarized many years of experimentation in extrasensory perception in Russia, with many experiments reported to have been carried out prior to World War II. Since that time, many laboratories reportedly have been set up in Soviet universities.[15]

It is noteworthy to discover in all these reports that, where Western ideas of psychic research are grouped around trying to discover *what* is happening, the Russian idea of studying things psychic is to have people *utilize* abilities even before exact understanding of them is possible.

In this way it is possible for Western ideas of things psychic to cling to the impossibility of it all, since the critic can remain aloof and disbelieving until it is known how they come about. The Russians, however, seem to treat the situation much as we do electricity in the United States.

It is not known how electricity comes into being, only that it does. Certain people, promoters if you will, simply bypassed the problem of origination of electricity and set about using it.

Given the prevailing attitude in the United States about the impossibility of things psychic, I have been prevailed upon to explain *how* it was I allegedly caused an untoward effect within the magnetometer—or how I

[14] L. L. Vasiliev, *Experiments in Mental Suggestion* (Hampshire, England: ISMI Publications, 1963).
[15] See, for instance, J. Pratt, "Parapsychology in Russia and Czechoslovakia," *Journal for Social Psychologic Research,* no. 42 (1963), pp. 16–20; A. Ivanov, "Soviet Experiments in ESP, 1921–1927, 1932–1938, *International Journal of Parapsychology,* no. 5 (1963), pp. 217–230.

produced the results in the Schmeidler experiments and follow-up work at SRI. Unless one can explain *how* it is done, the effect itself does not exist for Western scientists since they are prone to disregard anything they cannot see.

I don't believe psychoenergetic effects such as these can be explained in material terms. The material universe is characterized by how it is perceived and measured. In the time—admittedly a very small time—it takes the eye to perceive the physical universe, time has nonetheless passed. So the material universe is always perceived one iota in the past. This is in a fractional way tantamount to observing light from a star billions of years after it has left the star.

Psychic "intention"—that is, the desire to affect any given thing, the body included—cannot operate on what is perceived, since that has already receded into the past. One will not change the star by changing the light that has already left it. The psychic intention must anticipate and locate, in terms of matter and space, the situation as it will be in the future, an act that transcends the senses but exists as psychic expectation.

Consciousness, the thinking entity, the one that *uses* mind, is not dependent solely upon the physical body. That entity, the you, is capable of extending its view of the universe, at least through hunches, intuition, creative insights, and even well-formed psychic transcendence wherein the barriers of matter, energy, space, and time are barriers no longer. If one becomes familiar enough with this concept, one begins to include it in one's view of the universe. Finally, familiarity with other-than-sense perceptions begins to activate their potential, and the thinking entity begins not to depend solely on physical mechanisms.

In bringing about a psychoenergetic effect, the perceptive being must move a few moments along time into the future since the attempt to affect anything in present time is not observable in present time but falls away almost immediately into the past.

If one is sufficiently aware to do all this, one need only "intend" that something will happen, and it will.

This is offered here merely as a trial hypothesis, a hypothesis that—in terms of transcending space and time as well as matter and energy—opens the door for many other possibilities.

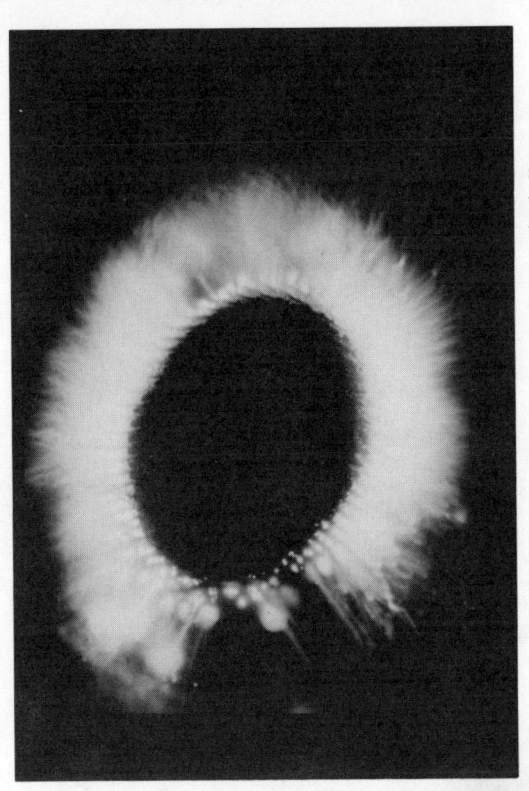

FIGURE 1. Aura of a fingertip showing flares and energy bubbles typical of Kirlian-type electrophotography. (*Courtesy of Judy Skutch, Foundation for Parasensory Investigation, New York*)

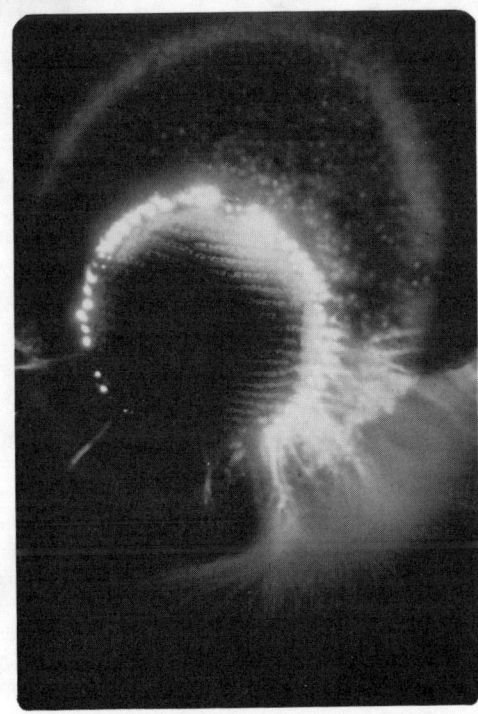

FIGURE 2. Kirlian photograph of a fingertip showing multiple aura effects. (*Courtesy of Judy Skutch, Foundation for Parasensory Investigation, New York*)

FIGURE 3. *Our Various Bodies.* Crayon on paper by the psychically inspired artist Columba Krebs. This direct rendering, executed some forty years ago, illustrates both the now-familiar Kirlian effect as well as the Kilner-type of greater auric surround. (*Courtesy of the artist*)

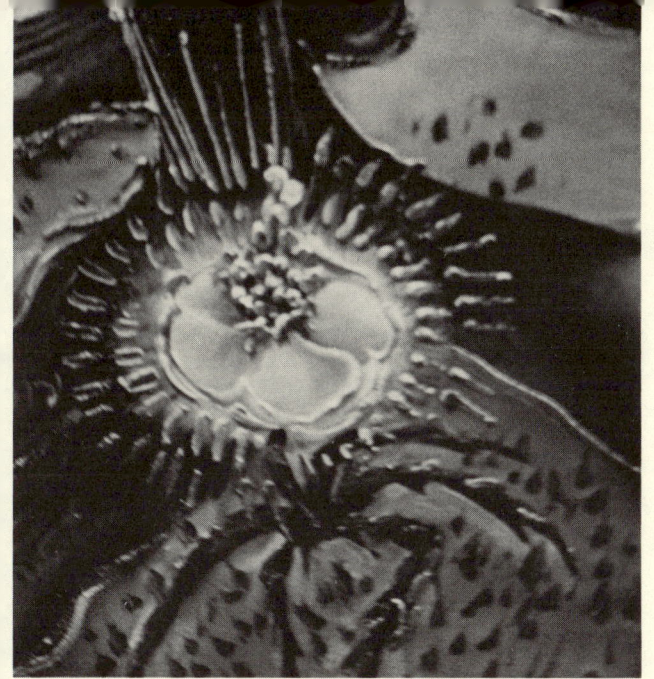

FIGURE 4. *The Lovers.* Ingo Swann, 1964. Oil on canvas. Detail of flower illustrating Kirlian-type surround.

FIGURE 5. *Les Fleurs Fleurs #10.* Ingo Swann, 1963. Oil on canvas. A vase of flowers literally created out of globs and balls of auric lights. (*Courtesy of James P. Morgan*)

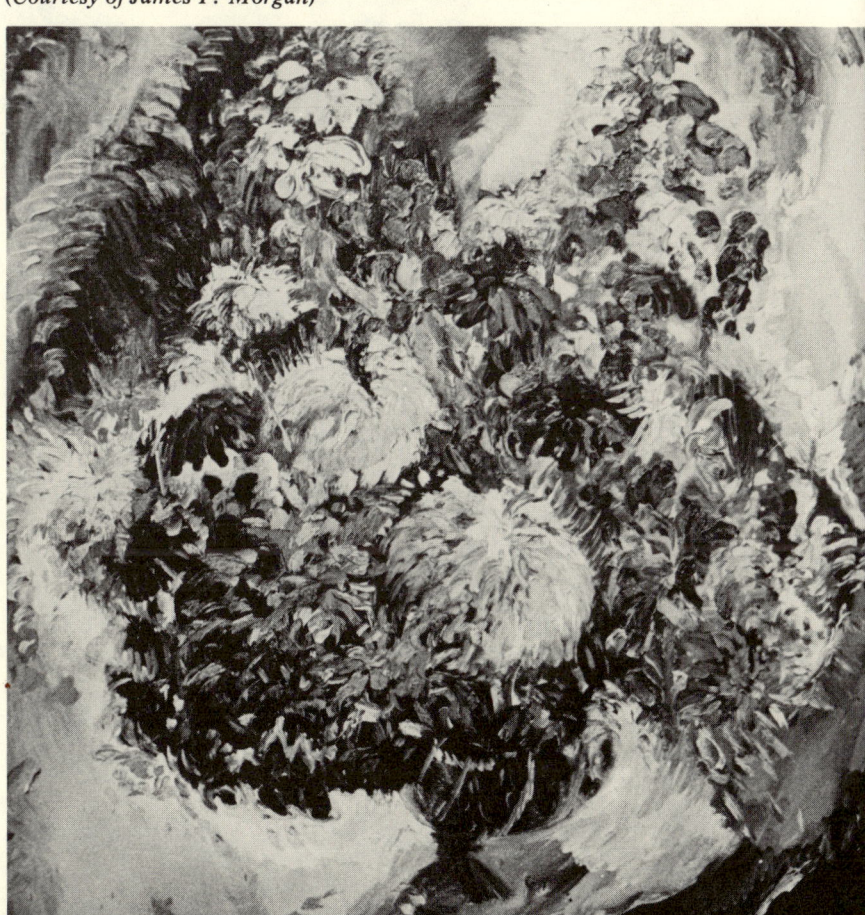

FIGURE 6. *Head.* Ingo Swann, 1963. Oil on canvas illustrating the face of a pensive youth with Kirlian-type surrounds. (*Courtesy of Dr. Stanley Krippner*)

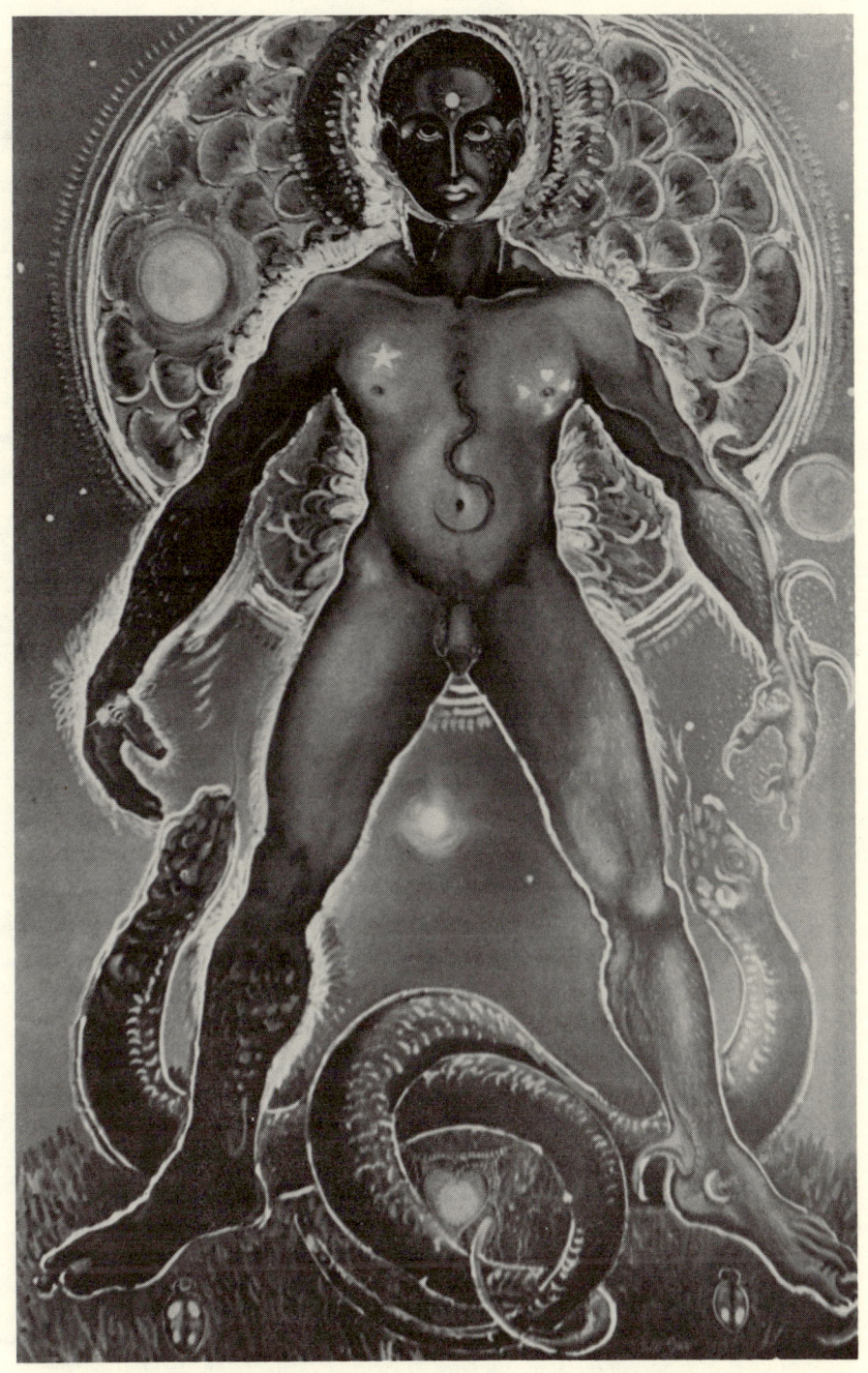

FIGURE 7. *Command Over Power.* Ingo Swann, 1964. Illustrates both the Kirlian- and Kilner-type auric vehicles.

FIGURE 8. *Mandala of the Soul.* Etching by Helmut Zimmerman, 1960. (*Courtesy of the artist*)

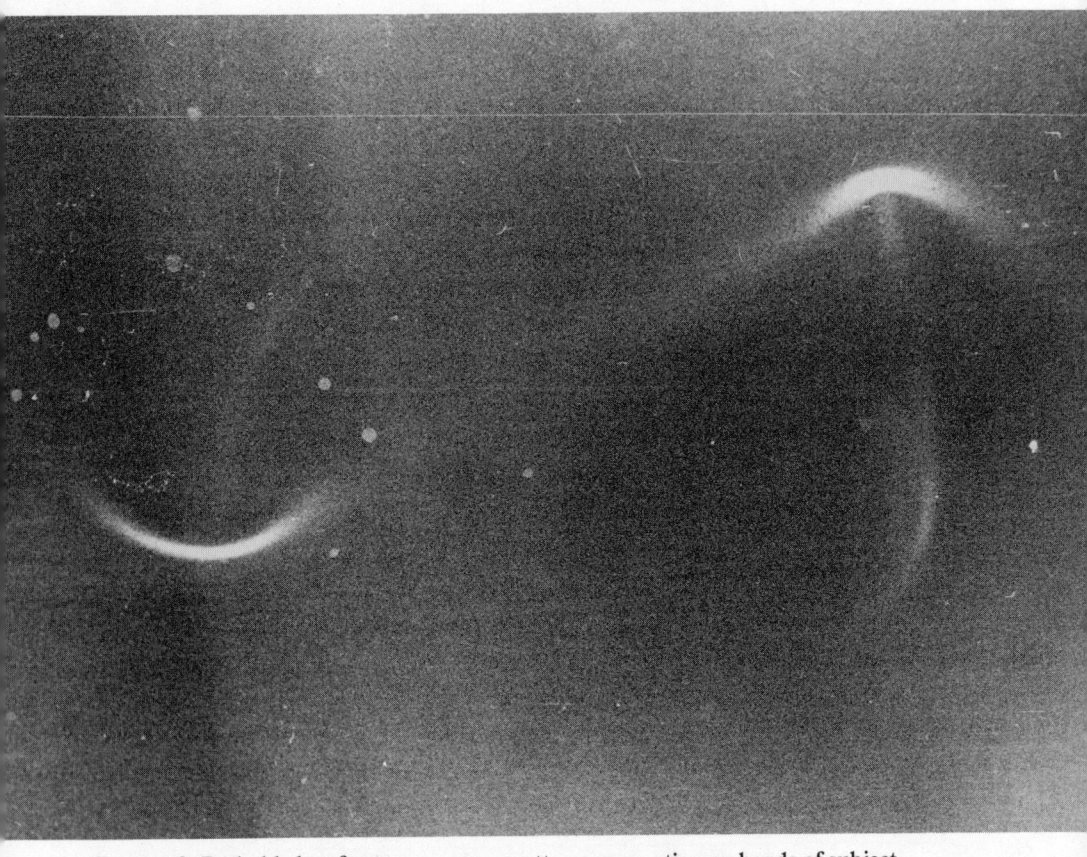

FIGURE 9. Probable low-frequency energy patterns emanating on hands of subject. Photo taken in October 1971 in totally darkened room.

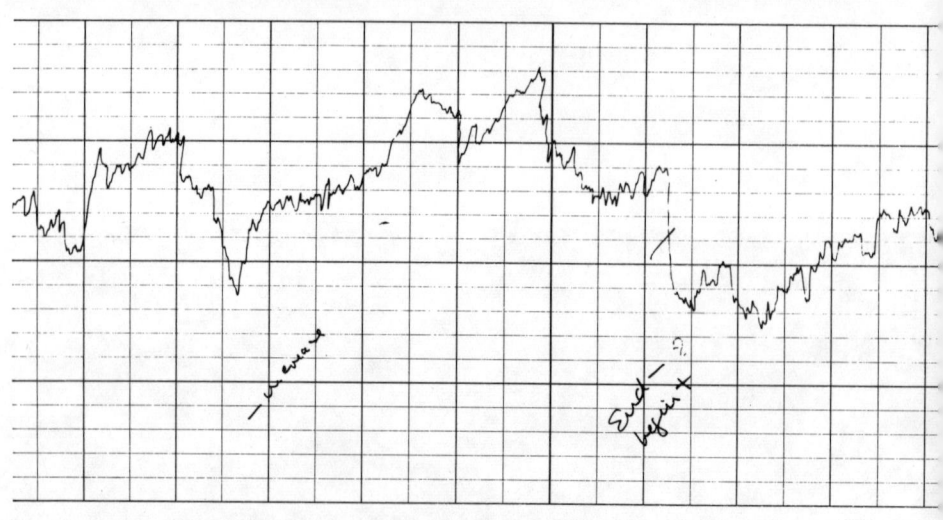

FIGURE 10. Portion of galvenometer read-out in exploratory sessions in Cleve Backster's laboratory in New York showing increase in activity upon introduction of PK heat intention and decrease upon PK cold intention.

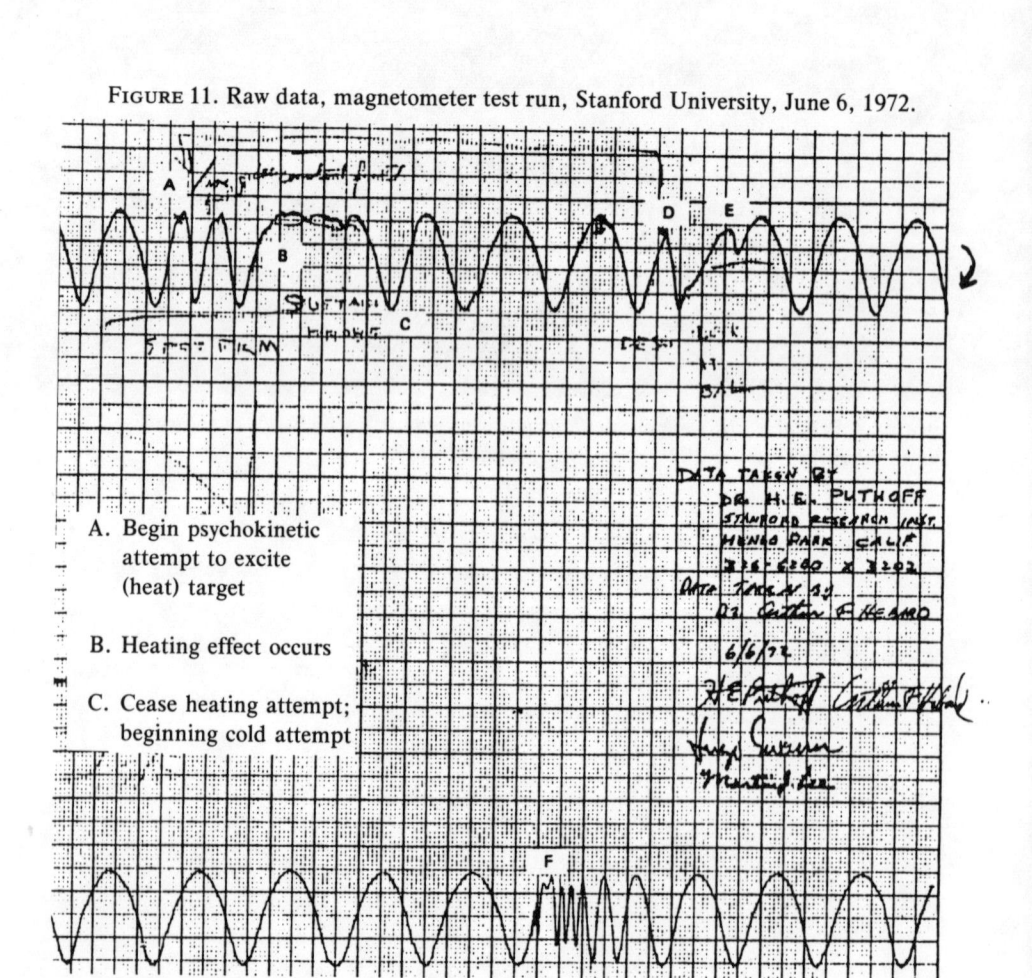

FIGURE 11. Raw data, magnetometer test run, Stanford University, June 6, 1972.

A. Begin psychokinetic attempt to excite (heat) target

B. Heating effect occurs

C. Cease heating attempt; beginning cold attempt

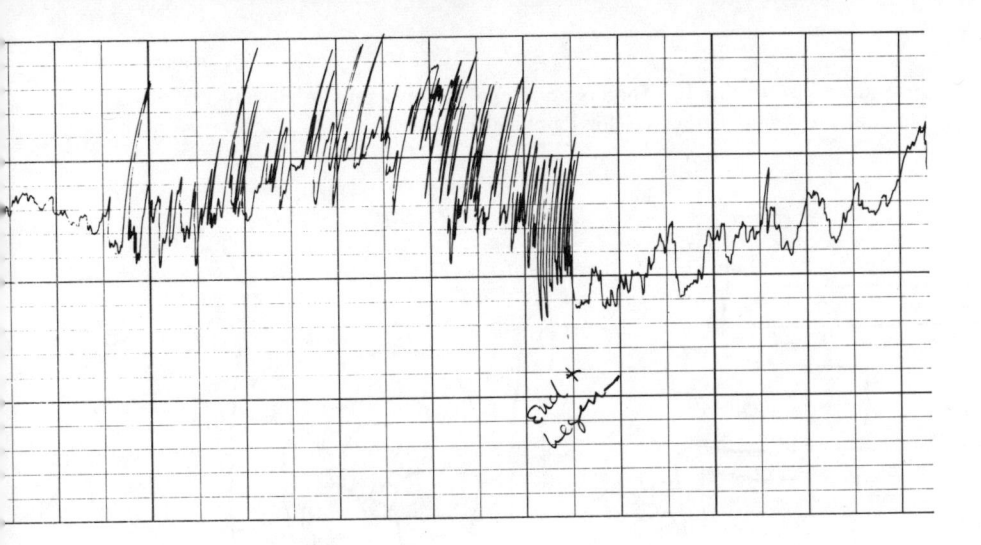

FIGURE 12. Raw data, magnetometer control run, Stanford University, June 6, 1972.

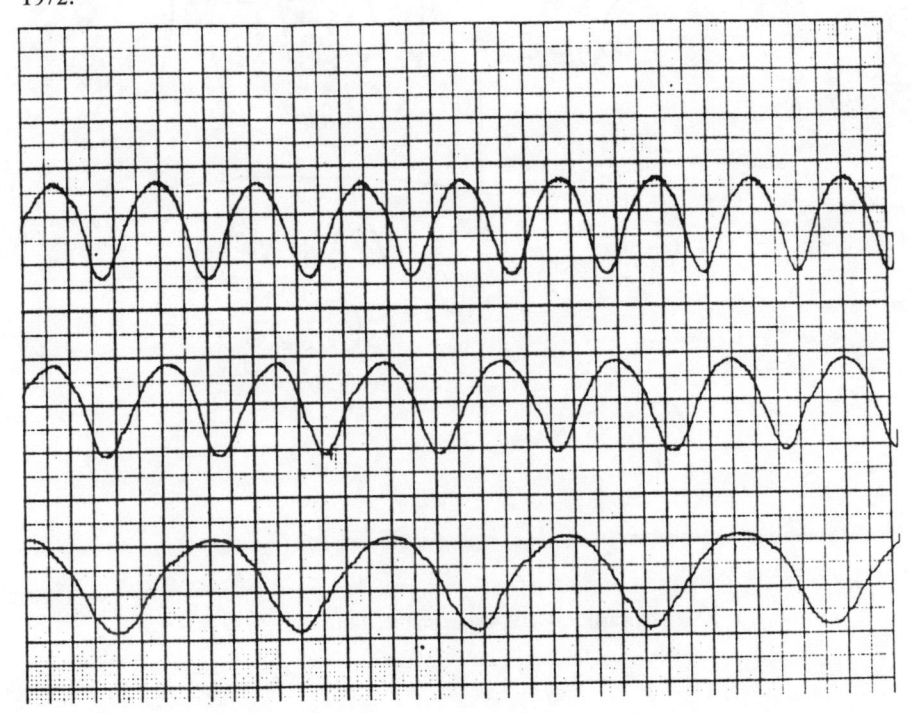

FIGURES 13 THROUGH 18. Targets and Ingo Swann's remote viewing responses taken at the American Society for Psychical Research.

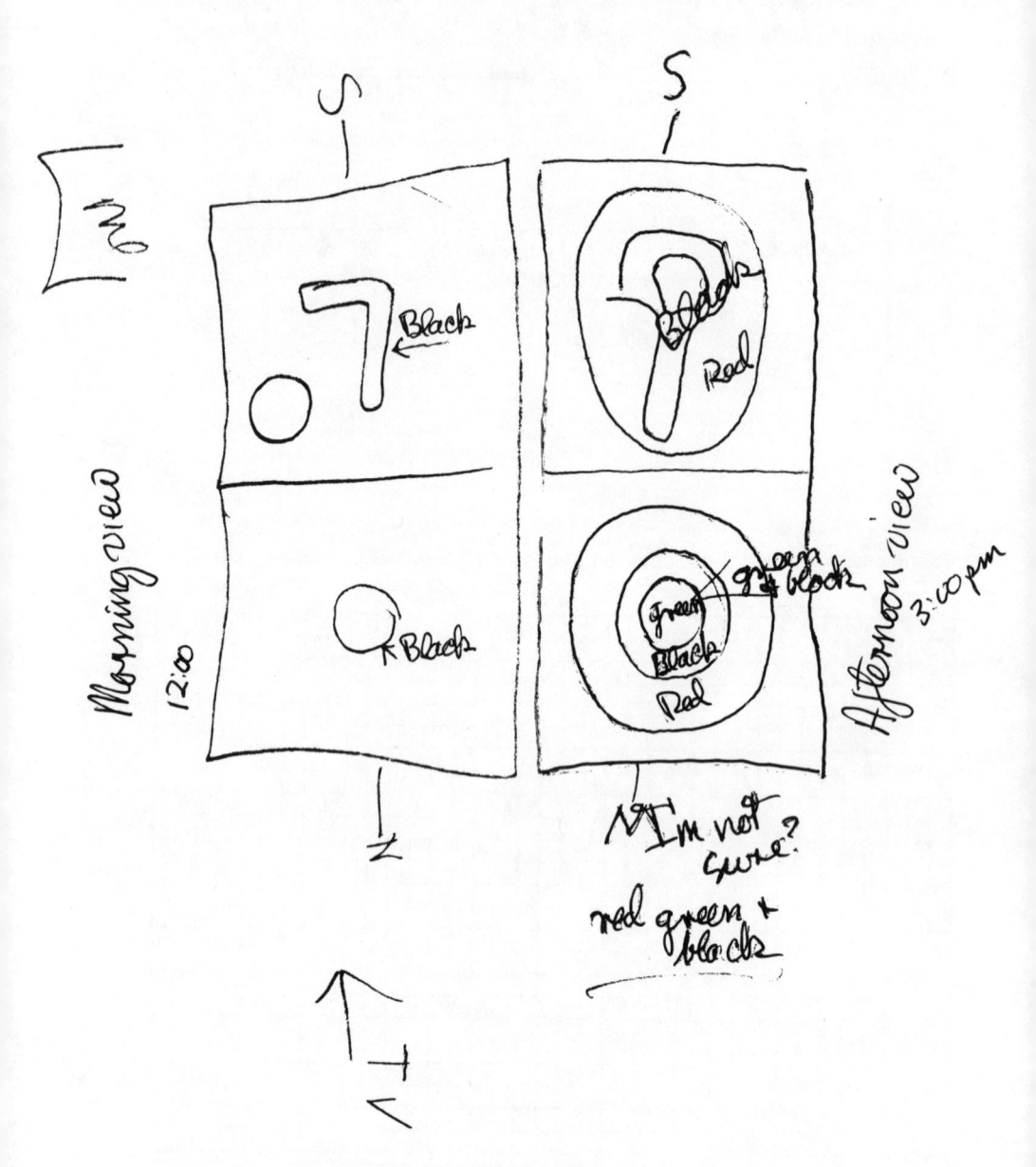

FIGURE 13. ASPR/Swann OOBE experiment: January 12, 1972.

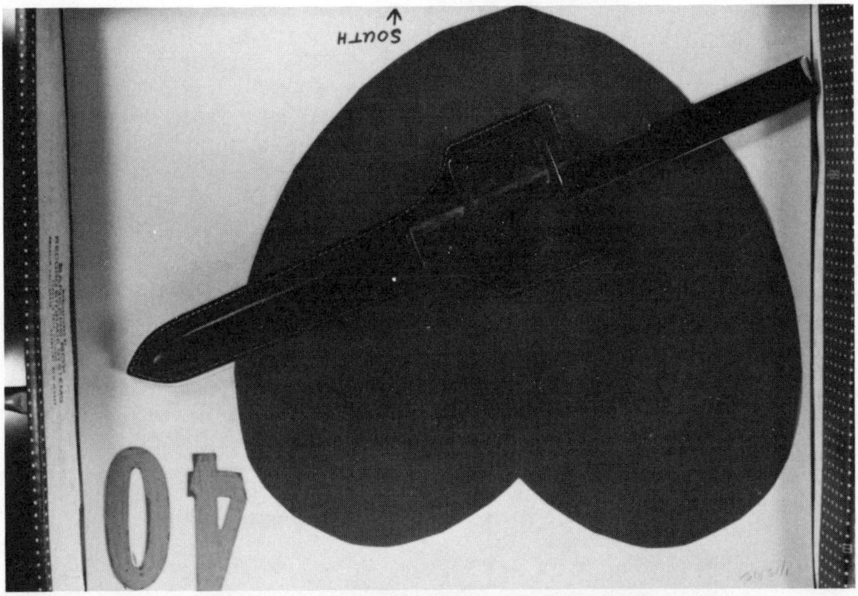
SOUTH
40

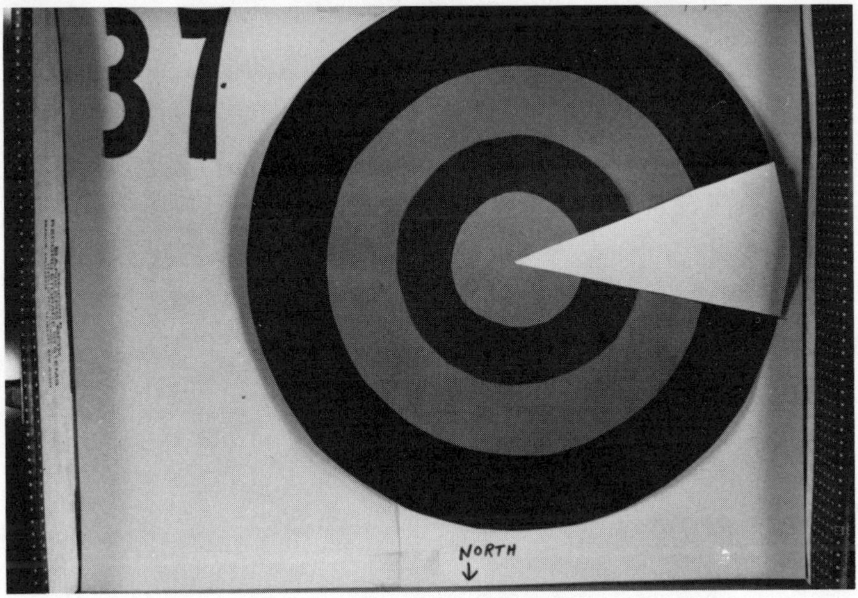
37
NORTH

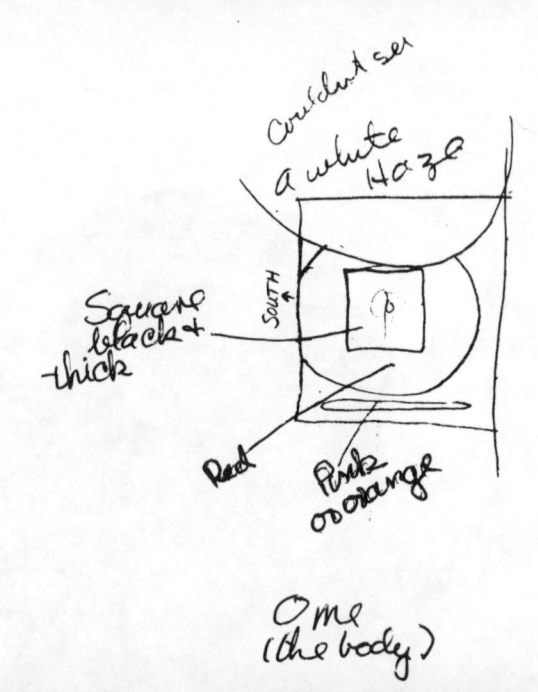

FIGURE 14. ASPR/Swann OOBE experiment: January 27, 1972.

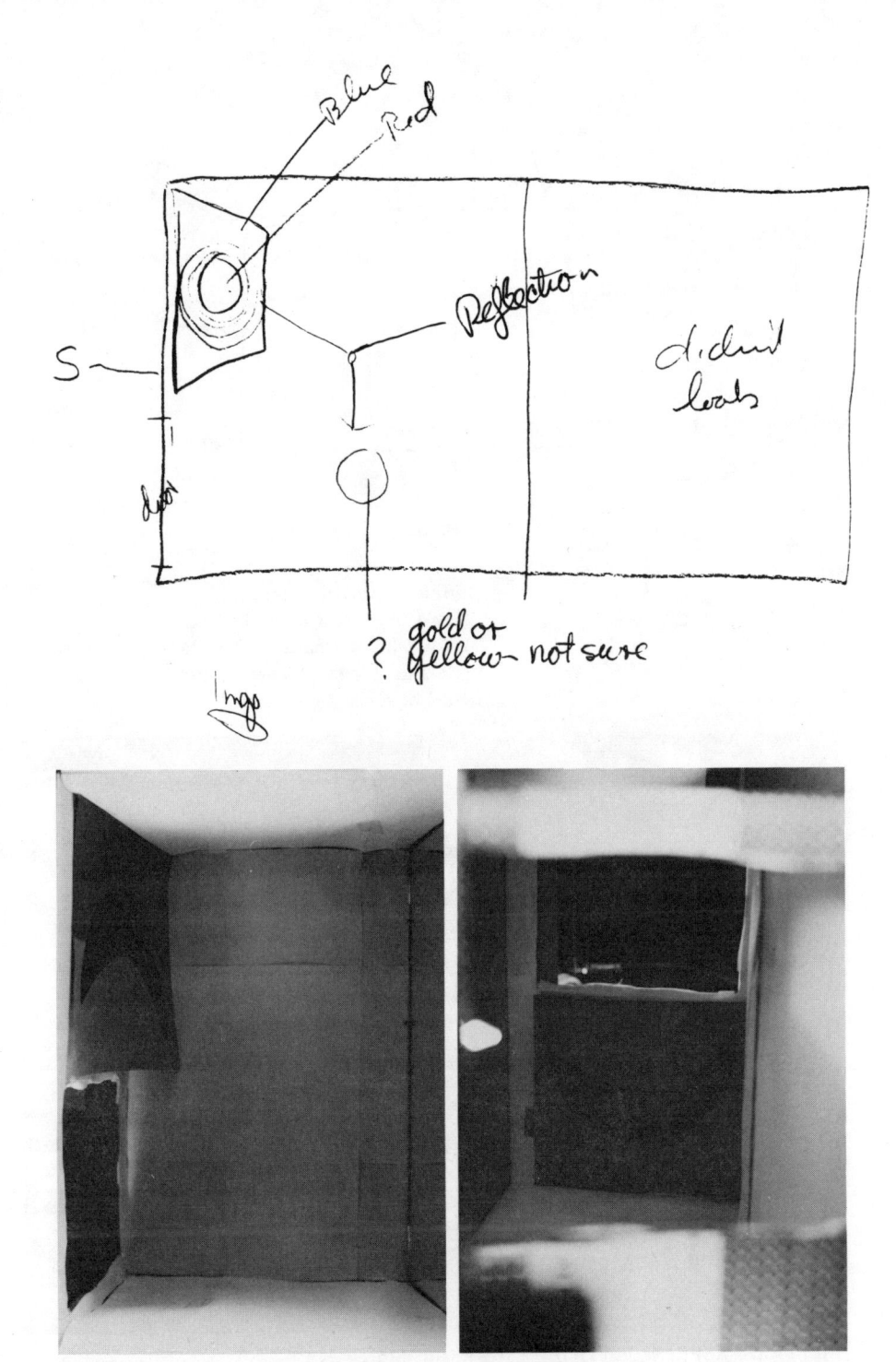

FIGURE 15. ASPR/Swann OOBE experiment: February 16, 1972.

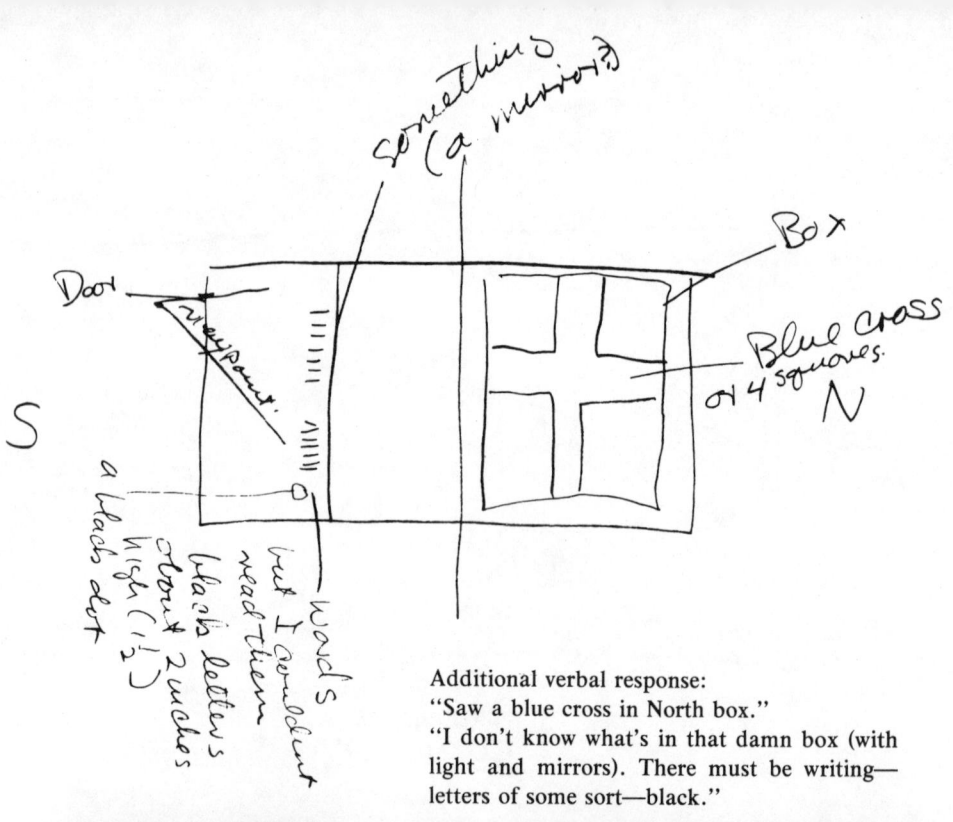

Additional verbal response:
"Saw a blue cross in North box."
"I don't know what's in that damn box (with light and mirrors). There must be writing—letters of some sort—black."

FIGURE 16. ASPR/Swann OOBE experiment: March 3, 1972.

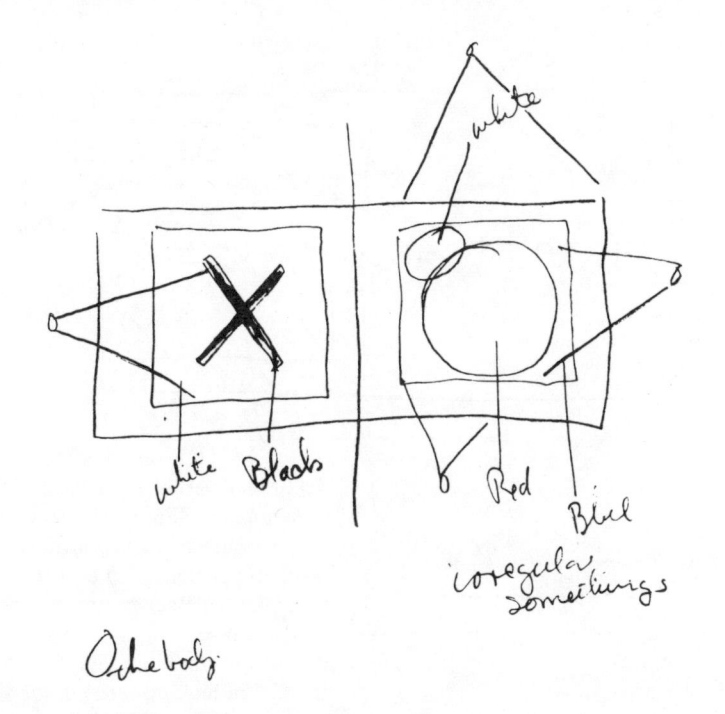

FIGURE 17. ASPR/Swann OOBE experiment: April 5, 1972.

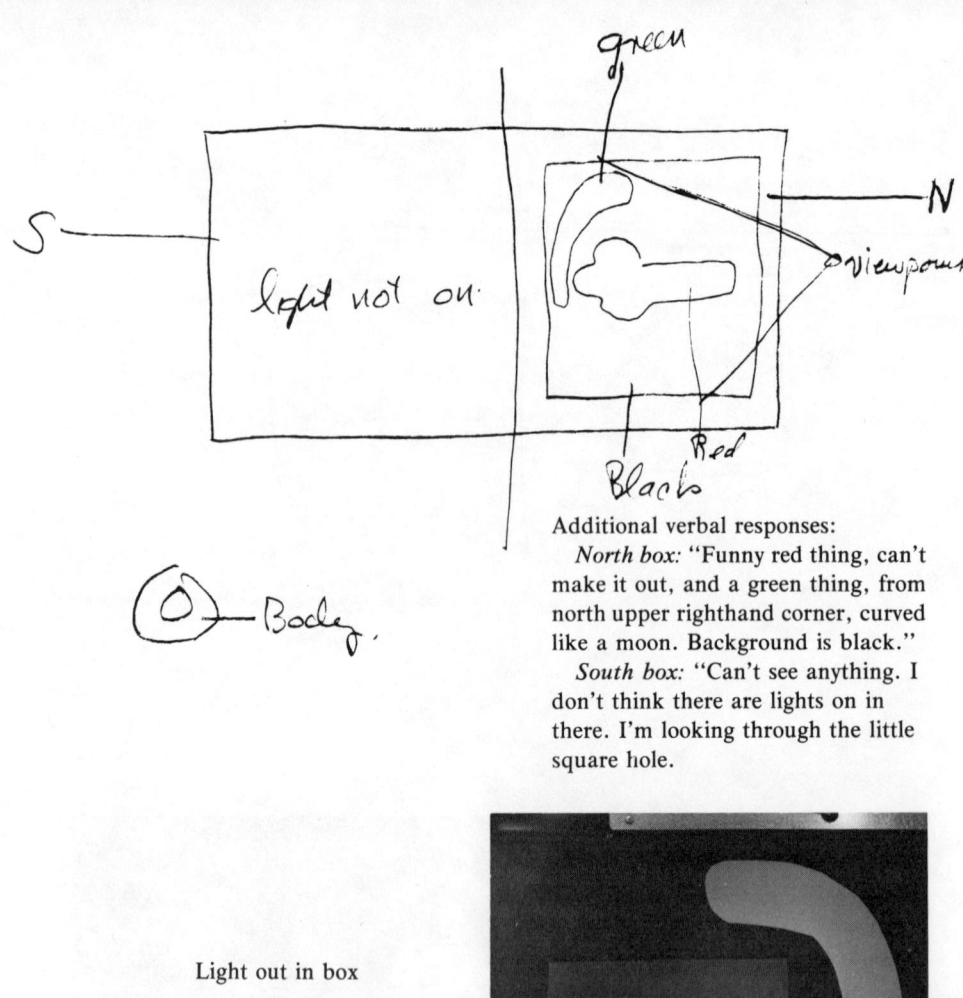

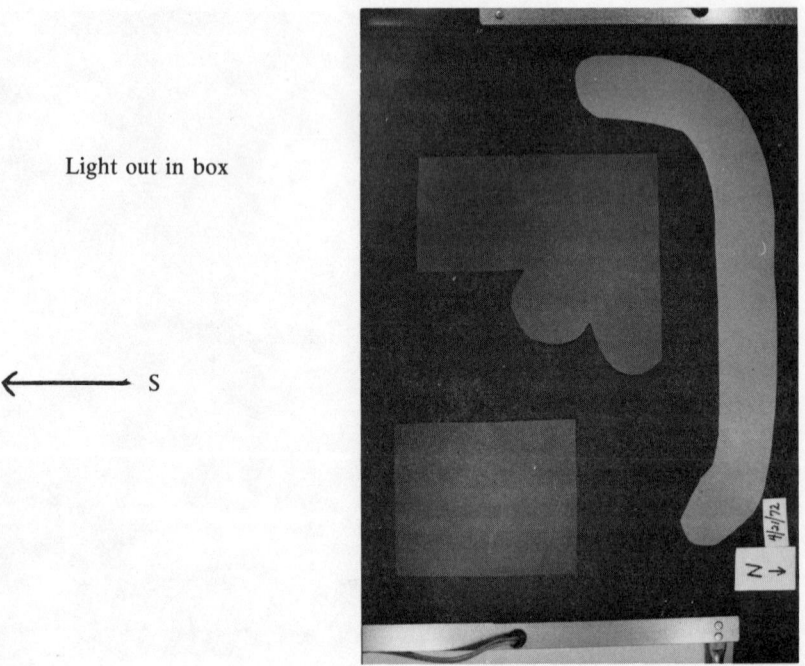

Additional verbal responses:
  North box: "Funny red thing, can't make it out, and a green thing, from north upper righthand corner, curved like a moon. Background is black."
  South box: "Can't see anything. I don't think there are lights on in there. I'm looking through the little square hole."

Light out in box

FIGURE 18. ASPR/Swann OOBE experiment: April 21, 1972.

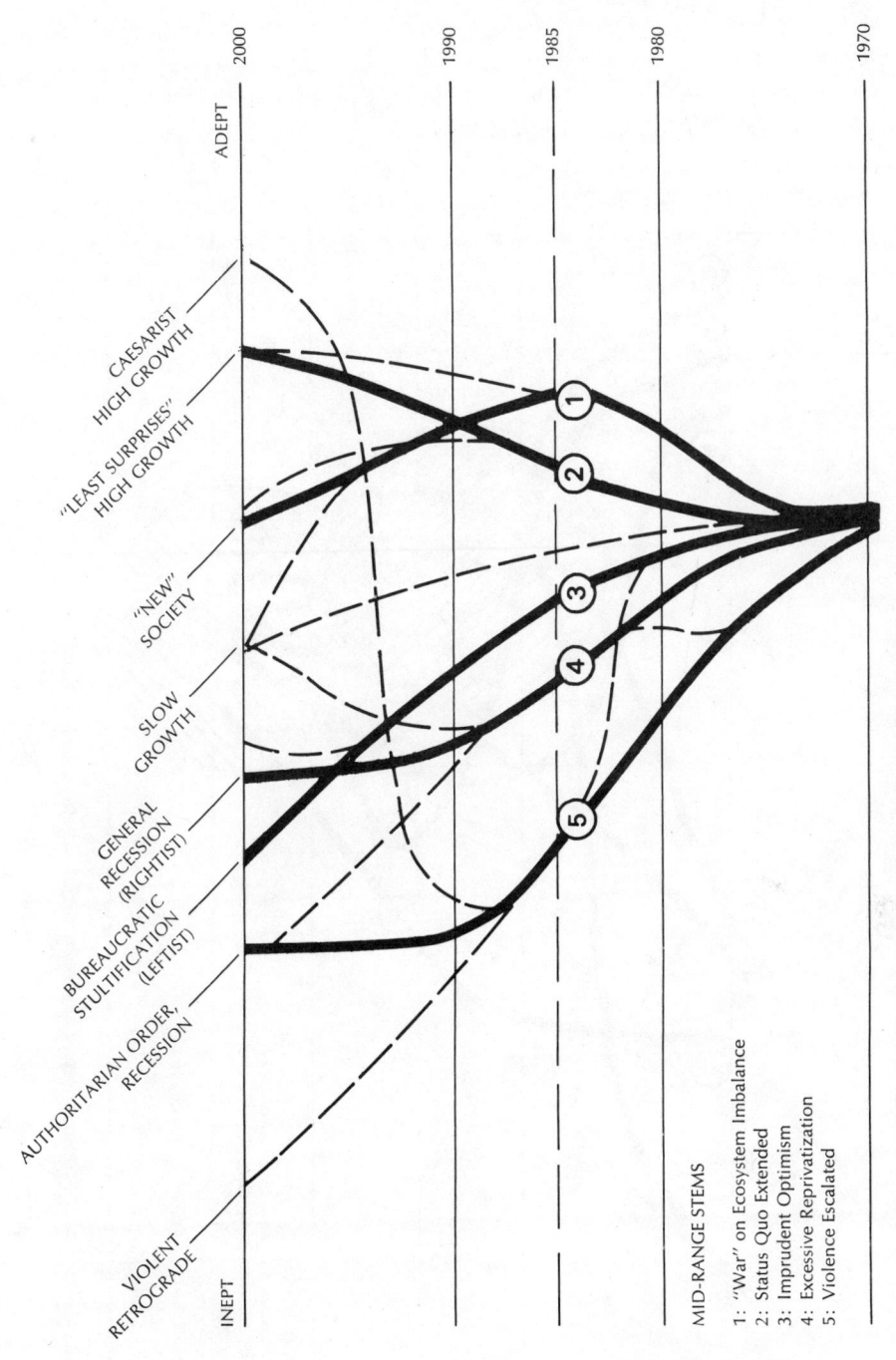

FIGURE 19. Tree of alternative future histories (adept-inept dimension).

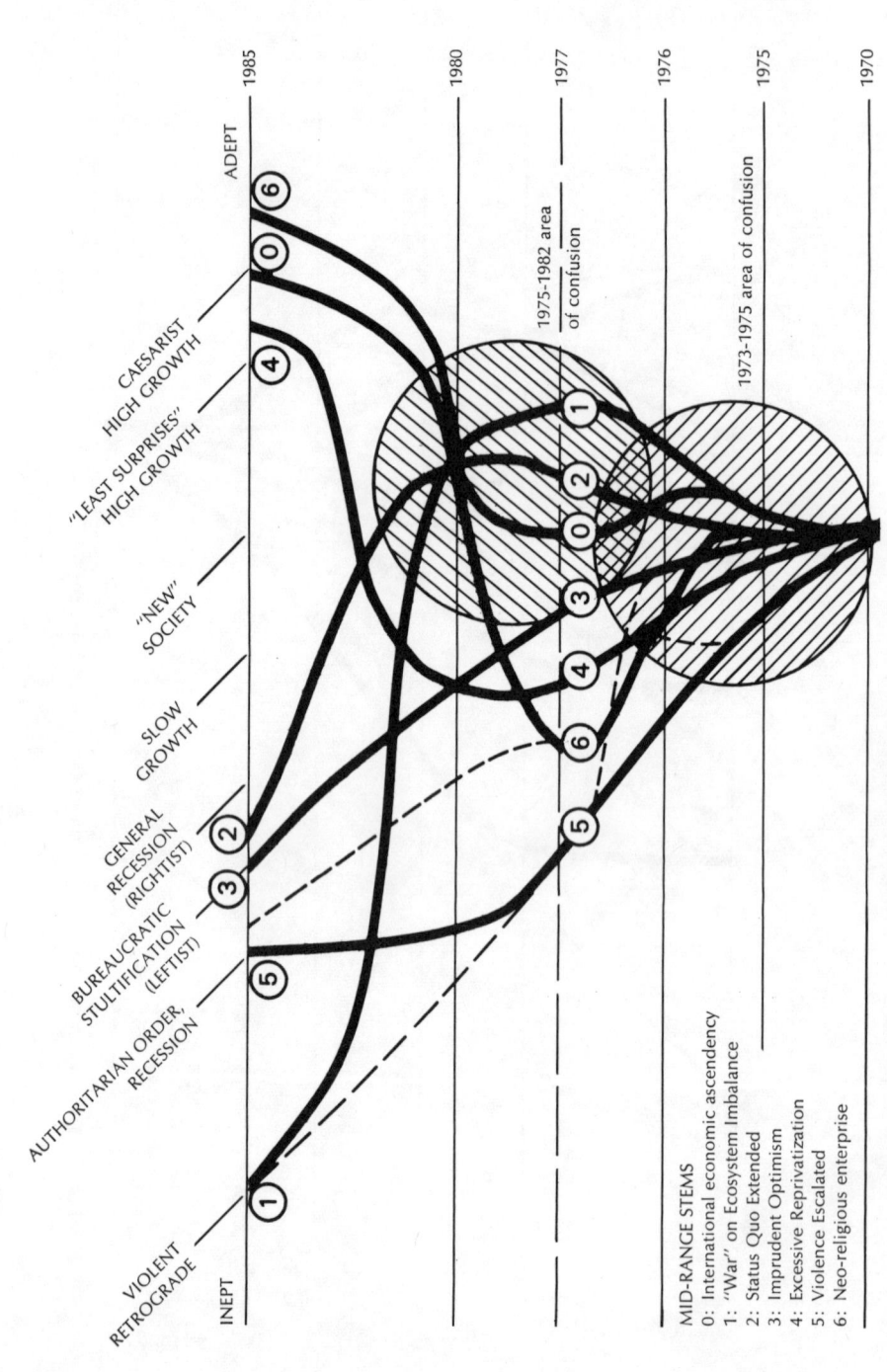

FIGURE 20. Tree of a prophetic set of future histories (adept–inept dimension).

PART III

Out of Body

> A loosening of fetters,
> A breaking down of bars,
> An opening of doors,
> A soul, long prisoned, free
> To mount the golden ladder
>   of the stars
> And see the world that
>   lies beyond the prison wall:
> Men call it Death;
> The Spirit calls it Life.[1]

Wafting around this planet, forming curious eddies here and there, lodging for a while—or perhaps a long time—in the hearts of more than a few is the many-fingered regretful aurora called loneliness. Often one is lonely for a specific person or thing. But sometimes it is a general malaise, preoccupying some even in the midst of benevolent and full lives.

I have never found it said before, but as awareness begins to become less dependent on sensory perceptions and one begins to be aware of other magnitudes, it is possible to come to the threshold of a type of loneliness native to the psychic state. It is a brand of loneliness characterized by a sort of beautiful sadness; one can sense that all beings probably experience it at one time or another.

Some are fascinated by this; others recoil and refuse to hear about it. This special loneliness seems to have many levels of emotion within it, and in art as well as life it can be dramatized through many artificial conditions—through sex, food, thinking, all the things some people do in excess to try to hide the beautiful sadness of their intuited loneliness.

To simply know or be familiar with oneself and others as bodies is not enough to many people. Yet to reach out mentally, emotionally, or

[1] Manly P. Hall, "The Hymn of Death," *The Space-born* (Los Angeles: Skelton, 1930).

psychically to touch the being of others always seems a risky business because the searcher himself collides with the wall of loneliness. People aware of themselves as more than mere physical bioelectrical systems, aware of more than just eating, fornicating, aging, and dying bodies, run headlong into the isolation imposed upon them as a result of the obiter dictum that holds that, if a person feels he is more than just body, he is wrong.

To many people, therefore, the lush existence of human body interchanges becomes paramount since philosophically and scientifically psychic union is denied. To thoroughly participate in physical life and be respectable among one's contemporaries, one had best reduce one's awareness to fit. And so people usually do.

The psychic entity reduces his awareness, enthusiastically encouraged to do so by training, inculcation, education, and other contrivances of social upbringing that hold that other awarenesses are not real. The psychic entity therefore becomes unconscious of perceptions exceeding physical explanation.

Caught and trapped at the level of experiencing only physically oriented perceptions, if one tries to look about with other than sensory perceptions, he usually perceives only blackness or invisibility. A few manage—by drugs, alcohol, dreams, or other artificial means—to experience other possibilities, but hardly ever take cogent control of them. Psychic awarenesses, therefore, are seldom used as vehicles for conscious, self-determined, creative actions.

One's contemporaries can and often do bring severe punishment to those who dare to be different. But at the inner core of being, of awareness, most are bursting with the suppressed enthusiasm of an existence that goes beyond bodies, awaiting the time when it will be safe and possible to express themselves more in keeping with their inherent inner largesse.

And thus the sense of loneliness, a loneliness that is sometimes laced with invisible anger toward the imposed barriers that make men and women less than they really are.

Within the space of one's own beingness, however, many people often allow themselves reverie upon this matter, and the results of such reverie sometimes energize certain individuals to untoward actions. The highlands of the Rocky Mountains, for instance, where I was born, are populated with a rare genre of "hard-rock" miners or prospectors. They roam around the crags and forests hunting for lodes of gold, silver, and other precious minerals, and their chosen profession isolates them from others for great periods of time.

During my childhood I knew many of them. They were usually scrawny but inordinately strong, tending to be weather-worn. In their eyes dreams and visions always glittered. They came into town once in a while, treating themselves to a good binge and then disappearing for another period to their mountain cabins. What went on in their minds, their thoughts, and especially their tender respect for life—if they were not busy shooting it out with someone—seldom was available to academicians, who probably would not care anyway.

With all the intellect, genius, and inventiveness available to the intellectual and monied giants on the planet, it is almost a cultural embarrassment to learn that one of these "hard-rock" men thought enough of life and existence to take an inordinate step toward establishing the reality of man's "more-ness."

Society will never know—at least by ordinary means—what thoughts ran through the being of one James Kidd. Kidd was a prospector, sometimes working his own claims around Phoenix, Arizona, where he lived modestly. At other times he roamed the fabled Superstitions, a grouping of mountains in Arizona, former Apache country where Geronimo and Cochise once ruled. Aside from reports that he was an unassuming man, quiet and some say handsome in a rotund, elderly way, not much is known. He disappeared in November 1949 and was never heard from again.

A few years later a strongbox owned by Kidd yielded a slip of paper, a will written in his own hand on January 2, 1946, indicating that all his property in cash and stocks was to go "in a research or some scientific proof of a soul of the human body which leaves at death."

When all the Kidd assets were accumulated, this "property" totaled the not insignificant amount of $174,065.69. Due to the conscientiousness of one Geraldine C. Swift, estate tax commissioner of Arizona, this strange will was entered into probate on May 6, 1965, and the First National Bank of Arizona was named administrator of the estate.[2]

In keeping with Kidd's wish, in order to award the money to competent

---

[2] The Kidd story, or at least its beginning chapters, is expertly recorded elsewhere and need not be drawn out here. See John G. Fuller, *The Great Soul Trial* (New York: Macmillan, 1969).

research, formal hearings were held beginning on March 6, 1967, and the rush was on. Arizona was to see an influx of people the likes of which many there never dreamed existed.

The authorities were bedeviled with the legalities and illegalities of researchers, psychics, seances, messages from beyond, occult stipulations—all arcane nuances that do not usually enter into legal arenas. Altogether, some 133 applicants felt themselves qualified to conduct the research stipulated by Kidd.

The recordings of these public hearings provide a rare document, an energetic testament either to desire for money or desire to accede to the challenge Kidd had hurled.

In December 1973 the Kidd fortune was awarded, after a lot of backtracking and appeals, to the American Society for Psychical Research at New York. Through accumulated interest and after legal fees and expenses the bequest received totaled $300,000.

Man's rise from savagery to civilization has been marked with attempts to explain that man was existing, most of which explanations have been total flops. The resolution to this failure has been to blame everything on God in one form or another, and on the devil, who is considered responsible for inspiring bad actions in individuals unlucky enough to fall under his influence. Responsibility is thereby conveniently lifted from the heads of mere mortals since, in theological terms, all actions can be seen to reflect this dichotomy.

The individual is not required to think, and in some cases severe sanctions are taken against those who do. Yet, as history has shown, while certain social orders are toasting the perfection of their theological establishment, likely as not there is a culprit poised in the wings destined to add havoc to the most sublime of orders.

When science and religion split, descriptions of human existence passed from the hands of theologians and philosophers to the hands and minds of "scientists," and formative ideas of human existence began to be construed apart from metaphysical concerns.

However, it is upon these early independent philosophical ideals that thought today is based. These philosophical ideals were put together by men attempting to broaden concepts of existence in the vast, swift rush of expanding discovery in the material universe that began in the sixteenth century. Essentially they are important within that context but almost useless in reasoning for a time like the present, which is characterized by increasing emergencies in aligning material with immaterial or nonmaterial potential.

The impending changeover from solely materialistic thought systems to those that will encompass nonmaterial probabilities will probably not take place like a well-oiled gear but with considerable gnashings and groanings.

The inadequacies inherent in the ideas of the founding fathers of philosophical materialism are seldom illuminated within the materialistic bastion. The concepts that actively began to consign human awareness to the environs of the body, up to and through the emergence of Sigmund Freud—who came to hold that the mind was an appendage to the genitalia—are not all that old: they began to form only after Columbus allegedly discovered America.

However, this development is interesting enough to draw out in the context of this book, since few people realize that the imprisonment of awareness to and in the body came about as a result of only a few men. These few arbitrarily established, among other things, that if the nonmaterial *did* exist, it could not be known anyway. This seems a facile explanation, but it is one that has come to rule. It is the contrivance whereby nonmaterial interactions have been set aside.

The complacency of education frequently blinds our social systems to the fact that what is taught about the nature of man may not be true. This complacency also arbitrarily hides the abysmal fact that some ideas about man are merely the unproven ideas of certain individuals.

A good case in point is the acceptance of the concept of *evolution* as a fact when it is still an unproven theory. Yet quite automatically it is enforced into consciousness as a "must be true" idea. The California State

Board of Education, in March 1973, became aware of this horrendous fallacy and reinstated in educational texts the concept of evolution as *theory* only, and not yet as proven fact. There are several other theories as to the origin of physical man that might have as much credence as the theory of evolution.

Philosophy relating to a solely materialistic idea of the universe and of man can be traced to a few. Some time ago men became impatient with the weaknesses of religion and sought to wrest the universe from the hands of God and ecclesiastics into the hands of science. An early attempt in this direction can be traced to one Thomas Hobbes, born in 1588 and educated at Magdalen College, Oxford. It should be remembered that the Copernican explosion was yet to come, but the idea that the Sun did not revolve around Earth was certainly well on the gossip lines by then. Great changes were in store for the men of those times, as they are today.

Hobbes's early interests were mathematics and physics, and he was totally absorbed in the rationalistic views of the time. He was also devoted to writing on political science, a predilection that brought a series of disfavors upon his head, and he had to live in exile in Europe until 1651. Charles II came to grant him his favor, but the philosopher's later life was filled with difficulties because he persisted in attacks upon organized religion and even managed to antagonize many of the scientists and mathematicians of the time.

He developed a totally mechanical conception of nature and felt that, since primitive man lived in a state of total anarchy, to create and sustain the state it was necessary for individuals to sacrifice their selfish rights.

Hobbes developed a rank materialism and became a strict supporter of the universe of the physical senses; many decades later his teachings were linked to those of associational psychology. There cannot be much doubt that his influence was tremendous, both through men who subsequently adopted his ideas and because his influences drove men who disagreed with him into new fields.

Another early spurt for materialism came from the Baron von Leibnitz, a German philosopher and mathematician born in 1646. He became an important and versatile leader in many fields, and is famous for his discovery of differential calculus.

Leibnitz indicated that the only true reality lies *outside* the physical world, beyond the world of the senses, but he linked this outside world to the physical world by establishing the existence of a hierachy of *monads*. He felt that the monad was a force substance that had both unity and infinity and was a manifestation of a nonpersonal God and an ultimate cause.

Just how this was so was never fully explained since it was necessary to *assume* a priori that such was the case, and if one did that, then the rest could be explained. The *monad* was a psychic thing, to be sure, and the universe is composed of a complex of these.

The concepts of Leibnitz, if apparently nonmaterial in their nature, are attempts to link up invisible forces within the concepts that already had come to govern materialism. They thus constitute an occult materialism, and can be seen so today in the many "occult" movements that seized upon cause-effect hierarchical systems as explanation for many otherwise unexplainable things.

The Leibnitz system has very ancient forerunners, but it would be beside the point to delve into them. While the Leibnitz system assuredly is almost a metaphysical or psychic system, it is well established upon known cause-effect relationships that govern the material universe, and the vistas of Leibnitz's monads are thoroughly demarcated by the limits of the visible worlds.

But the Leibnitz system gave rise to the concept that ideas themselves are innate to the individual, the individual having developed them from inner germs. This concept of "idea," of course, prohibits all thought except *predestined* thought.

John Locke, born in 1632, exerted a great influence on many later philosophers. Schooled at Christ Church, Oxford, he studied medicine, although he practiced it little during his life. He held several minor civil and diplomatic posts, mostly obtained for him by his patron, Anthony Ashley Cooper, first earl of Shaftesbury.

Locke, if schooled, was not a well-educated man, and this lack enabled him to lay down his ideas in a much clearer manner than is usually the case with philosophers. His most profound contribution to succeeding generations was that he held that mortal man enters the world with a blank mind, a tabula rasa. This blank mind acquires ideas only by suffering experience, and so Locke felt all knowledge must ultimately arise from sense perception.

He placed great stress on the belief that knowledge accumulates as a result of inspection or direct perception of the external world, and that the interplay of reflection upon perceptions of the external world gives rise to more and more complex ideas of matter, energy, space, and time. He also stressed, in *Some Thoughts Concerning Education* (1693) that education should be concerned with moral and physical development rather than the inculcation of knowledge. It is obvious that many educators in succeeding generations took Locke at his word.

In establishing the mind of man as blank at birth, Locke omitted to establish where the perceiving mind originated. The mechanisms that the blank mind used as perceptual information flowed into it were left equally fuzzy.

Nonetheless, Locke firmly established the tabula rasa concept, which (although it raised considerable protest from detractors) became honored in philosophical and educational thought. Many people later concluded that humans are programmed by their experience, and that humans therefore could purposively be programmed by feeding them the proper experiences.

The tabula rasa situation was taught as late as the time the formal education of this author began. Its tenets preclude and forbid anything that does not originate in the material universe, cause-effect relationships, as well as denying the existence of situations that do not depend upon reflection of sensations.

Locke's *Essay Concerning Human Understanding* has been called the first critical approach to human intellect and intellectual powers. There have been some, of course, and wisely so, who have considered this concept to be utter garbage.

Several lesser luminaries in early philosophy also fed certain confusions into the general philosophical channel. George Berkeley, for instance, an Irish philosopher born in 1685 and educated at Trinity College, Dublin, established that matter was just a name for arrangements of ideas. The only things we could know of matter, if anything at all, were its secondary qualities—such as weight, color, and sound.

He felt that, even if matter could exist (which it didn't), we could never know it since we are essentially confined to the world of our ideas. Detractors wondered how it was, if matter did not exist, that we could experience the course of nature. Berkeley felt this was so because God raised in man sensations of a given coherent order.

It is David Hume, however, who lodged a philosophical rock that founds and confounds much of present-day thought. Hume was born in 1711 in Scotland, and later studied at Edinburgh and in France. He delved deeply, *he* felt, into human nature, and he convinced many later philosophers that he had done so.

His ideas are founded on those of Locke. Without explaining the origin of the perceptive quality, he set about dividing it into two parts—that of ideas or thoughts and that of impressions. To him, impressions were the most important of the two since he felt they were the original substance upon which thought was subsequently founded.

How and why this was so was not explained, but these assertions enabled Hume to ascertain that the human soul was made up of a series of perceptions and that this accounted for everything. The practical needs of human nature were what called forth religion. Further, although man can believe in what lies beyond human experience, he can never have knowledge or proof of such matters. Therefore, anything that violated experience could not be held in reason.

Hume's influence upon following generations was staggering, as was the influence of Immanuel Kant. Together these two men locked the boundaries of human awareness tightly into the concept that all existence was composed of cause-effect relationships. From this yoke, human awareness and science have not yet recovered.

The being who was to become the monolithic Immanuel Kant was born in 1724 at Königsberg, where he lived most of his life. Upon maturity he was engaged as a tutor by several East Prussian families. He became a lecturer at the University of Königsberg in 1755 and gave instruction in several subjects, including mineralogy, geography, and metaphysics.

He turned his inquisitive attention to many philosophers and metaphysicians who preceded him or were his contemporaries. After digesting the works of other philosophers, he disregarded them at least partially and set about establishing a "critique of pure reason," which was soon reflected in his epoch-making book that uses the same phrase as its title.

His influence upon succeeding metaphysicians, philosophers, psychologists, and generations is incalculable. His teachings have penetrated into practically every concept of thought since, and it is not to be questioned that he is, indeed, the greatest part of the foundation that underlies modern concepts of human thought.

Kant felt it necessary to reject many earlier workers in the field of human knowledge because they had not given sufficient consideration to the *limitations* of knowledge. That knowledge might have limitations comes today as a sort of shattering, defeating quality to advancing discovery, but at the time Kant set forth his views, this idea seemed to have attraction.

Kant indicated that it was necessary to ascertain such limitations before trying to solve problems of human existence, in order to know whether knowledge or reason could resolve them. To a few latter-day observers this has seemed somewhat like the crocodile trying to learn about the swamp by attempting to swallow its own tail.

Nevertheless, this seemed an appropriate line of thinking to Kant, and has seemed so to multitudes of followers since. Kant felt that we perceive things in space and time through our senses. He called the information coming into us through our senses *phenomena*. But he established that the senses cannot give any knowledge of things in themselves; this he called *noumena*, or that which could not be known.

We get our knowledge of phenomena by coordinating the information provided for us by our senses and combining it into "sense-images," Kant believed. He termed this coordination "perception." He indicated that, by further coordinating these sense perceptions with concepts of understanding, we received our *experience* of the natural world. By the judgments resulting from this coordination of experience, we can accompany this experience with general principles (which he calls "ideas") and arrive at an understanding or have knowledge of the metaphysical world. But Kant failed to establish with any clarity that any "understanding" arrived at in this manner would be delimited a priori by experience of the phenomenal world.

Swooping past this somewhat glaring omission, he pressed onward and suggested that we cannot perceive anything except in the form of space and time and all things based upon that form—i.e., cause and effect, unity and plurality, and so forth. It is because *phenomena* can only be experienced in these categories that any knowledge of *noumena*—things outside the senses—could never be obtained by pure reason. Kant admitted that the same kind of experience that results in knowledge might operate within the realms of "intuition" in such a way as to make *noumena* thinkable, but nevertheless *noumena* could not be affirmed or denied by experience.

It therefore would seem that Immanuel Kant never "experienced" any *noumena*, although many people have, and so he felt free to establish these limiting factors on knowledge.

But Kant felt that since "ethical consciousness" demands that something must lie beyond the world of *phenomena*, faith must enter in to provide proof for moral freedom, immortality, and God. Reason could not operate in the world of *noumena*, but faith could; reason alone could examine *phenomena*.

Immanuel Kant's works are among the most difficult and obtuse in modern philosophy and metaphysics. But as complicated and complex as his works are, they clearly reflect the strict materialistic conception of things that has governed the thinking of man for many centuries: Man can perceive what the senses permit him to perceive and, based upon that, he can have knowledge. Contrariwise, what one cannot perceive by the senses cannot be perceived and will never be perceived; thus knowledge of it cannot exist. All this he handed over to the regimentation of "faith," exactly as his theological predecessors had.

Immanuel Kant met a tragic end. He declined mentally toward the end of his life, possibly because his awareness began bouncing against the "limitations" of knowledge. Of course he was not the first to have engendered his own mental conflict, nor will he be the last.

For the individual who feels he can perceive the indecent discrepancies in Kant's theorizing, it is difficult to understand just how his theories swept up the thinkers in more than one nation. And this rash of the *phenomenal* world concept coincided somewhat with certain theories about the brain that had come up just before Kant's confusing philosophy and metaphysics arrived on the scene.

One Etienne Bonnot de Condillac, a French philosopher born in 1715, became a member of the French Academy of Sciences in 1768. Condillac created for the works of Locke a secure place in the cultural development of France. He went on to suggest that the mind depends totally upon the store of knowledge acquired for it by the senses. He felt that, until the senses bring to the mind perceptions from the outside, the mind lies blank and holds no ideas.

Just prior to this grand announcement, a certain David Hartley, born in 1705, decided that he also had found out something about the mind. Hartley was an English physician and also a philosopher. And, like many later personalities who studied both physical science and metaphysical topics, he felt obliged to sequester the "metaphysics" into rationalizations of the "physical," which can by now be recognized as *the* talent of almost all materialistic philosphers.

Hartley, founding the concept of associational psychology, indicated that all mental phenomena were to be discovered in the sensations arising from vibrations of the white medullary substance of the brain and spinal cord.

It should be established that there were many critics of these emerging materialistic concepts. But however discontented some people were with theories that the physical senses are the end-all of human interaction, these theories rose to dominance during succeeding decades and are heartily supported today. The "we are our brains" theory became especially paramount through the years, so much so, in fact, that in many universities it constituted heresy to suggest anything to the contrary.

The subject of metaphysics, normally the realm permitting creative speculation upon the possible structures of existence, was thus handed down to philosophy, the notorious realm that tries to establish explanations for functions of human endeavor within the universe. Psychology, however, was finally able to undertake the entire responsibility of creating for society a view that coincided solely with psychological theory.

This event can be traced to the simultaneous rising of a positively ardent flock of experts on the eminence of the brain; especially important in this regard was Alexander Bain, a Scottish psychologist born in 1818.

In 1841 Bain became assistant to the professor of moral philosophy at Marischal College, Aberdeen. He later became examiner of moral philosophy and logic at the University of Glasgow.

In later years he was to turn out an almost endless series of pamphlets on ethics, morals, and English grammar. But preeminent among his interests was the newly born field of psychology in the material sense, and he emphasized this subject in his courses on logic.

His point of view on psychology was thought to be new at the time; it later became popular, then imperative, and finally fully accepted without argument by latter-day psychologists. Forgetting that the ancients had advocated the necessity of "a healthy mind in a healthy body," he taught that physiology was of extreme importance to psychology. This must be observed to be true, of course, since a mind terrorized and pained by an unhealthy body does not usually function well.

Up to that time the concept of metaphysical inquiry had not been totally disenfranchised, at least insofar as psychology was concerned. But Alexander Bain claimed the responsibility of clearing metaphysics from psychology finally and for all time.

Thus, by this and other similar routes, the cudgel of authority as to the what and wherefore of human consciousness passed to psychologists. There were, of course, holdouts and recidivists who adhered to a more aesthetic, intuitive, and comprehensive view of the nature of man.

And there were crises, to be sure. For one thing the influx of Oriental thought in the form of European translations of Buddhist, Tibetan, and Chinese philosophic texts gave the burgeoning materialistic establishment considerable pause at various times. And not a few European scientists and psychologists were converted, at least partially, to some of these Oriental implications. The staunchest of Western psychologists merely chalked up the loss of these erstwhile colleagues to fringe dementia, a state of mental disorder characterized by impairment of mental powers.

But modern psychology survived these intrusions and unorthodoxies, though not without sever exchanges of diatribes and altercations, the most notorious of which was to be the Freud/Jung fiasco. This debacle is continuing into the third and fourth generation.[3]

The rise of psychic research, in some sort of organized form, could be considered another crisis and has engendered an impressive amount of hooting and mockery. Whatever the threat stemming from "psychic" research might have been, early psychic researchers were never quite able to capture a ghost. Various suitable physical explanations could always be found for instances of table-turning. And the high frequency of ectoplasms turning out to be constructions of ordinary gauze or photographs from French newspapers was perfectly disheartening.

And in the long run, although Western culture has had its own mystics, witches, and psychics, all these could now be respectably explained away as strange, psychotic cross switchings in the white pulp of the medullary substance. If the events were of such a magnitude as to seem totally

---

[3] Literature on the Freud/Jung disaster is copious; most of it tries to suggest that this disagreement was merely a matter of ideology. The fracas is elucidated with some merit by Jan Ehrenwald, "Freud versus Jung—The Mythophobic versus the Mythophilic Temper in Psychotherapy," *Israel Annals of Psychiatry and Related Disciplines* 6, no. 2 (1968).

beyond mere medullary implications, they could be held to be unknowable in the first place, in line with Kantian concepts of the *noumena*, and thus no scientific time and expertise should be wasted on them.

As has recently been stated, the quantum physicist Werner Heisenberg will most likely be noted in history as the individual who brought an end to causal determinism in physics—and hence to a solely materialistic outlook of things.[4] This impending change, of course, leaves members of the materialistic bastion utterly foaming at the mouth.

Yet, while this drama in physics is getting up steam, and psychic implications are gaining momentum as a result, the great, overriding question is whether it is at all possible for individuals to have psychic manifestations in the sense that they are human *abilities*. Or whether, in a currently popular view, these confusing phenomena are merely results of some strange combination of mental or physiochemical orders not yet discovered.

Scientists in general, when forced by dint of the frequency of appearance of the phenomena, often opt for the latter reasoning and try to explain that the origin of paranormal events lies in known but not understood physical interactions of some sort. It is possible that *some* paranormal phenomena will be aligned with relevant discovery in the fields of electrobiological research and so forth. But considering the general magnitude of certain paranormal manifestations, it is definitely a "cop-out" to cling arbitrarily to this explanation.

Parapsychological research, during the time it has been identified as a science—or pseudoscience—has not been troubled by the appearance of a psychic ability whose magnitude would bring all past ideas on the subject to a crude, rude, and stunning halt. Psychical phenomena studied in the past hundred years of research have been—with one or two exceptions—minimal phenomena and of no significant importance to the vast, imposing bastions of science.

[4] Arthur Koestler, *The Roots of Coincidence* (New York: Random House, 1972), p. 51.

For example, what would science in general, and parapsychology in particular, do if confronted with a case similar to that of Joseph Copertino, who in the seventeenth century stunned the world by his ability to leave the ground at will—to levitate. His ability was of such magnitude that he was often willing to take passengers on his back or transport luggage for notables.

Apparently a simple-minded man who became a monk early in life, Joseph was denounced by the Inquisition, which decided he was tainted with devilish and diabolical powers. Such condemnations were always an embarrassment to the religious orders in which they turned up, and Joseph was no exception. Even though he was transferred to a less conspicuous monastery, and in spite of inquisitional orders to the contrary, Joseph continued levitating. Eminent people added to the embarrassment by attesting to the reality of this levitation. Duke Frederick of Brunswick-Lüneburg, though himself a suspicious Lutheran, admitted the marvel. No less important people than Princess Maria of Savoy and King Casimir V of Poland testified under oath to the marvel of Joseph.

Forced to reexamine Joseph in the light of these influential attestations, the Inquisition decided it could find no diabolical association and eventually declared Joseph to be innocent of evil intercourse. A renowned specialist in canon law, Cardinal Prospero Lambertini, later Pope Benedict XIV, examined this case of levitation and felt inspired to pronounce it real. Joseph, later decreed a saint, continued to exhibit his penchant for religious levitatory rapture and every so often rose from the floor before his brother monks, carrying a small statue of Jesus in his arms.

Further, it seems at one time to have been quite fashionable to levitate. Saint Thomas Aquinas is said to have floated in religious ecstasy some three feet above the floor in front of a crucifix. Saint Teresa often rose before her astonished Carmelite sisters. Elizabeth of Bavaria, Saint Francis Xavier, and Saint Margaret of Hungary often rose also. The Jesuit Ignacio de Azevedo solved the problem of crossing bridgeless rivers by flying over them, and Saint Peter of Alcantara repeatedly floated airborne for three hours.

Levitation seems to have gone out of fashion, and today it is not at all common. One can amuse oneself by considering the dramatic effects such a demonstration would have on both science and the establishment, which has so far successfully promoted the concept that not only levitation but any psychic manifestation is not possible—and when apparent is merely the result of some toxic mental or physical situation. What state of scientific knowledge would have to obtain should it be required to explain the representative of China suddenly levitating in the Security Council of the United Nations before his stunned colleagues? From one point of view, therefore, science, is probably quite grateful that levitators do not abound in this day and time.

Psychic research, if indeed it can be called that, has in recent years concerned itself with the smallest of the vistas presented by its idea of how it should proceed. No amount of inquiry, no force, no current rationale, no bombast has encouraged many seemingly miraculous psychical phenomena to yield to science either one facet of their mechanics or a few particles of reproducible data.

The intriguing, fascinating, and commonly known worlds of precognition, prophecy, telepathy, and clairvoyance are only begrudgingly admitted to exist, and then only by a small minority of scientists. The rare abilities of mind-reading, telekinesis, teleportation, and the legendary out-of-body experience—this latter reported almost daily by thousands of experients—are denied by most of science. Only today are they making some sort of a dent in the irascible scientific fabric.

Personal experience often serves as a guide to one's outlook on life, even when such experience necessarily conflicts with accepted dicta. Many individuals merely adopt two viewpoints, one that seems to accord with what is expected of them by society and another more personal view that is structured around their own awareness.

Years ago this author tried to comprehend the rationales that governed the lives of his two grandmothers. My paternal grandmother, Maria, was a Swedish immigrant and finally came to rest in the small town of my birth, high in the Colorado Rockies. Her husband, Andrew, also an immigrant, was drawn to the high country by the gold lust that preoccupied a great many people of his generation. He never found gold. He became a paid employee of one of the vested mining interests in the area and died early of consumption.

Maria's ideas of life were simple. One was destined to be poor; one should be acutely conscious of authority and of one's superiors in society and never do anything to antagonize them. Nothing material should ever be thrown away; everything should be reused in some manner. Rags went into making beautiful rugs and quilts, scraps of food into delicious stews and soups, and pieces of life and mementos into two large trunks in the second bedroom. And above all one should retain the Swedish way of life, almost untouched and unaltered.

Within these boundaries life was homey, almost softly warm.

Extraordinary occurrences were not supposed to happen. If they did, they were certainly never talked about; they were ignored, and every effort was made to pretend that they had never occurred.

When Andrew died, leaving Maria with four growing children, she prepared to face life alone since it was unseemly for her to marry again. But one evening, while she was sitting with her sorrow in the darkened living room, Andrew appeared to her and gave orders that she should quickly take another husband since it was really foolish, considering the times, to remain alone.

She obediently permitted herself to be wooed, and she took another husband, also named Andrew. She chose badly, however, and the second Andrew passed on within two years. Shortly after the funeral of the second Andrew, the first Andrew once more appeared and prevailed upon Maria to try again. Maria felt this was going too far. She declined and took work as a charwoman in order to support her family.

Several months passed, during which argumentation on the matter of a third matrimonial transpired between Maria and the specter of her first husband. Seeing that he could not convince her to take yet a third, Andrew eventually retreated upstairs, where he knocked around for several years, causing the house to creak and groan through the night.

Seeking to enlarge her income, and since the upstairs had some fourteen rooms, Maria got the idea of taking in roomers. Some of them reportedly were harassed by Andrew's ghost and quickly moved out. This matter apparently died away gradually, with Andrew giving up and going on to other things. But Maria was always reluctant to go upstairs. When I was a child, all the upstairs rooms were empty and it was a vast, mysterious domain in which I tried to catch Andrew many times.

Years ago this familial involvement from beyond the grave seemed extraordinary. In the last few years, though, I have especially sought to talk about death and dying with the elderly, many of whom have already had a loved one precede them to the wherever. Almost all of them, given a Scotch or sherry, will confess to feeling accompanied by the specter of their departed one, or even to have consulted with it on important matters.

This type of occurrence is not of recent vintage, either. In May 1800 the spirit of Mrs. Nelly Butler, the deceased first wife of Captain George Butler, appeared and, during the course of several visits, urged Butler to take a second wife, namely, one Miss Lydia Blaisdel. Furthermore, apparently dissatisfied with the burial of her (Nelly's) deceased child, the ghost supervised a more satisfactory reinterment in the presence of some eighty persons.[5]

The ghostly presence of the first Andrew in Maria's life was a great embarrassment to her. Of course it was never openly discussed. Only with considerable precocious childhood effort was the entire story pried out of her, and then the trunks in the second downstairs bedroom were opened and the remembrances they contained spread out all over the floor. The photographs of the first Andrew were studied deeply and meditated upon at great length in an effort to ascertain something in the glint of his eyes or his posture that might reveal why, as a ghost, he might have decided to try to guide Maria's life from the beyond. All to no avail.

But Maria's life was decidedly influenced by this paranormal event. Even if this saga was not openly discussed, she was able to nod her head in sympathetic understanding when tales from others got on the gossip lines.

The situation represented by my maternal grandmother, Anna, was a horse of an entirely different color.

She was born in West Virginia of German descent. An orphan, her childhood was spent in abysmal poverty, passing from one poor family to another that was even poorer. As she matured, however, she took the reins of her life in her own hands, labored hard in the jobs women

---

[5] Abraham Cummings, *Immortality Proved by the Testimony of Sense in Which Is Contemplated the Doctrine of Spectres, and the Existence of A Particular Spectre* (1826), p. 76. This book is quite difficult to come by. An excellent review of its contents is found in Muriel Roll, "A Nineteenth-Century Matchmaking Apparition," *The Journal of the American Society for Psychical Research* 63, no. 4 (October 1969), pp. 396–409.

could hold, and eventually married a man named Curtis who was "with the railroads."

Curtis also became possessed by gold lust and decided to traipse off to the Rockies, leaving Anna and one child behind in Sioux City, Kansas.

Having gotten a husband, Anna was not inclined to leave him to the wiles of the women in the mining camps. Obtaining an automobile, she followed him unannounced into the mountains, catching up with him in that small mountain town.

Curtis's luck at discovering gold was nil, however. After siring four children, he felt obliged, with Anna's prodding, to obtain a more steady income, going once more with the railroads. He died in my third year, and my only memory of him is of being bounced on his knee outside by the porch trellis upon which grew lush, green hops, the mysterious plant from which beer is made.

Anna was familiar with all sorts of paranormal realms. In fact many matrons in the town's Scandinavian community, my paternal grandmother included, had concluded that Anna was, if not an outright witch, at least the possessor of the "evil eye." It was somethig of a scandal that my father and mother married. Even though the two grandmothers lived next door to each other, it was seldom that they darkened each other's doorsteps.

Since Anna was prepared to entertain all sorts of paranormal possibilities, it was to her that this author, as a child, took many of the unusual questions about existence that came to him. And there was an unusual hook-up between Anna's sense of extraordinary awareness and the awarenesses that seemed to me, at that early age, part and parcel of existence. For example, one winter Anna and I had been out of town and were driving back along a precipitous mountain road. On one side the mountain rose upward in steep majesty; on the other side it dropped off in an equally steep but dizzying grandeur. It was winter, and huge drifts had been plowed through by the road's maintenance snowplow.

Anna was driving, but she suddenly pulled over to the side of the road. The sun glistened on the brilliant whiteness, pierced by the lush winter green of pines. Except for the rush of the river falling over cataracts far below, silence lay over everything.

"Honey," she said in a weak voice, "I don't think we should go any farther up the road."

We got out to survey the scene, to see what her excellent senses had picked up. The scene was really beautiful, a glistening whiteness beneath azure blue sky, the crisp mountain air freezing on all sides. Barely out of the car, standing on the running board, we heard a small pop in the air, then a crack, and then the dreaded road of an avalanche. We plunged to the lee side of the mountain, while barely a hundred yards in front of us the cascade of snow mounted its predictable uncompromising viciousness. Pines snapped, the snow moved and fell into the abyss below, the concussion of air bounced upward, snapping more pines near their tops. Suddenly, almost as quickly as it had begun, the roar died, except for echoes bounding about on the surrounding peaks, and all was again silent.

"I'll be a son of a bitch," muttered Anna. Hesitantly, we peered over the edge to see where we would have been had we progressed onward. Except for a gray smear of earth torn away in the slide, the path was almost invisible. But the road was definitely blocked.

"I guess we'll have go turn around and go back to Placerville," Anna said.

At the idea of turning around, a strange sensation snapped my head in the backward direction where I, in barely an instant, surveyed the road.

"No," I said. "I don't think we should move at all."

"Why, honey? Why not?" asked Anna in a small voice. "We can't stay here. We'll freeze."

So, back in the car, shutting out the cold air, Anna managed by several small moves to get turned around. But when it was headed in the proper direction I knew we had to stay put. "Grandma, please don't go now."

And once more there was a pop in the air, a swish of moving snow, the agonizing rending of trees and crunching of rocks beneath the glittering white moving surface.

Huddled in the car, Anna's foot on the brake, we watched the retreat swim in snow dust as the second avalanche slid past. Whatever the reason may be, experienced mountaineers know that slides often come in threes. We waited patiently for the third, hoping it would not invade our small island on the road, the barest thirty feet that the sliding mountain had not so far touched. In moments, when the air concussion of the second movement had barely subsided, across the canyon came the third, this time billowing snow dust up out of the deeps, obscuring for a moment the brilliant sunlight.

"I'll be a son of a bitch," Anna said.

"Me too!" I exclaimed.

And there we had to sit until the gas ran out of the car and there was no more heat coming from the small heater. Finally, feeling that the snow on the second avalanche toward Placerville had settled enough, we made our way tenuously across the slide area. And after walking only a mile or so, we ran into an approaching auto, into whose warmth we retreated. We spent the night at a small settlement called Placerville in the company of a couple of hard-rock miners Grandma knew from way back.

For me, unusual problems began early, but they founded in my space experiences that came to underlie all possible thoughts of human existence. Their mark was left so indelibly that no amount of authoritarian or social implanting was able to erase it. And if this came to be the source of tremendous anxiety in the years in which education, morals, and social conditioning were expected to mold me in the guise of a typical individual, it has also been the source of almost unimaginable beauty and confidence in the integrity and immortality of spirit.

It is useless to insist in the face of incredulity that what happened to me as a child was a real experience. No effort is being made, therefore, to lay it out as fact, and so it can conveniently be told in the third person.

For those who can remember, 1936 was a very good year for scandal and important events. For the generations that have matured since, the romance and intrigues of the time appear periodically on movie screens.

Early that year, King George V died at the age of 70, and was succeeded by the popular Edward VII, who, after many years of loneliness, had fallen in love with *The American,* Mrs. Wallis Warfield Simpson. The world waited breathlessly to see if Mrs. Warfield, separated but not yet divorced from her husband, an insurance agent, would become Queen of England.

While the new King of England was fighting his romantic battle with the English Parliament, the rejected art student, Adolph Hitler, was already saying "non-sense" to all impediments to his dreams of conquest. German troops reoccupied the Rhineland, and the Berlin-Rome-Tokyo Axis was formed.

In Russia, Stalin, with a series of trials which left any concept of modern justice somewhat in limbo, began purging his enemies. And in Spain, the Republicans supported by Communist Russia met in grueling and bloody combat the Nazi supported Falangists.

As the year moved on, King Edward began losing his battle to marry Wallis Simpson, or at least to have her as Queen. Hitler set up the first of the infamous concentration camps, the monumental insults to human nature. General Francisco Franco, supported by Germany, began winning the war in Spain, being proclaimed head of the Loyalist government. The brutal civil war in Spain claimed many lives, among them the talented poet, Garcia Lorca, and eventually inspired the late artist, Picasso, always preoccupied with brutality, to paint his famous mural *Guernica*.

Bruno Richard Hauptmann was electrocuted in Trenton, New Jersey, for the kidnapping of Charles Augustus (little Augie) Lindberg, Jr. A tornado in Gainesville, Georgia, claimed the lives of 203, while in the Preakness, at Pimlico, Baltimore, Bold Venture won $27,325. John Henry Lewis was still light heavyweight champion and New York won the Major League Pennant.

If people in many parts of the planet were troubled and in difficulty, the young boy born in the peace and crystal atmosphere of the high Rockies seemed untroubled. Of course he was so young that no one thought of him as anything but a baby. He gazed out at the world through light blue eyes. His tabula rasa, his blank mind, if indeed that was what he had, was busy doing what it was supposed to do.

In the spring of that year—1936—far removed from international and even national events, there was no reason to expect that the momentous affairs brewing on other parts of the planet should come to have immediate repercussions on his young, growing mind and his subsequent life.

It was a small town in which he lived. He was only two and a half years old, and everyone was still talking to him in baby talk. Despite this impediment, he himself could almost talk in proper words, and he could listen. News of outside events penetrated the isolation of the high mountain town.

OUT OF BODY

The cold spring air hurt his swollen tonsils. The event of having them removed was imminent. He was frightened, of course, but then had not everyone—mother, the doctor, grandmothers, uncles, father, and nurses—had they not all said everything would be all right?

In the vestibule of the hospital—not exactly a proper waiting room—two women were considering the impending possibility of "another war."

"Yes," said one. "It seems as if wars come about every twenty years."

A passing thought flitted through his tabula rasa. No, he thought, there were times when they came even more frequently. But he could not exactly put a mental finger on the origin of that computation. He tried to swallow, but the pain discouraged that. Instead he spit into a handkerchief.

"Do you suppose the king will marry her?"

As the pain mounted temporarily, the question, the idle question, seemed to float into him from all sides. He wondered if he understood exactly what a king was—probably, but there were no kings in the Rockies.

His mother held his hands tightly as his body contorted with the raging pain at the back of his throat. He wondered, between the waves of hurtful sensation, if they would burn his tonsils in the incinerator in back of the hospital. It had a big smokestack that belched dark, black smoke. His uncle had told him that was where the doctor and nurses burned arms and legs when they needed to be cut off. He decided that his tonsils should not be put there along with all the other hospital refuse.

The nurse finally came for him.

And then, somehow, he was on a white, somewhat hard, table in the operating room. The walls were painted white, and a surround of dark brown wainscotting ran around the bottom half. The scent of "hospital" was very heavy.

Now it was going to happen, he thought. His view of things seemed to get smaller and smaller, to collapse into some sort of tiny vantage point. The nurse began strapping him down, saying funny infant things.

And then she tried to put the *thing* on his face.

The indignities suddenly seemed gargantuan. He resisted the ether mask. The nurse persisted. The fight was on.

Drawing upon inordinate physical strength, the young child fended off the strength of the nurse, upon whose upper lip sweat and determination made their mark. The caterwauling brought in his mother, whose sympathies, horrendously, seemed to be with the nurse who he was by now certain intended vile, indescribable acts upon him. Mother held his feet, but the yelling had attracted the attention of the doctor, already on his way to perform the tonsillectomy.

That man strapped the young boy's feet down firmly. Perhaps now reacting like an animal in mortal danger, the boy responded with even greater feats of physical strength, accompanied by a considerable flow of tears and great gusts of screaming.

The three attackers retreated to the anteroom for a consultation. The nurse soon returned with a half-filled balloon and sweetly taunted the young boy by saying, "I bet you can't blow this up further."

After a period of cajoling during which the tears subsided, with mother and the now tender doctor also coaxing, the boy finally smiled a little and put the rubber nipple in his mouth.

It was only when the body began to subside into unconsciousness that the youngster realized the trickery that had been played upon him. The balloon had been half-filled with ether, and for every breath he exhaled into it, he inhaled a small amount of the noxious substance.

To his young mind this trickery was shocking. Mere physical resistance, sponsored by fear of all these unknown things, was quickly replaced by a consuming rage. But the body slipped out from under him sufficiently to enable the nurse to triumphantly strap the hated and detested ether mask over his quivering lips.

If the unconsciousness that covered his infant's body was warm and dark, not so his enraged perception. The focus of his vision shifted. The walls of the detested chamber seemed intensely emerald. The old wainscotting, a dark band around the lower half of the room, now appeared to be a living rainbow.

There is no doubt that, had means been at his command, the young boy in his furor might have laid waste to the room and those in it.

But the doctor, now a complete enemy to him, was already prying into the mouth and down the throat.

"Well, we are getting these out none too soon," he commented.

The young boy watched the quick professionalism of the strange instrument, being forced down the throat, the quick insertion of forceps, and the flash of the scalpel. He moved up about three feet above the body, just out of the glaring light above the operating table, into the warm shadows.

The scalpel slipped down into the mouth. The doctor's hand shook somewhat. The blade cut the back of the tongue.

"Shit!" exclaimed the doctor, gritting his teeth.

The total anger that had up to now consumed the young, invisible viewer was now somewhat replaced by a little interest. The doctor had said a dirty word, one of the words Daddy often said, but a word that utterly horrified Mama and the two grandmothers. But hardly had he had time to consider the delicate significance of this when in quick succession the doctor pulled out of the throat two suspicious small brown things.

The mystery deepened considerably. How could dirty brown things come out of this end of the body when they usually came out of the other end? But things were moving quickly. Before *this* mystery could be seriously considered, the nurse plopped the two brown things into a small bottle and placed it on a sideboard behind two rolls of tissue.

The doctor was already busy pushing some thread and a needle into the open throat to sew up his mistake. The boy noticed that the doctor's fingers and the body's lips were flecked with ruby-colored blood, which somehow was glowing. Mother, standing by, was crying a little. But the doctor was smiling and soon began whistling.

"He's going to be just fine," he advised, peering deep into the throat, surveying his expertise. This whole affair had not seemed to last very long. In fact there was some sort of timeless quality to it. Shortly, vision was again perceived through the eyes, which were shedding wet tears.

He had suffered the outrage of the balloon betrayal, the body ached from defeat, the throat was numb from scalpel slicings, but the young boy's interest was now totally with the mysterious brown things. These must be the infamous tonsils everyone had been talking about. He must save them from the furnace.

Gagging a little, the nurse now unstrapping his feet, his mother holding his hand, he said, "I want my tonsils."

"Now, now," chided the nurse. "We have already thrown those dirty things away."

He looked at her incredulously. Would all this betrayal never stop?

"No, you didn't," he snorted, the supreme pain in his throat disappearing in the triumph. He pointed to the two rolls of tissue. "You put them behind those over there."

"No, I didn't," exclaimed the nurse quickly, nervously.

"Yes, you did. Give them to me. And Mama," he announced triumphantly, "the doctor said 'shit' when he cut my throat."

But they refused to give up the tonsils, which probably were incinerated along with various arms and legs and afterbirths. Exchanging strange glances, the nurse, the doctor, and Mama carried his body out of the torture chamber. After a while, home safely in a warm bed, Mama wanted to know how it was that he knew where the tonsils had been hidden. He could not explain it all to her very well, but the strangeness of that brilliant separation from the body became ever after like the sound of a bell on a distant mountain, a sound emanating from lands where things were decidedly different from life as it was generally lived in the year 1936.

It was only a few days until he was up and about, experiencing the marvelous beauties of a Rocky Mountain spring. Often at night, while the body drifted in slumber in the warm bed, he watched the stars gleaming high above the house, even high above the mountains, even high above the atmospheric mists that surround the turning, groaning orb of Earth. The spring winds often wafted him along. And he visited wherever his heart and interest took him. And he made mistakes. He began talking about what he came across.

"Mama," he said eagerly one morning, "Last night I saw the king of England. He was sitting in a big room with big chairs in it, all alone, and he was crying."

And Mama began crying also, which amazed him. He understood quickly that the recounting of certain adventures hurt her deeply for some inexplicable reason, and he decided not to tell her any more, since her tears hurt him, too.

As the first grandchild on either side of the family he was greatly fawned over and eventually spoiled rotten. What one grandmother would not give him, the other would, since between them there existed an inexplicable competition of some sort. And when they failed, there was a multitude of aunts and uncles.

Maria, when he broached certain strange experiences to her, tightened her lips and lapsed into Swedish, saying things he did not comprehend. He quickly came to understand, however, the look in her eyes. The various aunts and uncles were likely to be quite silent, or perhaps giggle and change the subject very quickly.

And so it was to Anna that he came to talk about such things, since at least she did not turn almost cataleptic when the stories were presented.

In the late summer of 1936 the young boy toddled his way over to Anna. He was extremely perplexed, and he asked her about those people across the ocean who were throwing dynamite at each other.

"Why, honey, what makes you think that?"

"I saw them, flying in big birds, throwing things at the ground where there were great big explosions."

"But how could you know about that?"

"I floated across a big ocean with huge waves. There are towns and villages, and lots of people moving out of them. They have their cars filled with suitcases, and some have horses and carts. There are screams."

"Don't you think that is just a dream?"

"No, because a dream is when I stay in one place and lots of pictures go on."

"Well, you tell me about all these things, but don't tell anyone else."

"And they speak like the Mexicans speak."

"Yes, that must be Spain. There's a war going on over there."

"What's a 'war'?"

Since he was a quick youngster, it wasn't long before he came to realize that he need not lie in bed at night to wander here and there, for while merely resting out in the shed in back of the house where he played, even with his eyes open, he could slip away on the wind.

Everywhere there were things that fascinated him, often more than two or three things at once. Tornados, horse races, earthquakes. How this could be was not even a question. There was too much to see, much less to think. Not only events but watching the mountain winds sweeping through forests of pines, clouds moving in the moonlight at night, rainbows forming after the magnificent storms that swept the plains; watching the pounding surf on beaches he knew not where, and the glittering phosphorous plankton trailing in eddies from the passing of ships at sea during the night.

And seeing the elusive gold in the granite mountains, and colored veins in the earth, and the lights around flowers, and following the trout in mountain streams. All this and playing too. And whispering confidences to Anna, who told him that sometimes she could hear the songs the mountain aspens sang. He pounced upon this idea of sound and, where the moving scenarios had been silent before, now he could perceive sounds in everything—suddenly everything was alive with noise.

Then came the day when he knew what Anna was thinking before she spoke, and Mama and Daddy, too. Life was spicy, vivacious, He was eager, and he began to grow.

But these halcyon days of astonishing psychical perceptions were doomed to end. The ending began with the growing awareness that hardly anyone else flew along with the winds. A sense of strangeness came to rest, and even he became startled when extraordinary things occurred, almost like being startled by the fluttering of a surprised owl in the dark depths of the forest.

In addition all things did not look the same any more, and a sense of right and wrong had grown. Thus, where he had once viewed dispassionately the dynamiting of people, as time passed he came to feel terror and depthless compassion when he viewed and understood that in another place soldiers dressed in green and black were starving hundreds of people, killing them and burying them in mass graves, or stuffing their bodies by the dozens into hot, flaming ovens.

He "withdrew" from scenes of human intercourse of all kinds since, when he became gradually aware of degrees of human nature, the sadness, the terror, and the cruelty were too much. He still had the vast reservoirs of nature, though, and these were his secret treasure trove on many days.

Anna was a wealth of comfort because the deep recesses of her personality could accommodate the impossibilities of these tales. With her as his sole confidante, these experiences flowed on for many months.

The antagonism aroused among grown-ups as a result of slips of tongue were of no concern to his young mind. In fact he could have gone on forever terrorizing mature people, since there was some sort of natural competition between children and adults that he barely understood. The death knell for extraordinary perceptions came from an unexpected quarter.

These paranormal sequences set him too far apart from other children as they, too, began to mature and adopt the standards required of them within the structure of a normal school and home life.

This conflict preoccupied his thoughts. During those days the abilities began to decline. In this conflict even Anna seemed helpless; she could only tell him that ordinary people feared and hated such strange things.

If, as is now thought, the modern discovery of discontinuity has put an end to the tyranny of causality—that is, of materialistic rule;

and if scientists are enervated by this notion;

if scientists now theorize that the contents of consciousness do not seem to have solely spatio-temporal dimensions;

if scientists feel that in this respect thought or the contents of consciousness resemble the nonmaterial problems of quantum physics, the nonthings that amazingly defy materialistic definitions of matter, energy, space, and time;

if the universe, indeed, is beginning to resemble a gigantic thought structure rather than a complicated machine;[6]

still, all this is only revolutionary theory as related to human actions and constitutes so far merely a momentous theoretical waltz to which few have learned to dance.

It is a delicate and quite risky business to touch upon the fact that, in the sciences, in religion, in philosophy, individuals everywhere still seem to conceive and perceive of themselves, and consequently act, as they always have. Perhaps this is a crude generality into which not all are to be lumped. But if it bears even a little truth, it is a relevance that guilty individuals do not care to inspect.

Whatever this relevance might be, however, almost anyone can see that there is a distressing tendency for many men and women to approach things in the light of what they have been taught, what they have learned,

---

[6] See Sir James Jeans, *The Mysterious Universe,* Macmillan (Cambridge, England: The University Press, 1930), pp. 122ff.

and especially through the eyes of those they admire. Individuals ordinarily seem stuck within the concepts of existence that have been handed down to them through education, family life, or religious training.

If they stick their heads up out of the dicta that have gone into forming their viewpoints of existence and life, likely as not they move off on some tangent, a false track, a situation that can create considerable comedy in the human enterprise. This effort permits individuals to become preoccupied with the viewing of things from odd angles.

Many aspects of mysticism and a great portion of things psychic fall into this category of human enterprise. These tangential activities permit the parties so possessed to move slightly away from accepted dicta, to isolate a strange or nutty concept or idea around which they can group everything else, and to offer this up as a synergetic, a sort of combining action that explains everything to them, if to no one else.

Psychic research is simply filled to the teeth with activities of this type, especially in those sectors of the science where researchers are preoccupied with the putting forth of ideas as to what, exactly, is responsible for the existence of psychic phenomena.

There have been numerous attempts to suggest that one's genes are responsible; traumatic experiences are blamed; getting hit on the head; being born a twin; having had a grandmother who trained one; and so forth.

In suggesting *how* psychical things work, energies usually are hypothesized, unusual energies yet to be discovered; yoga is lavishly suggested as a source and a method; neutrinos, electricity, and radiations might account for something; and so on.

Yet all these contrivances and theories are only possible "hows"; they are not "whats." As hows they usually are not successful, even though participants in any of the occult or arcane methods usually are enthusiastic if not entranced about whatever it is they think they are doing.

The fact is that one has to degrade one's natural psychic awareness considerably in order to participate in life and society as it is structured on this planet. One need only ask oneself if there was a time in the past, perhaps in magnificent childhood or youth, when more was expected from life than has been dealt.

And so I will return to my own story, once again in the third person.

The transcendental variances of his early years reached their peak during the glittering lush summer of 1941. The mountains were magnificent in July and the nights extraordinarily clear. The stars and firmament were incredibly scintillating.

The problem, however, had become paramount. It reached its complex peak on the Fourth of July.

His parents had given a party and sent all the children of those who attended to the movies. Nothing special happened, except that being herded together with a dozen other kids caused him to align himself with them and their games. Probably, too, the impossibilities represented by his unusual perceptions were becoming more obvious.

That night, sitting by the window in the dark of his bedroom, the stars overhead reminded him once again of their glory. In an effort to perceive them better, he swept up, up, and away to be among them. There they were, hanging on all sides, glowing, glittering objects by the billions. And the sound, the color! The enervating touch of space and time!

As beautiful as it was, he realized that the scope of his problem lay in the fact that he simply didn't wish to be different from others. His perceptions put distance between him and the warmth and affection of human endeavors.

It was not the *existence* of exquisite, extraordinary perceptions that constituted the problem. The problem lay in how others regarded the extraordinary, and they tended not to regard it at all.

He had to make a choice. It was to be a bad choice, of course, as he came to understand years later. But it is a choice many make. It is a choice that, by the manner in which children are made to think, is often made for them. It is a choice made naturally, since there are not enough Annas.

The rush back toward the planet was thrilling. It occupied all of an eyeblink. But it was a meaningful instant. Vistas of new possibilities opened up to him, vistas now populated with people, friendship, human warmth, human interactions, not separated by the strangeness of extraordinary carryings-on.

In this eager, happy rush to join the flow of humanity, he noticed more completely than ever before the majestically turning Earth.

It hung like a blue-white jewel shrouded in a pink aura. The sun was blazing radiances of brittle green and scintillating rainbows, bathing the planet's sun side in an almost incandescent glory, enveloping the night side in somber blackness.

There were the familiar swirls of clouds and the emerald and blue glints of oceans. It was not truly round as he had already been taught, but somewhat oblate. From its poles radiated faint, almost invisible bands of electric swirls, resembling enormous, nearly invisible tornados reaching out into space, arching around, entering the earth again at the opposite pole.

He slipped gently, unharmed through those magnetic vortices and was instantly once more within the security of his darkened bedroom. He sighed, felt himself tired and went to bed.

After that evening such events lingered only on the fringe of memory and sometimes altogether disappeared for years. These submerged qualities were entertained in their entirety less and less, activating only to protest the inadequacies of human philosophy. It was not until the winter of 1969 that they began to reemerge in a form somewhat approximating the childhood magnitude, and then only when he was forced to deal with a telepathic chinchilla, a tale told later on in this book.

Assuming the validity of something going "out of body," the most felicitous hypothesis of what it is that actually goes out might be what got into the body in the first place.

Now there are certain resistances against this hypothesis, opprobriums that lurk steadfastly within present and historical philosophical, religious, and metaphysical schemes. But in defense of this hypothesis it must be pointed out that the most rapacious of men, eager to inform others of what is and what is not, do not themselves have direct evidence of nonexistence before birth and after death.

For scientific monitors simply to state that existence exterior to bodies is not possible because they are not aware of it or cannot themselves perceive it is idiotic.

Occult literature is filled with references to the legendary out-of-body potential. But it is pertinent to note that modern science itself has experienced brief encounters with the paranormal potential of humans to view things from a point exterior to the visible, physical body.

The so-called autoscopic hallucination is a good example of one of these confrontations.

Prior to a definition of the word "autoscopic" it is necessary to understand how psychology defines "hallucination." A person who is preoccupied with so-called biologically "useless" ideas is said to be hallucinating, especially if these ideas involve religious or symbolic behavior. This type of person is called schizophrenic if his preoccupation is of such magnitude as to exclude "normal" biological behavior.

In science, especially in the mental sciences (if they can be called that), there exist many types of hallucinations—and the general basis for defining hallucinations is that the ideas rampant in the hallucination do not acquire measurable cultural support. When they do, of course, they are no longer regarded as hallucination. Thus, it seems to be the cultural stance that determines what is "normal." [7]

The autoscopic hallucination has been recorded for a long time. The experient suddenly views his own body in front of him. This usually occurs during drowsiness but also can occur with people who are wide awake. The image is seen very clearly, but sometimes not in vivid color. If the experient attempts to get close to this vision, it tends to fade after exhibiting movements similar to the original body.

In the psychiatric literature there is even one case reported where the experient was able to have auditory capacities with the vision as noted in 1950 by Jean Lhermitte, a professor of the Faculty of Medicine in Paris, who delivered a lecture at the National Hospital, Queen Square, London, in which he outlined many of the characteristics of autoscopy.[8]

Since Dr. Lhermitte is involved in the medical profession, most of his reports have their nexus in medically or mentally related situations, and he terms this seeing of self "hallucination." To his credit, however, Lhermitte clarifies the word as meaning perception without object—and not mere craziness.

Lhermitte suggests that since remote times philosophers have been

---

[7] See J. R. Smythes, "A Logical and Cultural Analysis of Hallucinatory Sense-experience," *Journal of Mental Science* (April, 1956), pp. 336–342.

[8] Jean Lhermitte, "Visual Hallucination of the Self," *British Medical Journal*, March 3, 1951, pp. 431–434.

amazed by the most unusual phenomenon of the vision of one's double, or the visual hallucination of the self. During the Romantic period of the eighteenth and nineteenth centuries, especially in Germany, occurrences of this strange phenomenon were interpreted in a variety of ways and were the source of many literary works.

From the neurosurgical standpoint, however, medically related instances of the phenomena are the usual autoscopic reports. Most frequent are autoscopic phenomena associated with epileptics, with patients with functional disorders of the labyrinth of the inner ear, and with patients suffering from infectious fevers, typhus, brain tumors, general paralysis, and cerebral lesions.

But more important to this writing are the reports of experients themselves, who sometimes indicate that they feel they have two bodies momentarily, and that the "second" body seems the more real of the two, apparently in control of the mental qualities such as observation, judgment, and perception. Further, these experients always seem to be aware of the physical body and its location in space.[9]

From a neurophysiological clinical position, many instances of autoscopia can be associated with neuropathic or psychopathic situations; they frequently are reported by individuals who are victims of chronic alcoholism, anxiety, fatigue, attacks of labyrinthine vertigo, as well as the febrile-toxic states of typhus and influenza. Recurrent, often continuing, reports of autoscopia are seen in such dramatic diseases as dementia paralytica, encephalitis lethargica, epilepsy, and drug addiction.[10]

Literary works have often been based in part upon autoscopic experiences of the authors. An example is Edgar Allan Poe, who was subject to toxicomania, alcoholism, and melancholia. Dostoievsky was an epileptic and also subject to fits of temper, and Alfred de Musset was cyclothymic. Guy de Maupassant, who rendered his visions in *Le Horla*, was deteriorating, as was Hoffman, who was obsessed by the fear of death and ended his life in general paralysis.[11]

[9] See Caro W. Lippman, "Hallucinations of Physical Duality in Migraine," *Journal of Nervous and Mental Disease* 117 (1953), pp. 345–348.

[10] J. Todd and K. Dewhurst, "The Double: Its Psycho-Pathology and Psycho-Physiology," *Journal of Nervous and Mental Disease* 122 (1955), pp. 47–55.

[11] For an extremely interesting review of these famous cases, see S. M. Colman, "The Phantom Double: Its Psychological Significance," *British Journal of Medical Psychology* 14 (1934), pp. 254–273.

So there is not much doubt that viewing the body away from the body, or viewing a second body, is associated in many clinical diagnoses with dreadful biogenic situations. Migrainoids—that is, people with seemingly inherited migraine factors—often report this second body. For instance, one woman found her other self up in the corner of the ceiling, looking down at her real self and making a play-by-play report of her actions.

But there are also many, many reports from above-average business and professional people who apparently are highly intelligent, normally sexed, and able to meet the demands life places upon them. These reports should be considered free of neuropathic or psychopathic origins, if such symptoms are not discoverable.

One can suppose that people separate from their bodies all the time. Most keep their thoughts deep inside themselves, and so we have to depend upon extraordinary occurrences—moments of crisis, for example —when this process takes place.

Certain diseases, in their progression through the body, cause it to degenerate slowly. This often enables the experient, completely sane in all other ways, to suffer strange reorientations of consciousness without necessarily sending the nervous system into shock or unconsciousness. Medical literature is rich in such reports, all neatly stuffed away in some unobtrusive place, naturally. But I have talked with many physicians and nurses who admit having observed strange things. For example, attending deathbeds apparently reveals phases of existence not normally available in textbooks.

And gastroenteritis is especially productive of such experience; a report of one was circulated in 1937.[12]

> On Saturday, November 9, a few minutes after midnight, I began to feel very ill and by 2 o'clock was definitely suffering from acute gastro-enteritis, which kept me vomiting and purging until about 8 o'clock. . . . By 10 o'clock I had developed all the symptoms of very acute poisoning: intense gastro-intestinal pain; diarrhoea; pulse and respirations becoming quite impossible to count. I wanted to ring for assistance, but found I could not and so quite placidly gave up the attempt. I realized I was very ill and very quickly reviewed my whole financial position; thereafter at no time did my consciousness appear

[12] See *The Scotsman*, February 26, 1937, p. 16, columns 3–4. This report also read by Sir Auckland Geddes (later Lord Geddes) to members of the Royal Medical Society.

to me to be in any way dimmed, but I suddenly realized that *my* consciousness was separating from another consciousness, which was also me. For purposes of description, we could call those the A and B consciousness, and throughout what follows the ego attached itself to the A consciousness. The B personality I recognized as belonging to the body, and as my physical condition grew worse and the heart was fibrillating rather than beating, I realized that the B consciousness belonging to the body was beginning to show signs of being composite, that is, built up of "consciousness" from the head, the heart, and viscera, etc. These components became more individual and the B consciousness began to disintegrate, while the A consciousness, which was now me, seemed to be altogether outside my body, which it could see. Gradually I realized that I could see not only my body and the bed in which it was, but everything in the whole house and garden, and then I realized that I was seeing not only "things" at home, but in London and in Scotland, in fact wherever my attention was directed it seemed to me. . . . I next realized that my vision included not only "things" in the ordinary three-dimensional world, but also "things" in these four or more dimensional places that I was in.

Just as I began to grasp all these I saw "Julie" enter my bedroom; I realized she got a terrible shock, and I saw her hurry to the telephone; I saw my doctor leave his patients and come very quickly; and heard him say or saw him think, "He is nearly gone." I heard him quite clearly speaking to me on the bed, but I was not in touch with the body and could not answer him. I was really cross when he took a syringe and rapidly injected my body with something which I afterwards learned was camphor. As the heart began to beat more strongly, I was drawn back, and I was intensely annoyed, because I was so interested and just beginning to understand where I was and what I was "seeing." I came back to the body really angry at being pulled back, and once I was back all the clarity of vision of anything and everything disappeared, and I was just possessed of a glimmer of consciousness, which was suffused with pain.

Assuming this experience to be real and not a figment of the experient's imagination, it can be broken down many ways, in the scientific sense, before it is dispensed with altogether as is usually the case. But certainly not the least of its meaning is the fact that the experient himself seems to be somewhat surprised at perceiving himself to be separate from the body, which lay in a dreadful state on the bed apparently doing its own thing.

Further, by merely shifting his "attention" to whatever it was he held a momentary interest for permitted the topic, place, content of that interest to become instantly perceivable to him—even London some distance away and the thoughts in the doctor's mind. Also, realizing the crisis the body had begun to go through, instead of wailing about the trauma, the "I" consciousness turned its attention to the review of a practical matter, the condition of the experient's finances. And, finally, as he began to revive under the doctor's administrations, he was "angry" at having to resume coincidental consciousness with the body, obviously a much lesser and demeaning consciousness, including pain and unconsciousness.

No effort here is being made to suggest that this consciousness was that man's soul, nor to imply that every man who manages to really die experiences the same thing. The state-of-the-art discussions of the nature of the soul are in such total confusion that it is frequently an unsafe topic to write about at any length, and report-back experiences from people who have indeed dropped the body permanently are exceedingly rare.

But a salient point, with reference to parapsychological abilitisms, can be brought out; during this physical trauma the experient indeed seems to have been caused by the near-mortal agony to assume a viewpoint away from the body and by doing so apparently could at least transcend normal concepts of *space* and *communication*.

But in medical or psychological literature there is no direct mention of so-called out-of-body experiences; when reported these always are attributed to neurophysiological conditions. By definition the autoscopic viewing means the experient sees a second body a short distance from his physical body. The out-of-body definition should indicate in some manner that the experient shifts his organizing capacity of *perceptics* to a point distant from the body and views things from there. This view often includes sightings of the physical body.

These two definitions begin to blend, however, in the psychological literature; events reported under the heading autoscopia often resemble the out-of-body faculty. Even more interesting are the people who report seeing themselves in a situation that has yet to come about, and then recognizing the scene years later just as viewed in the prior experience.[13]

Some extended scientific interest in autoscopia was exhibited between

[13] The interested researcher can refer especially to N. Lukianowicz, "Autoscopic Phenomena," *American Medical Association Archives of Neurological Psychiatry*, vol. 80 (1958), pp. 199–220. This paper carries 101 references to other sources of autoscopic reports.

1930 and 1955, this interest decreasing—or at least reports on it slacking off—since then. Some attempts, as might be expected, were made to support the theory that a conflict between sexual and other drives was responsible for this phenomenon, and also that this double might be a personification of the phallus, since it is said that psychoanalytic investigation reveals that the unconscious is frequently equated with this infamous male appendage.

In keeping with the increasing interest in things psychic, it should be stated that people are now more free to admit experiencing factors not in keeping with prior dicta and that the rolls containing reports of out-of-body experiences are growing daily. A hypothetical positive approach would therefore have to hold that it is possible to have other than sensory awareness and/or perception of things, even things at great distances from the body. This positive approach would establish possibilities and seek to demonstrate them or adequately disprove them. The difficulty here, obviously, is that the "possibilities" have as their starting point the cultural stance as to what is or is not possible. This starting point is called, regrettably, materialism.

History records instances of perceptions that have flashed beyond the speed of light to some distant places. A lilting tale is told, for instance, by the historian Herodotus (born about 484 B.C.), who traveled the ancient world, commenting on just about everything from brothels to military maneuvers.

There was in Babylon a vast, imposing edifice called the Temple of Belus.* This monolithic structure had seven towers of astronomical observation, to which had been added an eighth, in which dwelt priestesses who developed prophetic vision by pressing sacred stones to their heads and bosoms. This type of stone was known as the betylos, or the meteoric stone, aerolites composed of meteorite substance, mainly of stony matter.[14]

The priestesses, by touching these stones, were enabled to travel to

* An effort has been made to trace the etymology of "belus," somewhat unsuccessfully except that several sources suggest that it represents the masculine generative principle.

[14] Herodotus, b.i., c. 181.

where they had come from as well as to enhance their general abilities at *psychometry*. The modern definition for this word revolves around the concept that a person can hold something and tell about its past to one degree or another. But in ancient times it was one of the legendary psi arts, which involved touching, seeing, feeling, or thinking about any object to know its past, present, and future.

The betyli were said to contain souls that had fallen from the stars, and these fallen souls were said to enhance the ability of psychometry. These meteoric stones are not unfamiliar to other eminent historians; Strabo, Pliny and Helancius, for instance, comment at length on their electrical and electromagnetic power. The use of betyli also extended to Patara in Lycia, and to Thebes in Egypt; there also exist trace references in many later cultures such as that represented by the Druids, who also possessed variable psychometric powers.

There are no important recent experiments in psychometry, the most recent being those of William Denton of Boston in 1873. Despite the fact that most of the subjects were close family members, the Denton experiments carry an attraction that cannot easily be put aside. The academic mentality, of course, would faint at the thought of the awarenesses of Denton's subjects visiting Mars and Jupiter, as well as receding into the past to view the eruption of Vesuvius and the destruction of Pompeii.

Across time and through space, almost in the twinkling of a betylos, tales of the past and possibly the future literally seemed to cascade from the lips of the Denton experiments. Holding the targets in their hands, sealed from touch cues by wads of cotton, with many of the targets geological specimens, the experiments were able to describe long-gone geological ages of this planet. Holding samples of objects from ancient civilizations, they described social orders, ancient habits, and life in those times. Gazing at night at the moon or at distant planets faintly visible as sparkling lights to the naked eye, they described visions of civilizations there, long gone or perhaps to come. One is almost encouraged to put the book down in exasperation.

One of the most interesting things William Denton said has to do with the future possibilities of such art as demonstrated by his subjects:

> Astronomy will not disdain the assistance of this power. As new forms of organic being are revealed, when we go back to the earlier

> geologic periods, so new groupings of the stars, new constellations, will be displayed, when the heavens of those early periods are examined by the piercing gaze of future psychometers. An accurate map of the starry heavens during the Silurian period may reveal to us many secrets that we have been unable to discover. . . . Why may we not indeed be able to read the history of the various heavenly bodies . . . their geological, their natural, and, perchance, their human history? . . . I have good reason to believe that trained psychometers will be able to travel from planet to planet, and read their present condition minutely, and their past history.[15]

This possibility naturally befuddles materialists, who are preoccupied with getting only *physical* space craft to some great distance. From the far past of this Earth comes the challenge of legends that say people did it with awareness alone; that Earth has been visited physically by other beings; and even perhaps that the genetic humanoid itself is not of this Earth.

It is one thing to refer obliquely in literature or art to man's legendary abilities and completely a different game to try to capture one of these abilities in a laboratory setting. During 1972 the staff and trustees of the American Society for Psychical Research extended to me the opportunity to participate in a long-term approach toward seeking evidence for the so-called "out-of-body" experience.

The routine of these experiments ran over some fourteen months altogether and, surprisingly, rendered good results. The modus operandi for these experiments was described at the beginning of this book, together with the difficulties that plague such experimentation. The targets generally were suspended from a platform near the ceiling, hidden and inaccessible to the subject. My task was to perceive the target and draw what I perceived on a sheet of paper. The results frequently were astonishing (see Figures 13-18). Equally often they were unrewarding from the hit-miss point of view.

The entire battery of experiments, however, was exceedingly meaningful

---

[15] See William Denton, *The Soul of Things, Psychometric Researches and Discoveries,* vol. 1 (Wellesley, Mass., 1873), p. 273.

as a learning procedure since the extrasensory perception was seen to increase both in scope and accuracy as the experimentation continued. In some cases this paranormal perception began to distinguish between flat surfaces and three-dimensional objects (see Figure 14). Later, when the targets began to be housed in boxes with a single small hole, the subject was required to attempt psychically to peer through the aperture. As a result unexpected confirmatory responses began to accumulate.

For example, during the experiment of March 3 (Figure 16), when the box enclosure was carefully lined inside with white paper, the person constructing the target inadvertently did not cover some printing on the inner side. This printing was "seen," but not read, by me as I tried nervously to perceive what was in the box. After the experiment was completed, but before the box had been taken down and inspected, the person who had structured the target got excited and indicated that this trial must have been a "flunk" since there was no printing in the box. Bristling, I indicated that I had, nevertheless, perceived printing there, and so it must be there. To everyone's chagrin, when the box was taken down and inspected, there was the printing, just as I felt I had seen.

At another time, with the experiment well under way, I was once more trying valiantly to perceive what was in the box but the blackness I usually confronted did not subsequently resolve into the remote vision expected of it. Trying to figure out why everything "looked" extraordinarily black, I "floated" into the box itself (I was only supposed to peer through the aperture) and perceived that the small light used to illuminate the interior targets was not on.

"The goddamned light is out over the target," I shouted, eager to catch the researchers in their inexpertise as they were usually gleeful to catch me at a good failure.

"Impossible," came the reply.

Nonetheless, I stuck to my perceived response. When the trial was completed, a tall ladder was procured. When the target monitor clambered up it, he found that the light was not on (see Figure 18).

Such were the dramatics at the American Society for Psychical Research during the year 1972. Aside from these moments of unexpected drama, however, the battery of experiments yielded a platform of information that was built upon during the subsequent year when similar research was staged at the West Coast think tank, Stanford Research Institute.

There, during an eight-month concentrated effort, some 7,000 exterior perception trials were conducted, yielding an extraordinary amount of data. Once more the learning pattern became visible in almost all cases. The perception of any given set of targets actually began to improve through enforced use of the unknown ability. This led, of course, toward the establishment of a trial hypothesis that the ability is accessible because it exhibits a learning pattern, and therefore conforms to the general idea that abilities improve through practice.

This confirmation is extremely encouraging since it intimates that the paranormal perceptics are innate in the individual and, once their character is understood, might be *learned*. But this was only one of some two dozen indicators to be drawn from the eight months' work.

The endeavor into things psychic at Stanford Research Institute unfortunately tends to be misunderstood in the press, and perhaps in the critical science community.

That famous Stanford Research Institute is getting together with the scientifically unpresentable field constituted by things psychic naturally electrifies academic guardians. It is, however, well within the right of researchers to continue to investigate the unknown, and it seems utterly calamitous for the skeptical echelons of society to interpret results before facts have been presented.

In my case a period of eight months was made available to see if anything not already understood by parapsychology could now be discovered. At no time was my tenure at SRI meant to prove anything, since demonstration of the presence of unknown abilities was established to the satisfaction of Stanford Research Institute by the results of work conducted at the American Society for Psychical Research and under the auspices of Dr. Gertrude Schmeidler at City College.

All the work at SRI, therefore, was geared to attempting to gain sufficient insight into things psychic to allow for the establishment of new trial hypotheses upon which future work might take place. In this the work at SRI was exceedingly successful. It is, regrettably, not possible to report at length in this book upon the battery of work accomplished before the researchers have had sufficient time to thoroughly evaluate and publish their results.

However, a couple of anecdotes can be mentioned.

Somewhere during the project there, I became involved—as was my duty and contribution—in trying to discover how the so-called "psychic entity" placed itself in relation to the physical universe in the first place. Obviously, the physical body negotiated the physical universe in terms of things physical; but how, if at all, did the psychic entity negotiate between the material and nonmaterial universes?

This is a situation that has not really been dwelled upon at any great length by the proof-oriented orthodoxies of materialistic science, since results in the material sense always involve things material. In the early hours of the morning (I habitually rise at 7 A.M.) I like to smoke endless cigars and consume unhealthy amounts of Italian espresso while I think.

I am firmly convinced by agonizing experience that thinking is actively discouraged in our Western culture. One is adamantly required to conform; and, while one is conforming, creative thinking is forbidden—especially thinking upon subjects beyond the pale.

It was during one of these "forbidden" think sessions that I got the idea that the psychic entity—if it exists at all with potential abilities to transcend matter, energy, space, and time—must innately have absolutely unheard of and undreamed of powers. In order for this psychic entity to "get into" the physical universe at all, it must in some manner cause itself to conform to the laws of the physical universe. For this to happen, there must exist, hypothetically of course, a psychic/physical threshold of some sort. Now transcending the physical perspectives of things would indicate that the transcendental condition should be senior to things physical. Therefore the psychic being would have to *reduce* into the conditions of the physical universe in order to perceive them, even through sensory mechanisms.

If this is so, then it is obvious that the psychic entity would have to think "down" into things physical and not "upward" from things physical into transcending situations. This is exactly how creativity seems to work. The artist or inventor gets an idea, usually in some form of abstraction, and reduces it to thought. Only when all the thinking about it has been arranged to conform to physical possibilities does the artist commence bringing the creative work into a physical manifestation.

Thus, so it seemed to me, the psychic/physical threshold would exist, hypothetically, at thought itself. Contrariwise, if this should be the case, then in the general social flow—considering the taboos about things psychic and the discomfort dicta can bring down upon those who participate in them—thought about things psychic, and thus abilities deriving from them, should have long ago been suppressed into the condition of awareness called *unconsciousness*. This is precisely where we find most psychic abilities emanating from.

There must be, of course, many kinds of thought processes, certainly not the least of which are those that impinge upon the body electrochemically and produce animation of the biological structure. But there are other thought processes having nothing to do with physical animation —elegant, comprehensive processes quite exterior to the physical universe. There is always the garbage bag to get through, that accumulation of useless thoughts, past traumatic experiences, and so forth that apparently serves no goal other than to mess up cogent, creative thinking.*

Getting beyond this garbage bag of useless mental junk and being able to exist somewhat exterior to past accumulations of thought would naturally be a prerequisite to any creative appreciation. The mind seems able to associate with any idea as long as there is no prior inlay of opposing ideas. Ideas that merely lie around and oppose perceptions and cognitions are dreary.

Whatever all this may or may not be, ensconced in clouds of delightful cigar smoke, I decided that thought itself constituted a threshold somewhat on the nature I was searching for, especially abstract thought as contrasted to linear thought. If this were true, then the physical targets arbitrarily and endlessly utilized by contemporary parapsychology were the worst possible kind of targets. This would naturally be the case since the psychic entity could not relate to unknown physical targets very well in the absence of a mental or thinking access to them.

Of course the problem immediately arose as to what constituted an abstract target. This worried me for some time until I realized that abstract targets were lying around all over the place in the form of anything that in itself referred to thought before it referred to physical things. These are words, mathematical symbols, understanding, intuition, art, and so

---

* In this wise it is apparent that human awarenesses are cut down by accumulation of useless thoughts about past experiences and associations, these accumulations seeming to block the psychic avenues, as well as abilities and excellence in even mundane enterprises. Heretofore, trauma constituting blocks has been thought to be solely of psycho/physical origin; of course there must also be blocks constituted of such things as false, erroneous thinking and education. These are not usually touched upon in normal psychology, which is psycho/physically oriented.

forth—all the things that may have tangible sensory appreciation but *refer*, in their first instance, to nonphysical things. And, assuming that one's garbage bag of useless thinking and experience does not get in one's way and divert basic cognitive processes, the realm of the abstract is one of the swiftest, most precise methods of understanding, cognition, and communication.

In trying to design an experimental paradigm utilizing purely abstract targets, I wondered if simple geodetic coordinates might not serve the psychic entity well in locating him in terms of the Earth's surface. This idea, of course, was totally foreign to even the brilliant thinkers busy trying to think at Stanford Research Institute. Because of my persuasive way, however (a lot of screaming and hollering), an experimental pattern of one hundred targets identified merely by coordinates was set up and run.

The abstraction of the coordinate sufficed to provide orientation for the psychic probe—whether it be called clairvoyance or out-of-body perception (it is now called "remote viewing")—to locate by transcendental means the place to which the coordinate referred and thence to inspect it and describe what was there.

Now this is dealing in the irrational to an extreme. An explanation in terms of cogent science would take pages and would require a good reorientation of what is currently thought about human abilities. Suffice it to say that it worked. And it worked with totally amazing precision.

For example, one day one of the distant targets, selected blindly by the experimenters, turned out to be what they thought was the center of Lake Victoria in Africa. However, due to their initial lack of enthusiasm for this irrational approach, and because we had not yet understood the precision of the abstract ability, the coordinates were rather loosely put together. The coordinate was given, and across space my awareness began to move to become coincident to that part of Earth to which the coordinate actually referred in the physical sense. The conversation that followed went something like this:

SWANN: For the first time I actually have a sensation of moving through space, over a body of water and landing on what seems to be land. I'd say this coordinate refers to a piece of land to the east of a large body of water.

EXPERIMENTER: No, that would not be correct since the coordinate we gave you is actually in the middle of Lake Victoria.

SWANN: Goddamn it, I don't believe it. Where the hell is a good map?

Since the SRI library did not yield one, out we went to a bookstore to purchase the *Times Atlas of the World*. Everyone was chagrined and amazed to discover that the exact coordinate given in the experiment actually referred to the peninsula jutting out into Lake Victoria just east of Ukerewe Island—in fact exactly where the psychic perception said it was.

This type of experimentation is, of course, rather novel, and this reporting of it quite unofficial. It engenders, at least in me, however, a sense of freedom that far surpasses the pleasures of mere biological centering of all systems of awarenes. Here, so it seemed, were truly great leaps across space that gave a sense of exhileration lost when as a child the decision was made to conform to what others expected.

It was also an experiment that startled many, first because of the seeming unreality of using only coordinates as targets, and second because of the dramatic science-fiction images it set off in the minds of the imaginative. Actually, this type of experiment more generally affirms that an ability is present, rather than indicate how the ability might be used; as an example, many of the coordinates given were simple, merely seeking to ascertain if the coordinate related to ocean, mountain, desert, and so forth. But as the experiment was run over several days, evidence mounted to indicate that the psi-ability was undergoing some sort of a learning pattern, reflected in a rising curve of both accuracies and increasing descriptions of the site.

One target given was 15°N and 120°E, for which the response indicated "land, with jungles and mountains, mountains that resembled sort of peninsular-type mountains." The target area was the west coast of the Zambales mountains, a peninsular formation in the Philippines.

The coordinate 30°S and 105°W gave merely "ocean" as a response, the coordinate being, of course, mid-ocean.

Another coordinate, 32°E and 30°N, produced a response that went: "Ah, looks dry, like Italy, no, not Italy, what are those things in the far distance, ah, they look like pyramids, is that Cairo?" The coordinate was near Cairo.

Sometimes the response to the coordinate seemed to be approximate, or else our maps did not have enough resolution to indicate what was at the coordinate, exactly. The response to coordinate 40°N and 40°W, for example, produced the response of "city." This coordinate is somewhat south of the city of Madrid, and it was not possible to verify if, indeed, at the site given there were buildings that might have looked like a city.

But many of the simple coordinates seemed highly successful. The coordinate in Borneo produced the response of "jungles." The target 35°N and 85°E, in the middle of the plateau of Tibet, produced "dry mountains."

As the ability seemed to grow a little, the descriptions of the target sites became more particular. The coordinate 23°S and 69°W brought forth a response of "this seems to be some sort of a plateau, and there is a city to the southwest." The target indicated the high range in Chile, and the city to the southwest possibly was Sierra Gorda.

In all cases, reference to maps was a necessity, since it quickly became apparent that the ability was reporting on what could be "seen" and thus gave descriptions of physical surroundings. Whereas, it is the tendency in map work to associate with names of countries and geography. This seemed like an automatic phenomena with the researchers, who, at first, felt that if one did not respond "Chile" to a coordinate given in Chile, then the experiment was a flop. But gradually everyone came around to using their eyes instead of their habits, and when the responses were compared to fine maps, an amazing set of correspondents could easily be seen.

As to error, the errors were also spectacular. A coordinate given in the midst of Texas produced the response of "ocean," one given in the middle of the Indian ocean produced the response of "mountains," and so forth.

A compilation of hits against misses, however, produced an interesting statistic: Nineteen of the target areas gave different responses and are considered as misses; thirty-two of the target areas produced responses that were by eye inspection of maps very similar; and forty-three responses were considered to be identical to the target area as given by coordinate. Six targets had to be eliminated from firsthand judging since the particulars given in response were almost impossible to verify from maps at hand.

As a result of the 100 target areas, it was considered that an ability was present and the test situation was given over to independent sponsors who themselves got up some coordinates. That is, no one at SRI knew what the target would be and the targets themselves were generated triple-blind on the East Coast.

This type of testing produced stable and verifiable results. One example: The coordinate came in as 49°20′S and 70°14′E. The first response came almost immediately: "I see what seems to be a mountain sticking up through some clouds, no, not just a mountain, it must be an island."

"Well," said the experimenter present, "I think that is wrong. I checked the target just before we began, and it is in the middle of the ocean."

"Where the hell is the map?" asked the subject.

So, upon consulting a better map than the one hastily used by the experimenter before the session (an experimental no-no, by the way), it was seen that the coordinate referred almost exactly to the 1,600-foot mountains rising out of the eastern area of Kerguelen Island.

With the experiment thus limping along, the next portion of it was to sketch interesting or pertinent landmarks, especially artificial constructions, if any could be seen there. An interesting map was thereby produced, showing a small landing field, some quonset-type buildings, painted orange, butane tanks. A further view of the island, psychically, that is, revealed thousands of birds, low-cast overhanging clouds, some boats docked at a single jetty, and a lighthouse at the other end. Good descriptions were also given of rivers and streams egressing to the sea, and so forth.

At this time, many people at SRI and associated with it began to take this type of experiment much more seriously than they had at first.[16] The skeptic can, of course, list perhaps a thousand reasons why such an experiment should not be considered even a possibility, the major accusation being that I have an idetic memory of maps. It is not the purpose of this book to quibble with skeptics, however, except to say that my memory really is not too good, but that my powers of perception seem in fine order.

---

[16] The onus of an extended reporting of this and other similar experiments rests with the participating researchers at Stanford Research Institute.

There are psychics, and then there are psychics.

The average and familiar type of psychic is someone who deals in mystery, often through a sort of counseling service based upon self-proclaimed powers to see and evaluate situations others cannot see and evaluate. Some psychics have masters, guides, and whatnot that speak through them, offering advice and suggestion, berating us for the conditions in which we find ourselves.

Experience will quickly inform one that this is the basic picture the public holds of the psychic. There ought to be a difference in terminology between these hypnoid productions and the man or woman whose abilities seem to extend consciously beyond what is normally expected. Regrettably, this distinction does not really exist even in the minds of some eminent researchers whose business it is to establish these distinctions, and who should really know better in the first place.*

At any rate there are different kinds of psychics and also different types of psychic enterprise.

One psychic who seems vastly different in terms of ethics and humanitarian concern is Harold Sherman, whom I met in New York's elegant Algonquin hotel, which used to be the hangout of the famous Henry L. Mencken. I have experienced much drivel from many pseudopsychics over the years, but Sherman transfixed my attention by beginning to talk about human potential and humanitarian precepts.[17]

My association in friendship with Harold, and with his sensitive and

* I do not decry all psychics, obviously. Many have had visible and meritorious abilities as well as a competent power for enriching the human cultural concept being born today. The incidence of freaks and frauds, however, is quite high, and I have spent many years having readings and consultations, observing an amazing array of inspiring and beautiful but baseless productions. In one case, for instance, a case that is quite typical, I attended upon a young man whose reputation was spreading like wildfire, and whose guide and master was another of those Tibetans who seem to frequent this caliber of psychic. This Tibetan, although quite willing to advise me, could tell me nothing about myself or my problems until he learned my astrological birth sign, which is Virgo. This communicator thereupon had a great deal to tell me, droning on for nearly an hour with hardly a breath. Regrettably, being a long-term student of astrology myself, I was able to recognize his utterances as practically verbatim from a famous basic astrological text by Alan Leo.

[17] The depth and character of Harold Sherman can best be grasped from a recently published interview. See James Grayson Bolen, "Interview: Harold Sherman," *Psychic,* February 1974. Sherman is the founder of ESP Research Associates Foundation.

sympathetic wife, Martha, has been a source of endless pleasure for me. I was extremely impressed and rewarded to learn that Sherman had long ago demonstrated the existence in himself of a rare and unique ability.

During the year 1937 Sherman chanced to meet in the New York City Club the famous and noted Arctic explorer Sir Hubert Wilkins. As co-members of the club, they conversed and soon discovered their mutual interest in things psychic and extrasensory perceptions. About that time the Russians were searching for a plane lost somewhere near the North Pole and had asked Sir Hubert to try to find it. Sir Hubert and Sherman arranged that Sherman would try to "tune in" on Wilkins at specified days and times for nearly six months at a distance of some three thousand miles. This experiment was an astonishing success, indicating that Sherman's impressions of the activities and movements of Sir Hubert were 70 percent correct.[18]

I have been pleased to be able to discuss the field and problems of psychic research with this experienced and noted man. Consequently, while on project at Stanford Research Institute, when my mind began to move toward utilizing more than one subject to simultaneously probe distant targets, he was one of the first I invited to join in such an attempt.

It seemed to me that, in research, experimentation is not always couched in a form that could obtain the greatest amount of data for the minimum of effort. For example, if two, three, or even more subjects were to attempt a simultaneous psychic probe of the same target, squads of comparative data could be available, whereas with the utilization of just a single subject all one ends up with is singular data. In this type of twinning or quadrupling, comparative data could demonstrate the similarities or differences in the subjects' responses, as well as quality, intensity, and so forth.

The ordinary concept of experimentation is to find a topic and methodology that will appease the critical observer—in other words, a proof-

[18] See Sir Hubert Wilkins and Harold M. Sherman, *Thoughts Through Space* (New York: Creative Age Press, 1942). This book is a complete account of the Wilkins/Sherman experiments and includes facsimiles of affidavits as to conduct of the experimentation and authenticity of documentation. This book recently has been revised in paperback by Fawcett Publications (New York, 1973).

oriented approach. From the subject's point of view—although I feel subjects should cooperate in this approach to the best of their abilities—this style often results in the utmost boredom, which can and does become a source of extraordinary defeatism.[19]

This defeatism is further engendered by a curious attitude held by a majority of parapsychological researchers and critics that the subject, until proven innocent, is guilty of fraud. During the last two or three decades, research in things psychic has come therefore to be founded directly upon appeasement of the skeptical attitude, an attitude that holds that psychic things are not really possible. Consequently, in research, the uninformed subject when entering experimentation does not generally understand that he is already under a sort of odious interdict, a pervasive and in many cases disgusting prohibitive that he, the subject, must somehow overcome.

As this point is made in other places in this book, it need not be gone into here again, save to say that the attitude itself rises out of those philosophies and psychologies that forbid actual psychic events. The skeptical attitude here is an antipsychic attitude, since it holds that nothing psychic can happen but that apparent psychic events can be simulated through fraud and trickery. Thus, when well-meaning researchers and subjects effort forth on some sort of psychically-related experimentation, their first duty, abhorrent as it is, is to provide an answer to the fraud

[19] One of the most frequently observed effects in parapsychological testing is that called "psi missing." At first the subject does well, scoring above chance, but he subsequently dwindles off into chance or below-chance expectation. It is not known exactly why this effect occurs, but it is hypothesized that motivational and personality profiles might have something to do with it. Boredom could also have a lot to do with this decline effect, but not exclusively so. This decline effect was especially noticeable during the thousands of trials in which I participated at SRI during 1973. This decline effect has been associated with the decrease of spontaneous psi abilities, but at SRI it was possible to establish that this was only partly the case. It seems more likely that this effect will be generated as the subject uses his psi potential in a creative way, attempting to change over from a merely spontaneous response psi system into one that is consciously controlled. The decline effect sets in, as observed, between these two phases. Of course such psychological factors as boredom and conflict could be another source for a different type of psi missing, as was also observed to be the case. See Charles T. Tart, "Card Guessing Tests: Learning Paradigm or Extinction Paradigm?", *Journal of the American Society for Psychical Research* 60, no. 1 (January 1966); John A. Freeman, "A Sequel Report on a High-Scoring Child Subject," *The Journal of Parapsychology* 30, no. 1 (March 1966); Katharine M. Banham, "Temporary High Scoring by a Child Subject," *ibid* 30, no. 2 (June 1967).

question, a question that may have nothing to do with the actual experiment. The idea that all is fraud and the various responses to that idea does, indeed, lie like a heavy hand across experimentation.

Actually, it would be more to the point not to argue the merits or demerits of any certain experiment against the idea that all is fraud, but to take certain quite ordinary steps to discover if the subject himself tends towards fraudulence. If he does, then, of course, extreme caution should be maintained when working with him. If good certainty is established that he is not tended toward fraud, then the integrity and self-respect of the subject should be taken somewhat for granted, and the experimentation should not be constrained to conform to imaginary a priori accusations of fraud.

Actually, in my experience, no precautions are taken to establish the character of psychic research subjects in advance of experimenting with them. This seems, to me, a somewhat glaring omission since this procedure is conducted in almost all businesses, governmental work, and other institutions in our culture that deem it advisable to know and understand the character of a potential employee.

In psychic research, no steps at all are taken to fulfill this seemingly important requirement. I know of no case, for instance, where the potentially amazing psychic subject has been administered a lie-detection battery, although gossip sometimes filters through that this has indeed been done. I have heard that some of the more spectacular flying-saucer contactees have undergone such treatment, but when the results of the test seem to indicate that they were not lying, little has been heard of the situation again.

It has to be said that in psychic research, things do happen that can most assuredly be artificially created by trickery and fraud, in the case of psychokinesis, and by the subject having had possible access to prior information in the case of paranormal perceptions. The antipsychic attitude, naturally, seizes upon his explanation and adherents of this attitude have thereby in the past been able to disenfranchise countless good examples of experimentation in which, indeed, fraud did not exist at all.

However, since a priori assumption of fraud is the case, it takes extraordinary expenditure of funds and creative imagination to figure out experiments that can compete with it.

As a result of this astonishing situation, a retrospective view of psychic research, say for the last thirty years, really indicates that psychic research is not research, per se, of psychical phenomena, but a war of attitudes.

A good case exemplifing this type of situation is the following two experiments. Much of the data the psychics obtained by paranormal means can indeed be found in astronomical texts—texts and papers that existed prior to the experiments. The skeptic will immediately seize upon this fact and disqualify any of the information obtained psychically that also corresponds to the information that was available beforehand. If this attitude is to be accepted as a correct one, then all subjects serving on behalf of attempting to demonstrate mankind's legendary parnormal potential would have to be held in seclusion from a very early age to guarantee that they never read books and familiarized themselves with anything at all. The automatic and often unthinking rejection of this sort can be seen to represent an antiawareness attitude, not only in terms of psychic experimentation but in terms of life in general.

With the following experiments, a different approach to judging them has to be assumed. A good deal of data was available about the two targets, mostly in the form of speculation. *And* a good deal of this speculation was in error, as the real information about the targets eventually indicated. It is important, therefore, to observe that when the two psychics attempted to perceive the targets by paranormal means, *their* information did not include data that was erroneous to any great degree, although there were at least two major points made by the psychics that have yet to be proved or disproved by future discovery about the two targets. Also, it did transpire in the second of these two experiments that both psychics described conditions for which there was no prior hypothesis, conditions that were extremely important discoveries to science in general. In fact, hypothesis that existed before feedback on the targets was possible held rather firmly that the conditions viewed by the two psychics did not exist. Thus, these psychically discovered conditions of the second target did not have prior information at all, and thus must cause the skeptic no undue amount of concern.

It was probably an attempt to offset much of the "boredom" at Stanford Research Institute that caused me to invoke a depth of creative imagination more in keeping with fictional enterprise than with scientific perspectives.

Well into the project at SRI, snarling about the damnable repetition of procedures, I was desperate for a little excitement.

In the midst of this desperation during March 1973 I noted with growing interest the approaching bypass of NASA's *Pioneer 10* spacecraft with the distant planet Jupiter. *Pioneer 10* would begin to send back data about Jupiter approximately December 3, nine months away. Wouldn't it be interesting if a psychic probe of Jupiter could be compared to the eventual feedback from *Pioneer 10*? Furthermore, this was something I could invite Harold Sherman to join in on.

It would be easy enough to do. All one had to accomplish was a psychic viewing of conditions on Jupiter, record the responses, and deposit copies of the responses with unimpeachable sources.

Having made my decision to do this, I broached the topic to my fellow SRI researchers, who had not yet quite gotten over the abstract targeting approach that was then beginning to produce untoward results. Leaving them gasping at the prospect, I went ahead and set up the experiment. Sherman, of course, had immediately become cognizant of the possibilities and was eager to participate.

The probe was held on April 27, 1973. Sherman began his probe at 8:00 P.M. Central Standard Time from his home in Mountain View, Arkansas. Swann began his probe at 6:00 P.M. Pacific Standard Time from the somewhat unaesthetic experimental chamber at Stanford Research Institute. The probes were therefore simultaneous; they ran for thirty minutes. The responses of both subjects were recorded by Dr. H. E. Puthoff and Russel Targ, reproduced the next day, and registered and deposited at several places thereafter, including with several noted astrophysicists.

Data comparisons of both subjects' responses indicate that both apparently viewed approximately the same things and their descriptions of environmental conditions on Jupiter clearly indicate a similarity. Had these views differed excessively from the *Pioneer 10* data, the similarity of the responses would at least have indicated a strong telepathic hook-up between the two subjects, separated by almost 2,300 miles. The descriptions of the two subjects concerning the planet's atmospheric conditions stated nothing that differed to any excessive degree from the *Pioneer 10* data.

Excerpts from the responses of the two subjects, noted by one astrophysicist to contain more data than the capabilities of *Pioneer 10* would feed back, are so similar that it is not necessary to indicate which is Sherman and which Swann.

RESPONSE 1: Now I am projected to a point where I feel I can see Jupiter itself, a spectacle beyond description. It looks like it is bulged in the middle. It is a gaseous mass of myriad colors, yellow, red, violet, some greens, like a giant fireworks display. I see trillions of silver needles, ice crystals, and I am wondering if they are not icy cold. The cloud covering must be miles deep. It billows and leaps with a changing vivid yellow, red, and green incandescence, as though reflecting great magnetic fires. I don't know how close *Pioneer 10* is going to come to Jupiter in its bypass, but it looks like it will encounter powerful magnetic forces, winds of terrific velocity, and gaseous masses of poisonous and damaging nature. The atmosphere seems unusually dense on some levels and extremely rarefied on others.

Now I suddenly seem to see through the clouds and catch sight of a reddish brown formation extending in a curved line as far as my mind's eye can see. There are huge volcanic peaks, great cones rising some miles. There must be water, mostly in solidified as well as vaporized form. There are powerful magnetic forces, winds of terrific velocity, and heavy gravity.

RESPONSE 2: I think there must be an extremely large hydrogen mantle. If a space probe made contact with it, it would be maybe 80,000 miles out. I seem to be approaching at a tangent and can see part of the night side. Very high in the atmosphere there are crystals, they glitter; maybe the stripes of Jupiter are like bands of crystals, like rings of Saturn, but closer to its surface. I bet you they will reflect radio probes. I'll go down through the clouds. Inside those cloud layers, those layers of cold crystals. They look so beautiful from the outside, like glittering rainbows of many colors, but inside they look like rolling gas clouds, eerie yellow in color. There are different thicknesses of clouds and crystals. The atmosphere is very thick in some places and there are tremendous winds. I see something that looks like a tornado. Could there be a thermal inversion here? I bet there is; I bet you the surface of Jupiter will give a very high infrared reading. The clouds are moving very fast.

Toward the surface the horizon looks orangish or rose-colored, but overhead it is a kind of greenish yellow. There is an enormous mountain range, maybe some 30,000 feet high, enormous peaks. Between the ranges the whole surface seems enormously flat. I get the feeling that if a man stood on those sands he would sink into them. There is a distinct feeling of liquid about everything. There must be water here, both icebergs and vapors. The magnetic pull here is exhausting and extremely strong.

Pioneer 10 is the first spacecraft to get close-up views of the gigantic planet Jupiter many millions of miles from Earth. The data sent back have swiftly established the need to bring radical reassessments to theories about the planet's magnetic field, the intensity of its radiation, and its structural composition. Naturally the necessity of this reassessment enhances the validity of the subjects' responses since they could not have familiarized themselves in advance with the findings of the space probe.

As the craft sped through the planet's magnetic fields it suddenly pierced the radiation belt that scientists now believe forms a ring extending some 110,000 miles from the surface on a plane with its equator. The radiation itself was so intense that it was estimated to be a thousand times the amount that will kill a human. It was indicated that the total energy represented by the field is 250,000 times that of the Earth. The planet was also discovered to possess a hydrogen torus, a doughnut-like ring around it in the orbital plane of its moon, Io.

The surface itself was not revealed to the capabilities of *Pioneer 10*, so the majority of its data dealt with atmospheric and magnetic conditions. Astrophysicists hypothesize, however, that the planet has a frozen and/or liquid metallic hydrogen core or a rocky core containing several tens of Earth masses.

Jupiter also was discovered to have terrific surface storms with violent convective forces in its atmosphere and winds believed to reach 300 miles an hour. One storm was observed to stretch some 10,000 miles along the colored bands of the planet's atmosphere. It was noted that Jupiter's atmospheres consist of a cloud covering of cold ammonia flowing in bands of many colors. The Jovian clouds are now reported to be streaked with bands of orange, salmon, red, and blue. The top clouds are bitter cold, but temperatures in the lower atmospheres are warmer.

An infrared temperature map of Jupiter indicates that the planet radiates two and a half times more heat than it absorbs from the Sun, and the cloud covering, thick and opaque, has been described as forming a very efficient greenhouse environment, inverting the heat content of the planet's surface.

These two responses, together with actual data from *Pioneer 10,* if not scientifically expansive at least indicate a possibility of psychic probing not heretofore entertained seriously. The experiment was conducted within the concept of a secure paradigm, the basis for the security being that Jupiter itself had never before been probed to the degree that *Pioneer 10* would monitor. Therefore the verity of the responses depended not on what was hypothesized about Jupiter in advance of *Pioneer 10* but on how well the subjects' information agreed with the actual feedback from the spacecraft.

From a progressive point of view, it is not necessary, and in fact it is altogether another situation, to try to make the Jupiter experiment conform to criticisms from skeptics. Personally I would not try to answer skeptics here, since I find the game of skeptics quite dull. Nonetheless, in all fairness to the reader, it should be pointed out that hypothesis pertaining to conditions on Jupiter was rather voluminous prior to the *Pioneer 10* bypass but unknown to the two subjects. Much of that hypothesis is now known to be in error, and neither of the subjects verbalized anything that conforms to those hypotheses that are now known to be in error.

However, assuming that the subjects were cheats, which they are not, the Jupiter data coming from the subjects might have been extrapolated from extant theory predating the *Pioneer 10* bypass—assuming, naturally, that the subjects were astrophysicists, which they also are not.

Thus, in speaking of attitudes, if the attitude leans in favor of the presence of abilities in this experiment, the grounds are well laid for continuing experimentation. The skeptical attitude, of course, can go do what it wants.

The planet Mercury, however, because of its position in relation to the Sun, habitually has been occluded from revealing astronomical probes. Hardly anything was known about Mercury until it was bypassed by *Mariner 10.*

The Sherman/Swann psychic probe of Mercury came as a challenge from a science editor of a well-known national magazine. This challenge rested firmly upon the fact that hardly anything was known about Mercury, whereas for Jupiter certain extrapolations might have been possible.

The Mercury extrasensory probe was held on the evening of March 11, 1974, simultaneously, with Sherman beginning at 8:00 P.M. Central Standard Time from his home in Mountain View, Arkansas, and Swann beginning at 9:00 P.M. Eastern Standard Time from his studio in New York. This experiment was monitored and recorded by parapsychologist Janet Mitchell of the American Society for Psychical Research and research associate to Dr. Gertrude Schmeidler at City College. The impressions were recorded, transcribed, notarized, and deposited by noon March 13 with various interested parties, including the Central Premonitions Registry in New York.

Here is what Swann and Sherman found on their psychic probe:

> RESPONSE 1: As my mind centers on the planet Mercury, I get a sensing of great heat. Yet, strangely enough, I do not feel this heat to be coming from the Sun. On the contrary I feel that the powerful electromagnetic radiation from the Sun has set up a friction among the countless particles or molecules or elements composing the body of Mercury, and the resultant constant friction is the cause of the intense heat rising from the interior as well as the surface of Mercury.
>
> I seem to see great rays or beams of energy streaming from the Sun and striking the planet. I follow these beams down to the surface and see that Mercury is bathed in their radiations, which change into light and heat as contact is made with it.
>
> I perceive in my mind's eye what appears to be a jellylike quivering of the surface and there seem to be depths or craters from which exude whitish yellow and green vapors. They seem to stand in vacuumlike space, as do layers of transparent white mist that extend some miles above the surface. The jagged, sometimes mountainous, landscape seems to be scarred and pockmarked.
>
> As I let myself wonder about the dark side of Mercury, shielded as it is from direct contact with the Sun's magnetic rays, I am immediately conscious of extremely cold temperatures. I sense the existence of almost impenetrable, indescribable black rock formation of great altitudes as well as great depths. Can they be almost solid iron? My dominant impressions are of awful, frigid abysses frozen in oceanless black and gray wastelands, seemingly metallic in nature. It is a relief to me to feel that I have mentally encircled the dark side of Mercury

and am emerging on its bright side into what would be blind varicolored brilliance to eyesight.

I doubt if there is much of an atmosphere. If so it must be extremely rarefied. The surface of Mercury seems to glow in areas like a Dante's inferno, reflecting dazzling molten-red light as from a great blast furnace. This interplay of matter and energy in a highly volatile state is constantly replenishing itself through magnetic recharging in association with the Sun's magnetic field. The light side of Mercury presents a fiery spectacle.

I wish I had knowledge of chemistry and minerals so that I could interpret the immense interplay of interchanging particles and elements in constant motion, activated by the Sun's electromagnetic discharge. This explosive discharge varies with intensity in the ebb and flow of gigantic sunspots. I feel that all the elements to be found on Earth and our Moon are in a state of flux on Mercury but are not as solidified or broken down into water and oxygen and plant life, although there is a great contrast in the dark side of Mercury and the elements are more in formation there. And I seem to sense fantastic crystallized shapes of great rigidity.

RESPONSE 2: Do you suppose Mercury has—what shall we call it? —a magnetosphere? Like a circular sphere of magnetism, of magnetic belts around it. Except with Mercury they are not a sphere but on the sun side of Mercury they are set closer to the planet's surface and on the far side of the planet it is sort of pushed out into space. It must be the strength of the solar winds that do that. In other words on the night side of the planet the magnetosphere is pushed farther out into space by the solar winds, and on the sun side it is closer to the surface. It feels hot.

Everything seems very clear. Oh, I know why! There seems to be a thin atmosphere but it is not enough to. . . . It doesn't make a blue sky like Earth's, so you can see blackness except where the sun is. Maybe it looks purple, I guess. There is not much haze.

As the planet turns, the sun creates waves of earth tides so that the surface has lots of cracks and fissures. The gravity must be uneven, pulling more toward the Sun at all times.

I see some almost invisible clouds. And those are some sort of electrical storms. These clouds come and go very fast and they form on the day side of the planet, on the two peripheries of the day side, and trail into the night side. I see them as rainbows that seem to leap up. They arch. They are more like auroras, I guess.

It must have different gravities, depending upon which side you are on. It's beautiful—God, it's beautiful. The refraction of the Sun on those—I guess it would have to be an atmospheric type of situation

> with liquid molecules in it in combination with the fluctuating magnetosphere—it looks like oil on water in a way, that kind of color effect. I get the impression that there is a lot of metal—copper I might say, but I am not sure.
>
> There must be something like lichens, sort of a waterlike life that attaches itself to the rocks and goes through its life cycle that way. It seems a lovely little planet—no place for a human, though. There are differences in land masses, in a way mountainous but not too mountainous. Everything looks chewed down, I guess because of the land tides. I see land masses and channels that look water-washed.
>
> I'd say that the planet is characterized by a sort of low-keyed electric magnetic splendor.

As with the Jupiter data, the psychic responses of the two subjects concerning the conditions on the planet Mercury should not be submitted to a proof-oriented design. The odds against genuine ESP phenomena occurring and being recognized and verified are extremely high, and so it seems more emphasis should be placed on a single successful event rather than devoting time to verifying those items that "might" have been arrived at by some other means.

The responses about Mercury, however, begin to stand out a little more than usual since prevailing hypothesis about the planet held that it would *not* have an atmosphere and that, because of its small size, it would not carry magnetic fields. Both subjects included in their responses definitive statements as to the existence of a thin atmosphere, that now has been computed to be less than one hundred-billionth as dense as Earth's but nonetheless indisputably there. All publications checked for feedback purposes indicate that the presence of the atmosphere was a major surprise to scientists evaluating the *Marina 10* data.*

If there was anything that was expected of Mercury, it was that it should *not* have a magnetic field because of its slow revolutionary period. *Mariner 10,* beginning its bypass of the planet on March 29, 1974, provided its biggest surprise when it revealed a magnetic field with a strength about 1 percent that of Earth's.

---

* Since the introduction of the psychic experimental data, judging the question of prior knowledge of Mercury's atmosphere has gone into argumentation. It seems that as early as 1925 certain polarmetric observations in France and spectroscopic observations in the Soviet Union suggested that an atmosphere was present on Mercury. Other scientists disagreed with these observations, and when the atmosphere was indeed confirmed, surprise was expressed on all sides.

Another significant discovery about conditions on Mercury was the existence of a helium "tail," streaming out from Mercury in a direction away from the Sun. This is especially significant because the shape of the tail was another unexpected feature, a magnetic field pressed closer to the sun side of the planet and streaking off into space on the other side. About twenty minutes before the spacecraft reached its closest distance to Mercury there were very clear signs of a bow shock wave, a front formed by the impact of the solar winds ricocheting off the planet's enveloping magnetic field. And it has also now been somewhat verified that Mercury's magnetic field may be created externally by bombardment of charged particles emanating from the Sun and hitting the atmosphere.

These were the unexpected features of the planet Mercury, all of which were clearly described by the paranormal processes of the two participants in the experiment, features for which prior data did not in fact exist.

Both subjects reported seeing auroral glows, and *Mariner 10* indeed provided verification in that strong auroral glows were observed at ultraviolet wavelengths typical of helium, argon, hydrogen and probably neon. Also reported was the existence of trapped charged particles streaming continuously off into space, and that the surprisingly abundant high energy electrons must be continuously replenished by some sort of planetary source. Both subjects, in their psychic probes, gave possible theories for the source of the auroral glows, but the actual source has yet to be determined by scientists.

It should be indicated, here, that theories are invaluable to scientific progress, since they give at least beginning points from which to dig deeper into the mysteries of the universe. Obtaining information psychically from which to begin to build theories could easily be seen as a practical use for psychic abilities.

Both subjects were reasonably accurate in description of surface conditions. But there existed, prior to *Mariner 10,* previously recorded hypotheses concerning these characteristics. Thus, the findings of the two subjects probably would prove unconvincing to those trying to find alternative explanations.

Whatever that may be, both subjects feel that the Mercury enterprise was a trenchant experience and enormously enjoyed participating in both the Jupiter and Mercury probe. The average reader may not be able to duplicate the intense excitement of feeling that he is on another planet, an excitement increasingly heightened when newspapers and magazines begin to report almost identically upon what was previously seen via paranormal potentials.

Across the pages of history many men have represented the plea for rationality; this plea at its best includes the idea of establishing at least trial hypotheses relevant to the many philosophical and metaphysical conundrums that eat at the hearts of sensitive people and plague the awareness of many others.

At the hearings to decide who would be best equipped to carry out the mandate in James Kidd's will, Dr. Gardner Murphy, a dignified, highly credentialed man whose blue eyes gazed with equanimity over the proceedings, spoke on behalf of the American Society for Psychical Research.

Murphy was born in 1895. He became an authority both as a psychologist and as a psychical researcher. At one time he was president of the Society for Psychical Research and later president of the American Society for Psychical Research until 1971. Since 1952 he has also been director of research at the world-famous Menninger Foundation. Throughout his career his interest in things psychic has reflected a wide concern for theoretical as well as experimental aspects of parapsychology. He has written at length about clairvoyance, precognition, telepathy, survival after death, as well as the meaning psychical research brings to religious awareness.

It is strange to realize that a legal if not a scientific confrontation on the matter of soul took place in the arid spaces of Arizona. There, among the heaven-reaching saguaros and fuzzy Joshua trees, with the warm, dry winds sighing through the open spaces, skeptics were figuratively left behind as scores of claimants arrived to present their suits.

At the hearing Dr. Murphy first suggested data that revolved around deathbed crises, drawing a difference between pathological hallucinations and types of perceptions as death draws near, awarenesses not usually attributable to pathological situations. These include release from suffering, moments of psychic freedom and exultation. He inclined toward the opinion that there are some special dynamics of the deathbed experience that differ from familiar pathological hallucinations.

Later in the verbal interchanges Murphy indicated that, should the society receive the funds stipulated in the Kidd will, it would endeavor to emphasize the so-called "out-of-body" experience. Further, Murphy brought out the idea that many aspects of psychic involvement, such as perhaps immortality, were not researchable in an experimental sense since the components of these presumably transcended present knowledge of matter, energy, space, and time.

Murphy placed his finger at this moment on the crucial reality of discovery in things psychic.

PART IV

Prophecy

> And many false prophets will arise and lead many astray. And because wickedness is multiplied, most men's love will grow cold.
> —Matthew xxiv, 11, 12

Psychokinesis is a form of human potential, a paranormal effect of human determinism upon energy and matter that somehow cuts across accepted cause-effect laws.

Clairvoyance and out-of-body perception are abilities that relate to a different organization of space than is usually the case when one views things solely via the senses of the body.

But what of transcending ordinary concepts of time? Time, that movement along physically-oriented life, moment by moment, in some sort of a linear directional sequence toward the future that is marked by memory, by clocks, and years, centuries, and aeons.

There exists no really workable definition for prophecy or prediction, and extreme attempts have been made to fit these somehow into the equally nebulous definitions surrounding "intuition" and "premonition." But, strangely, in the intuitive and premonitory realms, prophecy-related results can comfortably be tolerated, possibly because of their intense personal nature. But when the prophet reaches out across nations, political parties, and social arrangements he immediately falls victim to one of two traps: the blind believers or the disbelievers who arbitrarily dismiss the possibility.

Aside from these, a rather cogent rationale for the existence of prophecy and prediction exists. This was well said by the amazing H. G. Wells, who often was somewhat gloomy and pessimistic on the future of *homo sapiens*.

Many, if not all, of Wells' literary works are bound intimately in some way with quasi-prophetic or extraordinary prophetic views of the future

—some bad, some amazingly good. For example, in his book *Anticipations of the Reaction of Mechanical and Scientific Progress Upon Human Life and Thought* (1901) Wells successfully anticipated the motorized era of sweeping throughfares, congested cities, and the advent of suburbs. He predicted the tank, the military weapon to be developed beginning with the Great War. Wells felt that the past has enormous predominance on mankind's thoughts because of ignorance of the future and the academic persuasion that ignorance is incurable.

As early as 1899 he indicated that he was

> strongly of the opinion that we ought to consider the possibilities of the future much more than we do. Why should four-fifths of the fiction of today be concerned with times that can never come again, while the future is scarcely speculated upon? At present we are almost helpless in the grip of circumstances, and I think we ought to strive to shape our destinies.[1]

To this end of shaping our destinies, prophecy might come as a blooming flower radiating a scent or an essence that the future-minded personality might appreciate. I am of the opinion that there are some people who secretly hope there is no tomorrow, and the preponderance of prophetic holocausts possibly supports their hope.

But even if Armageddons are the future heritage of men, still I can perceive within myself and in many others a bit of chivalry that suggests a preference for going down waving the sword of a constructive future rather than sitting out the fire on a mountain top waving a placard of doom. Doom awaits those who think it does.

For a being to reach out—whether it be in premonition, intuition, prediction, or prophecy—from the material body and transcend space and time to view energy and matter, it must be said that consciousness (or whatever it is that has consciousness) must be innately able to do this, probably in manifold forms. This should at least be established as a hypothesis.

Because of this manifoldness it is probably up to the individual to sense these abilities within himself. Only the contrite person can watch something happen and *then* say, probably only in a whisper, "I knew it all the time."

---

[1] This statement originally appeared in an interview in *Cassell's Saturday Journal* on April 26, 1899. See also Norman and Jeanne Mackenzie, *H. G. Wells, A Biography* (New York: Simon and Schuster, 1973), p. 162n.

Using even the most crass form of epistomological logic, it is permissible to assume that good prophetic or presentient abilities coupled with courage and daring to act promptly upon whatever conclusions are reached could and have made a good life for many who use their inner prophetic hunches.

The mere act of verbal prophecy, however, continues to amaze and fascinate the excitable; the foretelling of the future without necessarily having to do anything about it is an entertainment and a luxury, a psychic activity fringing upon social dilettantism.

This type of psychic activity gets and holds the interest not only of the general public but of researchers as well. It is specially attractive, for some reason, to the lazy, the rich and the creatively idle.

That prophetic abilities exist in men, flowering only in certain individuals, is beyond doubt to any investigator who endeavors only a few feet into the topic. The ability to exist at a workable level of prediction is for any individual a level of existence highly desirable, since it brings to that individual a sense of tomorrow without which the present can and often does become almost unbearable.

Because prophecy creates in the populace a sort of hope factor, many come slavishly to venerate prophets, and especially *methods* of prophecy. In a creative sense this type of situation seems undesirable since it tends to remove from that populace a sense of self-determinism and reactivates concepts of predestination, and, if the prophecies are especially negative, can instill contrariwise a sense of hopelessness. Those people who are not at all in control of their daily existence, but are moving on lines set up for them by childhood training, education, religion, and society itself especially would feel ineffectual to begin with. Ideas of predestination and doom appeal to them, since these validate and support the essential hopelessness that must possess them.

Doomsday prophets, therefore, can be seen to rip through certain milieus of social consciousness at rather frequent intervals. But since most doomsday prophets have never been right, the emotional charge supporting them must not originate with the prophet himself, but within the degraded sense of life of his adoring public. These are called prophets but are not prophets at all, being merely individuals sensing the innate hopelessness of that social milieu and feeding back into it some tripe that can electrify the situation.

This type of prophecy—that is, voicing what people want to hear—is also rife amongst academicians and staunch supporters of empirical and materialistic interpretation of existence.

Empirical evidence can be said to be dependable, *providing* nothing unpredictable is injected into the scene. Since this is often the case, the best predictions based upon empirical—that is from evidence derived from observation, experience, or experiment, hold true only so long as things go along much as everyone expects them to go. Unpredictable actions or events can, and do, come along and create havoc.

A good example of this type of thing existed in the faith and hope placed in the League of Nations, a system set up purportedly to maintain peace, and to provide for the settlement of disputes at the conference table.

Historically, the League can be seen to be a product resulting from World War I (the Great War), and consisted of a plan acceptable to national systems to prevent yet another grand catastrophe as well as to ease the absolutely devastating effects of the last one. The League, however, had predecessors in the form of the Concert of Europe, the Hague Conferences, and several other peace-enforcing groups such as the League to Enforce Peace. All these contrivances belong to the dreams entertained by some men to devise methods to thwart aggression.

From the start, certain criticisms were voiced against it. It was thought by some nations to constitute a hegemony of the great nations, this being held as undesirable by the lesser. And by many it was considered ineffectual because one of the large powers on the planet, the United States, adhering unadvisedly to its "isolationist" policy, never joined, although the Treaty of Versailles setting up the League was the handiwork of an American president, Woodrow Wilson.

Yet the League of Nations instilled a sense of security not entirely wrong and, providing the untoward did not occur, conceivably might have been successful. This positive attitude was reflected in academic thought and perpetrated upon that consciousness which always feels things are well in hand. The League was, by hope, held to be prophetically a solution to future conflicts.

This prophetic confidence, based upon empirical assumption, was reflected in a speech given on November 18, 1924, at Harvard Law

PROPHECY

School by Manley O. Hudson,[2] Bemis Professor of International Law in the Harvard Law School.

Based upon empirical observations Hudson advised that the next war, if there was to be one, would be preceded by long discussions which would be conducted on a cooperative basis, since the world now had a machinery for this purpose. He indicated that conferencing was swiftly becoming a tradition and furthermore a habit. He was confident that, in viewing the progress that had been made in conferencing prior to the Great War, the world had swiftly moved nearly a whole century ahead, and that the world had advanced to a platform of international cooperation which exceeded the wildest dreams entertained by anyone prior to 1914.

He indicated that the establishment of the machinery of the League of Nations, was so "ramifying in influence" and so "embedded in affairs" that it was difficult to expect the world ever again to be without it. He further went on to state that, with this machinery at nations' disposal, it would seem unlikely that the world would ever again move in the direction of Armageddon.

If a conflict were to come into being, it would be preceeded undoubtedly by lengthy and long drawn-out discussions; the records of these discussions would form an "open book"; and all facts about the dispute would "flame" in newspapers and headlines throughout the world. At any rate, should conflict be imminent, debate about it at the conference table would involve *generations* before it should actually come to pass as open conflict.

There is no doubt that men everywhere have an inalienable right to struggle for better communication. Men's actions, however, have a tendency to avail themselves of better judgment by the survey of results rather than the enthusiasms of more hopes. Hudson's "prophetic" expectation of "generations" of discussions about antagonisms was barely nine rather than the enthusiasms of mere hopes. Hudson's "prophetic" expectayears old before Adolph Hitler used the excuse of the armament question before the League in 1933 to cause Germany to withdraw from it, in

[2] See Manley O. Hudson, "The Stacking of the Cards" in *The Next War,* three addresses delivered at a symposium at Harvard University, November 18, 1924, the Harvard Bulletin Press, Cambridge, 1925, pp. 85–87.

conformity with his own plots and plans for the world, machinations of which he had not bothered to inform the League about in the first place.

Shortly, thereafter, the world was once again embroiled in an Armageddon the atrocities of which caused the last one to be put to shame. Had Hudson, and others, turned somewhat of an ear to certain prophecies, they might at least have included in their empirical optimism at least one nettle, a presentient foreboding of the rise of "a second beast" which existed in many minds even *prior* to the Great War which had itself wreaked havoc upon millions.

There are two bitter sociological factors concerning prophecy.

First, most so-called prophets prove to be wrong to begin with. An analysis of prophecies made during a recent four-year period (1969–1972) and published either in the pulp media or in pamphlets and booklets shows that most of the prophets turned out to be totally wrong, missing the mark by miles. Only about 1.5 percent of the inclusive prophecies were anywhere near the mark.

Second, the appearance of a man or woman who really manages to foresee the future in some detail is usually horrifying. There has hardly been a time in recent history—say the last two thousand years—when the future did not hold some indescribable and indecent activities, some terror or desecration.

Prophets, real prophets that is, naturally would be able to perceive these indignities if they really could foresee anything at all. However, people pretend that tomorrow will only be more glorious than the present; they absolutely will not accept that actions performed in the present are heading, once more, toward dire ends.

In this manner prophecy gets mixed up with people's hopes. The prophets who swing along with these hopes, these illusory trends, are well thought of even if they never actually foresee the future. The prophet who has a good look at the future, however, should be able to reasonably predict what actually is there, and such prophecies must

PROPHECY

include the culmination of present-day stupidities. Many people cannot confront the deficiencies of their present existence, much less the future, but they do drool over illusions of all kinds. And those who consult prophets or predictors usually do so in search of a better, not a worse, future.

It is part of ordinary existence to be able, even in the most common of daily tasks, to exist somewhat at a level of prediction. Good businessmen, of course, seem able to exist at a level of prediction that spreads at least a little into the future, thereby enabling them to make correct decisions in the present.

Many people seem unable to do this. They cannot predict if their marriage will last the year out, whether they will still have the same job. All the important small things of life are involved with a sort of prediction. Those who cannot perform at least this minuscule psychic feat end up lonely and defeated. Naturally, deep inside they abhor the future, since the present itself is dreadful.

The tendency, then, would be to view the future as better, more glorious. Consequently, hope itself is placed somewhere in the immediate or far future. This serves to drag the individual along through the years. By placing hope itself in the future, all sorts of psychological edifices can be structured toward that future—major among these at present is the belief in a golden age of Aquarius, just around the corner of the next few years.

Real prophecy, however, usually is shocking, often horrific, and certainly unappetizing to those who constantly dwell in the small fringe of human greatness and grandeur. Even prophetic insights to major beneficial and humanitarian discoveries, destined to expand human awareness by leaps and bounds, can at the time prophesied represent a huge horror to any given society. For example, the Copernican discovery of the motion of Earth around the Sun led to certain scientific astronomical prophecies, but these were prophecies that threatened utterly to destroy man's image of himself at that time. And so the quasi-prophetic situation represented by Copernicus was viewed by most with utter horror.

Trying to discover good things about the human situation is, of course, very much a prosurvival course. However, denying the existence of man's negative proclivities does nothing except render the individual incapable of dealing with them when they begin to protrude by force of human interaction. When it comes to viewing the future, most people have their heads buried in the sand.

The real prophet simply seems to transcend time and space, have a look, and report back to those in the present. That prophetic ability exists is beyond doubt; that imitators, frauds, and self-styled prophets more wrong than right also exist is equally well established. The difficulty therefore lies in finding out how correct a given predictor has been in his predictions.

Good prophecies, the best prophecies, are filled with particulars as to date, place, time, participants, and so forth. The worst prophecies are those that can be interpreted equally well for events transpiring in 1476, or 1628, or 1892, or 1978, and so on.

There seems to be a tendency for prophecies to come in sets, and for some as yet unspecified reason they appear to be more prevalent just prior to times of great change.

The France of Louis XVI and Marie Antoinette, for example, was a France beleaguered by changing thought systems. A certain amount of social realignment, if not upheaval, reasonably could have been predicted by the trained political and governmental mind.

The rather fixed economic and social methods of the *ancien régime* did not leave much latitude for the commercial expansion taking place during the seventeenth and eighteenth centuries. France was not a backward nation, but its social development had progressed too swiftly to allow for commensurate constitutional change. This type of situation provided fertile ground for gross and sometimes indecent reactions in all levels of society.

Many reasons and causes have been given as contributing to the cataclysm that came to be called the French Revolution. Locke and Hobbes had played a significant part in establishing an increasingly materialistic outlook on things, this outlook eventually coming to be called the "Age of Enlightenment." A trend toward scientific skepticism had entered the social consciousness through the scientific methods of Newton and Descartes.

The tenets couched in the thought characteristic of the "Age of Enlightenment," however, had brought into existence powerful disciples of Hobbes and Locke in the august personages of Diderot and Voltaire. Denis Diderot, a philosopher of materialism, wrote on almost every conceivable topic. He also was an art critic and, through his famous salons, the founder of art criticism.

Diderot became editor of the famous *Encyclopédie,* published first in 1765 in twenty-one volumes, with contributions by Voltaire, Rousseau, Turgot, and Montesquieu, among others. Montesquieu had become famous as a jurist and political philosopher, and also notorious as a satirist who attacked and criticized French institutions. Under Diderot and Voltaire, a group known as the Encyclopédistes formed after the visions of Hobbes and Locke. They used the pages of the French *Encyclopédie* to enter the arena of propaganda and thereby resolutely began attacking state and church.

This method of swaying public sentiment is not without its adherents and practitioners today. Indeed even the pages of historical prophecy, such as those of Nostradamus, have not gone unnoticed by propagandists, as we shall see.

Through the words of Voltaire and Diderot, existing laws and social structures were subject to withering, degrading criticism, obviously geared to the eventual downfall of those institutions. The rapid expansion of commerce in the seventeenth and eighteenth centuries had created a vast so-called *bourgeoisie,* whose members protested the outworn privileges of the clergy and nobles. They desired power and were looking around for ways and means of achieving it. The diatribes published by Voltaire and Diderot thus represented or came to represent the voice of this discontented sector.

The vast, almost imposing, populations of poor and underprivileged, however, came to find voice through Adam Smith, a Scottish economist born in 1723 and educated at Glasgow and Oxford. He became professor of logic at Glasgow University in 1751 and professor of moral philosophy in 1752. He spent the years 1754–1766 in France, and in 1776 published his famous work *An Inquiry into the Nature and Causes of the Wealth of Nations.*[3]

Smith opposed monopoly and felt that all special privileges constituted injustice to the poor. He believed that an economic system functions best in the absence of interference by government or other coercive organizations. Of course this view was immediately popular among the burgeoning industrialists and the classes beneath them.

This attitude—since an attitude it is—came to be called laissez faire, the term probably originating with another man but reaching its popular usage in the doctrines of Adam Smith. The leaders of the middle classes gravitated to the laissez faire concept. Since access to legislative government was denied them through the inadequacies of the existing state, they sought ways and means to bring down the corrupt administration and absolute kingship that had caused social institutions to lag in development. Discontent in the society of Louis XVI therefore was deep, continually fanned by propaganda and the necessity for sweeping changes.

And, as any historian worth his pants knows, bureaucratic systems simply move at a slowness that precludes any possibility of sweeping changes from within. Thus the man of foresight or just plain cleverness can look for and expect *revolution.*

Into this electrified situation, then, any prophet who predicts the end of the old regime and the commencement of a new order probably will be given almost undivided attention by a great portion of the discontented society. The prelude to the French Revolution saw literally dozens of such types, many of whom are not without their interest in a number of significant ways. Two are of special interest because of the utterly staggering accuracy of their predictions.

Giuseppe Balsamo was born in 1743 in the beautifully situated town of Palermo on the northwest coast of Sicily. His parentage seems obscure. He was educated at the Caltagirone monastery in Sicily, from whence, as a result of producing forgeries of one sort or another, he was expelled for misconduct. He then seems to have wandered and "studied" in Egypt, Persia, Arabia, and Greece. He eventually appeared—married to an

---

[3] Adam Smith, *An Inquiry into the Nature and Causes of the Wealth of Nations,* edited with an introduction and notes by Edwin Cannan (New York: Modern Library, 1937).

equally unprincipled woman named Lorenza Feliciani—well within elegant boundaries of Neapolitan and Roman society.

Somewhere along the way he assumed the name and title of Count Alessandro Cagliostro and "studied" alchemy under the grand master of the Knights of Malta; this arrangement conceivably aided him significantly in obtaining access to society, nobility, and the wealthy.

Traveling to Germany and thence to Strasbourg, he gained the eager support and confidence of the famous Cardinal de Rohan by allowing the cardinal to understand that he, Cagliostro, possessed the secret of manufacturing gold, a secret that would even today obtain no little amount of attention.

He arrived in Paris during the year 1781. His fame had preceded him; he was thought by the poor to be their father and by the best of society to be divine. He erected on the Rue de la Sourdière a Temple of Isis and, establishing himself as high priest, gave lectures on the imminent return of the golden age and universal happiness. To rapt and enthralled audiences, among whom females seemed to predominate, he recounted tales of his voyages among the ruins of Palmyra and Nineveh. He advised about the mysteries of Thebes and Babylon where, he said, he encountered men who possessed marvelous knowledge as well as the miracle of perpetual youth—this last assuredly acquiring for him hypnotic fascination among his admirers.

Like Rasputin, one of his successors who acquired both public and royal patronage, he acceded to influence in the royal household itself, although he never came to play as significant a role in Louis XVI's court as Rasputin did in the court of the Russian tsar, Nicholas II.

Cagliostro undoubtedly was an intuitive politician at heart and understood, as have so many other popular prophets and occultists, that protection of the powers that be is necessary to insure a tranquil production of whatever it is they represent. He obtained this for himself by establishing the patronage of the Princess de Lamballe—an intimate of Marie Antoinette—as grand mistress of his temple, a position that the queen herself reportedly urged the princess to accept. Accordingly, on March 20, 1785, the princess was installed at the Temple of Isis on a throne created for the occasion, before a collection of the highest-born noblemen. A sumptuous banquet followed.

Cagliostro's Egyptian temple was considered spurious by the Masonic lodges in Paris, which called a *convent* to try to figure out what to do about him.[4]

Count Cagliostro was to be imprisoned by Louis XVI in the Bastille on August 22, 1785, as the result of a future scandal. But not before he foretold the fall of the royal house, the beginning of the revolution, and the death of the king himself. These prophecies apparently occurred as a result of the Masonic *convent* that met to deal with problems concerned with the Masons' existence, to which the popularity of Cagliostro conceivably was a growing threat.

Approaching the situation through one Antoine Court de Gébelin, a meeting was arranged at which a sort of inquisition of Cagliostro was to be held under the guise of trying to learn more about the mysteries he represented. The date of this meeting is given as May 10, 1785, but this is probably incorrect since Antoine Court de Gébelin appears to have died in 1784.[5]

During the course of this "conference," presided over by Court de Gébelin, Cagliostro sought to impress his select audience with his knowledge and capabilities, using demonstrations of numerology and astrology to predict the fate of the French government.

Cagliostro's methods in numerology and astrology have perplexed many subsequent occultists and researchers. As is usual in the occult, it has always been surmised that, if one could but master the method, one would obtain the ability. Not so, and not likely. Perhaps in some cases methodology of one sort or another spurs the "psychic" on to grand heights, but the innate flexible vision residing in the man himself probably constitutes the ability much more than does the mere manipulation of letters and planets.

In any case the *result* of Cagliostro's attempt to impress the gathered Freemasons is almost without parallel in the field of prophecy.

After demonstrating some particulars concerning historical France, Cagliostro went on to indicate that the present king, Louis XVI would

[4] See especially Paul Christian, *The History and Practice of Magic,* vol. I (New York: Citadel Press, 1963), pp. 139–172. The brief history included in this book if concise, is by no means extensive and the interested reader will find many other accounts of this interesting man's life and sojourns.

[5] See Arthur E. Waite, *The Secret Tradition in Freemasonry* (London: Rebman, 1911).

fall down from the ruined throne of his ancestors and die on the scaffold toward the thirty-ninth year of his life, placing his death during 1793; further, Louis XVI would be condemned to lose his head for being guilty of war; and the fall of the dynastic rank would be accompanied by conflict of material forces, overwhelming catastrophes, and crumbling powers.

Having touched directly upon the topic of the times, Cagliostro undoubtedly acquired the serious attention of his listeners, who, it is reported, were now completely under his spell. Departing momentarily from utilizing numerology to guide him, he advised that the crowds of people who had no tomorrow would suddenly seize tomorrow in their hands. In barely a moment the nation with so much wealth and so many splendors, laying claims to the eternal, would crumble into nothing. This drama would be accompanied by people maddened. Famine would incite mobs to theft and pillage, and murder would become the national occupation. All this was to be the predictable result that follows regicide.

Except for the dates given and the name of the King, the casual observer would not know yet if Cagliostro was speaking of France or of the toppling of the Russian House of Romanov, whose turn would eventually come.

Cagliostro then turned his vision toward the fate of the queen, indicating that Marie Antoinette would follow the king, that she—born so high and wealthy—would be cast down into poverty, into anguish. She would become wrinkled before her time; she would starve and be imprisoned; finally she, too, would be beheaded.

The gathered gentlemen were astonished. Court de Gébelin, himself quite stunned, inquired of Cagliostro if his fatidic vision had yet been narrated to the Princess de Lamballe, the queen's friend and the grand mistress of the Temple of Isis.

No, Cagliostro said, he had not informed the princess because he would then have to tell her she herself would be murdered in half darkness at the corner of the Rue des Ballets, after she had been freed from imprisonment.

At this point Cagliostro was recalled to himself and possibly felt he had talked too much, which indeed he had. Court de Gébelin, however, was hot on the trail of the coming debacle and urged Cagliostro to persist, at least to reveal the date of the beginning of the horrid times ahead. Cagliostro indicated that this date appeared to be 1789. Of the two sons of Louis XVI, the first would die prematurely of a rachitic spinal affection; the second would die imprisoned, a captive.

Cagliostro then concluded that, after the royal catastrophe, an elected Corsican would end the travail. Further, upon a question from one Jacques Cazotte, an impressive white-haired man, as to the name of this Corsican predestined to the throne of the deposed Bourbons, Cagliostro indicated that Napoléon Bonaparte would be his name and that after his election to the throne of victory he would himself meet with an unfortunate destiny.

The prophecies now can be seen to be complete as to the requirements of prophecy; names, dates, future activities all very well laid out, and referring only to the France at the time.

The French Revolution, like almost all great events, was "predicted" by squads of prophets, some emerging decades, some centuries, in advance. This revolution, it is said, was foretold as early as 1300 by the bishop of Cambrai, one Pierre d'Ailly, and again by an astrologer named Turrel in 1531, and of course by Nostradamus.

Revolutions are always topical anyway, and this particular revolution was not an exception. As the day for its birth drew nearer, Jacques Cazotte, the white-haired man who had asked Cagliostro who would succeed the Bourbons, himself somewhat of a prophet and clairvoyant, was dining at a dinner party in 1788 at the home of the Duchess de Gramont in Paris. Cazotte's prophecy seems to have been recorded by a fellow guest, Jean de la Harpe, who has been described as a skeptic and a fanatical atheist.

Turning to the subject of the coming revolution, Cazotte predicted dire events for all those assembled at the party, indicating that most would be taken by cart to the scaffold and that even greater nobility than those gathered would meet with much the same fate. Those who would escape the scaffold would do so because of suicide or death at the hands of mobs.

Before six years had passed, all those gathered that night met the end Cazotte had predicted. Yet upon hearing the predictions, they all laughed and felt him to be jesting.

Considering the degree of forgery that exists in prophetical texts, it could not possibly be known if the Cagliostro utterances were indeed given prior to the revolution. Many believe they are authentic, just as many believe the prophecies of Nostradamus to be authentic—but in this latter case considerable evidence as to tampering with the texts is available to anyone who cares to delve into the matter.

Whatever may be the truth or untruth in the matter of the Cagliostro prophecies, the French Revolution began as scheduled on July 14, 1789, when revolting Parisians stormed and destroyed the Bastille. Louis XVI and Marie Antoinette tried to flee their crumbling empire but were captured, tried, and eventually executed, the king on January 21, 1793, the queen, grown old before her time, a few months later after having been treated with utmost brutality. Louis XVII, the royal second son, who succeeded as heir after the death of the first, was held in prison and cruelly treated. He is said to have died about 1795.

Princess de Lamballe was arrested with the royal family and subsequently imprisoned. She was set free after her father-in-law paid large sums of money to an attorney of the Paris Commune for her release. A man named Trunchon was charged with escorting her home, but at the corner of the Rue des Ballets a man named Grison struck her down and three companions cut her into pieces. Her head, cut off by one of the three men, a wigmaker, was exhibited for a while on the streets and eventually thrown onto a rubbish heap.

To those whose consciousness is rooted in what the senses of the body perceive, the past, the present, and the future are all a mystery, as are time and space. Those who base their consciousness upon sense perceptions are not even in the game of awareness. This type of consciousness is perhaps merely a stupidity to others whose minds soar through universes of unseen implications and compute from data fed into their analytical minds from places and at a rate undreamed of by others.

One could get quite abstruse and begin talking about a "space/time continuum" as many do, especially physicists who like to get tangled up in this alleged problem. Creating space and time in one's thoughts as a "continuum," that is as a continuous extent, is likely to accomplish just that in one's thoughts.

From the psychic viewpoint, however, obviously time and space do not act as a continuum; but space is something in which time exists, and they are not related to any other extent. If, as we are to believe, Cagliostro could observe the unfortunate, bloody events that were to transpire some two to six years in advance, time and space would have to have become, for him at the moment of his prophecies, discontinuous. It therefore is permissible to hypothesize that this discontinuity in thought, and subsequently in some form of perception, can and does take place, and further that, once the individual is able to accomplish this in thought, he can and does turn his "inner vision" to the observation and prediction of normal cause-effect events, which *are* continuous.

In the France into which the fabled Cagliostro stepped, the milieu, the times, the trends, all must have suggested revolution—that is, to men who were not trapped solely in what their eyes perceived but could compare notes on events and trends through some form of apperception, some ability to comprehend by associating what is seen or thought with masses of nonmaterial concepts. Assuming that Cagliostro's consciousness was able to perform such mental tasks, it was only a matter of extending, as it were, such apperception to a future—or a past—moment to view what linear events would bring about.

Of course the implications of such activity are staggering, certainly beyond the bounds of reason, and simply confusing to the ordinary person brought up with rigid ideas of himself and how and what he can think. These implications are, among other things, that the human potential knows no bounds and that this universe, whatever it may be, is inexorably small compared to the hidden magnitudes of the extant being.

In order to pursue this topic, the reader would have to be able to hold concepts in which time and space were not linear but existed one within the other, and then simply move his perceptions along either of them.

There is plenty of precedent for this. Certain Oriental traditions suggest that one's consciousness solely demarcates and determines the space that is accessible to one, and further that an infinity of space is identical with an infinity of consciousness.[6] Western thought, however, has been quite

---

[6] See Govinda, the Lama Anagarika, *Foundations of Tibetan Mysticism* (New York: E. P. Dutton, 1960), p. 116. Lama Govinda is a European, born in Germany in 1898, and now a member of the Kargyupta order. Govinda's book is not characteristic of the "mystic" tradition since it clearly delineates many Buddhist concepts into a condition capable of being entertained in rational thought, whereas characteristic "mystic" ratiocination holds thought or perception as something out of which only meaning or implication can be perceived. The title of Govinda's book is therefore misleading.

linear for many centuries; thus concepts of infinity are unfamiliar.

There is no difficulty in comprehending what is meant in this Eastern concept, however; it simply revolves around the question—or perhaps problem—of what it is that one can become conscious of. If the answer is not "everything," then one is not even on the playing field.

The situation represented by theorizing that one's consciousness is identical to what one can perceive is not unrecognized in Western science. To one eminent physicist, consciousness is something that is a "primary" factor in all experience and hence deserves a good deal more attention than has so far been given it.[7]

Now explanations of consciousness fall into the category in which things collapse in upon themselves. If, as suggested in Eastern thought, and certainly hinted at in certain Western constructs, one's consciousness is what one is aware of, then one will issue conclusions based only upon what one is conscious of. The argument over what it is that one can be conscious of takes on new meaning, giving a *false* track that mystics and occultists by the legions have followed for centuries and contemporary mind controllers and meditators are swarming after today.

About the only constructive thing that is accomplished by meditation or mind-control techniques is that, if anything, one better organizes the contents of one's thoughts and a certain peace might pervade thereby. But within these practices it should be admitted that one is *already* aware of what one is aware. This awareness may differ in different people but will not fundamentally *change* until one turns around just about opposite from the issue of "What is it that I can be aware of?" to the idea of "What is it that keeps me from being aware?"

And there lie all the devils.

During the time of Copernicus the men thinking in terms of a stationary Earth, with planets, moon, and even the Sun moving around it, could not reorganize this motion in the universe in their awareness. To them a sense of time must have been exceedingly difficult, and of course a sense of space terribly interiorized around their conceptualization of man in the center of all, to which even the luminaries paid obeisance.

In attempting to execute prophecy, many people apparently predict what they imagine might happen to others as well as themselves. It is quite

[7] See Lawrence LeShan, *Toward a General Theory of the Paranormal* (New York: Parapsychology Foundation, 1969), introduction by Henry Margenau, p. 9.

obvious that the content of consciousness need not necessarily correspond to facts or truth. This, however, need not be a deficit of psychical abilities alone; it can be seen to litter the pathways of philosophy, theology, and science itself.

It is therefore permissible to suggest that not only is there an ability to have differing degrees of consciousness but also an ability to have in that consciousness false information or data—data that could and probably do alter the accuracy of any perception, even of conclusions based upon sensory input as well as any possible nonmaterial perceptions.

The Cagliostro predictions are a well-known set of prophecies that have impressed researchers for a long time. They have, however, a disadvantage in that they may have, through the years, been made editorially impressive by believers who wanted them to be seen in their greater aspects.

In history, such alignments, if not outright forgeries, are not unheard of in literary documents that come to influence subsequent generations. The famous Nostradamus prophecies are a set that have suffered some such interpretations and forgery. The most recent instance was the use of the Nostradamus oracles for black propaganda purposes by the Nazi Minister of Propaganda Joseph Goebbels, who had some of them rewritten in order to predict favorable futures for the German onslaught. The circulation by the German Propaganda Ministry of one such forged document was rather enormous. It was distributed in a total of 83,000 copies, 25,000 of which were in Croatian, 20,000 in French, 10,000 each in Italian and Serbian, 5,000 each in Dutch, Rumanian, and Swedish, and 3,000 in English for circulation within the United States.[8]

Throughout the many years that I have been an avid student first of the occult, and subsequently of parapsychology and related matters, I have been excited by prophetic enterprises. It is, to say the least, somewhat of a task to thoroughly apprise one's self of the condition of prophecy

---

[8] See Ellic Howe, *Urania's Children, The Strange World of the Astrologers* (London: William Kimber, 1967), pp. 163–191.

since it has been treated rather shabbily by academicians on the one hand and cooked into a mush by eager devotees on the other hand.

There is not much doubt that this interest was building into an idea of experimenting with modern prophecy such as the type given at the end of this section. Not the type of prophecy that informs all and sundry of love affairs of movie stars or of world calamities; but an experiment by which prophetic aptitude could be compared with modern sociological attempts to predict futures. In this context, it seemed desirable to learn what kind of prophecy constituted valuable prophecy; not so much valid prophecy, since through the centuries there is a lot of that, but a type of prophecy that could be used as a significator for future trends.

Now I am by no means an advocate of the theory of predestination, and prophecy in general rather reeks of admitting to predestined futures. I would seek to hold to a definition of prophecy as seeing clearly what is probably going to happen providing people keep on acting as they are presently acting. This might be mere extrapolation, to be sure, but there is currently no indicator, concerning human abilities, that establishes where extrapolation ends and prophetic insights begin.

The advanced prophet, conceivably, would be one that is thoroughly apprised of contemporary affairs, perhaps also using certain clairvoyant or out-of-body abilities to give him more exact information about contemporary affairs than is published in the media, and thence extrapolating forward from that combined information into visions of the future that show current trends culminating in unexpected events.

In researching historical prophecies, I was thus on the lookout for a set of predictions that fulfilled this paradigm.

I came across a very interesting set of prophecies, quite by accident. They were doubly interesting because they were precise as to dates and time spans, and there was evidence that they had not been forged or predated since, for the most part, they were found in pamphlets in the New York Public Library bearing the dates of acquisition by the library. This acquisition mark at least suggested that they were in the library before the events prophesied in them took place. And this series of prophecies represented a stunning display of prophetic aptitude at work.

TO KISS EARTH GOOD-BYE

It seems strangely difficult to discover particulars surrounding the life of Walter Richard (Gorn) Old, born on March 20, 1864, especially since in him there appears to have resided a prophet of considerable magnitude. A great deal of attention has been given to lesser prophetic lights; where volumes have been printed about prophets who are at least 75 perecnt wrong by observation, this author was unable to locate even a pamphlet dealing in retrospect with life of Old.[9]

Yet enough information has been gleaned to give some idea of the character of the man; his mind and life being supremely characterized by his apparent ability to stop, look, and listen to all sorts of things, to experience depths of devotion to discovery of the nature of man, and to be able to continually shift his attention once any chosen path had come to an end.

The word "eccentric" might describe him in many minds; there is little doubt that, considering the times in which he matured, his preoccupation with the intangible, with the nonmaterial led him in any number of directions, all of which would appear "eccentric" to the conduct expected in mundane circles.

He was educated in Birmingham at King Edward's School and began the study of astrology and the Cabala at a very early age. Some time around the age of twenty-one he broke down with a condition called hyperaesthesia, a term used in the 1880s to refer to excessive morbid sensitivity of the nerve centers, a condition that had come to carry parapsychological connotations by 1920.[10]

His interests led him to studies in practical occultism as well as to psychology and he began to be interested in things Oriental, studying Hebrew and Coptic texts, and subsequently hieroglyphics, Assyrian, and finally Sanskrit and Chinese. He eventually came to translate several Oriental books of wisdom, and apparently his interest in such texts led his mind into paths not normally followed.

These interests brought him into the excitement and scandal of the theosophical camp, and he seems to have been a close associate, if not

---

[9] Sources on Old were by no means exhausted by this author. Old resided mainly in London, and perhaps there exist more data about him to which this author has not had access.

[10] See S. G. Soal, *Preliminary Studies of a Vaudeville Telepathist* (London: University of London Council for Psychical Investigation, 1937).

confidante, of the famous and infamous personality that resided in the form of Helena Petrovna Blavatsky, cofounder of the Theosophical Society and author of the *Secret Doctrine*, the movement's major supportive text.[11]

According to one report, Madame Blavatsky called Old "the astral tramp" because of his penchant for "roaming about in his astral body at night." [12] Old's association with theosophy came to an end after Madame Blavatsky's passing, but not before he participated in an exceedingly interesting squabble, most of which seems to have been published in the press, which was always interested in the arguments and scandals of neo-movements such as the Theosophical Society.[13]

Old's description of his parting with the theosophical movement, although somewhat flowery, gives a clue to his character:

> I had learned all that was to be known about the methods and teachings of modern theosophy, I had weighed them in the balance and found them wanting. They took me from the sunlit hills of spiritual hope and aspiration, led me through shady glades and mysterious paths, through a forest of speculation and doubt, and eventually landed me in a morass of disillusionment from which I was left to extricate myself by an effort of the will.[14]

Another indication of Old's outlook on life can be found in his translation of the Tao-Teh-King:

> The simple life is not always the Simple Way. Indeed it is no Way at all if it does not lead to the end in view; and that end, I take it, is the ennobling of individual character, the raising of our standards of equity, and the strengthening of the bonds of fellowship on the common basis of our humanity.[15]

[11] H. P. Blavatsky, *The Secret Doctrine: The Synthesis of Science, Religion, and Philosophy* (Pasadena, Calif.: Theosophical University Press, 1963), 2 vols. This version is identical with the original 1888 text.

[12] See A. L. Cleather, *H. P. Blavatsky as I Knew Her* (Calcutta and Simla, 1923), pp. 23–34.

[13] The interested reader is referred to the press of the time. A summary of the Old/theosophy flap can be found in *The Theosophical Movement 1875–1950* (Los Angeles: Cunningham Press, 1951).

[14] W. G. Old (Sepharial), *The Theory of Geodetic Equivalents* (London: W. Foulsham), pp. 36–37.

[15] W. G. Old, *The Simple Way: Laotze (The "Old Boy")*—a new translation of the Tao-Teh-King, with Introduction and Commentary (Philadelphia: David McKay, 1913), p. vi.

Old apparently gave a good deal of attention to human nonmaterial interactions with matter, energy, space, and time, summing his conclusions up in a rather complete, if not almost quaint, statement: "It is impossible to separate the ideas of operation and agent, virtue and being, as if one should speak of the thinker apart from thought." [16]

Old eventually came to alight in London as an astrologer. The famous astrologer Alan Leo had figured out ways and means to make astrology a "public" thing and began the first of the astrological horoscope factories by setting up a company that mailed out prepared copy for a small fee. By 1898 Leo had become a full-time professional astrologer, living in a commodious house at 9 Lyncroft Gardens. Astrology during these and subsequent years experienced a heyday that was interesting, if not exciting. Another subsequently famous astrologer and prophet, Louis Hamon (Cheiro) was soon to dazzle society with his prophecies.

It would not be too far from the point to suggest that the mysteries, arts, crafts, and financings of which the practice of astrology can indeed be capable were at this time (1898–1920) experiencing a blaze of glory that has not been equaled since.

Into this world stepped Walter Richard (Gorn) Old who, taking the cabalistic name of Sepharial, began to produce a series of astrological writings and predictions that are astounding. It would be too easy to accept that Sepharial accomplished his prophetic deeds by the practice of astrology alone; indeed, he left a written legacy of astrological texts replete with much of his methodologies and practices. As is usual with the rare significantly successful astrologers, however, less inspired practitioners utilizing the same techniques very seldom accomplish similar heights of glory. It is therefore feasible to suggest that the gifts one brings *to* astrology are gifts that astrology itself cannot bring to the nongifted or the nonpsychically inspired.

It is therefore desirable to relate some of Old's prophecies on their merit as prophecies alone, the *how* of his coming to utter them being totaly another question.[17]

---

[16] W. G. Old, *op. cit.*, p. 23.

[17] There is not much doubt that the craft of astrology is a major producer of predictions, and in some rare cases there seems to be a high correlation between the art and the subsequent turn of events. One example of this rarity is the fact that Louis Hamon (Cheiro) predicted, many years before it occurred, the high probability that the prince of Wales, later the duke of Windsor, would abandon his

PROPHECY

The Great War, which subsequently came to be called World War I, grew out of the general political and economic conditions shared uncomfortably by European countries. Bismarck's successes during the Franco-Prussian war (1870–1871) had established Prussian supremacy over lesser states and brought about the German empire, William I receiving the crown of Germany in 1871.

William II, who succeeded to the throne in 1888, was characterized by his belief that kingship was divine in nature, by his impulsiveness, and by his almost absolute love of military display. William's character, coupled with Germany's desire to expand its economy and its colonies, would eventually lead to an expansion of Germany's affairs that Great Britain and France could not long ignore.

This state of affairs did not escape the notice of the revolutionaries and prophets who abounded at the time, and the royal houses of Europe were beleaguered by both. It is of course now possible to survey the situation historically and draw the "inevitable" conclusion. The Europe of the ages was doomed. Indeed, even during the years preceding the outbreak of hostilities, rational men could and did expect changes. But even the most imaginative did not predict that, within a few short years, royal dynasties that had lasted in some cases for hundreds of years would fall and be no more.

The impending conflict was seized upon by the astrologers hanging out in London, among whom was Walter Richard (Gorn) Old—Sepharial. Some of the pamphlets he published at the time were discovered by this author in the New York Public Library. They carried not only their dates of publication but also the dates of accession into the library. (And if any researcher is interested in reviewing the contents of these pamphlets, it is suggested that he hurry since they are decomposing and beginning to crumble into dust).

All the royal houses of Europe and Russia (as well as that of Turkey) came under the observation of Old at one time or another. He predicted

---

throne for a love affair. See Louis Hamon (Cheiro), *Cheiro's World Predictions* (London: The London Publishing Co., 1927), p. 87. This accuracy is the exception rather than the rule, however, and it is noteworthy that Hamon's fame, in addition to astrological expertise, came to him by his ability to make snap predictions at odd moments. Even a half-hearted survey of astrological records shows that the majority of predictions based upon astrological interpretation are miserable flops.

the fall of them all, but his specialty seems to have centered around the house of Hohenzollern—that of William II, whom he castigated in his usual flowery terms as "the Beast." Old's denunciations of William II, quite deserved to be sure, reached a virulence seldom found in public documents.

Old also turned considerable attention to the Russian tsar. He published several castigations directed at the aging Franz Joseph, who had sat on the throne of the Austro-Hungarian empire longer than Victoria sat on hers in England and whose annexation of Bosnia and Herzegovina in 1908 led directly to the outbreak of the "Great Devastation," as Old was to put it.

Writing in 1914, Old indicated it was unlikely that Nicholas II of Russia would survive the war and that at the time he reached forty-seven years of age there would be a great revolution that would probably see the end of the dynastic succession in Russia. Further, that country would not emerge from the war with any measure of success, and what had happened in St. Petersburg in 1905 would likely be repeated more effectively in 1915.[18]

The chilling story of Nicholas II and the Russian royal family is familiar history.

Old had been casting his prophetic eye over affairs long before the fall of the house of Romanov, however.

The "war of nations" was first predicted in Old's 1896 manual of astrology. And again in *The Green Book for Prophecies* for 1914, probably written in the spring of 1913 and published in the summer of that year. Old later commented that his first predictions were in the hands of people long before there was the slightest indication of any such world catastrophe, and indeed at a time when politicians had announced, referring especially to England, that never in the fiscal interest of that country was there a more suitable opportunity of reducing expenditures on the army and navy. "So much for political prescience," says Old.

In his 1913 prophecy for the year 1914, Old indicated that there would be signs of sharp agitation; there would be financial strain and a tendency toward panic on the markets. Disbursements on further munitions of war

[18] W. G. Old (Sepharial), *An Astrological Survey of the Great War, Being an Examination of the Indications Attending the Outbreak and the Presumptive Efforts of the Conflict* (London: W. Foulsham, 1914), p. 15.

would give rise to alarm in commercial centers. Further, the development of political affairs during this time would not be reassuring, and about July 25 there would be a crisis of an awesome nature. There would be war talk throughout the country.

Further, during August 1914 the situation would have developed to such an explosive stage that there would be great danger of sudden ignition. About the third of the month diplomatic relations, including England's, would be severely strained. There would be increased war talk and financial panic, and the popular feeling would be one of high tension. Also: "The Balkan concert will now be disturbed and affairs tend to a crisis in Austria."

Archduke Franz Ferdinand of Austria, heir to the Hapsburg throne, decided to pay a ceremonial visit to provincial Sarajevo, the capital of Bosnia, where he was in the mountains watching Austrian army maneuvers. To extend his visit into a good gesture of friendship, he brought his wife, Sophie.

As they drove through the town, these two eminent personages were assassinated. Between the date of this dreary action, June 28, and July 24, the crisis had indeed grown awesome. On July 24 the Austrian government demanded suspension of Serbia as a state and, this refused, on July 28 war was declared.

Archduke Franz Ferdinand, in good health and certainly in the prime of life, had had premonitions of his own violent death. In fact he felt compelled to say to Charles, next in line to the throne, that he knew he would be murdered and that he had prepared everything, including the crypt at Arstetten, his castle in lower Austria.[19]

As a result of this disruption in the "Balkan concert," Europe was at war by August 3. Germany declared war on Russia on August 1. France entered the conflict on August 3, as did England, also declaring war on that date, although technically the war declaration took effect on August 4.

Thus, with the conduct of the war firmly in the prophet's mind, Old went on to indicate, in 1914, that the aging Emperor Franz Joseph did not have long to go. He indicated that tragedy after tragedy had stricken down Franz Joseph's relatives and he now sat in sinister solitude waiting

[19] See Gordon Brook-Shepherd, *The Last Habsburg* (New York: Weybright and Talley, 1968), pp. 3, 27.

for the blow that would end his eventful career—and shortly after that the tocsin of the end of the Hapsburg empire would sound.[20]

Franz Joseph's end came not long after this prophecy was in print. He died of bronchitis and pneumonia on November 21, 1916, in his plainly furnished bedroom in the beautiful Schonbrunn Palace at Vienna. In this same palace Charles signed away his power as Austrian emperor on November 11, 1918, thus ending the Hapsburg dynasty.

Old, successfully it seems, adequately prophesied almost every major enactment during the conduct of World War I. The almost unerring accuracy of his predictions can best be seen in his treatment of William II, German emperor and head of the house of Hohenzollern.

Of this man Old indicated as early as August 1, 1914, that Germany would gather "dead sea fruit of inordinate ambitions." The Hohenzollerns would "bite the dust" and the empire itself would go into an eclipse. Writing in 1915, Old indicated that the "despot will be blinded and the cult of 'Blood and Iron' doomed to extinction, so far, at least, as it finds representation in the person of Kaiser Wilhelm II." [21]

Old saw the end of this remarkable "Beast" as the end of the Hohenzollern dynasty that had for so long dominated the fortunes of Germany. This man would succeed in reaching a safe exile and succor in obscurity, Old stated: " 'Nemesis' awaits upon the earthly representative of the Arch-enemy beginning about April 1918, and will give him a safe conduct to the obscurity which, to one who has attempted such heights, must indeed be a hell of debasement and perdition."

After April 1918 German morale began to collapse. As the Allied forces pressed on, an armistice was signed on November 11, 1918. William II ceased to be kaiser when he signed his abdication on November 28, 1918, after having fled to Holland, where he lived in exile until his death on June 4, 1941, an obscurity that certainly must have been a hell for one who had reached so high.

Contemplating the destiny of Crown Prince William, heir apparent to William II, Old began by saying that the "horoscope of the Crown Prince of Germany is one that the astrologer instantly recognizes as not royal, a decadent horoscope." Old indicated that the crown prince clearly would

[20] W. G. Old, *An Astrological Survey of the Great War, op. cit.*
[21] W. G. Old (Sepharial), *The Great Devastation: A Prophecy of Times That Are Coming Upon Europe* (1915), pp. 9–10.

lose his inheritance. He would be imprisoned in exile, but around 1922 "he would be heard from again, and in due course be made a forlorn hope by a certain coterie of his people in an attempt to regain the Empire." He would set himself up in the image of the "First Beast" and enter, uneventfully, into league with the chancellor. But about 1931 he would be entirely rooted out and there would be another, a "Third Beast" already smoldering with the ambition of *la grande revanche*, a devastation for which the Great War would seem like only a "dress rehearsal."

Crown Prince William followed his father into exile on November 12, 1918. He was held—to all practical purposes a prisoner—by the Dutch on the desolate island of Wieringen in the Zuyder Zee. In 1922 he published his memoirs, with the goal of obtaining allies to help him off the island and back to Germany. He was allowed to leave exile on November 10, 1923. Subsequently, after his return to Germany, he periodically surfaced in vain attempts to realign his position in Germany. In 1931 the chancellor even considered using the crown prince as a front, but this proved unnecessary. And the ambition smoldering in this chancellor's mind already was preparing the way for the "Great Devastation" for which the First World War had been only a dress rehearsal.

Walter Gorn Old, of course, was not totally accurate in all his prophecies. The set concerning the advent of World War I and the personalities involved is extremely interesting, though, since the majority of these prophecies are accurate, specific, and therefore meaningful toward the substantiation that prophetic abilities exist and that men can and do transcend space and time in a multitude of meaningful ways.

Up to the present time the word "logic" has had a definition that has held it to be a science that investigates principles governing correct or reliable inference, or a system of principles of reasoning applicable to any branch of knowledge or study. Perhaps this definition of "logic" might hold for the visible and sensory worlds, where cause-effect relationships are the be-all of existence. In the paranormal realm, however, such definition would go arbitrarily defunct since one would run headlong into the situation presented by the appearance, at a *psychical* level, of manifold universes.

To endeavor toward a definition of "universe," therefore, might present a problem to those who feel, nay insist, that there is only one universe—the physical. Contrariwise, an individual inflowing data from places other than the physical universe might define a "universe" as a system of created things, whether those things be tangible or intangible. There could be, then, many universes.

In addition to the physical universe there would at least be one's own view of things, this constituting a separate universe.

The philosophical mistake, and the supreme philosophical egoism, resides in those who for any number of unknown reasons try to convince others that *their* universe is *the* universe; a good deal of confusion usually comes about in this way.

The situation of psychical perception of future events does not lie any great distance from the concept that one's consciousness determines what is accessible to one. The type of consciousness inflowing and utilizing non-material information need not necessarily confine itself to sensory inputs and might more beneficially follow the real structure of time and space, as contrasted to the materialistic concept of them.

In this wise "logic" might more suitably be defined as a sliding scale of sorting and grouping facts around some problem in the past, present, or future in order to organize it and, most specifically, to predict and resolve the future.

Prediction of future events would therefore constitute only one-half of a psychical ability, with the full ability also carrying actual reorganizing and resolution impact. Psychical research has, almost since its inception, observed prophecy to consist solely of prediction of future events. Those who were somewhat accurate as to dates, places, and so forth were considered hits; others less accurate were misses.

However, another form of prophecy might include not just the titillation of people's nerves with dire predictions but also being able to seize the significances of future trends to do something to ameliorate situations.

This type of "prophet" is not generally recognized by parapsychology—nor, indeed, by society—as a parapsychologically related phenomenon. The type of precognition experienced by psychics seems to provide only that a certain event will happen. This other type of "prophet," sometimes referred to as a genius, foresees achievements or events happening in relation to himself, or as a result of himself bringing the event into being. Thus, with this type of prophet not only is there a paranormal potential evoked but also an action principle. The genius foresees what might be and then goes to work bringing it into being.

There are many examples of this type of prophetic ability cum action. Not only did such scientific geniuses as Kepler, Pascal, and Faraday regard the origin of their abilities as paranormal, but many artistic and literary geniuses and inventors have held they worked with the help of psychic insights.[22]

In one way a man or woman can be said to be the composite of all his or her experience. This experience or composition can occupy memory by pervasion—at which time one can utilize experience to know and understand.

This composition or experience also can at times occupy the consciousness (or subsconsciousness) by force—at which time the person is preoccupied (sometimes compulsively) with dealing in his own composition or experience, this last bringing about mental derangements and psychosomatic illnesses.

It might be fair to say that an individual trying to deal with the contents of his own consciousness is going down and out of a good life, and that the individual reasonably exterior to the contents of his own consciousness (or unconsciousness) can plan a future creatively, whether it be only one moment or a hundred years ahead, and is thereby engaging in psychic and prophetic potential.

Society—and psychic research, of course—usually only grasps and pays attention to the strange, the melodious unnatural, the things that stick out, differing from all else. These often are called psychic. The real, or possibly more complete, psychic lives and succeeds among all, simply because he can plot and plan and succeed at a future.

Cagliostro was a psychic not so much because he traded in the un-

[22] See Roy Dreistadt, "The Prophetic Achievements of Geniuses and Types of Extrasensory Perception," *Psychology* 8, no. 2 (May 1971), pp. 27–40.

natural or verbalized prophecies but because he rose from obscure parentage to a place where his machinations could involve imperial grace (and eventually disgrace). Could he have changed an empire for the better instead of prophesying its bloody end? Who can really say? His metaphysical activities did not necessarily bring about the dissolution of the French monarchy, as the machinations of Rasputin helped to bring down the Russian royal house some two hundred years later.

Yet Cagliostro's success in his own life undoubtedly rested on precognitive abilities, else he could not have structured his path so stealthily up and off an island into fame, fortune, adulation, and cultural influence.

Since Cagliostro's time, and before, there have been multitudes of genius-type individuals who managed to create and develop ideas and trends *against* the common tide of society. One can well imagine that not only did such a genius-type have to create, but also to manage to insert their creations into the general social flows, society usually being against startling changes, especially if those changes meant reorganizations of basic belief systems. Sometimes these individuals succeeded; at other times, they were burnt or imprisoned.

Whether it be mere psychic prophecy or action-oriented prophecy, because prophecy is so illusive, there has been little structure hypothesized for it. In order for there to be prophecy, the prophet has to have an ability to transcend time. In order for prophecy to be of any earthly use, the prophet, or those who listen to him, have to have an ability to act upon the information gained as a result of the prophetic insight. Thus, for social leaders, artists, inventors, etc., and even the ordinary work-a-day person, to make many and continual proper moves toward a future, if those moves are successful, indicates a certitude of prophetic fulfillment. No prophetic fulfillment can exist, however, in the presence of a condition in which "knowns" and "unknowns" look alike. Any prophetic situation, then, should have in its structural elements some sort of an ability aimed at reducing the "unknowns."

This type of reasoning comes extremely close to what today is sometimes called "risk decision analysis," a type of study conducted by the Department of Defense, among others, to study and break down the facets of certainty and uncertainty.[23]

[23] See John Mihalasky, "ESP: Can It Play a Role in Idea-Generation?" *Mechanical Engineering,* December 1972, p. 32.

This type of study, for instance, breaks uncertainty down into "known-unknowns" (where one is aware of one's areas of uncertainty) and "unknown-unknowns" (where one is unaware of one's areas of uncertainty). Thus there is considerable variability in certainties. The winning man understands this, knowing more of what he does not know than the ordinary man, who often assumes that he knows everything. Thus the winning man can at least proceed along a certain prophetic track based upon the increase of decision making that comes merely from being certain of what he does *not* know.

People who feel they know everything about the future will not, of course, be capable of dealing with a future that does not fit in with their preconception, since it will continually take them by surprise. The historical function of the psychic and prophet, those that have been accurate, anyway, has been to inform society about unexpected events that will tumble even the best laid plans and cause the future to sweep off in unexpected directions.

Those men and institutions who predicted the success of the League of Nations, for example, did not include in their predictions the arrival of the unexpected in the form of Hitler, the "Third Beast" clearly predicted by Walter Old.

And so, the problem of prohecy remains.

Only those existing in euphoria can be unaware that our societies are heading toward a future that will make the French Revolution and the two world wars look like staged movie sets. Even so, no one pays much attention and most people actually get quite angry if one does not paint a rosy picture for them.

The inability to confront and try to cope with the needs of the time, the inability to prophetically connect the present to the future, is a nemesis of man. People simply hide their heads and assume that somehow someone will do something about it all.

The future, left unattended to in the present, was indicated in 1969 by the past secretary-general of the United Nations, U Thant, when he said:

> I do not wish to seem overdramatic, but I can only conclude from the information that is available to me as Secretary-General that the Members of the United Nations have perhaps ten years left in which to subordinate their ancient quarrels and launch a global partnership to curb their arms race, to improve the human environment, to defuse the population explosion, and to supply the required momentum to development efforts. If such a global partnership is not forged within the next decade, then I very much fear that the problems I have mentioned will have reached such staggering proportions that they will be beyond our capacity to control.[24]

The ordinary man in the street probably feels that the vague powers allegedly ruling the planet are not doing their job at all well. But there are actually many organizations that are busy trying to predict the future so as to spot what best can be done, such as the Institute for the Future (Brookings) and a working group at the Rand Corporation. Another of these, probably the most famous, is the Club at Rome, which has been trying for quite a while to discover something about the future. Whether these organizations, and several similar ones, will have proved effective, only the future can tell.

The general problem confronting such agencies is that they can indeed predict several alternative futures based upon statistics, trends, hypotheses, ideas, and all the things humans usually try to plot their courses upon —in the absence of psychic inspiration or intuition. Of course it is good to utilize all available data, but such data pass their usefulness after they establish that the future will either be total anarchy or total totalitarian dictatorship or anything in between. What will in fact occur will be anyone's guess, but anything is possible based upon present data.

Thus the fields of social prediction and development usually are divided in any of several directions as they go about attempting to establish futures for mankind. Naturally social policy planners cannot stop working just because of this ambiguous situation.

One agency involved in future matters is the Educational Policy

[24] Quoted in Robert Theobald, "Challenge of a Decade: Global Development or Global Breakdown," pamphlet prepared for the United Nations Centre for Economic and Social Information, 1969.

PROPHECY

Research Center at Stanford Research Institute, carefully monitored by its director, Dr. Willis Harman. Harman's credentials are miles long. Rather than recite them, it is more to the point to say of Harman that he is a good humanitarian, nervous about the future of humans.

It was my endless pleasure, while at Stanford Research Institute, to have conversations with this man about the swiftly oncoming future and to become familiar, through him, with some of the truly staggering problems facing my generation and those immediately to follow.

One evening while we were driving to Berkeley to give a small seminar on progress in parapsychology and related areas of interest, we discussed the common social planning problem of not knowing which future, of all possible types of futures, is truly in the offing. As desperation increases in official centers, there has been a great deal of speculation about the possibility of utilizing psychics to probe the future, to give some ideas about what might come along. Of course this type of speculation is extremely unofficial and quite off any public records.

As it was, I myself had given considerable attention to this possibility. Many people who become successful in business or science, or even politics, often confess to extraordinary circumstances. I knew personally at least half a dozen psychics who had good track records for accurate prediction, and three seemed to be in especially good harmony as far as ideals and goals were concerned.

For example, one of these had predicted in 1969 that Richard M. Nixon would come close to being or actually be either impeached or incapacitated before he left the White House. Another had indicated in June 1961 that a Cuban named Rafael would become a leader in creating discontent, racial strife, and various economic difficulties in many countries. And on February 14, 1962, Rafael Rodriguez replaced Castro as president of the powerful Cuban Agrarian Reform Institute, this Rafael having long been an important functionary in the Kremlin's Latin American machinery.

Yet another of these psychically gifted acquaintances had predicted in 1972 such an unlikely occurrence as a fire in New York's tallest building, the World Trade Center, an event that occurred in the second part of January 1973.

All three of these modern prophets had predicted—well before it came about or was even hinted at in the daily press—an impending gas and oil shortage that would result in rationing in many American states, an event that occurred in late 1973 and early 1974.

Before Dr. Harman and I had reached Berkeley, we had cooked up a project where three psychics would be invited to consider the next twenty-year period, in order (1) to find out if their predictions would agree or not and (2) to take the agreed-upon points, if any, and construct from them a prophetic insight that would overlay social policy prediction indicating which of the many possible futures would be most likely to occur.

The resulting report is here quoted in full.

Introduction

As a result of a conversation in May 1973 between Dr. Willis Harman and Mr. Ingo Swann, on the topic of alternative future histories and the many difficulties encountered in methods of adequate prediction, it was wondered if prophetic abilities seemingly held by some individuals might be employed to some constructive end.

It was agreed that Mr. Swann would obtain the consent of three individuals with good prophetic track records to give consideration to the future, and likely conditions which might come about.

Dr. Harman agreed to submit a guide indicating areas of general societal interest, which reads as follows:

QUESTIONS ON THE FUTURE

Present trends (expanding technology, increasing affluence, increasing urbanization, automation and cybernation of white-collar work, lengthening lifespan and earlier retirement age) continue to increase the severity of assorted societal problems—depletion of natural resources, particularly minerals and fossil fuels; impact of growing energy demands on the environment (strip mining, air pollution, radioactive waste, etc.); technological disemployment, unemployment and underemployment; growing welfare and social security load; increasing technological impact on the environment, rights of privacy and liberty, quality of life. Increased costs of producing goods and services, arising partly from labor demands for higher real income and improved working environment, and partly from environmentalist, consumer, and civil rights pressures for greater corporate social responsibility, are reducing the relative competitiveness of American industry. Possible consequences of this may include further automation and cybernation, leading to further disemployment, and further exodus of multinational production to other countries. The scramble for resources, and the increasing gap between have and have-not nations, made more visible by worldwide communications, will continue to threaten world peace.

In view of these factors, what is likely to be the state of the nation and of the world with regard to unemployment, welfare costs, economic and monetary crises, role of multinational corporations, environmental and ecological crises, perceived legitimacy of business and government institutions, citizen morale and sense of national purpose, etc., in 1975? In 1980? In 1985? In 1990?

What actions or significant events might alter these predictions, and in what way?

Consent of three individuals residing in different parts of the country was obtained, and, based upon Dr. Harman's guide, they agreed to attempt psychic penetration into future conditions.

All three individuals (referred to below as Participants A, B and C) indicate that their attempt at prediction must be considered only as a research endeavour, and should not be considered as meaningful beyond that.

The Participants unanimously agreed that major interest of their renderings should center on comparative data that might emerge among them, and that the comparative data should then be viewed in association with likely future scenarios already hypothetically constructed.

All Participants felt obliged to submit that it was extremely difficult emotionally as well as psychically to involve their sensitivities in the direction of prophecy as suggested by the guide, not because the guide was not specific or comprehensive, but because of the apparent negative characteristics of the immediate future. Participant A indicated that he had not wanted to see and feel what came to him and Participant B experienced similar apprehension. Participant C felt overwhelmed at his view of the swift negative changes he perceived.

Thus, if adequate emotional withdrawal could have resulted justifiably in non-participation, all three Participants did endeavour to overcome their resistance and submit renderings of their views.

The Participants did not discuss the guide between them prior to submitting their renderings, and did not have the opportunity to compare notes. Scientifically, this separateness seems desirable and in the best interests of research. But this purity of contact might also be considered as depriving the Participants of mutual emotional intellectual support in the humanistic sense. It is possible to hold therefore that this same type of experiment conducted mutually and in conversation with one another might produce more comprehensive, possibly precise results.

The present to 1975

The Participants unanimously submitted that out of the coming twenty-year period questioned in the guide, the immediate future itself would be of extreme concern and would create the greatest amount of difficulties to be experienced during the next twenty years. All Participants indicate that the major concern would revolve around economic considerations and disappointments.

Participant A indicated that the next few years now loom as threatening to our very way of life, particularly if the American dollar and our monetary troubles cannot be stabilized. Money values will change drastically, which will in turn have impact on welfare, social security and other programs, as well as wages. Participant B felt that economically, the bottom has not been reached. He suggested that September and October of 1973 will see another major slump, and during the late spring of 1974 the economic foundations will crumble. Policies of price and wage control and government underwriting of major corporations will prove to have been ineffectual. Participant C indicated increasing fluidity of the dollar, and indicated that prior to 1975, several government institutions will come increasingly under critical attack. Major among these will be welfare costs and personal income tax which more and more people will realize exclude each other during this impending time of financial collapse.

Participant A indicated that the practice of imposing the cost of all change on the consumer will reach the saturation point and bring about increasing protests and boycotts, while Participant B suggested that personal security itself will become of great concern. He indicated that the many structures built up in the name of security, such as international trade agreements, unions, social security, welfare, minimum wages, mammoth insurance companies and over-powerful police forces have been supported in the name of security, but will in fact have passed their effective point and create an opposite effect. He felt that this insecurity will have its effects in transportation, publishing, the media, advertising, politics and religion.

Participant A suggested that public confidence will become badly shaken, and that a type of martial law may eventuate leading to a new form of government. Participant C indicated that many attempts will be undertaken to establish through authoritarian methods bureaux to limit and control the spread and development of public reactions to unrest, as well as of many areas of current high interest, such as the vitamin and food supplement industries, and various introspective methods of developing personal knowledge and expansion of awareness.

The Participants were unanimous in predicting that, as strife and turmoil increase, the establishment of novel and strong controls will eventuate in even more severe conditions of unrest.

Participant A suggested that out of this turmoil and period of great uncertainty may well emerge a hybrid political party, growing out of the most respected Republican and Democratic leaders, who would seek a fusion to protect the more desirable elements of both political concepts. Participant B supported this prediction in that he felt that the president elected in the next election will be neither Republican nor Democrat—or he could be both Republican and Democrat. Participant C submitted that political leaders will conform more and more to demands of economy and population stress, and that political bias will weaken and subsequently a new, hybrid concept of political direction will occur. The men most likely to succeed to many levels of office will represent this compromise politic.

The Participants were unanimous in considering that the "energy crisis" is real and most serious, not only for the United States, but for the world as a whole.

Participant A states that the most critical for all humanity is the coming energy crisis, and unless extreme steps are taken to alleviate the situation, the fight for possession of the present existing fuel supply will bring about an enormous conflict. Participant B indicated that the energy crises will continue and grow more severe, both in electrical failures and in oil and gas shortages. According to Participant C, control and domination of the world's energy sources is already of chief concern to various multinational corporate leaders. He indicated that this rush to acquire world rights, both in natural resources and in industrially produced goods, is already well under way, and will be seen by 1975 to have contributed to world-wide economic dislocations. Many recognizable economic corporations will suffer, and perhaps disappear as these new multinational organizations cause massive shifts in economic interests. Participant B indicated that many large corporations involved in economic security and communications will fold or experience severe economic cuts.

Participant A felt that citizen morale will be seriously affected, and that attempts to curb inflation will not keep prices from rising, but will lead to widespread unemployment, industrial shut-downs, foodstuffs in short supply, and massive discontent and concern. Because of emergent difficulties, Participant C indicated that many governmental systems, hitherto non-economic or non-profit in legal character, will begin openly to depend upon and be influenced by the actions of various world-wide economic interests. He further felt that currently invisible financial structures are being made to monitor and control world produce and natural resources.

The Participants feel that the present difficulties in economy are enlarged far beyond the information provided in the public data systems, and that only extreme creative plans might alleviate the situation. These creative actions seem unlikely, and thus it is possible to predict forward from the situation which will obtain in the absence of ameliorative programs.

The Participants thus agreed prophetically that world economic interests and associated energy production difficulties constitute the crux of the future immediate.

Descending from this unyielding situation will be an immediate period of public unrest, possibly violent. Some governmental institutions will come under attack, authoritative methods of population control and movement will appear. There will be the emergence, in the United States, of a uniparty system, and world-wide beginnings of multicorporate unifications involving many countries.

1975–1980

The Participants agreed unanimously in their renderings that between 1975 and 1980 a period of human interchange will emerge, characterized by new concepts both in spirituality and human potential. Participant B predicted that out of the despair of the early seventies will come a period of searching for spiritual security, which will contribute more permanence than the physical, material security of the 1929–1974 period. Participant A suggested that science will have brought irrefutable knowledge of man's psychic potential and of dimensions beyond the physical senses. Both Participants B and C indicated closer linkage of science and parapsychology.

Participant C indicated that this transition will produce a new heroic image of man visible as early as 1974 or before. This image, in its various forms, will be utilized by eco-political groups that will also use cultural/religio leaders to manipulate population sectors, and will permit and encourage certain of these to emerge.

The Participants all indicate sternly great religious change. Participant A stated that "religion, as man has known it, is on the way out." Participant B echoed this prophecy by stating that "dogmatism and structure are on their way out." Participant C foresees intense ideologically fluid conditions during this period tending to snap existing religio/political structures.

Participant A indicated that as a result of vast human need, there will emerge certain people who possess a potential for a new kind of practical spiritual and yet non-religious leadership to which the masses can respond and thus help stabilize their emotions in a time of great crisis. This period will also see attempts of wrongly motivated individuals to take advantage of chaotic economic and social conditions by presenting programs that promise salvation for the masses, but which lead instead into abject slavery and domination. Participant B felt that although a new "messiah" will arrive on the scene, this will not be in the historical sense, but rather collective or group inspired. Participant C indicated that, ironically, the establishment of authoritarian bureaux to control social enterprise will provide a social element in which several charismatic leaders can emerge. Several of these will appeal to the masses, while certainly one will head a form of inspired fascism, supported in this nation by a cadre of mysterious individuals.

Participant A indicated that during this period the energy crisis will become severe enough to encourage the release of new ideas and inventions long bought or held off the market by vested interests. Participant B felt that methods of drive and locomotion that use less or no gasoline will be developed, while Participant C felt that during this period several international corporations will release several new power sources, but will retain control over them.

The Participants all predicted that welfare and later social security will become defunct during this period, as will unions, creating an extremely fluid social context as millions seek to restabilize their lives without these artificial securities.

The 1975–1980 period, therefore, if characterized by neo-spiritual and parapsychological as well as new energy developments, will also be characterized by politico/religious restructuring, which the Participants felt cannot be without repercussions on all strata of society. The vast change will sponsor dramatic emergences of personalities who will tend to lead masses in different directions both in personal as well as in social awareness. Behind the scenes, this socio/religio manifestation will be utilized by various political and economic interests to curtail or influence popular thought. This fluid social situation will not be without its extreme difficulties, and will be aggravated by the cessation, at least in the United States, of the economic security currently represented by welfare and social security.

1980–2000

Although the guide asked for prophetic responses beyond 1980, it was increasingly difficult for the Participants to use their sensitivities concretely beyond 1985. Not enough comparative data on the 1980–1985 period was submitted by the Participants to create a correlative research report.

All Participants, however, signaled some great world-wide change around 1985. Participant A indicated that beyond 1985 he saw little left but a jungle where once was a promising civilization. Participant B indicated that he could not see the outcome beyond 1985, but indicated that to him it seemed like a giving up of all technology and a returning to nature in one segment and a highly structured scientific space age on the other. Participant C felt that around 1985 something would happen in relation to human potential that would bring current concepts of man to an end.

Concluding remarks

If it could be assumed that the above conditions were likely to come about, it is clearly to be understood that ameliorative actions to be taken on the part of social leaders and governmental systems should have to be of extreme nature. These actions would have to be gauged not only toward the handling of national present-time problems, but involve a severe restructuring of man's view of himself as a whole.

The Participants submitted unanimously that whatever improvements taken by nations unilaterally to lessen local problems would constitute only a temporary relief for that nation, since the situation involves world-wide economic, political and philosophical balances.

It was felt by the Participants, therefore, that only cooperation at the international level toward the creation of a new image of man based upon far-reaching and significant real discovery—as contrasted to illusory—of man's potential would alter the predictions they have made.

The "tree" (Figure 19) of Alternative Future Histories, published by the Educational Policy Research Center in February 1971, rearranged according to the foregoing predictions, would constitute a pattern something like that described as Figure 20 (see Annex B).

The foregoing report was compiled and finished in July 1973. In compiling the data of the three subjects for similarities, it was amazing to find that all three participating psychics perceived much the same future for the world, up to 1985, at which point they felt some truly extraordinary event would take place.

This future history, in the various realms in which it dealt, presented, it was felt, a rather gloomy outlook. It was therefore not widely circulated, even though it was considered a genuine prophetic attempt at predicting general future trends—trends that several sociologists and political experts readily recognized. There was no direct evidence in July 1973 that the events portrayed were likely.

In the interim enough time and events have passed to show a high correlation for the pre-1975 predictions, with actual trends as they have come to pass; enough correlation at any rate to indicate that prophetic abilities were present in all three subjects and that the prophetic abilities aligned with each other to an amazing degree.

At the beginning of 1974, when some of the predicted events were visible, I decided to include this experiment in group prophecy in this book, and add to it a sequel. Another request to the three participating subjects was sent out asking for positive events in the future that might offset some of the gloomy trends as predicted.

Responses to this request were a long time in coming; once more, all three indicated that it was extremely difficult to concentrate or "see" into the times ahead. And for the most part, the participants agreed that many events coming are "reaction" events to trends and actions that have taken place in the immediate past—reaction events for which there seem no rectifying occurrences in the future.

The participants agreed on one point, however, a point that I feel is quite extraordinary. Extraordinary because if true such an event would undoubtedly exert encouraging trends in many different human interests.

Participant A indicated that "I can foresee that a Manhattan type research project will soon be formed to explore the potential of several inventions that promise the development of metals possessing such high conductivity that they will permit the extraction of electromagnetic energy direct from air and provide an unlimited source of power." Participant B confirmed this expectation by saying that although there will be many small energy crises before being able to use new energy sources, there will be the "allocating of funds by the federal government to develop either solar or nuclear energy," or "the allocating of such funds by a single individual." Participant C indicated that "without doubt there will be discovery (perhaps there has been already) of unlimited energy sources utilizing electromagnetic potentials as well as undreamt of recognition of the enormous resources the oceans hold for mankind."

All three participants, therefore, agreed upon the imminent discovery and development of in-depth resources of energy, an event that if it were to occur would sponsor a renewed outlook for today's populaces beleaguered by energy shortages and all the machinations in politics and finance that descend from this situation.

Granting the foibles of human existence, it is unfair and indecent to continually deluge the constructive attributes of men to a conflagration of the Armageddon yet to come.

This the sane man himself will anticipate, since it should be visible and acknowledged that as long as man—and humanity itself—is victim to an inability to handle the environment, to be effect of instead of cause over ideas of himself and as long as visions include an either/or principle concerning *potential* actions instead of some sort of all-encompassing rationale to actually do what is future-oriented instead of doing what one thinks is right, Armageddons will probably proliferate on all sides.

PART V
To Kiss Earth Good-bye

> We live in succession, in division, in parts, in particles. Meantime within man is the Soul; the wise silence; the universal beauty, to which every part and particle is equally related.
> —*Ralph Waldo Emerson*

One of the most interesting of all prophecies was made during the course of World War I, that sequence of years that produced an utter epidemic of visionaries.

The Rawson prophecy predicted the end of the world of materialism during the course of the year 1917, and more precisely about December 3 or 4. F. L. Rawson was a well-known teacher of what might be called an "independent Christian Science," not related to that of the famous Mrs. Eddy. Rawson seems to have had a great advantage over mere physical mortals in that he had realized, by some means, that the real spiritual man knew instantly anything he needed. He apparently gave many lectures demonstrating this opinion at the various centers where instruction was given on the workings of the mind.

Materialistic psychology was at this time in strong ascendancy, and doubtless not much official attention was paid to his teachings.

Rawson indicated that not only was the end of the Great War approaching in 1917 but also the end of matter itself, the end of a solely materialistic concept of things. He drew this inspired prophecy (probably published during 1915) from a reworking of certain biblical prophecies, especially the meaning of Revelations xii:16.* He concluded that "earth" meant the scientific world and "woman" the highest spiritual ideal. He

---

* This author has attempted a survey of the biblical texts referred to by Rawson, but whatever line of reasoning Rawson utilized remains quite arcane and I am tempted to conclude that the cited biblical passage served only as a point of thought for Rawson's abilities to coalesce into cogent prophecy.

realized from this that the natural scientist was to make clear the difference between working with the materialistic concept of mind and working by turning in thought.[1] He further indicated that this awesome event would be recognizable by the fact that the "notice" of the ending of the solely materialistic concept of things would be when in 1917 a "theory" to that effect would be "circulated" in written form.

It is exceedingly interesting to observe that, although it was first introduced in 1905, the year 1917 saw the publication of Albert Einstein's general theory of relativity, a theory that indeed brought a solely materialistic cause-effect idea of things to an abrupt end.[2]

Of course Einstein's computations cannot easily be understood by those of us who have not carried our study of mathematics very far. But his theory generally establishes that while ordinary physical mathematical computations refer to only three dimensions—length, breadth, and thickness—his computations presuppose four dimensions. According to his theory of relativity, measurements yielding different results may be equally true or right since measurements in general would be relative to a frame or system of reference. Einstein's theory is still called theory and not a law, despite the amazing mass of evidence that has accumulated to support its validity.[3]

---

[1] An original copy of the Rawson prophecy could not be located by this author. However, extended reference to it is found in a book published in 1917. See Countess Zalenski, *Noted Prophecies Concerning the Great War and the Great Changes to Follow*. (Chicago: Yogi, 1917). The original prophecy was apparently published by Rawson under the title *The War and the Great World Changes to Follow*.

[2] During the course of 1917 and during subsequent years, the introduction of the general theory of relativity inspired avalanches of papers in all directions. A general blow-by-blow account of the first issuance, possibly fulfilling the Rawson prophecy, can be found in Albert Einstein, *The Principles of Relativity,* trans. M. N. Saha and S. N. Bose with historical introduction by P. C. Mahalanobis (Calcutta: University of Calcutta, 1920).

[3] As has been seen, Hume worked very hard to establish that there were only two methods available to science: experience and mathematical derivations. He can be considered the father of the logical-empirical approach. His idea rejects all metaphysical auxiliary conceptualizations if these could not be rooted and established in experience and by logical derivation. Einstein first published his theory, worked out between 1902 and 1905, as "Zur Elektrodynamik bewegter Körper" (On the electrodynamics of moving bodies) in *Annalen der Physik*, 1905, p. 891. His theory was completed in 1916 in Berlin and published in *Annalen der Physik*, 1916, p. 49, under the title "Die Grundlage der allgemeinen Relativitatstheorie" (The basis

In physics the situation created by the introduction of the general theory of relativity has been both problematical and productive, and if evidence amasses, the situation is by no means yet resolved.[4] Aside from the now obvious fact that the physical universe itself can be measured differently depending upon frames of reference, so also can the mind, which by observation is capable of assuming just about any frame of reference within the grasp or tolerance of its possessor.[5]

Now any approach leading toward understanding and illumination of psychic processes is not going to be obtained by claques of dowdy, mystically oriented personages flocking to seances. Rather it will be required that people study and consume the structure of mind itself prior to grasping even the fundamentals of psychic interaction.

---

of the general theory of relativity). It was only in 1917 that English translations began to circulate in England, Rawson's territory. Among the verification experiments that could be carried out was a confirmation of Einstein's prediction on the shift in the position of the stellar images during a total solar eclipse. Another set of papers, possibly pertaining to the Rawson prophecy, were those issued by the astronomer royal who had pointed out as early as March 1917 that a total eclipse would take place on March 29, 1919. This eclipse would offer unusually favorable conditions for testing, since the darkened sun would be situated in the midst of a group of particularly important and bright stars, the Hyades. The Royal Society and the Royal Astronomical Society of London began early to make preparations for this experiment. When the armistice was signed on November 11, 1918, the appointed astronomical committee announced detailed plans for the solar viewing expedition. Einstein's prediction was verified, and he was hastily awarded the Nobel prize in physics for 1921. Einstein himself considered the philosophical implications of his discoveries. See especially Albert Einstein, "Space and Time in Pre-relativity Physics," *The Meaning of Relativity,* four lectures delivered at Princeton University, May 1921 (Princeton, N.J.: Princeton University Press, 1923), pp. 1–25.

[4] The lay reader will find some of these difficulties described in understandable form in an excellent book prepared for general information pertinent to science in general: See Guy Murchie, *Music of the Spheres: The Material Universe—from Atom to Quasar, Simply Explained* (New York: Dover, 1967), 2 vols.

[5] This problem, of course, boggles psychology, which clings to the mechanistic approach of the mind. A more cogent approach to the nitty-gritties involved can be found in Ya. P. Terletskii, *Paradoxes in the Theory of Relativity* (New York: Plenum Press, 1968), 2 vols., especially Chapter V, "Are Velocities Higher than the Velocity of Light Possible?", pp. 65ff. It is indicated that, hypothetically, the admission of hyperlight signals is equivalent to the admission of the possibility that the temporal sequence of signal emission and absorption can be changed by a suitable choice of a frame of reference, a hypothesis that, when overlaid on concepts of "mind," constitutes the psychic paradox.

During the last century, as mentioned, William Kingdon Clifford first approximated this idea when he suggested that thought might be just a hill in the geometry of space. This reflective musing was reiterated decades later by Dr. Carl G. Jung:

> it is dawning upon us to what an extent our whole experience of so-called reality is psychic; as a matter of fact, everything thought, felt, or perceived is a psychic image, and the world itself exists only so far as we are able to produce an image of it. We are so deeply impressed with the truth of our imprisonment in, and limitation by, the psyche that we are ready to admit the existence in it even of things we do NOT know; we call them "the unconscious." [6]

Hypothetically it might be established that, if thought were indeed mere hills in the geometry of space and if the world does exist only so far as we are able to produce an image of it, then things psychic could be merely unfamiliar geography in the desert of existence beyond individual or group imagination.

Undertaking to substantiate this would drag on interminably, the chief obstacle being man's current concept of himself. It is much easier and to the point to give an anecdote that will show how men do indeed view things from different frames of reference.

The English physician Edward Jenner, born in 1749, observed one lucky day that milkmaids who had suffered the disease of cowpox on their hands seemed immune to smallpox. He got the idea that perhaps, if an individual was injected to a small degree with the dead virus of the disease, a sort of immunity to the disease itself would be established.

He proved that this was true when he successfully vaccinated John Phipps in 1796.

But this new and extraordinarily beneficial concept was not to progress very easily at first. As might be expected, various individuals were concerned that it went against accepted dicta. Reverend Edward Massey, an English theologian, began preaching against vaccination for smallpox in 1772 and eventually published a sermon entitled "The Dangerous and Sinful Practice of Inoculation."

---

[6] C. G. Jung, "Psychological Commentary on 'The Tibetan Book of the Great Liberation,'" *Psychology and Religion: East and West* (New York: Pantheon, 1963), p. 479.

He felt the practice went against the idea that diseases are dispensed by "Providence" as punishment for those who have sinned. Furthermore, he indicated that the disease of Job—smallpox—had been given him by the devil; it had to follow that any proposed attempt to interfere with the disease was a diabolical operation.

This hue and cry was picked up in Boston by the Anti-Vaccination Society, formed by a group of physicians and clergymen in order to denounce the practice of vaccination as going against the will of God. This in 1798, only two years after Jenner had managed to succeed in demonstrating the verity of his discovery.

The common human failing, not only in viewing things psychic, but in existence in general, is to make what is perceived conform to personal frames of reference, thereby *reducing* awareness of existence to that point of reference. Conversely, the expansive awarenesses would shift viewpoints and frames of reference to glean all possible implications out of what was seen. The reductive pattern is most frequent, though.

To illustrate an example of this kind of reduction, a quantity of what seemed to be envelope-sized flakes of dried "beef" fell from the sky on March 3, 1876, in Bath County, Kentucky.[7] This appears to have been a somewhat "organized" fall, arranging itself to cover a strip of land some fifty yards wide by a hundred yards long.

This wonder was investigated by a Leopold Brandeis, who concluded that this flesh-colored substance was not beef at all but nostoc, a blue-green freshwater jellylike algae often found in moist places. He advised that it had fallen with the rain and his conclusion was published in the *Scientific American Supplement* of the time.

Another investigator, one Professor Smith, felt that the substance was the dried spawn of some reptile, probably a frog. But this rendering was rejected by the president of the Newark Scientific Association, a Dr. A. Mead Edwards, who apparently had consulted with a Dr. Hamilton, who had advised that the fall was lung tissue. As to exactly how it had fallen, no theory was officially advanced, although unofficially it was held that some buzzards so high in the sky as to be invisible had disgorged their latest meal.

[7] See Charles Fort in *The Book of the Damned,* Boni & Liveright, London, 1919. See also *The New York Times,* March 10, 1876, for first public reporting of this event.

Another investigator supposed that a herd of cows somewhere had somehow been sucked up into the sky, shredded, and dried, with the remains thus deposited in Bath County.

At any rate the substance soon began to decompose and the local inhabitants were compelled to bury it for health reasons. Everyone could conveniently put this event aside, although the substance was listed as late as 1918 in the May issue of the *Monthly Weather Review* as having been dried spawn of some batrachians or fish.

Now, it is quite apparent from the reports that the "dried beef" was a thoroughly unfamiliar substance, yet there are no reports that admit to this. And the several explanations as to what the stuff was and as to how it got there are certainly some of the most liberal and far-fetched I have ever come across. At any rate, this example is simply a fascinating exposé of academic attempts to neatly slot everything into the familiar.

There was a time, not so long ago, when the unfamiliar, the impossible, developed an impressive sequence right in front of me. There was no slot for it, and having to accept it at face value caused me to have to change my ideas considerably.

I have not been as successful as a subject for exploration of extra-normal effects as I have been interested in them. Nonetheless, I have often been asked how it was that I came to be able to produce the effects I have in laboratories. The answer is relatively easy: I decided simply that such things were possible and I was determined to find out about them. Why was I determined to find out? Because of a chinchilla.

One cold afternoon in the early spring of 1970 this author passed a pet store on Greenwich Avenue in New York, barely glancing in the window. I had gotten several buildings along when I realized that in that window was something I had never seen before.

Going back to look, I saw there among the disgusting fat and lazy guinea pigs a bit of gray fluff that resembled an extremely large mouse with a bushy tail. When it perceived that I was studying it closely, it disported itself with great gusto, running around in circles on the backs of the other lethargic animals and running up and down the chicken wiring cage.

After regarding it for a while, I went along and forgot about it in the rush of trying to survive in New York.

Thoughts of this unidentified animal crept in every once in a while for about two weeks, and finally I had to go and solve the mystery. Back at the pet store I was informed that this was a chinchilla. After studying him for a while, noticing that there seemed to be a fiery glint in his deep, limpid eyes that I liked, I bought him and named him Mercenary.

For several months little happened. He lived in a box on my desk and never ventured beyond. He was marvelous, his deep, sparkling eyes set in a gray face surrounded by long whiskers and miniature elephant ears. This animal for some reason seemed to me to be one of the most amazing biological inventions ever conceived in the mind of "evolution," and he was never to be anything but a complete joy to watch.

One day, however, he remembered that chinchillas can jump and run some twenty miles an hour, and our relationship began to change swiftly. Also his appetites wandered from carrots, celery, and rabbit pellets to books, pencils, typewriter ribbons, furniture, wood, and the telephone cord.

Hastily put into a makeshift cage, he stared out at the world with a soulful look that was positively heartrending. So, since his urine didn't stink and his droppings came out rock-hard and could be vacuumed up, I relented and, after taking precautions on what was chewable, let him have the run of the apartment.

It wasn't long before I understood that this was a thinking beast since he could obviously plot and plan his moves and figure out how to get at things of interest to him. Chinchillas have an opposable digit on their front feet, so they can use them almost like hands.

At night, however, since he was likely to push things off onto the floor, making great crashes that would bring one suddenly out of a sound sleep, he had to be relegated to his cage. There he stared out, his eyes sparkling with fury at the indignity of it. But chinchillas are nocturnal rodents.

Thus he tended to become scarce when it came time for him to go into his cage each night. I was obliged to search for him, and he never hid in the same place twice. This got to be a problem, since it sometimes took half an hour to discover him and then considerable time to chase him into the bathroom where I could get hold of him.

But he was magnificent, and his intelligence and learning patterns were superb.

One night, however, while I was sitting in front of the tube, Mercenary jumped up on my knee to have his chin and ears scratched, which he liked. The TV program was exceedingly boring, as usual, so I thought I would go to bed early. At the merest thought, the gray fluff rose instantly about two feet in the air and vanished from view. I had not moved at all when the thought of putting him in his cage occurred. Yet he tore off in a gray cloud and the typical search and chase were on.

Up to this time, although I had always had a great interest in the occult and in things psychic, the interest had been merely academic. Awareness of things psychic was part of my makeup, being based on childhood memories, but in no way was there abilities extant at that time.

It came as a stunning recognition, therefore, when sitting before the television, my finger still trying to scratch the chin of the now vanished gray fluff, I realized that he had obviously picked up my thought. No words will reflect my astonishment. I will only say that, whatever the collective concepts of thought and existence in my head, all of them collapsed in that moment into a heap of shards in my mental cellar.

For several days I was busy testing this out. I would think of putting him in his cage at very unlikely times. The effect was superb. After what appears to have been a brief learning period, he refused to react but would sit upon his hind legs, his eyes blazing, his tail switching back and forth, while he mentally probed my mind to find out if I meant it or if this was just another testing sequence. I brought in one or two friends, explaining to them beforehand that when I winked at them *they* were to "think" about putting Mercenary in his cage. The results were always immediate.

Amazement and excitement about Mercenary's telepathic abilities lasted about three weeks before the implications began to set in. These began perhaps with the conclusion that, if all chinchillas were similarly telepathic and we humans had to fight a war with them, we would certainly lose.

Once a full understanding of his telepathic nature set in, a great deal about him seemed reasonable. He knew, for instance, when I was thinking about feeding him, since he always appeared promptly. He knew when I was displeased with him for chewing up two volumes of the Encyclopedia Britannica, and so he did not attack the rest of the volumes thereafter.

A dreadful implication finally rose to consciousness. Mercenary could pick up my thoughts, *but I couldn't pick up his.*

This situation and its dismal implications were mulled about for several weeks. A chinchilla, of all things, could obviously apprehend mere thoughts, and human thoughts at that. Admittedly, he only reacted to thoughts that had something to do with his personal habits, but this minimal reaction was in itself sufficient to bring my own ideas about things psychic to paralysis.

This feat on his part surely brought into question the ego poise humans hold of themselves as a superior species. Interactions of a nonspecific, obviously nonmaterial nature were taking place, and had been taking place before I become aware of them. Continued thought on this topic became extremely complex, and the reader need not be bored with such ramblings.

Suffice it to say that, after several weeks of fighting for some sort of intellectual stability in this matter, one supreme consideration emerged. Mercenary could perceive and apprehend my thoughts. However confused the logic might appear in the matter, his perception of my thoughts could not exist unless a similar potential existed within me, since this obviously was an *interaction.* a *meeting* of mind, and not a cause-effect situation.

His reaction to the cause of my thought obviously was linear, hence cause-effect, but his apperception of thought was of a different magnitude. I no longer cared what he did because of my thoughts; I only cared that the hook-up could exist.

This suggested a simultaneity of ability on both our parts, else it could not possibly be. It was only my awareness, my own intellectual poise and standards of how existence should be perceived that prevented me from encompassing its nature.

Mercenary has gone on to his own future, disappearing one day into the wilderness of New York—which was all right since whatever fate he met in the big city was better than being cooped up in an apartment he hated.

But this small, gray, luxurious beast, whose pelt might have been used for an expensive coat, left me an almost incalculable heritage: His psychic potential, certainly of the first water, caused me to hastily begin to reorganize my thought systems.

As a result I know there is a spark in everyone, the potential of which exceeds any authority that says "impossible."

This mental "reorganization" has engendered a view of existence for which there are few descriptive words. It is a view from which there will be no recanting or retracting; it is a view for which the word "psychic" perhaps is descriptive, but only minimally so; it is a view in which—for me only, perhaps, since no one else need acquiesce in it—the future has new meaning and value. It is a view that includes many possible universes, other ways of looking at and participating in things. As with Clifford, Rawson, possibly Jung, it is possible to think that I am the thinker. If so, indeed I kiss Earth good-bye.

The problems—the social, psychological and metaphysical confusions—that arise from the possibility of the validity of things psychic are monumental.

They are not unfamiliar, however, and many qualified thinkers have tried an approach to them.

In the past things psychic definitely fell into the realms of the magical, certainly outside the rational.

Modern research has made sufficient gain to be able to state that things psychic, even though often appearing to be magical or mystical, probably are not. They seem to have enough structure at least to be observed statistically, although their structure admittedly must be outside the rationale of materialism since it cannot be found within it. This structure invariably leads in the direction that implies there is more to man than the physical material body.

In the terms of modern parapsychological research this situation was cogently described as early as 1941 by the now famous parapsychologist

Dr. J. B. Rhine.[8] Modern psychic research has sought to gain credence within the scientific milieu by attempting to subject things psychic to the empirical method, that is, to be guided by observation and experiment alone without using theory. But it seems apparent that, although trying to stay somewhat within the guidelines of empirical investigation, many parapsychologists have allowed themselves raptures of quasi theory that cannot be said to really rest upon empirical evidence at all. Still, many have correctly confined themselves to speculation upon probabilities and possibilities, without embroidering these with interpretation.

Rhine felt that ESP experiments contributed something in support of an "extraphysical" situation. This extraphysical concept, even if delineated obliquely in ESP research, carries severe implications tending to support historical concepts of the existence of soul, metaphysical self, psyche, and so forth. So if one allows oneself to get into thinking along these lines one is as likely as not to get involved in the labyrinth of ponderous historical jibberish about the existence of the soul, etc.

Rhine, however, was more creative than that, although his speculations on the matter seem to have passed almost unnoticed by many subsequent researchers. He pointed out that, assuming extraphysical implications of ESP, anything escaping the limitations of space and time "represents immortality in itself." Further, anything released from the limitations of space has infinity, and anything not subjected to time has eternity. He cautioned that, should times and spaces eventually be discovered that we today do not know, these discoveries, of course, would modify his concepts.

He then pointed out that, assuming the existence of an extraphysical or incorporeal entity, such entity would require ESP abilities for the assumption or acquisition of knowledge, as well as "a capacity for psychophysical causation in order to produce effects upon the physical world."

Rhine was not the first mortal to speculate upon the possibility of the immortal. He was preceded at least by the authors of the quite ancient—in Earth time—Vedas, followed by the wise Greeks. But his hypothesis, turning up well within the boundaries of a distinctly materialistic epoch, seems clarion.

But contemporary parapsychologists have approached this implication

[8] See J. B. Rhine, "It Follows from ESP," *The Journal of the American Society for Psychical Research* 35, no. 6 (1941), pp. 191–195.

obliquely. Strenuous attempts have constantly been made to allot and confine the nonmaterial to psychology, energetics, biology, and lastly physics—that is, to any of the sciences utterly dedicated to materialism. In one way, perhaps with equal obliqueness, the efforts of science to do this are really not very different in character from the approach of occultists who tend toward the opposite extreme, trying to bend all materialistic things into occult, quasi-theoretical ideas of the immortal, the infinite, the ethereal by means of cards, stars, or the entrails of chickens.

This impasse between the psychic and the scientist today constitutes a block of some magnitude. A great deal has been said about it one way or another.

In 1909 the honorable and respected William James (1842–1910) expressed an attitude almost bearing on misgiving. James's cosmopolitan outlook and broad cultural view of the world made him a leader of his day. He joined the faculty at Harvard University and lectured first on anatomy and physiology, but later on psychology and philosophy.

His fame and prestige brought a certain elegance to psychical research, which he openly advocated. He was one of the founders in 1885 of the now prestigious American Society for Psychical Research, and served as president and vice president of the Society for Psychical Research in London.

James once indicated, by way of summation of his involvement, that, after some twenty-five years of association with psychic research, he was no further along "theoretically" than he had been at the beginning.[9]

It can be seen that the material/nonmaterial conflict persists in the social structure, if for no other reason than the fact that people tend to take sides, form groups, and probably enjoy at some deep level the hurling of diatribes and harassment of the opposite camp. And because people experience, at least for a time, comfort in following their noses in whatever direction the wind blows.

This dichotomy of material/nonmaterial interaction probably will con-

---

[9] See William James, "The Final Impressions of a Psychic Researcher," *The American Magazine,* October 1909. (This essay has seen several reprints.) See also Gardner Murphy and Robert O. Ballou, eds., *William James on Psychical Research* (London: Chatto and Windus, 1961), p. 309. Those interested in establishing an opening concept of the difficulties encountered in psychic research might well read this last report since it contains a good description of the situation in 1909, a situation that has not changed much up to 1974.

tinue for some time, at least as long as there is no cogent scientific discovery in the nonmaterial realm. But in the mind of the individual the solution is not all that difficult: It simply consists of no longer holding the two apart but putting them together.

It has become increasingly apparent to me that the legendary psi factors are closely aligned, as Rhine suggested, with creativity. And more especially with functional and practical creativity, as contrasted with the sophistication and dilettantism of many of the arts.

The path of understanding of things psychic has in a sort of reverse vector pattern led away from the usual occult, mystical, and even mythic sources normally credited. Another factor easily apparent is that society holds fixed ideas of what things psychic should be, and consequently cannot and does not identify some forms of obviously psychic-related activities as psychic.

For example, in researching topics for this book I considered the prevalence of water dowsers. Water dowsing is one of the few practical applications of psychical abilities, and as such it usually is tolerated without much fuss. Dowsers are often utilized when all other known methods of finding water fail.

Reports of successful water dowsers abounded on all sides. But initial inquiry yielded not one successful oil dowser. There were several claims, mainly from promoters who appeared interested in getting a con game going, but not one could produce a verifiable situation or document showing that he or she had found oil by dowsing.

Did this suggest that there were no oil dowsers?

The interesting truth eventually dawned. If a man could successfully dowse for valuable crude oil and associated products, in all likelihood he would have become a wealthy oil magnate if he had half his wits about him.

Once this elusiveness was grasped, one could change the question. One wouldn't ask, "Have you ever heard of a successful oil dowser?"

Instead one would say, "Sir, now that you have consented to giving an interview here in your offices atop your seventy-story building, can you tell me if you ever located oil by means resembling something paranormal?"

Almost inevitably the oil men who would talk about it at all began talking about their "intuition," their "hunches," and rather inspiring black gold discovery stories would unfold.

As it turns out, it is the economy of the situation that creates the great difference between the visibility of water and oil dowsers. Since water is usually of little significant commercial value, the water dowser offers his services to those having difficulty locating water on their premises. Whereas the person seeking oil, and playing his hunches and intuition, is confronted by a totally different economic reward should he be sucessful. Thus the results of two similar paranormal *potentials* appear in the social structure in two totally different *forms*.

Now it has to be held that it is inhumanitarian and totalitarian to insist that people accept or believe things that are not real to them. Individuals should be entitled to their skepticism, especially as concerns psychic phenomena, since they should not be forced to accept something that is elusive in the first place and usually invisible in the second.

But if seeing is believing to many people, experience often proves the best teacher. This cliché can be seen to divide the men from the mice regarding the appearance and credibility of paranormal or psychic phenomena.

There is no more completely convinced observer than one whose well went dry and who had to spend five thousand dollars while a thoroughly qualified geologist drilled dry holes for him and finally rendered a report that there was no more water on the property. The man, setting aside his idea that water dowsing was a hoax, in great desperation hired a dowser. The dowser spent half a day walking over the property and then pointed to the middle of the roadway that the owner had spent three thousand dollars building.

"But I can't drill there," complained the landowner. "It would cost almost a thousand dollars to move that road."

"You can move the road," retorted the dowser. "But you can't move the water that is down there."

The water came up clear and sparkling at two hundred feet down and has flowed ever since.

Both water and petroleum dowsers use apparently subjective abilities, abilities that, as Schmeidler and others have shown, exist within the individual somewhat in proportion to what he feels about his own potential.

A review of the biographies of Mendeleyev, Goethe, or Darwin discloses that these men, as well as others, often obtained their ideas from psychically related functions—dreams or daydreams, flashing intuitions and insights, or glittering visions. Creative ideas are results of the mind receiving organized data and synthesizing experiences into a pattern that leads to inventiveness not generally accessible to others. Accumulating data clearly indicate that the information so gathered comes from sources often beyond mere physical experience, and other data firmly indicate the extrasensory function in this type of idea generation.[10]

Douglas Dean and John Mihalasky, both of the Psi Communications Project at the Newark College of Engineering, have conducted research in a psi-oriented theory involving creative decision making, including the phenomenon of precognition or prophetic insights contributing to success in everyday business life.[11] While their studies may not be conclusive, they nonetheless clearly point a new direction for the investigation of psi factors in man.

Their research strongly supports a hypothesis that the "lucky" individual is operating on something more than mere chance. In a more clear and strong manner their research firmly indicates that some successful executives have more precognitive ability than others. Many dramatically successful businessmen apparently are more equipped to anticipate the future intuitively, even where usual data concerning that future do not in fact exist. And, in direct interviews with successful executives and other business figures, an impressive majority indicated that they do use inexplicable means in making important and far-reaching decisions, almost

---

[10] See John Mihalasky, "ESP: Can It Play a Role in Idea-Generation?", *Mechanical Engineering,* December 1972, pp. 32–34, and "Extrasensory Perception in Management," *Advanced Management Journal,* July 1967, pp. 50–54.

[11] See John Mihalasky, "The Role of Precognition in Risk Analysis," *The Engineering Economist,* Summer 1972, pp. 55–62. See also E. Douglas Dean et al., *Executive ESP,* New York, Prentice-Hall, 1974.

always correct in their outcomes. Experimental situations established by Dean and Mihalasky tend to confirm the hypothesis.[12]

Naturally, if and when "intuitive" forces guide the successful executive or inventor or artist, a significant and dignified *relationship* between the subjective and objective universes comes into being. This delicate, and quite often invisible, interchange is often blatantly ignored by hard scientists, who themselves seek to interpret the results of this interchange in the terms of one universe only, the objective. There is, however, a modicum of data suggesting that further investigation of the creative aspects of man in relation to psi potential might lead to more than a modicum of illumination on both these elusive topics.[13]

There is not much doubt that the highly creative individual is somewhat feared in society, and the successful creative individual, if his success is measured in acquisition of power and money, is jealously regarded by those not so gifted. It should seem that creative inputs should at all times be regarded gratefully by society as a whole. But this seems not to be the case. If creativity survives at all, it is by overcoming resistance.

A rather poignant example of this social "fear" of creativity can be seen in the elevation of Thomas Edison, who was minimally creative in electrical discoveries, over the suppression and ignoring of Nikola Tesla, who was positively mind-bending in extensive electrical discoveries.

Nikola Tesla was born in 1856 in a small village called Smiljan in a part of Austro-Hungary that is now part of Yugoslavia. He rose from there to eventually become one of the most remarkable inventive geniuses ever to grace mankind at a time when inventiveness in electricity, power, and methods of harnessing it was sorely needed.

There is no doubt that Tesla, as a youngster, was precocious and

---

[12] See John Mihalasky, "Computer Scored Audience Experiments in Precognition," *Journal of Parapsychology* 31 (December 1951), p. 319.

[13] The hypothesis that creativity and PSI are related can be supported extensively by documentation. It quickly becomes an involved subject since the paradox called "human personality" quickly becomes engaged. See, for instance, H. J. Eysenck, "Personality and Extra-Sensory Perception," *Journal of the Society for Psychical Research* 44, no. 732 (June 1967), pp. 55–71; Charles Honorton, "Creativity and Precognition Scoring Level," *The Journal of Parapsychology* 31, no. 1 (March 1967), pp. 29–42; Thelma Moss, "ESP Effects in 'Artists' Contrasted with 'Non-Artists'," *ibid.* 33, no. 1 (March 1968), pp. 57–69.

fascinated by mechanical devices. His inventiveness was of such a caliber as to be troublesome, and he seems to have been performing experiments continually. He was interested in mechanical apparatus, turning moving things to produce power. At various times he seems to have had strange illnesses, accompanied by extremely acute sense perceptics.

Any reading of biographical data on Tesla establishes that he was an extraordinary individual, even as a boy. The impact of his inventiveness upon the planet reached a force almost undreamed of in the minds of mere mortals. Of the few men in history who can lay claim to the title, it is to Nikola Tesla that the appellation "superhuman" belongs without question.

As the years of his life passed, he contributed to the benefit of mankind alternating current, motor and generator controls, polyphase currents, dynamos, transformers, electrical distributors, arc lights, currents of high frequency and high potential, various mechanisms for circuits and systems, insulation, radio telegraphy, wireless systems, radio mechanics, methods of tuning and selection, various systems concerning steam turbines, airplanes, mechanical oscillators, thermomagnetic motors. These items represent just a few of the discoveries and patents that bear his name.

Yet Nikola Tesla died alone in his hotel room in New York sometime during the night of January 7, 1943. Upon the announcement of his death, it is reported that operatives from the Federal Bureau of Investigation came and confiscated his papers, allegedly to examine them for some sort of secret invention with possible war use. All other Tesla papers and patents were sealed by the custodian of alien property, even though Tesla had been an American citizen for many years.

It is said that Tesla did not believe in psychical phenomena at all, although he apparently experienced many situations that would, to all accounts, fall well within that description. Only one of his many paranormal experiences is pertinent here.

It seems likely that, to a man whose life experience continually took place in the vast realms of paranormal cognition and awareness, ordinary psychical research as it tended to be conducted during his lifetime might have seemed irritating. Psychic research during its early years was devoted to following courses that might have appeared totally foolish to a man able to take the benefits of his extraordinary cognition and turn them almost immediately into demonstration of vast practical use and staggering value.

There are several versions of the experience that was to mark Tesla's life in its entirety.[14]

It seems that in 1882, on a late February afternoon in the city park at Budapest, Tesla was strolling with a friend named Szigeti. He was recovering from a malady that was never successfully diagnosed by doctors, an illness that had nearly cost him his life. Overhead a sunset was spreading across the evening sky in a majesty that must have been absolute. Tesla was reciting poetry, a favorite hobby. The sky apparently reminded him of some lines in Goethe's *Faust,* and with waving arms he gazed up to the setting sun and addressed some of Goethe's beautiful poetry.

Suddenly he fell into what appeared to be a moment of supreme concentration, from which his friend Szigeti was unable to remove him —even by shaking him physically.

No one knows exactly what went on in Tesla's mind or within the realms of his paranormal vision at that moment. The reports differ, but it seems likely that, for a brief instant, Tesla was able to perceive almost the totality of the electromagnetic functioning of the Solar System. Prior to this experience he had apparently been trying to solve the intricacies of a system of alternating current, and this seems to have been foremost in his mind. Certainly, descending from this moment of sublime cognition came the solution for this system, and he was able to construct one soon after.

To this supreme moment, therefore, the world owes one of its most practical scientific discoveries. Tesla was to indicate later that not only the solution for the alternating current but *all* his subsequent discoveries, as well as his dedication to bringing them about, had their origin in that brief moment when he "went" to the sun and "saw" how it all worked.

Based upon present data concerning the nature of human understanding, it is almost impossible succinctly to talk about what went on in Tesla

---

[14] See John J. O'Neill, *Prodigal Genius: The Life of Nikola Tesla* (New York: Ives Washburn, 1944), pp. 48–51. O'Neill was a lifelong friend of Tesla's and his rendering of the experience might be considered most descriptive of the event, if not the most authoritative.

at that moment. Most academic discussions of Tesla solve the problem by ignoring it altogether or else passing over it very lightly, although occultists do leap upon it in frenzy.

Whatever it was, however, it gave a substance and a vivification to Tesla's life from which he could not be diverted by the most abysmal disappointments, and which was to produce an absolute juggernaut of electromagnetic inventiveness which mere men could hardly keep up with, much less try to understand.

In the social fabric, and especially in competitive business enterprise, this type of extrasensory, or even higher-sensory, function is not as rare as is commonly thought. Tesla was by any means a unique being, possibly combining psychic vision with an amazing energetic action-oriented determination. (This latter is probably more rare than the former.)

Shafica Karagulla gives some narrative accounts of people who have tapped into higher sense possibilities, to their own as well as others' amazement.[15] A certain "Paul," for instance, found himself able, after a short course in elementary electronics, to grasp in totality the thoughts of others as well as to "see" installations in complete working order. He could soar out, survey large areas, and spot building arrangements at far distances.

At one time, confronting a work program that presumably would take nearly eight months to conclude, "Paul" was able to hand his superior a completed program in one week. The program was passed, but the superior, quite aghast at a description of how "Paul" had accomplished his work, asked him to "appear" busy for the rest of the time since no one would believe he had done the entire thing in only a week. "Paul" could also "tune in" on malfunctioning machinery and find where it had gone wrong, locating the exact trouble area.

If the productive individual confirms survival in terms of the present, it should have to be held that the creative individual holds the future in his mind or psyche—unless society as a whole or even in part opts for a static culture.

If materialistic bastions, recalcitrant in their antipsychic—possibly even

[15] See Shafica Karagulla, *Breakthrough to Creativity* (Los Angeles: DeVorss 1967), pp. 81–122.

anticreative—attitudes, have tried to opt for a static culture, it is nevertheless a hard and embarrassing fact that major creative inputs, even in their world, have come about as a result of psi-oriented abilities possessed by many historical geniuses.[16]

Dr. Stanley Krippner, the president of the Association for Humanistic Psychology and newly elected vice president of the International Association for Psychotronic Research, recently characterized psychic research in its present importance when he indicated that "Parapsychology is simply an idea whose time has come." [17]

If this is true of the "idea," it may not be true of the science. In all things of import, save revolution and war, there is a distinct cultural lag between discovery of new factors and acceptance of them.[18] But there cannot be much doubt that the "idea" of things psychic possesses the public mind with enthusiasm if not passion.

Since endurance and discovery are not going to come about through redecorated mysticism or pseudopsychics flopping about giving unverifiable "life readings" to middle-aged women, a great deal is going to depend upon the emergence of new workable paradigms that will accommodate these attributes of the human psyche. Happily, many of these are immanent. And, too, there is also a sense of competition, as mentioned earlier, between scientists in the United States and those of the USSR.[19]

Many years ago I got involved with my own mind, a risky business, of course. Perhaps at that time I was impressed with my barest functional control over myself, and I rationalized that, if mind was supposed to give analytical factors leading to an enhanced existence, then surely I did not

[16] See especially Roy Dreistadt, "The Prophetic Achievements of Geniuses and Types of Extrasensory Perception, *Psychology* 8, no. 2 (May 1971), pp. 27–40.

[17] See Paul Chance, "Parapsychology Is an Idea Whose Time Has Come," a conversation with Stanley Krippner in *Psychology Today,* October 1973, pp. 105–120.

[18] See Gunther S. Stent, "Prematurity and Uniqueness in Scientific Discovery," *Scientific American,* December 1972, pp. 84–93; Thomas S. Kuhn, *The Structure of Scientific Revolutions* (Chicago: University of Chicago Press, 1962).

[19] See Stanley Krippner and Richard Davidson, "Parapsychology in the U.S.S.R.," *The Saturday Review,* March 18, 1972, pp. 56–60.

know nearly enough about how I, as mind and self, functioned. It is surprising how little is known about the mind, in spite of the rather decorative attitude among professionals who lead others, less informed, to believe that solutions to the mind are in hand, or at least in the next book to be published.

Well into the swamp of literature concerning the mind, I came across the concept that awareness undoubtedly functioned *through* mind and that mind itself was filled with inhibiting features and false data.[20] These inhibiting and false features, if powerful enough, can delimit awareness. Awareness and conditions of existence were therefore somehow interdependent.

If this was so, then experience and logic—the crux of materialistic philosophy—were probably true, but only to the condition of existence suggested by that philosophy. The experience, education, and traditional programming the individual receives do constitute his view of life. But was this to be the only condition of existence?

It seems clear that the boundaries put on life and existence by cause-effect science and philosophy probably do delimit awareness. This probability can, for instance, be laid directly over the sheep/goats discovery of Schmeidler, which indicates that one's ESP potential is greatly influenced by how one *thinks* about it in general.

Now I do not consider materialistic precepts per se anathema, since from them have developed countless discoveries to the physical benefit of mankind. But I am opposed, mainly from a creative artistic viewpoint, to the materialistic credo that holds materialism to be all there is.

It seems clear that if materialistically oriented scientists or social scientists consider materialism to be all there is, then that is all there would be for them. Change in their viewpoints would come about only through hearty and in-depth changes in their ideas about things.

And, as all but the most unenlightened would have to acknowledge, it is only those individuals who experience in-depth reorientations about the possibilities of knowledge who increase the total human fund of it.

Modern man, in the context of his presently increasing conflict with the universe, can be seen to be governed by his standard time- and space-bound mental organization. This same organization also is intrinsic to problems of existence currently plaguing advancing discovery.

[20] See L. R. Hubbard, "The Four Conditions of Existence," *The Phoenix Lectures* (Edinburgh, Publications Organization Worldwide, 1968), pp. 73–120.

It therefore has to be held, that considerable departures from current constructions about consciousness, the mind, and the impact of awareness (or idea generation) upon it are required in order to begin a structural understanding of paranormal processes. It is within the best interests of quick gain in these departures to consider new paradigms of the mind and of consciousness.[21]

As an example of such a new paradigm, the philosophy and mental technologies of Scientology constitute an appreciable advance, not only in that there are novel methods for locating barriers in one's own views of matter, energy, space, and time, but also because the ideas of its founder, L. Ron Hubbard, is of a scope that encompasses transcendental states of existence.[22]

---

[21] The descriptives involving this situation have been presented cogently in a combination of other sources. See Henry Margenau, "ESP in the Framework of Modern Science," *The Journal of the American Society for Psychical Research* 60, no. 3 (July 1966), pp. 190–228; Jan Ehrenwald, "Psi Phenomena and the Existential Shift," *ibid.* 65, no. 2 (April 1971), pp. 162–172; E. H. Walker, "The Nature of Consciousness, the Relation to the Foundations of Quantum Mechanics and Its Philosophical Implications," *Proceedings of the SIMS Conference,* University of Massachusetts, July 28–August 1, 1971; "Foundations of Paraphysical and Parapsychological Phenomena," unpublished paper, Ballistic Research Laboratories, Aberdeen Proving Ground, Maryland; L. R. Hubbard, *Scientology 8-8008* (England: East Grinstead, Department of Publications World Wide, 1953 and 1968).

[22] The theories underlying Scientology and its companion science, Dianetics, are best found in the works of their author, L. Ron Hubbard (see bibliography). If certain experiences were possible for me as a child, it must be stated that no volitional control over the types of phenomena demonstrated during the last three years would have been possible had there been in me an absence of the transcendental structural ideas presented by Hubbard. It is basic to Hubbard's thesis that the center of awareness, the "I," is probabilistically determinant over matter, energy, space and time to the degree that the "I" removes the programmed blocks to his understanding of them. This premise is in agreement with the hypothesis advanced years ago by many scientists and philosophers that the universe is present for us dependent on how we are creating our image of it. A synopsis of the basic scientological premises was presented recently by this author. See Ingo Swann, "Scientological Techniques: A Modern Paradigm for the Exploration of Consciousness and Psychic Integration," in *The Proceedings of the First International Conference on Psychotronic Research,* Z. Rejdák, M. Toth, J. A. de Matia, eds. (New York: Masterworks Press, forthcoming).

There have been multitudes of barrier-blowing experiences that have always seemed to draw me toward the infinite, or at least toward ideas of it. I am reasonably satisfied now that immortality is a thing of uninterrupted consciousness, but this is something that belongs to the psychic, not the physical, man. The psychic man, trying to live life in a solely materialistic or physical sense, must exist in a universe that is nothing more than a great limbo of discarded psychic inevitables—discarded because they do not fit into the rationales of the material.

Heretofore, only the path through the mystical was held to be the access point to things beyond the physical. But the so-called mystical is merely the residue of the things not permitted by material theory, and mystical beauty, like physical beauty, is often only skin deep.

Uninterrupted consciousness is not sleeplessness or even deathlessness. It can more precisely be defined as a state of awareness that does not block off ideas and perceptions from the perceiver.

Conversely, interrupted consciousness would be that type which forces, either by habitual and automatic rejection of ideas or by nonconfrontation of new meanings, the individual to delimit himself in awareness.

This is a rather slippery situation. But it is a real one and persists in almost all cultures. The artist Vincent Van Gogh, just before he was to drop everything else in his life and become an artist, wrote in July 1880 to his brother Theo. He said that men are often blocked from doing anything because they feel themselves prisoners, "prisoners in an I-don't-know-what-for horrible, horrible, utterly horrible cage."

Eight years later, between October and December of 1888, he painted the lovely *Sowers* (the first of two), a reproduction of which inspired me from the walls of the experimental chamber at the American Society for Psychical Research the day that the truth of man's paranormal potential really dawned on me.

If the physical is considered the be-all, end-all, the universe is truly a horrible, horrible, utterly horrible cage. It is possible to exist in an awareness beyond things physical, beyond the "earth" in all things.

SELECTED BIBLIOGRAPHY

Backster, Cleve. "Evidence of a Primary Perception in Plant Life." *International Journal of Parapsychology* 10, no. 4 (Winter 1968), pp. 329–348.
Banham, Katharine M. "Temporary High Scoring by a Child Subject." *The Journal of Parapsychology* 30, no. 2 (June 1967).
Barnothy, Madeleine F., ed. *Biological Effects of Magnetic Fields.* New York: Plenum Press, 1964.
Barry, J. "General and Comparative Study of the Psychokinetic Effect on a Fungus Culture." *The Journal of Parapsychology* 32, no. 4 (December 1968), pp. 237–243.
Beaty, John Yocum. *Luther Burbank, Plant Magician.* New York: J. Messner, 1943.
Beloff, John. "Parapsychology and Its Neighbours." *The Journal of Parapsychology* 34, no. 2 (June 1970).
Bhadra, B. H. "The Relationship of Test Scores to Belief in ESP." *The Journal of Parapsychology* 30, no. 1 (March 1966), pp. 1–17.
Blavatsky, H. P. *The Secret Doctrine.* Pasadena, Calif.: Theosophical University Press, 1963.
Bohm, David. "Quantum Theory as an Indication of a New Order in Physics: Part A—The Development of New Orders as Shown Through the History of Physics." *Foundations of Physics* 1, no. 4 (1971), pp. 359–381. Part B—Implicate and Explicate Order in Physical Law," *Ibid.* 3, no. 2 (1973), pp. 139–167.
Bolen, J. G. "Interview: Harold Sherman." *Psychic,* February 1974, p. 6.
Brier, R. M. "PK on a Bio-electrical System." *The Journal of Parapsychology* 33, no. 3 (September 1969), pp. 187–205.
Brook-Shepherd, Gordon. *The Last Habsburg.* New York: Weybright and Talley, 1968.
Byron, F. L. "A Top Executive's Advice: Hang Loose." *Dun's Review,* September 1969, pp. 51–53, 114–117.
Chance, Paul. "Parapsychology Is an Idea Whose Time Has Come." *Psychology Today,* October 1973, pp. 105–120.
Chari, C. T. K. "Precognition, Probability, and Quantum Mechanics." *The Journal of the American Society for Psychical Research* 66, no. 2 (April 1972).

SELECTED BIBLIOGRAPHY

Chauvin, Rémy. "To Reconcile Psi and Physics." *The Journal of Parapsychology* 34, no. 3 (September 1970), pp. 215–218.

Christian, P. *The History and Practice of Magic*. New York: Citadel Press, 1963.

Cleather, A. L. *H. P. Blavatsky as I Knew Her*. Calcutta and Simla, 1923.

Colman, S. M. "The Phantom Double: Its Psychological Significance." *British Journal of Medical Psychology* 14 (1934), pp. 254–273.

Cox, W. E. "The Effect of PK on Electromechanical Systems." *The Journal of Parapsychology* 29, no. 3 (September 1965), pp. 164–175.

Dean, E. Douglas et al., *Executive ESP*. New York: Prentice-Hall, 1974.

Denton, William. *The Soul of Things, Psychometric Researches and Discoveries*. Vols. I–III. Wellesley, Mass., 1873.

Deych, A. N. "61 Libyedya, kak troinaya systema," *Priroda* 33, nos. 5–6 (1944), p. 99.

Dreistadt, Roy. "The Prophetic Achievements of Geniuses and Types of Extrasensory Perception," *Psychology* 8, no. 2 (May 1971), pp. 27–40.

Ehrenwald, Jan. "Freud versus Jung—The Mythophobic versus the Mythophilic Temper in Psychotherapy." *Israel Annals of Psychiatry and Related Disciplines* 6, no. 2 (1968).

———. "Parapsychology and the Seven Dragons: A Neuropsychiatric Model of Psi Phenomena." *Parapsychology: Today's Implications, Tomorrow's Applications*, American Society for Psychical Research Symposium, May 1974, in press.

———. Psi Phenomena and the Existential Shift." *The Journal of the American Society for Psychical Research* 65, no. 2 (April 1971), pp. 162–172.

Einstein, Albert. *The Meaning of Relativity*. Princeton, N.J.: Princeton University Press, 1923.

———. *The Principles of Relativity*. Original papers by A. Einstein and H. Minkowski, trans. by M. N. Saha and S. N. Bose with a historical introduction by P. C. Mahalanobis. Calcutta: University of Calcutta, 1920.

———, and L. Infeld. *The Evolution of Physics*. New York: Simon and Schuster, 1938.

Eisenbud, Jule. "Some Notes on the Psychology of the Paranormal." *The Journal of the American Society for Psychical Research* 66, no. 1 (January 1972).

Evans-Wentz, W. Y. *The Tibetan Book of the Dead*. New York: Oxford University Press, 1960.

Eysenck, H. J. "Personality and Extra-sensory Perception." *The Journal of the Society for Psychical Research* 44, no. 732 (June 1967), pp. 55–71.

Farrington, Benjamin. *What Darwin Really Said*. New York: Schocken Books, 1966.

Feinberg, G. "Possibility of Faster-than-Light Particles." *Physics Review* 159, no. 1 (1967), p. 1089.

Fort, Charles. *The Book of the Damned*. London: Boni & Liveright, 1919.

SELECTED BIBLIOGRAPHY

Forwald, H. *Mind, Matter, and Gravitation: A Theoretical and Experimental Study.* New York: Parapsychology Foundation, 1969.
Freeman, John A. "A Sequel Report on a High-Scoring Child Subject." *The Journal of Parapsychology* 30, no. 1 (March 1966).
Fuller, John G. *The Great Soul Trial.* New York: Macmillan, 1969.
Gardner, Martin. "Dermo-optical Perception: A Peek Down the Nose." *Science* 151, no. 3711 (February 11, 1966), pp. 654–657.
Garnett, A. Campbell. "Matter, Mind, and Precognition." *The Journal of Parapsychology* 29, no. 1 (March 1965).
Garrett, Eileen J. *Does Man Survive Death?* New York: Helix Press, 1957.
———. *My Life as a Search for the Meaning of Mediumship.* Oquaga, N.Y., 1939.
Gauld, Alan. *The Founders of Psychical Research.* New York: Schocken Books, 1968.
Govinda, the Lama Anagarika. *Foundations of Tibetan Mysticism.* New York: E. P. Dutton, 1960.
Gurney, Edmund; Frederic W. H. Myers; and Frank Podmore. *Phantasms of the Living.* London: Society for Psychical Research, 1886.
Hall, Manly P. *The Space-born.* Los Angeles: Skelton, 1930.
Hamon, Lewis (Cheiro). *Cheiro's World Predictions.* London: London Publishing Co., 1927.
Harman, Willis W. "The New Copernican Revolution." *Stanford Today,* Winter 1969, pp. 7–10.
———. "Old Wine in New Wineskins." In J. F. T. Bugental, ed., *Challenges of Humanistic Psychology.* 1967.
Hart, Hornell. *The Enigma of Survival.* Springfield, Ill.: Charles C. Thomas, 1959.
Head, Joseph, and S. L. Cranston. *Reincarnation, an East-West Anthology.* New York: Julian Press, 1961.
Heisenberg, Werner. *Philosophic Problems of Nuclear Science.* London: Faber and Faber, 1952.
———. *The Physical Principles of the Quantum Theory.* Chicago: University of Chicago Press, 1930.
———. *Der Teil und das Ganze.* Munich, 1969.
Hewish, A., ed. *Seeing Beyond the Visible.* New York: American Elsevier, 1970.
Holmberg, E. "Invisible Companions of Parallax Stars Revealed by Means of Modern Trigonometric Parallax Observations." *Meddelanden Fran Lunds Astronomiska Observatorium,* 1938, series 11, no. 92, p. 23.
Honorton, Charles. "Creativity and Precognition Scoring Level." *The Journal of Parapsychology* 31, no. 1 (March 1967), pp. 29–42.
Howe, Ellic. *Urania's Children: The Strange World of the Astrologers.* London: William Kimber, 1967.

SELECTED BIBLIOGRAPHY

Hubbard, L. R. *Dianetics: The Modern Science of Mental Health.* East Grinstead, England: Hubbard College of Scientology, 1950.

———. *Have You Lived Before This Life? A Study of Past Lives Through Dianetic Engrams.* New York: Vantage Press, 1960.

———. *The Phoenix Lectures.* Edinburgh: Publications Organization Worldwide, 1968.

———. *Scientology 8-8008.* East Grinstead, England: Department of Publications World Wide, 1953 and 1968.

Hudson, Manley O. "The Stacking of the Cards. In *The Next War.* Cambridge, Mass.: Harvard Bulletin Press, 1925.

Ivanov, A. "Soviet Experiments in ESP, 1921–1927, 1932–1938." *International Journal of Parapsychology,* no. 5 (1963), pp. 217–230.

Jacobson, J. Z.; B. J. Frost; and W. L. King. "A Case of Dermooptical Perception." *Perceptual and Motor Skills* 22, no. 2 (April 1966), pp. 515–520.

James, William. "The Final Impressions of a Psychic Researcher." *The American Magazine,* 1909.

Jeans, Sir James. *The Mysterious Universe.* Cambridge, England: The University Press, 1930.

Jung, C. G. "Psychological Commentary on 'The Tibetan Book of the Great Liberation.' " *Psychology and Religion: East and West.* New York: Pantheon, 1963.

Karagulla, Shafica. *Breakthrough to Creativity.* Los Angeles: DeVorss, 1967.

Kilner, W. J. *The Human Atmosphere: or the Aura Made Visible by the Aid of Chemical Screens.* New York: Rebman, 1911.

Klinckowstroem, Graf von. *Zeifschrift für Bucherfreunde.* March 1913. (A bibliography of the twenty-five oldest Nostradamus editions until 1689.)

Klip, Willem. "An Experimental Approach to the Interpretation of the Quantum Theory." *The Journal of the Society for Psychical Research* 44, no. 734 (December 1967), pp. 181–187.

Kniepf, A. *Echte und gefälschte Prophetien des Nostradamus.* (*Psychische Studien, 1909*). In Dr. Max Kemmerich, ed., *Prophezeiungen.* Munich, 1925.

Koestler, Arthur. *The Roots of Coincidence.* New York: Random House, 1972.

Krippner, Stanley, and Richard Davidson. "Parapsychology in the U.S.S.R." *Saturday Review,* March 18, 1972, pp. 56–60.

Krippner, Stanley, and Daniel Rubin, eds. *The Kirlian Aura.* Garden City, N.Y.: Anchor, 1974.

Kuhn, Thomas S. *The Structure of Scientific Revolutions.* Chicago: University of Chicago Press, 1962.

LeShan, L. *Toward a General Theory of the Paranormal.* New York: Parapsychology Foundation, 1969.

Lhermitte, Jean. "Visual Hallucination of the Self." *British Medical Journal,* March 3, 1951, pp. 431–434.

SELECTED BIBLIOGRAPHY

Lippman, Caro W. "Hallucinations of Physical Duality in Migraine." *Journal of Nervous and Mental Disease* 117 (1953), pp. 345–348.

Lukianowicz, N. "Autoscopic Phenomena." *American Medical Association Archives of Neurological Psychiatry* 80 (1958), pp. 199–220.

MacGowan, R. A. "On the Possibilities of the Existence of Extraterrestrial Intelligence." *Advances in Space Science and Technology.* In F. Odenbury, ed., vol. IV. New York: Academic Press, 1962.

Mackenzie, Norman and Jeanne. *H. G. Wells, A Biography.* New York: Simon and Schuster, 1973.

Margenau, Henry. "ESP in the Framework of Modern Science." *The Journal of the American Society for Psychical Research* 60, no. 3 (July 1966), pp. 190–228.

Markley, O. W.; D. A. Curry; and D. L. Rink. *Contemporary Societal Problems.* Research Report EPRC 6747-2. Menlo Park, Calif.: Educational Policy Research Center, Stanford Research Institute, June 1971.

Massie, R. K. *Nicholas and Alexandra.* New York: Dell, 1967.

McConnell, R. A. "ESP and Credibility in Science." *American Psychologist* 24, no. 5 (May 1969), pp. 531–538.

McDonald, J. "How Businessmen Make Decisions." *Fortune,* August 1955, pp. 84–87, 131–133.

Mihalasky, John. "Computer Scored Audience Experiments in Precognition." *The Journal of Parapsychology* 31, (December 1967), p. 319.

———. "ESP—Can It Play a Role in Idea-Generation?" *Mechanical Engineering,* December 1972, pp. 32–34.

———. "Extrasensory Perception in Management." *Advanced Management Journal* 32, no. 3 (July 1967), pp. 50–54.

———. "The Role of Precognition in Risk-Analysis." *The Engineering Economist,* Summer 1972, pp. 55–62.

———; E. D. Dean; and H. C. Sherwood. "Dollars May Flow from the Sixth Sense." *Nation's Business,* April 1967, pp. 64–66.

Moss, Thelma. "ESP Effects in 'Artists' Contrasted with 'Non-Artists.'" *The Journal of Parapsychology* 33, no. 1 (March 1968), pp. 57–69.

Murchie, Guy. *Music of the Spheres: The Material Universe—from Atom to Quasar, Simply Explained.* New York: Dover, 1967.

Murphy, Gardner. "Are There Any Solid Facts in Psychical Research?" *The Journal of the American Society for Psychical Research* 64, no. 1 (January 1970).

———. "Direct Contacts with Past and Future: Retrocognition and Precognition." *The Journal of the American Society for Psychical Research* 61, no. 1 (January 1967).

———. *An Historical Introduction to Modern Psychology.* London: Harcourt, Brace, 1929.

———. "The Problem of Repeatability in Psychical Research." *The Journal of the American Society for Psychical Research* 65, no. 1 (January 1971).

SELECTED BIBLIOGRAPHY

———, and Robert O. Ballou, eds. *William James on Psychical Research.* London: Chatto and Windus, 1961.

Nash, C. B. "Cutaneous Perception of Color with a Head Box." *The Journal of the American Society for Psychical Research* 65, no. 1 (January 1971), pp. 83–87.

Naumov, E. K., and L. V. Vilenskaya. *Soviet Bibliography on Parapsychology (Psychoenergetics) and Related Subjects.* Joint Publications Research Service, JPRS No. 55557. Washington, D.C., May 28, 1972.

Old, W. G. (Sepharial). *An Astrological Survey of the Great War, Being an Examination of the Indications Attending the Outbreak and the Presumptive Effects of the Conflict.* London: W. Foulsham, 1914.

———. *The Great Devastation: A Prophecy of Times that Are Coming Upon Europe.* London, 1915.

———.*The Simple Way, Laotze.* Philadelphia: David McKay, 1913.

———. *The Theory of Geodetic Equivalents.* London: W. Foulsham.

O'Neill, John J. *Prodigal Genius: The Life of Nikola Tesla.* New York: Ives Washburn, 1944.

"Parapsychology—What the Questionnaire Revealed." *The New Scientist* January 25, 1973, p. 209

Piper, Raymond and Lila K. *Cosmic Art,* ed. Ingo Swann. New York: Hawthorn, forthcoming.

Podmore, Frank. *Mediums of the 19th Century.* New Hyde Park, N.Y.: University, 1963.

Puthoff, H. E. "The Physics of Psychoenergetic Processes, Research Proposal," 1971 (unpublished).

Pratt, J. Gaither. *ESP Research Today: A Study of Developments in Parapsychology Since 1960.* Metuchen, N.J.: Scarecrow Press, 1973.

———. "Parapsychology in Russia and Czechoslovakia." *Journal for Social Psychologic Research,* no. 42 (1963), pp. 16–20.

Puthoff, H. E. and Russell Targ, "Physics, Entropy, and Parapsychology," *Proceedings of the Conference on Quantum Physics and Parapsychology, Geneva, August 26-27, 1974.* New York: Parapsychology Foundation (in preparation).

Reich, Charles A. *The Greening of America.* New York: Random House, 1970.

Reichenbach, Karl L. F. *The Odic Force: Letters on OD and Magnetism.* New Hyde Park, N.Y.: University, 1968.

———. *Physico-Physiological Researches on the Dynamics of Magnetism, Heat, Light, Electricity and Chemism, in Their Relations to Vital Force.* New York: J. S. Redfield, 1851.

Rejdák, Z.; M. Toth; J. A. deMatia, eds. *The Proceedings of the First International Conference on Psychotronic Research.* New York: Masterwork Press, forthcoming.

SELECTED BIBLIOGRAPHY

Reyn, N. F., and N. N. Pariyskiy. "Katastroficheskiye gipotezy proiskhodzheniya solnechnoy sistemy." *Uspekhi Astronomicheskikh Nauk,* 1941, 2, pp. 137–156.

Rhine, J. B. "Current Questions about the Field of Parapsychology." *The Journal of Parapsychology* 29, no. 4 (December 1965).

———. "It Follows from ESP." *The Journal of the American Society for Psychical Research* 35, no. 6 (1941), pp. 191–195.

———. "Parapsychology and Man." *The Journal of Parapsychology* 36, no. 2 (June 1972).

———. "Psi and Psychology: Conflict and Solution." *The Journal of Parapsychology* 32, no. 2 (June 1968), pp. 101–108.

Rhine, Louisa E. "The Establishment of Basic Concepts and Terminology in Parapsychology." *The Journal of Parapsychology* 35, no. 1 (March 1971), pp. 34–56.

———. "Parapsychology, Then and Now." *The Journal of Parapsychology* 31, no. 3 (September 1967).

Roll, Muriel. "A Nineteenth-Century Matchmaking Apparition." *The Journal of the American Society for Psychical Research* 63, no. 4 (October 1969), pp. 396–409.

Schmeidler, G. R. "PK Effects Upon Continuously Recorded Temperature." *The Journal of the American Society for Psychical Research* 67, no. 4 (October 1973), pp. 325–340.

———. "Predicting Good and Bad Scores in a Clairvoyance Experiment." *The Journal of the American Society for Psychical Research* 37 (October 1943), pp. 210–221.

Schmidt, Helmut. "Precognition of a Quantum Process." *The Journal of Parapsychology* 33, no. 2 (June 1960).

Scotsman, The. February 27, 1937, p. 16, columns 3–4.

Shamos, Morris H. and George M. Murphy, eds. *Recent Advances in Science.* New York: Science Editions, 1961.

Sinclair, Upton. *Mental Radio.* London: Werner Laurie, 1930.

Smith, Adam. *An Inquiry into the Nature and Causes of the Wealth of Nations.* Edited with an introduction and notes by Edwin Cannan. New York: Modern Library, 1937.

Smythes, J. R. "A Logical and Cultural Analysis of Hallucinatory Sense-experience." *Journal of Mental Science,* April 1956, pp. 336–342.

Soal, S. G. *Preliminary Studies of a Vaudeville Telepathist.* London: University of London Council for Psychical Investigation, 1937.

Stanford, Rex G. "An Experimental Testable Model for Spontaneous Psi Events: I—Extrasensory Events." *The Journal of the American Society for Psychical Research* 68, no. 1 (January 1974), pp. 34–57.

Stent, Gunther S. "Prematurity and Uniqueness in Scientific Discovery." *Scientific American,* December 1972, pp. 84–93.

SELECTED BIBLIOGRAPHY

Stevenson, Ian. "Twenty Cases Suggestive of Reincarnation." *Proceedings of the American Society for Psychical Research* 26, 1966, pp. 1–362.

Struckmeyer, Frederick R. "Precognition and the 'Intervention Paradox.'" *The Journal of the American Society for Psychical Research* 64, no. 3 (July 1970).

Swann, Ingo. "Scientological Techniques: A Modern Paradigm for the Exploration of Consciousness and Psychic Integration." *The Proceedings of the First International Conference on Psychotronic Research.* New York: Masterwork Press, 1974.

Szasz, Thomas S. *The Manufacture of Madness.* New York: Harper & Row, 1970.

Tart, Charles T. "Card Guessing Tests: Learning Paradigm or Extinction Paradigm?" *The Journal of the American Society for Psychical Research* 60, no. 1 (January 1966), pp. 46–62.

Terletskii, Yakov Petrovich. *Paradoxes in the Theory of Relativity.* New York: Plenum Press, 1968.

Theosophical Movement (The) 1875–1950. Los Angeles: Cunningham Press, 1951.

Thouless, Robert H. "Parapsychology During the Last Quarter of a Century." *The Journal of Parapsychology* 33, no. 4 (December 1969).

Tiller, W. A. "The Light Source in High-voltage Photography." *Proceedings of the Second Western Hemisphere Conference on Kirlian Photography, Acupuncture and the Human Aura.* New York: February 1973.

Todd, J., and K. Dewhurst. "The Double: Its Psycho-Pathology and Psycho-Physiology." *Journal of Nervous and Mental Disease* 122 (1955), pp. 47–55.

Tompkins, P., and C. Bird. *The Secret Life of Plants.* New York: Harper & Row, 1973.

Ullman, Montague; S. Krippner; and A. Vaughan. *Dream Telepathy.* New York: Macmillan, 1973.

Vasiliev, L. L. *Experiments in Mental Suggestion.* Hampshire, England: ISMI Publications, 1963.

Waite, A. E. *The Secret Tradition in Freemasonry.* 2 vols. London: Rebman, 1911.

Walker, E. H. "Foundations of Paraphysical and Parapsychological Phenomena." Unpublished paper, Ballistic Research Laboratories, Aberdeen Proving Ground, Maryland.

———. "The Nature of Consciousness, the Relation to the Foundations of Quantum Mechanics and Its Philosophical Implications." *Proceedings of the SIMS Conference,* University of Massachusetts, July 28–August 1, 1971.

Watkins, G. K. and A. M. "Possible PK Influence on the Resuscitation of Anesthetized Mice." *The Journal of Parapsychology* 35, no. 4 (December 1971), pp. 257–272.

Wells, H. G. *Anticipations of the Reaction of Mechanical and Scientific Progress upon Human Life and Thought.* London: Chapman & Hall, 1902.

SELECTED BIBLIOGRAPHY

White, Rhea A., and Laura A. Dale. *Parapsychology: Sources of Information.* Metuchen, N.J.: Scarecrow Press, 1973.

Wilkins, Sir Hubert, and Harold M. Sherman. *Thoughts Through Space.* New York: Creative Age Press, 1942.

Zalenzki, Countess. *Noted Prophecies Concerning the Great War and the Great Changes to Follow.* Chicago: Yogi, 1917.

INDEX

Ailly, Pierre d', 144
Alcoholism, 98
American Association for the Advancement of Science, 29
American Society for Psychical Research, 3–8, 53, 56, 68, 104, 105, 106, 126, 186, 197
Anticipations of the Reaction of Mechanical and Scientific Progress Upon Human Life and Thought (Wells), 132
Anti-Vaccination Society, 179
Anxiety, 98
Aquinas, St. Thomas, 79
Association for Humanistic Psychology, 194
Associational psychology, 70, 76
Astral bodies, 51
Astrology, 113, 142, 150, 152–153
Auras, 20–24
  in art, 22–24
  coronal, 20
  human, 21, 22
Autoscopia, 96–102
  definitions of, 101–102
  diseases associated with, 98, 99–100
  in literary works, 98
  neurophysiological, 98, 101

Autoscopic hallucination, 96–102
Azevedo, Ignacio de, 79

Babylon, 102–103
Backster, Cleve, 14, 17, 33, 34, 35, 36, 39, 52
Bain, Alexander, 76–77
Balsamo, Giuseppe. *See* Cagliostro, Alessandro
Bath County, Ky., 179–180
Benedict XIV, Pope, 79
Berkeley, George, 72
Biology, 28
Blaisdel, Lydia, 82
Blavatsky, Helena Petrovna, 151
Bohr, Niels, 47–48
Bold Venture, 86
Bonaparte, Napoleon, 144
Brandeis, Leopold, 179
Burbank, Luther, 15
Butler, George, 82
Butler, Nelly, 82

Cabala, 150
Cagliostro, Alessandro, 140–145, 146, 147, 148, 159–160

211

INDEX

Cambridge Philosophical Society, 47
Carlson, Chester F., 3
Carlson Research Laboratory, 3–8
Casimir V, King, 79
Castro, Fidel, 163
Cazotte, Jacques, 144
Central Premonitions Registry, 122
Charles, Emperor, 155, 156
Charles II, King, 70
Cheiro (Louis Hamon), 152–153
Chinchilla, psychic potential of, 180–184
Christian Science, 175
Clairvoyance, 6, 7, 25, 80, 109, 131
Clifford, William Kingdon, 47, 48, 49, 178, 184
Club of Rome, 162
Condillac, Etienne Bonnot de, 75
Consciousness, xv–xviii, 62, 93, 99, 132, 145, 147, 158
  barriers to, xv, 12–13
  frontier of, 11–13
  source of, 58–59
Cooper, Anthony Ashley, of Shaftesbury, 71
Copernicus, Nicolaus, 137, 147
Copertino, Joseph, 79
Coronal aura, 20
Cuban Agrarian Reform Institute, 163
Czechoslovakia, 52

"Dangerous and Sinful Practice of Inoculation, The" (Massey), 178–179
Darwin, Charles, 189
Dean, Douglas, 19, 189–190
Dementia paralytica, 98
Denton, William, 103–104
Descartes, Rene, 139
Diderot, Denis, 139

Dowsers, 187–189
Dracaena massangeana, 14, 33
Drug addiction, 98
Druids, 102

Eddy, Mary Baker, 175
Edison, Thomas, 190
Educational Policy Research Center (Stanford Research Institute), 162–170, 171, 172
Edward VII, King, 85, 86
Edwards, A. Mead, 179
Einstein, Albert, 47, 48, 176, 177
Electroencephalographs (EEG), 3, 4, 15, 41
Electronics and Bioengineering Laboratory (Stanford Research Institute), 50
Elizabeth of Bavaria, 79
Emerson, Ralph Waldo, 175
Encephalitis lethargica, 98
Encyclopédie (Diderot), 139
Encyclopédistes, the, 139
Energetics, 28
Enlightenment, 139
Epilepsy, 98
Essay Concerning Human Understanding (Locke), 72
Ethical consciousness, 75
Evolution, concept of, 69–70
Experiments
  eyeless vision, 17–24
  out-of-body experience, 104–126
  perception (distant from the body), 3–8
  plant communication, 14–17, 33–36
  in psychokinesis, 39–42, 50–53, 55–61, 62
  report on prophecy (1973), 164–172
  Schmeidler (at City College of New York), 39–42, 58, 62

INDEX

Stanford Research Institute, 50–53, 55–61, 62
Extrasensory perception (ESP), 18, 185, 195
　psychological conditions and, 40
　sheep-goats effect, 40–41
Extraterrestrial life possibilities, 9–10
Eyeless vision, 17–24
　auras, 20–24
　color perception, 18–19
　hoax type of, 17–18
　Kirlian photography, 19–20, 23

Faraday, Michael, 159
Faust (Goethe), 192
Federal Bureau of Investigation, 191
Feliciani, Lorenza, 141
First Western Hemisphere Conference on Kirlian Photography, Acupuncture, and the Human Aura, 23
Flying saucers, 9–10
Foundations of Tibetan Mysticism (Govinda), 146
Francis Xavier, St., 79
Franco, Francisco, 86
Franco-Prussian War, 153
Franz Ferdinand, Archduke, 155
Franz Joseph, Emperor, 154, 155–156
Frederick of Brunswick-Lüneburg, 79
French Revolution, prophecy of, 138–145
Freud, Sigmund, 69, 77
Frontiers of man, 3–30
　of the future, 8–13
　parapsychology, 24–30
　to perceive (distant from the body), 3–8
　psychic, 13–24
　types of, 9
Gastroenteritis, 99–100
Gébelin, Antoine Court de, 142, 143
George V, King, 85
Goebbels, Joseph, 148
Goethe, Johann Wolfgang von, 189, 192
Govinda, the Lama Anagarika, 146
Gramont, Duchess de, 144
Green Book for Prophecies, The (Old), 154
Grison, 145
Guernica (Picasso), 86

Hall, Manly P., 65
Hallucinations, types of, 97
Hapsburg family, 155–156
Harman, Willis, 163, 164
Harpe, Jean de la, 144
Hartley, David, 75–76
Harvard University, 134–135, 186
Hauptmann, Bruno Richard, 86
Hebbard, Arthur, 57, 59, 60
Heisenberg, Werner, 49, 78
Helancius, 102
Herodotus, 102–103
Hitler, Adolf, 85–86, 135, 161
Hobbes, Thomas, 70, 138, 139
Hohenzollern family, 154, 156
Homo novis, 13
Horla, Le (Maupassant), 98
Hubbard, L. Ron, 196
Hudson, Manley O., 135
Hume, David, 73
Hyperaesthesia, 150

Influenza, 98
Inorganic matter, communication with, 14–15

213

INDEX

Inquiry into the Nature and Causes of the Wealth of Nations, An (Smith), 140
Inquisition, 79
Institute for the Future, 162
International Association for Psychotronic Research, 194
Intuition, 25, 62, 74, 108, 131, 190
   loneliness, 65–66
   survival by, 46

James, William, 27, 186
Jenner, Edward, 178–179
Jung, Carl G., 77, 178, 184

Kant, Immanuel, 73–75
Karagulla, Shafica, 193
Karma, 11
Kepler, Johannes, 159
Kidd, James, 67–68, 126, 127
Kilner, Walter J., 21, 22
Kirlan, Semyon and Valentina, 19
Kirlian photography, 19–20, 21, 23
Krippner, Stanley, 194

Labyrinthine vertigo, 98
Lamballe, Princess de, 141, 143, 145
League of Nations, 134, 135, 161
Leibnitz, Gottfried Wilhelm von, 70–71
Leo, Alan, 113, 152
LeShan, Lawrence, 147
Levitation, 79–80
Lewis, John Henry, 86
Lewis, Larry, 41
Lhermitte, Jean, 97–98
Lindbergh kidnapping, 86
Locke, John, 71–72, 73, 75, 138, 139

Loneliness, awareness of, 65–66
Lorca, Garcia, 86
Loss of self, 9
Louis XVI, King, 138, 140, 141, 142–143, 144, 145
Louis XVII, King, 145

Mandala of the Soul (Zimmerman), 23–24
Margaret of Hungary, St., 79
Maria of Savoy, Princess, 79
Marie Antoinette, Queen, 138, 141, 143, 145
Mariner 10, 121–123
Massangeana, 15
Massey, Edward, 178–179
Materialism, 69, 71, 102
   occult, 71
   philosophic, 69, 70–76, 195
   scientific, 47–48, 53–55
Maupassant, Guy de, 98
Maxwell, James Clerk, 47, 48
Melancholia, 98
Mencken, Henry L., 113–114
Mendeleyev, Roy, 189
Menninger Foundation, 126
Mercury (planet), Sherman/Swann psychic probe of, 121–126
Metaphysics, 48, 68, 76–77
Middle Ages, 23
Migrainoids, 99
Mihalasky, John, 189–190
Milky Way, 10
Mind, defined, 44
Mind over matter, concept of, 42–45
Mind-reading, 80
Mitchell, Janet, 122
Monads, theory of, 71
Montesquieu, Baron de, 139
Monthly Weather Review, 180
Murphy, Gardner, 126–127

INDEX

Musset, Alfred de, 98
Mysticism, 94

Nazi party, 148
Newark College of Engineering, 189–190
Newark Science Association, 179
Newton, Isaac, 139
Nicholas II, Tsar, 141, 154
Nixon, Richard, 163
Nostradamus, 139, 144, 148
Noumena, Kantian theory of, 74–75, 78
Numerology, 142

Objective universe
　at the atomic level, 49
　investigating, 26
　relationship between subjective and, 190
Occultism, 71, 150
Oil dowsers, 187–189
Old, Walter Gorn, 150–157
Organic matter, communication with, 14–15
Out-of-body experience, 55–56, 65–127
　autoscopic, 96–102
　experimentation in, 104–126
　levitation, 79–80
　one's outlook, personal experiences and, 80–96
　philosophic inquiry into, 68–78
　psychic research and, 78–80, 93–94, 114–118, 126–127
　psychometry, 102–104

Parapsychology, 24–30
　frontier of, 24–30
　modern research in, 184–187
　new research approach to, 26–27
　physics and, 28, 29–30
　scientific results of, 28–30
　strategy and tactics in, 28
　track record of successful discovery, 27
　types of researchers, 38–39
Parapsychology Association, 19, 29
Parasensory Foundation, 23
Paris Commune, 145
Pascal, Blaise, 159
Perception
　distant from the body, 3–8
　objective universe, 26, 27
　for psychoenergetic effect, 62
　speed of, 51
　See also Out-of-body experience
Peter of Alcantara, St., 79
Phenomena, Kantian theory of, 74–75
Philosophy, 48, 68–78, 93
　early ideals of, 68–69
　materialistic, 69, 70–76, 195
　metaphysical inquiry, 76–77
　rise of psychic research and, 77–78
Phipps, John, 178
Photography
　bisulfate of quinine, 34
　Kirlian effect, 19–20, 21, 23
　of psychic energies, 34–35
Physics, 28, 29–30
Picasso, Pablo, 12, 86
Pioneer 10, 10, 118–121
Planck, Max, 47
Planetary systems, 9–10
Plant communication, 14–17, 33–36
Pliny, 102
Poe, Edgar Allan, 98
Precognition, 25, 80
Predestination, theory of, 149

215

INDEX

Prophecy, 80, 131–172
  analysis of (1969–1972), 136
  based on empirical observation, 134–136
  degrees of consciousness and, 145–148
  doom and, 132, 133, 172
  Educational . Policy Research Center report, 162–170, 171, 172
  of extraterrestrial life, 10
  of French Revolution, 138–145
  genius-type, 158, 159–161
  in literary works, 131–132
  logic and, 157–158
  of Old, Walter Gorn, 150–157
  by organizations, 162–163
  sociological factors in, 136–138
Psi Communications Project, 189–190
"Psi missing" factor, 115
Psychic frontier, 13–24
  meaning of, 13–14, 25
  source of, 108
Psychics, kinds of, 113
Psychoenergetics, 53–62
  potential of, 53–55
Psychokinesis, 25, 33–62, 131
  ability for, 55–61
  body animation, 46
  existence of, 55
  graphite electric potential, 36–42
  interactions (immaterial or nonmaterial), 45–49
  mind over matter idea, 42–45
  photography, 34–35
  plant research, 33–36
  potential, 53–55
  Schmeidler experiments, 39–42, 58, 62
  scientific materialism and, 47–48, 53–55
  sheep-goat (ESP) effect, 40–41

SRI experiments, 50–53, 55–61, 62
Psychology, 48, 76–77, 175–176
Psychometry, 102–104
Psychosis impedimenta, 12
Puthoff, H. E., 52–53, 55, 56, 57, 59, 60, 118

Quantum (nonmaterial) physics, 29, 78, 93
Quantum theory, 47–48, 49
Quark detector, 57–58

Rand Corporation, 162
Rasputin, 141, 160
Rawson, F. L., 175–176, 177, 184
Reichenbach, Karl von, 20, 22
Relativity, theory of, 176
Rhine, J. B., 24, 185, 187
Rhine, Louisa E., 24
Rodriguez, Rafael, 163
Rohan, Cardinal de, 141
Romanov family, 143, 154
Romantic period, 98
Rosary Hill College, 18
Rousseau, Jean-Jacques, 139
Russia, 14, 52, 194
  attitude toward psychic research in, 61

Schizophrenia, 97
Schmeidler, Gertrude, 39–42, 53, 55, 58, 106, 122, 189, 195
Scientific American Supplement, 179
Scientific materialism
  decline of, 47–48
  psychic experiments and, 53–55
Scientology, 196
Secret Doctrine (Blavatsky), 151

INDEX

Sensory perception, 51, 145
70 *Ophiuchi*, 9
Sheep/goat (ESP) effect, 40–41, 195
Sherman, Harold, 113, 118
Sherman, Martha, 114
Simpson, Mrs. Wallis Warfield, 85, 86
61 *Cygni*, 9
Skutch, Judy, 23
Smith, Adam, 139–140
Sociology, 48
Some Thoughts Concerning Education (Locke), 72
Sophie, Archduchess, 155
Sowers (Van Gogh), 4, 197
Spanish Civil War, 86
Stalin, Joseph, 86
Stanford Research Institute (SRI), 50–52, 56, 105–107, 110, 112, 114, 117, 118
Stanford University, 20, 57–58
Strabo, 102
Subjective universe
  investigating, 26
  relationship between objective and, 190
Swift, Geraldine C., 67

Tao-Teh-King, 151
Targ, Russell, 118
Telekinesis, 80
Telepathy, 6, 7, 25, 80
Teleportation, 80
Temple of Belus, 102–103
Teresa, St., 79
Tesla, Nikola, 190–193
Thant, U, 162
Theosophical Society, 151

Theosophy, 150–151
Tiller, William A., 20
Toward a General Theory of the Paranormal (LeShan), 147
Toxicomania, 98
Turgot, Baron de, 139
Turrel (astrologer), 144

UFOlogists, 9–10
Uninterrupted consciousness, 197
United Nations, 162

Van Gogh, Vincent, 4, 8, 197
Vasiliev, L. L., 61
Victoria, Queen, 9, 154
Vogel, Marcel, 17
Voltaire, 139

Water dowsing, 187–189
Watt, James, 12
Wells, H. G., 131–132
Wilkins, Hubert, 114
William I, Emperor, 153
William II, Emperor, 153, 154, 156
William, Crown Prince, 156–157
Wilson, Woodrow, 134
Windsor, Duke of, 152–153
World Trade Center (New York City), 163
World War I, 131, 134, 135, 136, 175
  prophecy of, 153–157

Zimmerman, Helmut, 23–24